I WANT YOU
TO WANT ME

I WANT YOU TO WANT ME

KATHY LOVE

BRAVA

KENSINGTON PUBLISHING CORP.
www.kensingtonbooks.com

BRAVA BOOKS are published by

Kensington Publishing Corp.
850 Third Avenue
New York, NY 10022

All Kensington titles, imprints, and distributed lines are available at special quantity discounts for bulk purchases for sales promotion, premiums, fund-raising, educational, or institutional use.

Special book excerpts or customized printings can also be created to fit specific needs. For details, write or phone the office of the Kensington Special Sales Manager: Kensington Publishing Corp., 850 Third Avenue, New York, NY 10022. Attn. Special Sales Department. Phone: 1-800-221-2647.

Brava and the B logo Reg. U.S. Pat. & TM Off.

ISBN-13: 978-0-7582-1857-5
ISBN-10: 0-7582-1857-5

First Kensington Trade Paperback Printing: September 2008

10 9 8 7 6 5 4 3 2 1

Printed in the United States of America

For Heather Graham and Connie Perry

*If these two wonderful women hadn't invited me
to New Orleans, I never would have been inspired
to write these books, nor would I have discovered one
of my favorite places on earth.*

Thank you.

Acknowledgments

This past year has been both my most difficult and my best.
As always it has been my friends and family
who've gotten me through the bad and celebrated with
me when things were good.

Okay, you Tarts, you know I love you!

A huge thanks to my family.
Mom and Dad, Cindy, Teresa, Darrell, and Gerry,
I love you.

Julie, Erin, Cat, Lisa, Chris, Kathy, Kate, Toni, Kristi,
and Amanda
Thanks for the phone chats, the laughter, and the
understanding.

Thank you to *The Impalers*, past and present
Special thanks to Brian Beeler,
the only original.
And to Craig Steggal, Michael Koerber,
Tim Perry, Paul Scali, Vince Reeves, Michael George, Roger
Sullivan, Johnny Relayson, Eric Knight, Greg, Matt Janice,
Allan Maxwell, Sonny Kane, and Andrew Autin
Who knew it took so many guys to create a
fictional vampire band!

And to my new friends in New Orleans,
Michelle, Jansen, Allison, Jennie, and Shelly

Also I want to thank my editor, Kate Duffy, and
my agent, Jenny Bent.
They've made this year much easier for me.

And finally, and most important, thanks to
my daughter, Emily.
She reminds me everyday what matters in life.
I love you, Boo.

Chapter 1

"Is there something wrong with the left breast?" Erika Todd asked her friend as she peered at the torso in front of her.

Maggie tilted her head, considering. "Yes. It's—crooked or something."

Erika's head tilted too. "Maybe it needs to be bigger."

"Or higher."

Erika sighed, throwing down the clay-encrusted towel she'd been using to wipe her hands, and turned away from the sculpture. "*Argh!* I just can't figure out what my problem is. I've been struggling with all of my pieces lately. And I'm getting more than a little frustrated."

"Maybe it's just a matter of getting used to your new surroundings. A lot has been going on for you in the past three months," Maggie said.

Erika shrugged. "I suppose, but it's all been good stuff. I should be feeling inspired, not . . ." She glanced back at her latest creation. "Lopsided."

"Well, you've been pushing yourself," Maggie pointed out. "Moving is hard. Maybe you just need to allow yourself a little break."

Erika nodded even though she didn't agree. She hadn't found the move hard. In fact, taking the apartment in Maggie and her husband Ren's building had seemed natural. The right move. She loved New Orleans. It spoke to her creativity.

All signs to the contrary. She frowned at the sculpture again. "Well, I don't have much time. My show is in a month, and I'd hoped to have three new pieces done for the exhibit."

It was Maggie's turn to simply nod. Her friend knew how important this show was to Erika. The Broussard, a renowned gallery in the French Quarter, was doing a show dedicated just to her work. She needed it to be perfect.

After years of struggling, working jobs she hated, living on macaroni and cheese and ramen, listening to her father tell her she had to think about getting a "real" job, things were finally falling into place for her, and she didn't want to lose momentum. This was her dream.

But maybe Maggie had a point. Obviously, working continuously wasn't creating the results she wanted either.

She surveyed the piece again, then sighed. "This piece is supposed to be called 'Fallen Angel.' Not 'Fallen Boob.' "

Erika dropped down onto the worn blue velvet chair she'd just purchased at a secondhand shop on Decatur. Maggie sat down on her sofa—an equally worn, yet lovely gold brocade sofa. Another secondhand find.

"You will get the pieces done, and they will be a huge hit. And you will gather rich patrons galore."

Erika laughed at her friend's certain optimism. "We can only hope."

"You will," Maggie assured her, with an encouraging smile.

Erika, with her artist's eye, assessed her friend. Maggie had always been cute—cuter than she ever gave herself credit for. But now, Erika studied her friend's profile as she'd just done her sculpture, but unlike her creation, she found her friend truly lovely.

Maybe it was the way her loose curls framed her face, accenting the softness of her cheeks and the delicate point of her chin. Or maybe it was the new style she'd embraced, clothes that displayed her rounded curves. Or maybe it was the happiness in her eyes, making them practically dance with unbridled joy.

"So where is Ren taking you this week?" Erika asked, knowing he was the one from where much of that joy stemmed.

Maggie's eyes brightened, glimmering happily in the lamplight. "I have no idea. It's a surprise."

"No hints?"

Maggie sighed. "Not even a tiny one. And believe me, I've tried every tactic imaginable to get him to slip." Then Maggie's cheeks reddened, giving Erika a pretty good indication what those tactics may have been.

Erika opened her mouth to tease her, when a knock stopped her. Before she could call for the person to come in, Ren strolled through the door from the glassed-in sun porch.

"You're back early," Maggie said, rising to greet him. He walked straight to her, pressing a lingering kiss on his wife's upraised lips. "Is everything set with work? Is your stand-in okay?"

Ren nodded. "Not me, but he'll do."

"Egotist," Maggie chided with a fond smile. Ren kissed her again.

Erika watched, a pang of envy tightening her chest. Not that she begrudged her friend the happiness she'd found. Maggie deserved it. Erika just wished she could find her own love interest. Her soul mate.

Maggie broke off the kiss, but didn't pull out of Ren's hold. Instead, they just gazed at each other for a moment. Watching the adoring looks on both their faces, Erika was struck by the need to capture that feeling, both in her art and in her life.

She quickly reached over to the end table that she'd painted cobalt blue and caught the strap of her digital camera. Before the couple realized she'd moved, she pointed and clicked.

Maggie made a small startled noise, while Ren turned to blink at Erika.

"You never know," Erika said, snapping another shot, "I may want to sculpt you two."

Maggie actually blushed. "I would hardly be a good subject."

Ren snorted, the sound somehow attractive rather than impolite. "You are a perfect subject."

Erika smiled at the conviction in his voice. Ren was thoroughly besotted.

"I, however," he added, "could never be an angel of any sort, fallen or otherwise."

"Well, I'm not sculpting just angels. I'm sculpting whatever strikes me. And you two did." Erika snapped another shot for good measure. "Maybe I want to capture true love. Or soul mates."

Ren smiled broadly at that, the curl of his lips giving him a slightly naughty and utterly charming look. "Well, I can accept that description."

He stole another kiss from Maggie.

Erika breathed a sigh, masking the sound of discontent by setting her camera on the coffee table. She'd never doubted that one day, after already accumulating an abundance of frogs, she'd meet her prince. But lately, maybe because of a dry spell, even from the frogs, she was beginning to wonder.

"Okay," Ren said suddenly. "Are you ready to go?"

Maggie smiled and shrugged. "As ready as I can be, given that I have no idea where I'm going. But then, I figured I didn't need to pack much."

"You, darlin', have a one track mind," Ren said, shaking his head in feigned dismay. He looked at Erika. "I think you should have warned me about her."

Erika shrugged, taking no responsibility for his choices. Although she did feel a little responsible for Maggie taking the initiative to go after him.

"You love it," Maggie said, and Ren kissed her.

"I love you," he muttered, his voice rough with emotion.

Another pang of longing pulsed in Erika's chest. The scene could have easily struck her as nauseating, but between her happiness for Maggie and her own desire for those same emotions, Erika just . . . wanted. Big time.

"Okay," Ren said, linking his fingers with Maggie's. "We'll see you on Wednesday."

"Have fun," Erika said as she walked them to the door.

She remained at the window, watching them gather their luggage and cross the courtyard toward the door that led to the street. They really were the image of newly wedded bliss. Of real happiness.

Erika didn't bother to disguise her sigh this time, there was no one to hear it but her new roommate, a big black cat she'd named Boris. And he wasn't paying any attention, curled in his usual spot on the back of her overstuffed chair, looking sullen. His usual expression. His only expression, really. Even in his sleep.

She gazed out into the shadowy courtyard for a few moments longer, then turned back to her apartment. Aside from the lopsided sculpture and the necessary mess of wet clay and bits of polymer and caked tools, the place was neat. Well, organized chaos anyway.

She, on the other hand, was another story. Her jeans were smeared with clay, her fingernails caked, her hair knotted back in an untidy and clay-spattered ponytail.

"And I wonder why I only have you for male companionship," she said, moving to stroke Boris's black fur. He opened one golden eye, then shut it again, obviously unmoved.

She supposed she should try to fix her sculpture, but she'd been working on this angel for nearly five days, and the poor thing was getting worse with each progressive attempt. Maggie was right. They both needed a rest.

"Although this is what you should be stressing about," she muttered to herself, inspecting the sculpture again. "Not your lack of a love life."

Erika knew that. Intellectually, she did. But emotionally, she craved what Maggie had found in Ren. And for some reason, she couldn't shake that longing, even with all the exciting changes in her life. Maybe because she was seeing her friend's happiness on a daily basis. Or maybe because so many other things had fallen into place lately. Wasn't it time for love to join in?

"Does life always have to be one thing or another?" she

wondered to the bored Boris. "A trade-off. My career is going well, so now I have to go without a love life?"

Erika pushed that train of thought aside. It sounded like her father's reasoning. Her father was a big subscriber to Murphy's Law. She, on the other hand, believed in positive thoughts creating positive outcomes.

And the positive thoughts she needed to work on now were about her art show.

"Focus on the now and the rest will fall into place."

Her mother had once said that to her in a letter, and Erika had tried to live by it. She was her mother's daughter, after all.

"So I think now what is required is a nice, long shower and a glass of wine."

She glanced back at the sculpture that looked more like a Picasso than an Erika Todd.

Maybe she just needed to start over. She wandered to her fridge, and poured a glass of wine. And maybe a nice, long bath and two glasses of wine was the way to go.

Something woke her.

Erika struggled upright, blinking around, trying to get her bearings. She was in the living room on her brocade sofa. Brushing the tangle of hair from her face, she fell back against the cushy, body-warmed pillows.

She must have dozed off as she'd been studying her work, analyzing, again, what might fix it. She glanced at the coffee table, where her second glass of pinot noir sat, half-empty.

Closing her eyes, she allowed herself to drift. Sleep was often as much a creativity sparker as work. Or at least she was going with that theory for now. The warm, enveloping couch felt lovely.

Then she heard it. A distinct bang directly above her head. Her eyes popped open, and she stared at the ceiling she'd painted sky blue when she'd moved in. She remained still, listening.

Just when she'd decided that she must have imagined the loud clunk, another noise echoed from above her head. The scrape of something being dragged across the floor.

She glanced over to her cat. Even Boris stared intently up at the sound. His ear twitched.

For once the grumpy cat was giving a definite reaction, but of course it was when she'd much rather have seen his usual bored or apathetic demeanor. She sat up, her eyes still locked on the ceiling as if someone was going to suddenly manifest from the floor above.

There was an apartment over hers. But it was empty. Empty and neglected, since Ren no longer rented the other apartments in his building—liking the privacy it gave him and Maggie. Erika knew she was lucky he conceded to letting her rent.

Her heart leapt, pounding in an uneven, breath-stealing way as she heard more sounds. The distinct creak of feet on a hardwood floor. A sound she easily recognized, because the old hardwood in her apartment squeaked the same way.

Careful to make no noise herself, she rose from the sofa and moved to the front door. Her apartment and the upstairs apartment shared the glassed-in front porch.

Her heart still pounding, she peeked out her window. Light from the courtyard illuminated a swath of the porch, leaving the corners shadowed in darkness.

Behind her, she heard footsteps. She spun, expecting someone to be right behind her. She jumped as she saw a figure in the center of the room. Then she realized it was her distorted creation. Before, she'd considered the sculpture to be frustrating, disappointing, and mostly a disaster. Now it looked almost ominous.

She sucked in a deep breath, trying to calm her rocketing pulse. *Calm down. Calm down.*

More footsteps. But overhead—not in the same room. Nothing was going to hurt her. The assurance didn't persuade her heart to stop hammering against her rib cage.

She looked back out the window, trying to angle her head

so she could see up the staircase to her right, which led to the upstairs apartment. The stairs, as much as she could make out, just ascended into pitch black.

Hesitantly, her hand went to the doorknob. She turned it slowly and eased the door ajar. Sticking her head out, she squinted into the darkness. And she listened.

Nothing. Not a sound.

She glanced around the door to Maggie and Ren's place, a carriage house across the courtyard. Aside from a dim glow from a lamp in the living room, their house was dark too.

She looked back up the staircase, debating whether she should go up and investigate. Peering into the menacing blackness, she decided that was a colossally stupid idea. Instead she pulled the door closed, carefully clicked the lock into place, and went in search of her cell phone.

"See," she said to Boris as she rummaged through her purse, then among her art supplies, only to find the phone buried under a pile of clay-caked rags. She grimaced at the grimy phone, then turned back to Boris.

"See, I'm not that foolish woman in the horror movies, who traipses off to investigate the noise from the attic."

Another creak sounded directly above her head. She quickly swiped off the worst of the filth and flipped the phone open only to see the faceplate wasn't illuminating. She pressed the On button. Nothing. She pressed again, harder. Still nothing.

She stared at the useless phone, knowing that even if she plugged it in, the battery would need a while to accept enough charge to even turn on.

"Okay, so I am apparently the foolish woman in a horror movie who has an ancient cell phone that never holds a charge." She snapped the phone shut. "Crap."

Now would be the time to regret not getting a landline turned on. She glanced toward the windows. She could go to Maggie and Ren's and use their phone. She debated the idea of leaving the security of her apartment, then decided she really had no choice.

"It's dumber to stay in here, listening to someone robbing the place," she told the cat. He blinked, but she wasn't sure if that was in agreement or not.

She rifled through her purse again, looking for her voodoo-doll keychain, which held Maggie and Ren's spare key. Then she tiptoed to the door.

"Wish me luck."

Boris had already curled back into an indifferent black ball of fur. She shook her head. "It couldn't have been a stray dog that showed up at my door, could it? At least a dog would care if I was going out to greet my imminent death."

She took a deep breath, then unlocked and eased open the door. Everything was quiet, but she didn't take the time to survey the murky corners. Instead she stepped out and rushed to the porch door, which led into the better-lit courtyard.

"Hey."

Erika's already tensed muscles reacted on instinct as soon as she heard the male voice close behind her.

She spun toward the faceless voice and hurled the object in her right hand. Without waiting to see if she made contact, she shoved open the porch door and propelled herself out into the courtyard, her legs pumping under her as she raced toward Maggie and Ren's carriage house. She fumbled with the keys, even as she ran. Thank God those weren't what she threw.

"Wait! Erika!"

The words, called out from behind her, took a moment to register in her panicked brain. But gradually she realized that the disembodied voice had just used her name. She stopped, the key poised to open the lock of the carriage house door.

Slowly she turned.

At first she couldn't locate the speaker in the shadows and greenery of the courtyard. Then a figure stepped forward into the glow of the courtyard's dim garden lights.

Erika squinted. *"Vittorio?"*

Chapter 2

He strolled closer, giving her a better glimpse of his lean frame, languid movements, and the sheen of golden hair.

"Yeah," he said, his voice a deep rumble, answering her question.

Not that there had really been any question there. She'd have recognized Ren's younger brother anywhere. She'd thought of this man innumerable times over the past several months. Yet now she could think of nothing comprehensible to say to him. Not even, *hello*. Not even, *you scared the crap out of me*.

"I'm sorry to startle you," he was saying, his words almost unintelligible through the still-thundering beat of her heart echoing in her ears. Although that wasn't just fear now.

She could only gape at him. *What was he doing here?*

"Do you have a towel?" he asked.

Erika frowned, not following that line of questioning at all. Then she realized his hand was pressed to his brow.

"Are you okay?" she managed, still feeling like she'd just stepped off the world's most frightening roller coaster only to discover her heart's desire at the bottom of the exit ramp.

Her heart's desire? She was more shaken than she realized.

"Aside from the blow to the head?" he asked, dryly. "Sure, I'm good."

She squinted at him. "Blow to the head?"

He held up an object. Erika blinked.

"That's my cell," she murmured, staring at the scratched black phone with its dead battery. Then she realized that was what she'd flung in her utter terror.

"Yes, I gathered that it was yours when you threw it at me."

Erika cringed. "You scared me. I didn't expect anyone to be in the upstairs apartment."

"I didn't expect anyone to be in the downstairs apartment."

"I've been renting it for about two months now," she said automatically, then she realized that she sounded apologetic. Which she had no reason to be.

"So a towel? Do you have one?"

Erika immediately started. "Oh. Yes, of course."

She stepped down from the carriage-house steps and headed back toward her place, making sure not to get too close to Vittorio. Something about him still made her feel wary—even as her body reacted to him. How was that even possible?

She was aware of him right behind her. She could feel him there, as if he were pressed against her, rather than a couple of feet away. The sensation surprised and unnerved her, although she wasn't sure why.

Vittorio had made the same impression when they'd met nearly eight months ago. Her body had never reacted to a man like it had when he'd touched her. A mere shake of hands when Ren had introduced them. But the electricity from the brief contact had been knee-weakening and more intense than anything she'd ever experienced. Well, at least for her. She had no idea if Vittorio had felt the same axis-tipping chemistry.

She pushed open her door and entered her apartment, letting him follow. She didn't look back as she headed to the small kitchen and grabbed a roll of paper towels.

"Here you go," she said, managing a small smile, despite

her body's current reaction to him. Her heart still pounded. She felt breathless.

He snatched the paper towels from her grasp, before she could even hold them out to him. He removed his hand from his forehead to pull one of the paper squares off the roll.

Erika gasped as she saw the gash on his temple, and realized he was bleeding, a lot, just above his left brow—the blood a deep red, vivid and horrible looking.

"My God, that looks terrible." She moved closer to inspect the wound. She gently pressed her fingers to his cheek, rising up on her tiptoes to see the cut better. "You should go to the doctor. I'll take you."

"It's fine," he muttered, jerking back from her and pressing the wadded-up towel to the cut.

"It doesn't look fine," she told him, sinking back on her heels and dropping the hand that she'd pressed to his cool cheek. A wave of rejection filled her. Ridiculous given that he was hurt. And by her, no less. He certainly had every right to be distrustful of her, and irritated too. "That looks like it needs stitches."

"It's fine. A bandage will take care of it."

"I have a Band-Aid in the bathroom. I think. And maybe some hydrogen peroxide." She turned to go search, but his deep voice stopped her.

"I'm fine." He sounded almost irritated now.

She ignored it. "It's no bother." She headed down a hallway which led to her bedroom and the bath.

Vittorio watched Erika disappear down the hallway. He gritted his teeth at the fact that even for just the briefest moment, his eyes had dropped down to look at the fit of the pastel plaid pajama bottoms she wore against her rounded derriere.

He wasn't here to be checking out Maggie's friend's rear end. He'd do well to remember that.

Lifting the paper towel from his wound, he inspected it to

see if the bleeding had lessened. Damn, head wounds bled a lot—even for vampires. But the bleeding was already stopping. And he certainly didn't need a Band-Aid. The cut would be healed by tomorrow night. Something vampires didn't share with humans.

He jammed the towel back to the wound, irritated with himself. Of course, being a vampire, he shouldn't have even been hit. His reflexes were usually impeccable. Hell, he could literally dodge a bullet. Yet he'd gotten beamed in the head with a frantically flung cell phone.

But the truth was he'd been stunned to see Erika dashing through the darkness. Stunned and unreasonably thrilled.

He'd not allowed himself to think about Maggie's friend since meeting her at the small jazz bar and restaurant where Ren had introduced them months earlier.

Oh, she'd popped into his mind at random and inappropriate times, but he'd shoved all images of her aside. He had no room in his life for her.

He'd returned to New Orleans with only one task in mind, and Erika with her pretty smile and intelligent blue eyes and totally perfect rear end. . . .

He groaned. *Do not let your thoughts head in that direction. Don't.* He'd be a fool to go there—even in fantasy.

"I have one Band-Aid," Erika said, materializing out of the dark hallway. "And I couldn't find any hydrogen peroxide. But I do have antibiotic ointment."

Vittorio, despite his little mental pep talk, drank in the sight of her. Her dark, almost black hair was piled onto her head in an untidy knot, escaped tendrils looking like swirls of ink against the pale skin of her long neck.

She walked straight up to him, her fingers capturing his, easing the paper towel away from the cut. Again she rose up on her tiptoes, and as before the position brought her close to him, her breasts almost brushing his chest.

He fought back a groan.

Her heat and her energy did touch him, spreading over his

body as if her long limbs were curled around him. For the briefest moment, he absorbed it, letting himself take that energy into himself.

Her fingers stilled against his, and she made a small noise in the back of her throat. Not a noise of distress, but one of pleasure.

Abruptly he stepped back, jerking his hand from her.

What was he doing? He didn't take a person's energy. Not like that. Not just a single person's. Damn, he had to create some space between them. Real space, not just the fluctuating expanse of physical distance.

"Erika," he said, then added, "It is Erika, right?"

Erika's face changed, a small show of disappointment, the slight pulling down of her beautifully shaped lips.

"Yes," she murmured, glancing down at the towel that had slipped from his hands to hers when he'd pulled away.

"I appreciate your offer to help," he said, keeping his voice cool. Pretending he wasn't aware of everything about her.

"It's the least I could do. I did hit you."

"True," he said, amazed at how condescending he could make the one word sound. But he did come from royalty— even if that was long, long ago and even if his father was only the fifth son of an earl. "Which is why I think you have done more than enough for me tonight."

Instead of looking cowed, which was what he'd expected from her, she frowned at his dismissive tone.

"Did Ren know you were coming?"

Vittorio raised an eyebrow. He didn't know whether to be annoyed or amused by her coolly asked question. "No, but I am his brother. I hardly think I need a formal invitation."

"True," Erika nodded. "But if you had told him, he probably would have told me. And thus, I wouldn't have been scared out of my wits, and I wouldn't have pitched my cell phone at your head."

"You could have asked before you pitched."

Erika laughed at that, the sound derisive, but it still managed to stroke over his skin. A shiver steeped with longing threatened him, but he suppressed it.

Do not react. He'd spent years practicing his lack of reaction. But despite his warning, his muscles tightened as he struggled with his body's response to her laugh, her voice, her lovely eyes. Her lips.

"Spoken like a true man."

Until she continued, he was at a loss as to what she was referring to. Although she was right, other parts, aside from his mouth apparently, were indeed acting like a true man.

"If I had taken the time to inquire who you were, lurking in the shadows, and you had intended me harm, you would have had the time to do so. The cell phone reaction still seems far more sensible to me—despite your injury. Of which I am sorry." She no longer sounded sorry, however. She sounded annoyed.

Good, Vittorio told himself. The sooner she realized how unlikeable he was, the sooner she would leave him alone to do what he needed to do here in New Orleans.

Then he realized she was staring at him as if she expected a response.

"Well, most people would have stayed inside their house and used the cell to call for help—rather than using it as a projectile."

Her soft pink lips firmed into a straight line. "Right." She shoved the Band-Aid and the tube of ointment at him.

"I'm sorry," she said, "I'm sure you'd like to be going. The company of a woman who is so stupid that she's unclear as to the proper usage of a cell phone must be intolerable to you."

He didn't move for a moment, even though he'd achieved the effect he wanted from her, as well as the out he needed. He certainly wouldn't be getting any friendly visits from his downstairs neighbor.

Yet he was oddly tempted to take her offering of first aid supplies, both of which she still held out to him. He wanted to soothe that injured look in her blue-gray, stormy eyes. Accepting her offering seemed like an appeasement.

Instead, he just muttered, "I'll be fine."

In fact, by tomorrow night the gash would be gone. Good thing she wouldn't be around to ask him about that.

He studied her for a moment longer. She stared at a point over his left shoulder, her lips and jaw still firmly set.

Still suppressing the need to mollify her, he turned on his heels and headed to the door. As he closed it behind him, reentering the darkness he both needed and despised, he briefly allowed himself to wish for a different scenario for the night. One where he could stay there in Erika's eclectically, colorfully decorated world—that suited her to a tee. Where he could touch her smooth, pale skin and lose himself in her warmth, in the color she would add to his gray, nighttime world.

But he couldn't. And if he was right about the reason why he was back here, he had to stay away from her. If there was any merit to his suspicions, no one was safe in his presence.

Chapter 3

"He is here." Orabella met Maksim's eyes in the reflection of her vanity mirror. She continued to brush her long hair, suppressing the giddiness that rose up in her chest.

Maksim strolled into the room, his long limbs loose and graceful, his muscles rolling under the fine material of his tailored shirt. He was a stunningly handsome man with thick dark hair and mesmerizing pale green eyes. But Orabella wasn't considering that at the moment, nor had that been her real interest in him anyway. Though it didn't hurt.

But what held her attention now was what he'd said. Those three words were far more thrilling to her than his pretty face and powerfully built body.

"You're sure?"

Maksim came up to stand behind her, regarding her in the mirror, his unusual eyes glittering as he rested his hands on her shoulders. "Of course I'm sure, my pet."

He leaned down to press his lips to the side of her neck. She leaned into the kiss, but her mind was focused on his revelation. Vittorio was here. She'd found him finally.

She hadn't truly believed he would be here. It seemed too easy. Too simple. Especially since he'd disappeared so totally for almost four months. But she'd banked on the fact he wouldn't be able to stay away from his brother for long. Vittorio had such an odd affinity for his half-brother. Personally, Orabella had little use for Renaldo. So like his damned father.

But Vittorio. He was here. A swell of giddiness filled her bosom.

She looked at herself in the mirror, watching Maksim as he pushed aside the collar of her robe. She always had deliciously beautiful men as her lovers, and Maksim was no different.

But in truth, she preferred blond hair, in the same shade as her own. Long, thick—again like hers, cascading over his shoulders. And dark eyes, midnight eyes.

She tilted her head to afford Maksim better access to her neck, but also to admire the way her long lashes, dark in comparison to her hair, made her eyes glitter nearly black.

She bit her bottom lip as Maksim nipped her, watching how the soft pink flesh pillowed around her white teeth.

Blond hair, dark eyes, full lips.

Her Vittorio.

"Why again must we watch this vampire?" Maksim murmured against her bared shoulder.

Orabella sighed, hating to be interrupted from her images of her perfect love. A creature who was an offshoot of herself. Perfect. Lovely. And hers.

"I've told you, darling," she said, her voice sharper than she intended, "he is obsessed with me."

Maksim lifted his head to regard her in the mirror. "If he is so obsessed, then why are you the one searching for him?"

She met his gaze, widening her eyes slightly, noting the pretty innocence it gave her features. "Haven't you heard of keeping your friends close and your enemies closer?"

Maksim straightened and strolled toward the bed, unbuttoning his shirt as he went. "In fact, I have," his voice low and almost distant.

Orabella wondered briefly about the flat tone, but then

dismissed it. Her mind was too filled with Vittorio to concern herself with her lover's petty moods.

"Was he with anyone?" she couldn't help asking. She needed to know—and the idea that he could prefer any other woman's company to hers made her ill.

"What does it matter?" Maksim collapsed on the bed, his shirt falling open to reveal his perfectly muscled chest and stomach.

"I'd hate to think he could be stalking another," she said, re-creating that wide-eyed, innocent look.

Maksim stretched, then raised a sardonic brow. "Is that because you are afraid he might have lost interest in you? Or because you actually fear for some other woman's safety?"

Orabella didn't have to feign her outrage—Maksim was far too smart. A flaw in a lover to be sure, but she still needed him. She couldn't have him being too suspicious of her actions.

She slammed down her brush and turned on her vanity stool. "You know I live in fear."

Maksim looked briefly as if he didn't quite believe her, but then his eyes softened. After all, why wouldn't he believe her? She did live with fear—she feared losing Vittorio. To lose him would be to lose half of herself.

"Well, I know where he is, and you are safe. In fact, why don't we leave now? Get as far from him as we can."

Again alarm pooled in her belly, cold and harsh. She shook her head. "No."

Maksim sat up from his lounging position, regarding her again with those strange, almost catlike eyes.

"Why? Staying near a man you dread makes no sense."

Orabella hated having to explain her decisions. So very irritating. Again, if Maksim didn't have the special abilities he did—both in and out of bed—she'd have long ago broken off their relationship. But she did need him.

She turned down her lips and regarded him with an expression she knew would gain her anything she wanted. And she wanted to stay as close to Vittorio as she could. She rose, walking slowly toward the bed.

"I feel better knowing where he is. And you will watch him for me, won't you? Protect me?"

Maksim's eyes roamed down her body as she approached him. She untied the belt of her satin robe, letting it part to reveal glimpses of her ivory skin.

Again, he raised a wry eyebrow, but she could see the hungry glitter in his eyes.

"Of course, my Bella."

She smiled, letting the robe drop to the floor, her own body reacting to his heated look. She crawled onto the bed and up his hard body.

After all, she did need the caress of a man's touch, the feeling of his mouth on her flesh, the stretch of his cock filling her. She needed physical love. And she needed what Maksim's loving could give her.

But her true love, her pure love was saved for Vittorio.

Her very heart.

Her darling son.

And he was so near.

Erika stumbled around her kitchen, her eyes feeling gritty and a dull ache at her temples. Sleep had evaded her most of the night, and this was the price. Feeling generally crappy.

She poured tea into a cup and sat down at her kitchen table, a round café-style table that she'd painted bright yellow. The color usually reminded her of sunshine and made her feel cheerful. Right now the color seemed glaringly bright and just made her head throb even more.

She glowered up at the ceiling, aiming her irritation toward the man up there somewhere, probably sleeping soundly and oblivious to the annoyance—and headache he'd caused.

"Not that he'd care anyway," she muttered, then took a sip of her hot tea. The sweet liquid tasted wonderful and she

waited for it to work its magic. Tea always calmed and relaxed her.

Not this morning, clearly. He had been so rude! She set her
cup down with more force than necessary. But more than
that, his cool attitude had goaded her into being rude back.
And she wasn't normally a rude person. In fact, she prided
herself on being quite nice.

But that man! She pulled in a calming breath, then reached
for the tea. After several sips, she did unwind a little.

"Okay, so let's be reasonable," she said aloud to herself,
and Boris, if he happened to be listening. "So you don't get
along with him. You can't expect to like everyone. And have
everyone like you."

That was all very reasonable and true, but there was another fact that was still adding to the continuing pain in her
head. She'd spent a majority of the night recalling all the
things she did like about him.

Okay, they were mainly physical, but despite her aggrava-
tion with the man himself, her body did react to his body.
Very intensely, in fact.

She sighed. Why would she be attracted to a man who was
so distant, so repressed? Those traits went against all the
things she looked for in a man. She liked her men fun and
open and kind, definitely kind. Serious was a bore. Her dad
was serious, and look at the relationship she had with him. It
was strained at best.

So why couldn't she stop thinking about Vittorio? Why
had she found herself thinking about him even from their
first short meeting?

Groaning with frustration she rose and placed her cup in
the sink. These were all thoughts and questions that had
plagued her last night. Nothing new and still no answers.

And really, she didn't want someone so emotionally cut off
in her life anyway. For a friend or lover. No sooner had she
finished telling herself that—*again*—when an image of Vittorio kissing her filled her head.

Growling, she shoved the image aside. She glanced over at the sculpture that had become the bane of her existence, and decided that with her headache and her irritation, she just could not face that too.

Instead she headed down the hall to get dressed. She needed to go out and remember why she loved this city. She needed to find her creativity. And she needed to think about something other than an unpleasant upstairs neighbor.

And maybe she knew where to go to get answers to the questions she'd had swirling through her mind since her run-in with said neighbor.

"Erika! Good to see you back, sweetheart!"

Erika smiled at the man standing in the doorway of the small room in the back of In Your Cups Tea Room. He was tall and a little thick in the middle, but he had sparkly eyes, highly arched eyebrows and a wide smile. Erika would classify him as cute—in a very camp way.

Philippe pushed aside the curtain that served as a makeshift door and sashayed into the room. "Where have you been?"

Erika smiled, deciding Philippe's brand of warm attention was just what she needed.

"Working."

He sat down across from her at a small table, then leaned in, his eyes filled with interest. "How is the show coming along? Henry and I cannot wait to go. I have a gorgeous vintage Bob Mackie pressed and ready."

Erika laughed. "Friday, October thirty-first. At seven p.m."

"Well, even I can remember that date." He wiggled his immaculately groomed brows. "Halloween. A very auspicious date."

"Let's hope."

"Have I been wrong yet?" He gave her a pointed look, and she laughed again. No. He hadn't. Since the first time she'd met him on a vacation down here nearly eight months before, he'd gotten her life eerily accurate. Right down to the sudden interest in her art and to her moving to New Orleans. He'd only seemed to be wrong on one topic.

"Speaking of which, let's see what your cards say today, shall we?"

Erika nodded as Philippe handed the deck of worn tarot cards to her. She shuffled them, concentrating on her question. *When would the prince that Philippe had predicted arrive?*

He'd mentioned this prince the first time they'd done a reading—and continued to do so with other readings. But as of yet, no prince, no knight, not even a page. Or even a court jester. Nothing. Maybe Philippe had simply been wrong. He was an amazing psychic, but even the best could have an off day.

She handed the cards back to him, and he arranged them on the table into a Celtic Cross. The large topaz ring he wore on his left index finger flashed in the candlelight as he flipped the first card.

"Oh, sweetheart, you are still struggling with your love life, aren't you?"

"Is it that obvious?" Erika smiled, albeit a little feebly, but she was not surprised he'd gone right to the subject bothering her. Philippe *was* good.

He reached out and patted her hand. "Only in the cards, honey."

She appreciated that. Knowing she looked outwardly desperate wouldn't help her headache.

He turned another card. "Well, dear, it's here. Finally. Lord, that prince of yours has been slow, hasn't he?" He frowned at the card. "Yes, he's definitely here now though."

Erika's heart jumped. "Are you sure? I don't think I've seen any prospects."

Philippe regarded her for a minute in the way he often did. She was sure he could read a person just as he did the cards. It could be a tad disconcerting—which it definitely was now.

"Oh, I think you have a prospect in mind."

As he'd been doing all day, Vittorio popped into her mind. But it couldn't be him. She hadn't met a man who was less interested in her. Heck, his feelings went beyond disinterest straight to dislike.

Philippe didn't wait for her to respond. He turned the card at the top of the cross. "Well, surprise, surprise. There he is."

Erika peered down at the card that had appeared in every one of her readings over the past two months—and in the first reading all those months ago. The card depicted a regal-looking man with long blond hair riding a white horse and carrying a sword straight in the air. A prince headed into battle.

"Your blond-haired, dark-eyed prince." Philippe sighed as if the beautiful man was real and standing right in front of them.

"Are you sure?" Erika still had doubts about the reality of this person. She certainly hadn't met anyone who fit that description . . . well, except her new neighbor. And while he did fit the look, he didn't fit anything else.

Philippe nodded, staring at the card. "This man is your soul mate. He's right here in the layout, as clear as day. A dark-eyed prince. Right there above you." He tapped the card below the knight, the card that represented her. But she didn't see that card. She only heard Philippe's words.

Right there above you.

Vittorio was literally above her apartment. But was she honestly supposed to be with Vittorio? And how the heck was she going to do that? He'd literally dismissed her last night. Dismissed her and then walked away without a backward glance. Not an auspicious start for soul mates, in her opinion.

Chapter 4

As Erika stepped out of the psychic's shop, she felt irrationally upset with Philippe and his reading. Which was hardly fair to him. He didn't make the future, he just foretold it.

Besides, what had she wanted him to say? She wouldn't lie to herself, and claim she wanted *no* love interest in her future. Maybe she just wanted the fair-haired, dark-eyed prince he'd seen over and over to turn into a knight with dark hair and pale eyes, just to rule out her boorish upstairs neighbor.

But no, Philippe couldn't even give her that. And now her prince was *right above her*, no less. All signs seemed to point to Vittorio. All signs, except the ones where he seemed to like her.

She sighed and headed toward her favorite bookstore, dying for one of the caramel lattes they made in the little café in the back. Decaf, because frankly her agitated body really didn't need any more stimulation. And her headache wasn't going anywhere soon—caffeine or no.

At least Philippe had assured her the art show was going to be a huge event. She should be focusing on that.

But no. She was focusing on a potential love interest who blatantly wasn't interested.

Lost, once again, in the rehashing of last night's encounter, she rounded the corner onto St. Louis Street and ran pretty much face first into another pedestrian. Right into his broad, very hard chest.

Stumbling backward, she immediately began to mumble her apologies while rubbing her nose. Damn, he had a seriously muscular chest.

But her words halted on her lips as she looked up at the man. Thick, black hair, chiseled, truly magnificent features, and striking pale green eyes. She knew she was gaping, but the man was stunning. Hadn't she just wished to meet a dark-haired, pale-eyed man—well, she'd thought knight, but this was weird enough. Armor would have just made it way too eerie.

"Are you okay?" he asked, his eyes locking with hers, intent and more than a little unnerving.

Erika dropped the hand still at her nose and nodded. "Fine. I wasn't watching where I was going."

"Well, it's hard to see around corners," he said with a slight smile.

A prickling of nerves ran over her—intense, causing goose bumps to rise on her bare arms.

She considered the feeling, testing whether the reaction was anything like the one she had to Vittorio. No. It wasn't. This was totally different. It wasn't attraction, but she couldn't quite read what the feeling was.

"I'm Maksim," the man said, holding out his hand, and when she didn't immediately accept it, he added, "I always think it's nice to introduce myself when I literally bump into someone."

"Well, technically I did the running into you," Erika reminded him, but she accepted his hand. "Erika."

"Nice to meet you, Erika."

He smiled at her, and again she almost wished her body would react to him. But the charming grin did nothing to her pulse. And this man was the definition of gorgeous.

"So you're sure you are okay?" he asked, still holding her hand. He tilted his head, the gesture cute and sexy all at once, which she could see in a very objective way, but couldn't react to. "No permanent damage to your nose?"

She smiled at him. "No, it's fine."

He nodded, but still didn't release her hand. He was clearly waiting for her to say something, waiting for her to make the first move here. And he was a total hunk, yet she couldn't.

She slipped her fingers from his. "Sorry again," she said, and started to step around him, but his hand on her arm stopped her.

Their eyes met, his pale ones holding hers.

She tried to speak, tried to break the eye contact between them, but couldn't. His gaze held hers. An intense feeling of confusion filled her, and her head seemed to feel—full. She didn't even understand the description, but that was the only word she could find.

She weaved, and his hand steadied her.

"Are you sure you are okay?" he asked again.

Erika nodded, able to look away from him this time. "Yes. Fine. Thank you."

He nodded, seeming reluctant to release her, probably because he was afraid she would fall or faint or something, and she wasn't totally sure she wouldn't. But he let go of her, and she did remain standing. That was good.

"Okay, then. Have a good day. Watch out for chests." He smiled once more and then moved past her, taking the opposite direction from where she was going.

She watched him as he strolled away, frowning at her own weird reaction. The man disappeared among a gaggle of laughing and chattering tourists. And just like that, the powerful dizzying sensation faded.

She frowned, confused. What had that been? Not attraction, that was for sure, which was really too bad, because she had a strong suspicion that if she'd wanted to she could have gotten a cup of coffee and a chat from that very handsome man. But she hadn't wanted it. At all.

Lord, she was mad. Totally mad. Letting a hot, charming

man walk away, while pining for, albeit an equally beautiful, but not even remotely charming—or even friendly—man.

She sighed and started down the sidewalk toward the bookstore.

Clearly she was altogether too stressed. She was not making good or rational choices. She needed to focus and get back to her work. Men could just stay on the back burner for the time being. She had much bigger things ahead of her. She'd do well to focus on them.

Maksim stopped as soon as he was out of sight of the woman. Erika Todd. He had her name. But that was about it. Entering her mind hadn't been the treasure trove of information he'd hoped.

Erika Todd knew nothing of Orabella, and she knew nothing about Ellina, which was both disappointing and frustrating.

For a split second, he lamented the fact that he had entered the mortal's mind. Mortals couldn't handle that kind of invasion. But then he shrugged it off.

Erika Todd would have some sort of residual damage from the mind-connect, but the harm was rarely permanent. And he had to give it a shot, didn't he? He'd certainly used his abilities for much less noble purposes—and frankly, Erika Todd meant nothing to him—just another mortal. And there were billions of them. He grimaced as a group of loud, obnoxious ones passed him, wearing green, purple and gold plastic beads and silly hats.

Unfortunately what he'd learned from Erika Todd was useless anyway.

Then he paused. Or maybe it wasn't.

She did know this Vittorio, object of Orabella's obsession. Not well, but she did know him. Maksim had seen a couple of uneventful encounters with the vampire. He supposed the cell phone incident from last night had been sort of eventful, but aside from being mildly amusing, it was of no import to him.

But this Erika was interested in Vittorio, which was bound to

be an issue for Orabella. He considered that for a moment . . .
it might be good information to know for the future. So he
wouldn't dismiss Erika totally.

Not to mention, he didn't know for sure if Vittorio wasn't
somehow involved in Ellina's disappearance. It seemed like a
long shot, but at this point he had to take long shots. He'd
been searching for her for two months. Someone had to know
something.

Maksim shifted to get out of the sun. Damn, he hated the
heat. Ellina had loved this city, which surprised him. Deca-
dence, sin, overindulgence—which this city had in abundance—that was his shtick, not his half-sister's. Ellina wasn't
so easily tempted. So what had drawn her here?

He shifted again, resisting the urge to tug at his T-shirt,
which sweat had glued to his body. Certainly not the oppressive
heat. He grimaced. Or the smell. Why had Ellina come here?

There were no answers yet. But he felt like he was on the
right track. At least with Orabella. She was definitely up to
something.

And she did know Ellina, he'd found correspondence from
Orabella to his sister. Innocuous missives, but upon meeting
Orabella he'd known she was far from harmless.

But thus far instead of getting answers, he was just finding
more questions. What was Orabella up to? Who was this Vittorio, and why was Maksim's petulant little lover so obsessed
with him? Oh, Maksim was fully aware that Orabella was
the one obsessed despite her claims otherwise.

Maksim wondered what he should report back to Orabella tonight. He wasn't stupid or conceited enough to believe that Orabella was just using him for his body. Well, he
was conceited enough—but definitely not stupid. She wanted
him for other reasons, reasons beyond tailing Vittorio.

He, on the other hand, suspected she *was* conceited, or at
the very least self-absorbed enough, that she wouldn't discover he was using her too. He just had to keep up the game
of being her smitten lover. A game he enjoyed in its deceit.

She wasn't the only one who excelled at using her lovers. But, if her motives for following Vittorio didn't yield any answers about Ellina, he didn't want her little mystery interfering with his own quest for answers.

The truth about Ellina was out there somewhere.

Maksim smiled to himself. How very Fox Mulder-ish of him.

He pushed away from the wall, whistling the theme to *The X Files* as he headed down the street to find some air-conditioning and a cold beer.

This was so ridiculous. Erika paced at the bottom of the stairs that led to the second-floor apartment. She hadn't even made it up them yet.

Okay, she had managed to walk up to the first landing, but once she got there, she'd turned around and headed right back down. There was something even more pathetic about that than just standing here.

Philippe couldn't be right about this. Or he was misunderstanding his own reading. Yes, Vittorio did fit all the specifics that the psychic had told her. Except the whole attraction thing, which seemed to be the key part of the prediction.

She placed a hand on the banister of the stairs that went straight, turned at a narrow landing, and disappeared overhead. And beyond those hidden steps was Vittorio.

She released the banister and fiddled with the plastic wrap covering the plate of cookies she'd made as a peace offering. Okay, "cookies" was generous. They were Rice Krispie treats, which was about all she could manage. She wasn't a good cook, nor did she particularly like to cook. She fiddled with the plastic wrap again. She wished she had something better to offer him.

"Oh, for heaven's sake, just go up there," she muttered to herself. The worst thing that could happen would be that he'd act as he had the previous night.

And she *had* gotten easily and uncharacteristically irritated by his rudeness. Which hadn't been fair, on her part. He'd been injured, and annoyed. Justifiably so, really.

At the very least she owed him another apology. He was Maggie's brother-in-law, and Maggie was one of her best friends. So she'd kill two birds with one stone. Smooth things over, and just see if maybe he was attracted to her—when he wasn't bleeding profusely from the head.

Her reasoning was sound, but still her feet remained planted on the worn wooden floor, the plate gripped in her cold fingers. What was making this so darned hard?

She pulled in a deep breath.

Okay, here was the truth of it, and she needed to be truthful with herself—if no one else. She was insanely attracted to him. An instant, undeniable attraction, a shock wave rippling through her like a hit on the Richter scale measuring beyond anything previously recorded.

That reaction made it a lot more difficult to face potentially encountering the same cool disdain she'd gotten last night. Dislike was something she never dealt well with—especially from a man whose mere presence sent her blood pressure rocketing out of the atmosphere.

But she had to. She knew she did. She had to know if Philippe was somehow miraculously right about this, and last night had just been Vittorio's pain making him seem so totally uninterested. And at the very least, she wanted to show him she was normally a polite, even-tempered person.

Staring at the staircase a moment longer, which was getting more daunting as shadows from the setting sun darkened the corners and cast strange shapes on the walls, she gripped the banister and took a step. Then another.

The hallway outside of Vittorio's apartment was murky, the waning light through dirty windows giving the whole corridor an unsettling air.

She fought the urge to glance over her shoulder, hairs rising on the back of her neck. Instead she focused on the door, rapping on the solid oak twice. She waited. No noise sounded from inside. No footfalls, no "just a minute," not even a shuffle.

Great. She went through that whole pep talk, and he wasn't even there? Crap. She'd have to get her nerve up again—and she didn't know if she could do that.

Okay, just one more knock. She couldn't do this again. He had to be there.

Just as she raised her hand to knock again, the door jerked open, her fisted hand coming close to bopping him in the nose. In the dim light, Vittorio grimaced at her through sleep-heavy eyes. His long hair was tangled and shoved haphazardly back from his face. Bare, muscled chest and flat stomach appeared over sweatpants slung low on his narrow hips.

"I'm sorry," Erika immediately said, even as her heart skipped wildly. An image of him lying in bed filled her mind, quickly morphing to a picture of her in bed with him. "I—I didn't think you'd be sleeping," she managed to mumble.

He frowned, blinking, then peered over her shoulder at the evening sky, which now nearly left them in darkness.

"I keep weird hours." His tone was flat, yet his voice still lent the words a beauty with its deep baritone timbre.

Erika stared at him, unable to keep from studying the shadows emphasizing the muscles of his chest and stomach. Chiseled and perfect. She immediately wanted to capture that perfection with her art.

But she managed to stop gaping and move her gaze up to his face, which was also a study in shadows and beauty.

Clearing her throat, she managed a smile. "I keep odd hours too."

He lifted an eyebrow, but didn't say anything. Instead he leaned on the door frame, crossing his arms over his chest. The movement caused his muscles to come to life. Erika's fingers twitched with the longing to shape over them like she would the smooth clay of one of her sculptures.

"I'm guessing you didn't come up here to discuss our sleep habits."

Erika's eyes returned to his, as did the sense of dread she'd been experiencing at the bottom of the stairs. Cool disdain—that was what she was getting. Crap.

"No." She offered him another small smile. "No, I came up to see how your head is." She reached forward to brush aside his hair to see the wound, but he caught her wrist, stopping her. His fingers cool, curled a tad too tightly on her skin.

"It's fine."

Erika nodded at the clipped response that didn't invite further questioning. Yet she didn't move, nor did he release her. Although his hold loosened and she could have sworn his thumb slid on the outside of her wrist like the briefest, faintest caress.

Crazy. She made a small noise in the back of her throat at the silly notion. The soft sound seemed to make Vittorio aware that he still held her, because he promptly dropped his fingers away from her.

Erika fought the urge to touch the place where his hand had been. Instead she stepped back from him. She should leave.

"Okay," she said feeling disoriented. "I just wanted to check." Check Philippe's theory, but as before she seemed to be the only one affected by Vittorio's nearness. Vittorio's expression was still remote, hardly filled with overwhelming attraction.

"I guess I should go, then," she added. She took another step backward, then remembered the plate of treats she still held.

"Oh and I made you these," she said, shoving the plate toward him. "You know, as a peace offering."

He stared down at the plastic wrap–covered squares as if he expected them to crawl off the plate and attack, perhaps sticking in his beautiful long hair.

Her fingers held the plate, tightening with the desire to touch the silky-looking locks. Was she utterly mad? This man was not interested in her—in the least—and she was fantasizing about touching his hair.

"I—" He still regarded the cookies with consternation. "I don't eat—sweets."

"Oh." She pulled the plate away from him. "Okay. Well, I did just want to say I'm sorry."

He nodded, saying nothing.

"About last night, I mean," she said, watching his expression.

A muscle in his jaw worked as if he was clenching his teeth. "As you've already said," he stated.

Erika nodded, not sure what else to say. It certainly didn't appear he was any more willing to forgive her tonight than he was last night.

Suddenly that uncharacteristic feeling of irritation swelled inside her again. Why did he dislike her so much? Okay, she had hit him with a cell phone, but it had been in an unusual circumstance. And she did feel truly awful about it.

But instead of just accepting that he wasn't going to warm up to her, she heard herself saying, "I know this is going to sound weird, but I'm actually trying to figure out if you are someone that my psychic told me I'd meet."

Vittorio straightened, and the remote look in his eyes shifted, but it wasn't to an expression she liked any better. His eyes widened with amused disbelief.

"Your psychic?"

Erika had received this reaction before. More than once. And she immediately regretted her honesty.

"I'm sure this sounds a little strange to you."

He tilted his head. "What did this psychic say?"

She hesitated. Was he genuinely curious, or did he intend to mock her?

"He's been predicting that I would meet someone who at least physically fits your description."

He nodded, his gaze leaving hers as if he was considering the idea. She still couldn't quite decipher what he might be thinking.

"And what else did this psychic say?"

Erika again debated what to tell him. But the lopsided, not altogether kind, slant of his lips made her stop. He just thought she was nuts. And he didn't appear to like her any better for her nuttiness.

"Forget it." She raised a hand in a gesture of defeat. "I just wanted to be sure your head was all right."

She started to leave, when his voice stopped her. "Thanks."

Erika didn't bother to turn around. She simply nodded, unsure if he could see it or not. And not really caring. He had a way of making her feel like a blathering idiot. Not a fun feeling when combined with her very irritating, and clearly irrational, attraction to the man.

She headed down the stairs, determined to let Philippe's prediction go—and to be nothing but polite in the presence of her upstairs neighbor, who she was beginning not only to want to shag, but to hate too. Talk about a doomed relationship.

Philippe had been so wrong.

She entered her apartment, shoving the door open with more force than necessary. And shutting it with the same needless force, although the slam did give her a small measure of satisfaction.

Sinking onto the gold sofa, she tugged off the plastic wrap protecting the marshmallow treats and picked the biggest of the bunch. She bit into it, forcing herself to focus on the crunch and the sweetness rather than her anger. But the attempt didn't last long.

"He is so . . . infuriating," she muttered around the cookie.

She took another bite, chewing with frustration.

"He doesn't know what he just sent away."

And she was pretty sure she wasn't talking about her cooking.

Chapter 5

Vittorio didn't move, listening to Erika's footfalls on the stairs. Then the jiggle of the old doorknob, then the slam of the door closing.

He'd angered her again, and he tried to find relief in that fact. But he couldn't dredge up even the smallest hint of anything akin to relief. Instead, he felt like shit.

He even wanted to tell himself she was likely a little crazy after the random announcement that her psychic had described someone in her future who fit his description. But a vampire finding someone nuts because they believed a psychic seemed more than a little paradoxical.

And then add that she made him cookies—or something that kind of looked like cookies. She made him *something*—and no one had done that in a long time. Not since he was a small boy, and Cook had made his favorite biscuits sprinkled with sugar and cinnamon. Oh yeah, he felt like shit all right.

Lord, he hadn't thought of his childhood in years, decades. The last two hundred years had obliterated the good memories of his past. Which brought him to why he was here. And why he had to create a barrier between himself and the sweet, beautiful woman downstairs.

He closed his door, a softer, more regretful mimic of Erika's door-slamming. He'd been stupid to even give her the very small hint of remorse that he had. Luckily, his "thank you" had done little to repair the damage his rudeness had done. Of course, standing here shrouded in darkness when he could be surrounded by her light didn't feel particularly lucky. Not in the least.

But he couldn't risk Erika's safety because he wanted her. That would be far crueler than his churlish behavior. And maybe, maybe, if he was wrong about being responsible for hurting people in his past, he could try to have some kind of relationship with her.

Even giving himself that much permission caused his body to react. His senses sharpening, his body aching.

"Damn it," he muttered to himself, frustrated with how easily he could lose control of himself when it came to her.

He was the king of control, having spent many years now controlling his appetites, his emotions, and thus his world. Or so he'd thought. But now he wasn't so sure. His control seemed to be sliding away—until he wondered if he ever had it at all.

He heard a noise below him. Erika. Her feet padding on the wooden floors, the clack of something, even the low, barely there sound of her voice—the words indiscernible, but the rise and fall of the tone fascinating to him. He imagined what she was doing. How she looked.

"Damn it!"

He strode to where he'd undressed the night before, his clothes a heap on the floor. He snagged his jeans, and changed from his sweats to the worn denim. Then he turned to the canvas satchel on a chair. Rooting around, he found a black T-shirt.

A bang sounded from directly underneath his feet, and he paused, the shirt halfway over his head. He listened for a moment longer, detecting the sound of Erika speaking again—the gentle, lilting tones like a caress all around him.

Longing gathered in his stomach, spreading downward. He wanted to be down there with her, hearing what she was saying—although he didn't doubt that it wasn't flattering to him.

Jerking his shirt on the rest of the way, he moved to look for his cell phone. Where the hell was Ren? He needed his brother here. At the very least, Ren and Maggie would provide a buffer between himself and Erika. Not to mention he really needed to talk to his brother about things that couldn't be discussed over the phone.

He paused in his search. Okay, that was worrisome, when he needed Ren's opinion on a problem. Even though Ren was older, Vittorio had always been the more rational one, the responsible one. Or at least he'd tried to be. But maybe he needed Ren's more extreme reasoning now. He definitely needed the one person who understood him and his past.

Finding the silver cell phone on the nightstand, he flipped open the cover and scrolled through his short list of numbers to Ren's. The line rang several times, before his brother answered.

"You have the worst timing in the world," Ren stated.

"I try," Vittorio said wryly, not in the mood for Ren's complaints. He had one of his own. But he did ask, "Why? What did I interrupt now?"

"Maggie getting naked."

Vittorio made a noise, not expecting that answer. Although knowing his brother, he probably should have.

"Then why did you answer the phone?"

There was silence on the other end, then a little hitch in Ren's breath.

"Oh, for Christ's sake," Vittorio muttered. "You aren't actually doing it, are you?"

"Not yet," Ren admitted. "So I'd appreciate it if you made this quick."

An image of what Ren would likely be doing to Maggie moments after hanging up the phone flashed through Vittorio's mind. Then the image morphed into himself and Erika with her soft, pink lips and stormy blue eyes.

Do not go there.

He gritted his teeth, forcing down a frustrated groan. "Where are you?"

"Maggie and I are in Italy. Vacation, little brother, something you should look into. What's going on?"

Vittorio had no idea how to explain what was going on. Nor did he really want to—not why he was in New Orleans, nor this crazy attraction to Erika. The intensity of it was irrational. A weird anomaly. Instead he took out his frustration on Ren.

"Why didn't you mention that Maggie's friend, Erika, was staying in one of your apartments?"

"Why would I?"

"Because I arrived here last night to stay in the upstairs apartment for a while and ended up scaring the shit out of her. She brained me with her cell phone."

As Vittorio could have expected, Ren laughed. "Her cell phone? That's pretty funny."

"Yeah, it was a laugh riot."

Ren's laughter dwindled, although Vittorio could tell he was still grinning. "So she assaulted you with a phone. I'm sure you're fine, what with being a big ole vampire and all."

"Yes," Vittorio admitted begrudgingly, "I'm fine. But I'm not happy about the whole thing. You could have told me she was here."

"Well, if I'd known you were coming I would have. And why do you care if Erika is there or not?"

Vittorio heard Maggie's voice in the background. Then Ren said, "You like her, don't you?"

Vittorio didn't suppress a growl. "What are you? A teenage girl? I don't like her—I don't even know her. I just— I just wanted to be alone."

"Okay," Ren said, but Vittorio knew he didn't believe him. "What do you want me to do about it? I can hardly kick out Maggie's best friend." Then he lowered his voice and added, "I'm sure as hell not going to do it with the potential of kick-ass sex in my near future. I don't think Maggie would be happy with me, if I did that. Not to mention, I don't want to. Erika is nice. You should talk to her instead of acting like a miserable hermit."

Vittorio growled again, both irritated with his brother's assessment of him and his response to getting rid of Erika. He'd known Ren couldn't, and shouldn't, make her leave, but . . .

Ah, hell!

"When are you coming home?" he asked.

"Wednesday."

Four more days. Hardly a long time in the life of a vampire, yet it felt like an eternity. He considered telling Ren why he was here, but then couldn't. Ren would be home soon.

And Vittorio could avoid Erika for that short amount of time—and then he'd have his brother and sister-in-law back to run interference.

"Okay," he said, mostly to himself.

"Okay. So play nice. And we'll see you then."

Abruptly, Ren hung up. He obviously had other things on his mind besides his brother being surprised by the harmless mortal woman downstairs.

Except she wasn't harmless. She had him seriously rattled. And he wasn't harmless to her either.

That was why he had to stay focused on finding out the truth. He rummaged around the darkness to find his wallet. And he had to start now. The more time away from Erika, the better.

Maksim followed Vittorio, staying a safe distance behind him, weaving in and out of the tourists crowding Bourbon Street. Just because he wasn't a vampire, didn't mean that Vittorio wouldn't sense him. Vampires were very good at detecting other paranormal creatures.

But it was clear Vittorio wasn't concentrating on anything but his own mission. His walk was fast and focused, his movements lithe and graceful with the inherent agility of the undead.

Irony, that. Zombies were such a clumsy lot, while the undead . . . poetry on two feet. He liked that about Orabella, among other superficial things. It was her personality that he found lacking. As well as her morals. The lack of morals didn't bother him as much as her personality either, come to think of it.

Vittorio turned off Bourbon onto a side street. Maksim waited a moment before following, just in time to see him step through street-dirtied plastic curtains designed to keep the cool air-conditioning inside.

AC. Hallelujah!

Maksim pushed aside the plastic, breathing a pleased sigh as a gust of chilled air blew over him. Even the stale scents of cigarette smoke and beer didn't dampen his pure bliss at the blast of cool air. But he only allowed himself a moment's joy before searching the dingy darkness of the small bar.

Vittorio was already disappearing into a small back room. Damn. Even though the area didn't have a proper door, it looked like a private portion of the bar, and was very tiny. Maksim would be noticed if he followed. Not to mention he'd be sensed. Demons had a particularly strong preternatural imprint. Easy to read in a closed space.

Instead he sat down at the bar in the main room, and waited. Vittorio would be out eventually. And Maksim would learn what had him nearly sprinting around the streets of New Orleans with that single-minded look on his almost angelically beautiful face.

"Sherri," Vittorio greeted the bartender, one of his longtime acquaintances. He hesitated to call her a friend, since they never saw each other outside of this shabby back room. But he supposed in a strange way, they were.

"Vittorio," she greeted with a smile. Her smiles always held a sardonic quality, as if she knew far more about you than she let on—and in many cases, he was sure she did. In fact, he was counting on it.

"You haven't been in for a while," she said, already reaching under the bar for a highball glass to make his drink.

"Been doing some traveling," he told her. That gave such a pleasant ring to what he'd been doing.

"Nice." She lifted the bottle of whiskey before pouring. "The usual?"

He nodded, sliding onto a barstool, pleased to see the room was empty. Too early for the type of crowd who came here. Vampires, the occasional werewolf and other forms of shapeshifters—and musicians, a sort of supernatural breed all their own. Ironically, Sherri was the only constant—and she was human.

She slid the whiskey on the rocks in front of him, but he didn't immediately take a drink. Instead he got right to what he'd come here for.

"Do you remember Amanda?"

Sherri frowned for a moment, searching her memory bank of late-night patrons. "Amanda? The one who fronted that band at The Purple Haze?"

Vittorio nodded. "What happened to her?"

Sherri gave him a surprised look, as if she couldn't believe he hadn't heard. After all, Vittorio had once spent plenty of time with Amanda.

"She was found dead in her apartment. God, that must have been at least three years ago now. I think they labeled it heart failure. You know, she had a cocaine problem for years. Well, of course you know that."

Vittorio nodded. Amanda struggled with drugs for years. When he'd first met her, she hadn't just restricted herself to coke. She mixed; whatever she could get. But he also knew she was doing a great job staying clean the last time he'd seen her.

But relapses were common. And maybe she had. Maybe she had just gotten careless. Fallen off the wagon, hard.

"But you know," Sherri added as she absently wiped down the worn bar top, "I recall hearing that they didn't find any drugs in her system."

Vittorio's muscles tensed. "Really?"

"Probably the damage was already done. Her heart just gave out or something."

Vittorio nodded again, even though he wasn't sure he agreed. She'd been killed. Possibly like Angela, Jessalynn. God, the list went on and on.

Nausea swelled over him like a warm, salty wave, threatening to drown him. Amanda made number twenty. Twenty women in as many years. Women he'd known. Women he'd helped—or thought he'd helped. They'd all trusted him. And now they were all dead.

Anyone looking at all these deaths, however, wouldn't necessarily find them unusual—after all, they were all drug users, some were prostitutes, others just living hard and fast lives. Prime candidates for early deaths. But even for a vampire who'd been alive for over two hundred years, the rate of unusual and premature deaths around him was high.

He glanced at his acquaintance on the other side of the bar. Sherri didn't realize just how lucky she was that they had only remained acquaintances. Friends didn't fare well around him. Maybe it was the natural course of things, or maybe it was something more.

He was leaning toward something more these days.

"And you remember Julianne, that little short girl from where The Impalers play?" Sherri asked, dragging him out of his thoughts. "I think she started there while you were still playing with the band."

"Yes," he said slowly, already dreading what Sherri would say about the sweet girl who'd moved here from backwoods Alabama. A girl he'd lent a sympathetic ear to on a number of occasions when he'd worked with the band. He'd even seen her some months ago while visiting Ren.

"Last April, she was found dead. Jumped out the window of her apartment on Decatur. You didn't hear about that?"

Vittorio shook his head, feeling numb. That's when he'd seen her. April. He'd been here for Ren and Maggie's wedding. He'd sat at the bar, after hours, and chatted with her. Something about her always called to him. She looked a little—lost.

"It was weird too," Sherri continued. "She was in here the night before she died. With her boyfriend, and they seemed quite happy. All sweet smiles like she always was. She certainly didn't strike me as someone who was going to hurl herself out a window the following night."

"What night was that?" He could feel nausea rising, making it hard to swallow.

"Early April, I think."

Vittorio nodded. She'd killed herself right around the time he'd seen her. Or she'd been killed.

Maksim waited. And waited. Frankly, demons were not known for their patience. But his frustration was compounded by the fact that he couldn't simply enter this vampire's mind, take the information he wanted, and be done with him. His mind-connect couldn't work with other preternatural creatures.

So he had to find out the answers he wanted, the old-fashioned way. Eavesdropping. Tedious—especially when he wasn't in the position to do so.

He leaned back on his barstool, trying to peer through the doorway that led to the back room. Vittorio still sat at the bar, his profile to him, nursing a drink and occasionally chatting with the female bartender back there.

The vampire looked decidedly ill. Although the lighting in this joint was hardly flattering. And the undead often did look a little peaked. But still Maksim got the feeling that it wasn't the unflattering lighting and lack of a pulse that made this one look unwell. Given Vittorio's rapid pace and intent look as he walked here, he had come to find out something. And that something apparently wasn't sitting well.

There was no way for Maksim to move closer without garnering notice, so he was stuck here trying to decipher any vibes he could pick up, which were diluted by the others in the bar.

Maksim sighed, pushing his lukewarm beer away. Well, if this vampire had any dastardly deeds planned for the evening, he wasn't rushing off to act on them. Frankly, he didn't look in any shape to do anything terribly dastardly anyway.

There was nothing to be learned here tonight. Maksim was better off going back to Orabella and trying to gather any information he could from her. And she would ask him to continue following this Vittorio. So there would be other times to figure out the deal with this vampire and his relationship to Orabella.

He fished around in the pockets of his jeans for a few dollars. He tossed the crumpled bills on the bar and strolled out of the narrow, squalid little hole-in-the-wall.

Vittorio sat in the bar for how long, he didn't know. Then he wandered back to Ren's house, taking the long way, the darker, dangerous streets away from the relative safety and lights of Bourbon Street.

Several shady-looking characters approached him, one asking for a cigarette, another asking for money, the third drunk, and itching for a fight. None of them worried Vittorio. This is where he'd spent much of his time when he'd lived here. Trying to help these people. And trying to save himself.

But all his efforts hadn't done an ounce of good. How hadn't he realized what was going on?

He unlocked the large barnlike doors that led into Ren's house. The courtyard was dimly lit and silent. The air was heavy and still, humidity hanging in the air like an entity unto itself.

Even as he told himself not to look, his eyes moved right to the windows of the lower apartment. Erika's apartment was dark. Hardly a surprise, it had to be after 3 a.m. She'd said she kept odd hours too, but he doubted they were as late as his. Most mortals' weren't.

Despite the horrible things he'd discovered tonight, he still found himself longing to see Erika. Was he mad? He couldn't risk being a part of her life. Or rather making her a part of his. What he'd learned tonight was enough to ram home that fact.

Julianne. She of all the women was proof he had to be careful. He hadn't been anything more to her than a sympathetic listener—someone to listen to her, period. She'd been a good girl, not part of the darkness he usually surrounded himself with. She was out of her element in the Big Easy. Shy, quiet and not suited to the wild bawdiness of Bourbon Street. But she'd come here and was determined to stay because of her love for a musician who worked at one of the many bars on Bourbon.

She hadn't been happy here. But her boyfriend hadn't struck Vittorio as the type to settle down into a mundane, domestic life. So to have him, she had to stay in his world.

Maybe she had really killed herself. Although she hadn't struck Vittorio as that type either. But he really didn't know. And somehow, awful as it was, her taking her own life was a better alternative to the one he'd come up with.

That women were being killed just because they knew him.

He dropped down on one of the wrought iron benches nestled among the overgrown magnolias and ferns and other lush greenery. Maybe he was wrong about everything. Twenty-one women dying was hardly a huge number when you factored in the number of years he'd been alive, and the lives they'd led. Maybe the deaths had been, if not natural, at least not abnormal.

He crossed his arms across his chest and closed his eyes, feeling every bit his two hundred-plus years. Sometimes he thought it would be almost lovely to have a natural death. Hell, he'd thought that a lot during his first years of vampirism.

Just then the still night air was filled with a brief shriek as loud and skin-crawling as what he imagined Julianne's cry to her death had been. Vittorio shot upright, all muscles tense, all senses alert, any feelings of weariness gone.

But it wasn't Julianne.

Erika!

Chapter 6

The horrible cry seemed to come from her apartment, but the acoustics of the enclosed courtyard made it hard to be certain. And now all was quiet again. Not even a hint of sound from Bourbon Street reached his ears.

Vittorio rose slowly, listening intently. He took careful steps across the flagstones, edging closer to the apartments.

Just as he reached the first step leading up to the glassed-in porch, another scream slashed through the silence. Vittorio leapt up the stairs and shoved open the old door, the hinges squeaking in protest, although the sound hardly registered as it was drowned out by another cry. Keening, broken and absolutely terrified.

Now there was no doubt from where the screams came. They echoed out of Erika's apartment like the haunted shrieks of a banshee.

A corresponding fear welled up inside him. What was happening to her? He tried the handle of her door. The knob refused to budge. He absently noted that it hadn't been tampered with, but he knew there were creatures out there who didn't need to break a window or a lock to enter a building.

Another horror-filled screech sliced through the darkness. Vittorio didn't hesitate. He concentrated, then he faded, becoming no more tangible than the shadows surrounding him.

He rematerialized on the other side of the locked door, trying to get his bearings. He'd not fed for days—not an un-usual thing for him. He could go long periods without steal-ing the human life force that he needed to survive. But the lack of sustenance made using his preternatural abilities more difficult. And more than a little disorienting.

He swayed slightly, as he tried to focus on something, any-thing, in the dark room to ground him. But before he could find anything, a shadow darted past his feet, pure black and low to the ground. He stumbled backward, more surprised than unnerved.

The pitch-black shadow skittered around the sofa, then leapt up and perched on the back of a large chair. Gold eyes peered through the dark, only to disappear, then slowly reap-pear, regarding Vittorio with an almost disdainful boredom.

It only took Vittorio a few moments to realize he was being stared down by a cat. He released a pent-up breath, amazed he had been so easily startled by the creature.

Another scream filled the air, reminding him of why he was really so rattled. The cry was close, deafening in its prox-imity.

Vittorio stepped farther into the room, focusing all his at-tention on locating Erika—and whatever was terrifying her so.

He spotted her on the sofa, her form barely visible. Her shout tapered down to small whimpers, the frightened sound no less disturbing.

"Erika?" he said quietly, rounding the sofa, moving guard-edly, watching for any other movement aside from the cat. But as he got closer, he realized Erika was huddled alone among the jumbled sofa cushions, her body curled into itself. Looking small and helpless.

He reached over to the end table and switched on the lamp. Soft yellow light pushed away some of the darkness. He leaned over her, seeing her eyes were wide open, staring unfocused, straight ahead.

"Erika?"

"Go away," she moaned, pulling her knees tighter to her chest.

He straightened, unsure what to do. He supposed he was the last person she would want to help her. But the paleness of her face, and the clear horror in her stormy gray eyes made it impossible for him to leave.

"Are you hurt?"

She didn't respond, her glassy stare still focused somewhere past him.

"Erika?" He pressed a hesitant hand to her shoulder. She jerked under the gentle touch.

"Oh God," she wailed. "Please don't hurt me!"

He immediately dropped his hand from her shoulder. "I won't hurt you."

"You are! You are already!"

He frowned, not understanding. Surely his light touch couldn't have caused her pain. And he didn't intend to threaten her, but he stepped back anyway, giving her space.

"Erika, please tell me what's going—"

Before he could even finish his question, another scream tore from her throat. Then another until Vittorio couldn't stop himself from reaching for her, pulling her against him until she was on his lap, her rigid body cradled against him.

"Erika?" He held her, smoothing his hand down the delicate curve of her spine, making soothing nonsensical sounds, willing her to calm.

Finally she did relax, her head nestling under his chin, her fingers lax and curled against his chest.

He held her, unsure what to do. Finally, he shifted her slightly, trying to see her face. Her eyes were closed, her breathing even.

Had she just been dreaming?

He held her for a while longer, allowing his own body to relax along with hers. She hadn't even been awake when she'd been gaping in terror at some dreamed villain.

He held her for a moment longer, savoring the feeling of her in his arms, her slight weight, the sultry scent of cinnamon clinging to her flawless, almost translucent skin. Her soft rear end situated perfectly against him.

He fought back a groan as his body reacted, much against his will. That was when he sensed her energy flowing around him, spinning like a fragrant, enticing cocoon, encompassing them both. He'd been able to ignore it when he'd been shaken by her screams. Now he couldn't. She smelled and felt too good.

He breathed in deeply, relishing the satisfying sensation of her delightful energy deep inside him. Then he froze, abruptly halting himself. God, what was he doing? He never took his energy like this—one on one. When he did feed, he went into crowds, taking from many. Keeping it impersonal, unemotional.

Quickly, yet carefully, he edged Erika away from him, arranging her on the cushions and sliding out from underneath her. But as he stood and started toward the door, Erika stirred.

"Vittorio," she murmured as she blinked up to catch him at the end of the sofa.

Then she immediately sat upright, her hand going to her chest, her eyes wide as she realized he was real. Not a part of another vivid dream.

"Vittorio?" Her voice was raspy from sleep. The sound brushed over his skin as powerful and enticing as her smell, as her energy. His nerve-endings tingled.

He didn't respond, his body in overdrive, his mind blank.

"What are you doing here?"

"I—I heard you screaming."

She frowned, clearly confused, then remembrance dawned on her face. "Oh, yes, I had the worst dream. Someone was trying to kill me."

He nodded, having deduced the nightmare had been something along those lines. "Yes."

He didn't know what else to say. He just knew he had to get out of there.

She brushed back her dark hair from her face and released a shuddering breath. "I'm sorry if I disturbed you."

Yes, she definitely disturbed him, but not in the way she meant. First he'd been terrified right along with her, and now he was painfully attracted to her. Oh yeah, she disturbed him all right.

She sat there for a moment, her gaze distant, fear still lingering in her eyes. Even though this look was much better than the wide-eyed, unblinking stare she'd had as she'd dreamed.

"I can't remember ever having a nightmare that horrible. And that realistic." She shivered, wrapping her arms around her midsection.

Vittorio's fingers twitched with the longing to touch her, to comfort her. But he couldn't. It might seem like a compassionate gesture, but really, it would be the height of selfishness.

She shivered again, but then forced a smile. "I don't think I'll be going to sleep again right away."

She slid her legs off the sofa and sat up, clearly trying to shake off the residual effects of the dream.

She stared at the coffee table, again in that way that indicated she wasn't really seeing the table. But he noted the plate of sticky-looking bars she'd made for him. Half of them were gone. And he felt a pang about that. She'd come down and eaten them herself. The unwanted offering. Somehow the image upset him. He should have just taken them. What harm would there have been in that?

"I figured, why let them go to waste."

Vittorio's eyes met hers, startled to realize she'd followed his stare and was explaining the missing pieces.

He met her gaze again, pulled in by the grayness of her eyes. Stormy blue at times. Then all dove gray and softhearted other times. And somewhere in between now. Shaken and uncertain.

He glanced back at the plate, then asked, "Are you okay now?"

She nodded, then her lips twisted into a pained grimace. "I hate to be this silly, but will you stay while I go check the other rooms? I really do feel—jumpy."

That was the least Vittorio could do. After all, until he saw her on the sofa alone, he'd thought her screams could have been caused by something he'd brought upon her. The idea sickened him, like the nausea from earlier in the bar.

"Let me check," he offered, heading toward her hallway.

"Thank you," she said in a small voice, but he didn't glance back in her direction.

The way she looked, delicate and scared, called to him. He wanted to hold her, protect her. But his presence would not give her protection. Even if he wasn't right about the deaths of the women in his past being connected to him, he wasn't the type of guy who'd be any good at playing the knight in shining armor.

Not to mention, he was simply too attracted to her energy. He wanted to sample it, to feel it inside himself.

He headed down the dark hall. The rooms were still, and he didn't sense anything there but the vibe of Erika herself. Her energy seemed to permeate the old walls, giving the whole apartment a new, warm feeling.

Yearning flared inside him, reinforcing why he had to get out of here, quickly.

Still, when he reached her bedroom, he flipped on the light, telling himself it was for her benefit—and certainly not his own curiosity. He paused in the doorway, surveying all the nuances of the room.

Her bed was piled with pillows and covered with a plush velvet duvet in a rich deep blue. Gilded lamps with bead-fringed shades sat on each side of the large bed. An oval mirror hung on one wall and a painting of cherubs took up a majority of the wall behind the bed.

The room could have reminded him of a baroque bordello, but instead Vittorio found himself appreciating the flow of colors and textures. It was a room that revealed the artist in Erika. Each piece of furniture complimented the other until the whole room radiated a feeling, a personality.

He tried to sense something amiss in the room. But nothing

was uncomfortable there. He focused on the other smaller bedroom that she was using to store her art supplies, and the bathroom.

There was nothing wrong—no residual energy from anyone else being there. Well, except for the cat. And he only had a distinctly disdainful air. Typical cat.

Vittorio headed back to the living room. Erika was no longer seated on the sofa. Now she paced, her arms wrapped around herself as if she was freezing. Her eyes didn't look any less haunted.

"Everything is fine." He kept his voice low, but laced it with conviction. She needed to believe she would be safe. There was nothing worse than not feeling secure in your own home. He knew that feeling all too well.

She nodded, but her arms tightened around her and she glanced at the hallway, clearly not believing him. He looked toward the front door, knowing that he shouldn't stay any longer. But he couldn't make himself go.

She pulled in a breath, then paced back to the kitchen counter.

"I'm sorry," she said, her tone frustrated, and he knew the emotion was directed at herself. "I know I'm acting ridiculous, but that dream . . . it was so vivid. So . . ."

She shook her head, unable to give words to the horrible images in her head.

Vittorio watched her a moment longer, her fear making the air heavy. He shifted, uncertain what to do, how to help her.

Finally, he moved to the sofa and sat. He patted the cushion next to him. "Come. I'll sit with you until you fall back asleep."

She gave him a weak smile. "I don't think that's going to happen again tonight."

He didn't say anything. He just tapped the cushion again.

Her eyes moved to his hand, but she didn't move. Probably not sure if she could really trust him. He couldn't blame her. But she eventually crossed to the sofa, her movements wooden.

She sank down, not touching him—for which he was grateful. She was too much temptation even without her body directly against his.

They were both silent for several seconds, then Erika turned to him, her knee very close to his. He could feel her heat.

"You don't have to stay," she said. "I appreciate you checking out the apartment. I'll be okay."

He knew he should take the opportunity to exit. But he couldn't leave her looking so distressed, so pale.

"Just lay down."

"Excuse me?" Her brows rose, her expression almost comical. A better look than the lingering fear.

He felt a smile tug at his lips. "It's four a.m. You need to try to go back to sleep."

"I really don't think that's going to happen."

"Try," he said, keeping his voice low, and slightly coaxing.

She considered him for a moment, then turned to arrange the jumbled cushions. She slid away from him, and settled down. Her body was stiff, and her legs were curled up so even her feet didn't touch him. The position didn't look overly comfortable, and he thought about suggesting they move to her bedroom, but immediately dismissed the idea.

He prided himself on good self-control, but being in a bed with her would test even his limits. Who was he kidding? She tested his limits by just breathing.

"Close your eyes," he murmured, trying to lull her with his voice. He half expected her to reject the idea. But she did as he asked, her lids fluttering shut.

Then he closed his own eyes. He started to draw in her energy, then stopped. He couldn't do this. It wasn't right.

He glanced at her, and her eyes were open, staring straight ahead. She was clearly reliving her dream. He could help her. He could take just enough of her energy to make her relax and sleep. Was that selfish?

Yes. But he couldn't leave her this way.

Slowly, he breathed in through his nose, his eyes never

leaving her. Her life force filled him, making every nerve ending in his body pulse and vibrate. The effect on his body was
like breathing in pure oxygen, like breathing in the best drug
ever made.

He held it deep inside himself, then breathed it out. Guilt
immediately filled him, even as he wanted to do it again.

He studied her, watching as his first breath calmed her, although she was still awake. He closed his eyes again and
breathed in. Euphoria, vivid, intense and so wonderful filled
him. He was floating, floating on pure bliss.

He exhaled, the release of air laced with the hint of a
pleased moan. His body quivered. God, he wanted all of this
woman. He wanted to be deep inside her when he tasted her
life force. He ached with that need.

He took more of her energy—but not as deeply this time.
Hard as it was to deny himself.

Then he looked over at her. Her eyes were shut, and for a
moment, he panicked. He'd taken too much. That was his
first terrified thought, then she sighed. He watched as her
chest rose and fell, her breathing even with sleep.

She was fine. Just fine. He released the pent-up breath he
didn't even realize he held.

"Erika?" he asked softly.

She answered him with a small, quite adorable, little
snore. His lips quirked into a slight smile. Guilt still filled
him, but he was pleased to see her calm and peaceful.

But he didn't allow himself any more time to watch her.
She was far too beautiful, and the temptation was too much.
He had to go.

He eased up off the sofa, making sure not to jar her. He
was pretty sure she wouldn't rouse, but he didn't want to risk
disturbing her. He walked to her room and pulled the thick
duvet off her bed and brought it back to the living room.

Carefully he draped the comforter over her. When he was
done, her cat, who'd watched from the back of a chair across
the room, jumped down from his perch and sauntered over

to take a spot on the puffy cover. He plucked at the velvet material until he'd arranged it to his liking, then settled down behind the curve of Erika's bent legs.

The cat regarded Vittorio with condescending gold eyes.

"I take it you don't much like me," he said quietly to the cat. "Good decision."

Vittorio turned to leave, then noticed again the plate of sweets on the table. Again, he pictured her coming back from attempting a truce, sitting down, and eating them. All the while disliking him.

He had to remember that was a good thing. He cast one last look back at her, and started toward the door. Then just as he would have dematerialized to his apartment, he stopped.

He returned to the table, and stared at the plate of treats she'd made for him. The thick cut squares glinted in the lamplight, the milky glaze holding together each piece of rice crisps. He picked up one of the squares, the coating sticking to his fingers.

Even though he didn't ever crave food, he bit into it. The crisps crunched, and sweetness flooded his mouth. Slowly he chewed, savoring the sticky, sugary flavor. He swallowed, then took another bite.

He ate one more bite, finding it hard to swallow, only because he was no longer designed to eat human food, not because he didn't want to keep eating.

Reluctantly, he placed the half-eaten treat back on the plate. He didn't allow himself to glance at Erika as he faded, just like he didn't allow himself to consider why it suddenly seemed important to eat what she'd made for him.

Chapter 7

"So what was he doing?" Orabella knew this particular moment, as she straddled Maksim in their bed, probably wasn't the best time to question him about Vittorio, but she couldn't help herself.

Maksim opened his eyes, regarding her with an ironic glint that stated he agreed with her unspoken logic. "Nothing of interest. Having a drink in a dingy little hole-in-the-wall."

Orabella nodded, then pivoted her hips, riding him like one of her deceased husband's prized ponies.

Maksim's eyes flickered shut as he moaned with pleasure.

"That's it, baby," he muttered roughly.

But Orabella didn't share his satisfaction. She was focused on other things.

What was her darling son doing here? Surely he knew she'd eventually come looking for him here. New Orleans was one of his favorite places. Just as he favored his dreadful, spiteful brother. And other dreadful creatures.

Did Vittorio want her to find him? The idea excited her. Her hips moved faster. She closed her eyes, picturing her son's angel face.

A face so like her own—which would ultimately make it impossible for him to deny or forget her. They were the same person, the only two who could truly understand each other.

But what if he was here for a different purpose? Some of

her pleasure waned. Vittorio always seemed to have a fondness for the women of the South. Another mystery to her.

And frankly, no woman he picked was good enough for him. No woman was good enough, period. The only one worthy of his love was his mother. He had to know that, deep inside, didn't he?

"Are you sure he wasn't there to meet someone?"

Maksim opened one eye. "It didn't seem that way."

She nodded and twirled her hips, pretending she was enjoying their sex as much as he was. Sometimes having a lover was such a nuisance.

But she did need him, for multiple reasons. Maksim could follow Vittorio. Vittorio would sense her instantly if she got within two hundred feet of him. And while that should have irritated her, because it did make it hard to get to him if he didn't want to see her, it also thrilled her. His awareness of her proved how connected they were. One soul in two bodies.

Her hips ground down hard on Maksim's, taking him deep. Vittorio was going to love her again. She would give him exactly what he'd missed all these years. He'd be thrilled.

She ground herself down onto Maksim, taking what she needed. What she needed for Vittorio. He'd be so pleased. He'd have to forgive her.

"Oh yeah, that's it, baby," Maksim growled, his words shattering her lovely thoughts.

She rolled her eyes in arrogance, then disguised the gesture as one of overwhelming bliss.

"Will you follow him tomorrow?" she couldn't stop herself from asking.

"Of course." Maksim's voice sounded as irritated as she felt.

"And tell me if he talks to anyone?"

"Yes." Maksim's large hands spanned the curve of her hips and took control of the pace, lifting her and impaling her over and over.

She had to admit, she did like it rough and his aggressiveness and rapid rhythm did feel good. She flung her head back and let her arousal rise. Maksim would report everything back to her, and she would know what her baby boy was doing. And eventually, she'd get what she wanted. She would use what Maksim was giving her, and then she would make Vittorio return to her forever.

She just had to keep Maksim blindly devoted to her for a little longer. She cried out as her release hit her, but before the last shudder quivered through her body, she wiggled off him.

"Where you going, baby?"

Orabella graced him with a coyly shy look. She licked her perfectly glossed lips. Demons loved naiveté. And he adored her ingenue act, never guessing it was just that. A show.

"I want to taste you," she said shyly, managing a blush.

Maksim rose up on his elbows, looking down at his penis. The sated organ began to swell and lengthen again. Sex was another thing demons adored. And Maksim was insatiable.

He glanced back to her, raising an eyebrow. "Well, who would I be to deny you your wants."

Exactly, she thought as she took his now huge and hard erection into her mouth.

Erika groaned as Boris woke her with a strident and demanding yowl. She tried pulling the covers over her head, but the insistent cat wouldn't cut her a break. He leapt onto her, landing smack dab in the center of her back.

"Get down, you pest," she groaned, her tone more tired than chagrined. Her cat seemed to have the market on that emotion. He yowled again. She wiggled and he jumped down, hitting the floor with a solid thud.

"Like you need any more food," she muttered.

He meowed once more, then gave up his vocal complaining and sat on the carpet, directly in front of her, regarding her with those unblinking golden eyes. Displeasure clear on his furry face.

Great, now the stare tactic. Groaning, she rolled over and sat up. God, her brain felt as if it was wrapped in a thick layer of cotton batting.

She pushed her hair back, and tried to decide what time it was. Sunlight flooded in through the windows and dappled the hardwood floors. Then all thoughts of time disappeared as memories of the night before penetrated her wooly, disoriented brain.

Vittorio. He'd been here. How could she have forgotten that for even a minute? He'd come down when he heard her reaction to her nightmare. She must have been loud. Her cheeks burned, embarrassed that she'd let a nightmare get her that upset.

Then again, that was no ordinary nightmare. Even with the warm, lemony light of the sun dancing around her, a chill stole over her skin. She'd never had a dream like that before. Shadows and horrible, disfigured beings coming after her. Pulling at her. Wanting to do things to her that she knew would be beyond awful. All of it had been so real, so vivid. Even remembering frightened her.

But then Vittorio had been there. He'd checked her apartment. He'd stayed with her until she dozed off again.

She touched the soft velvet of her duvet. He'd covered her before he left. Somehow that knowledge chased away a little of the chill prickling her skin.

She pushed away the cover and swung her feet to the floor. The worn wood was warm under her bare feet, helping chase away a bit more of the chill in her bones.

She looked around, wondering how long he'd stayed. Boris got up and began to twine himself around her ankles, the gesture nagging, certainly not affectionate.

"All right, all right." She started to reach down to pick up the plate of remaining marshmallow treats. Then something caught her attention. A half-eaten treat sat on the coffee table. She hadn't left it there.

When she'd returned from Vittorio's apartment with the rejected peace offering, she'd promptly sat down and eaten at least five of them. Drowning her frustration, hurt and disappointment in a moment of binge eating. And she hadn't left any half-eaten ones behind. Which meant Vittorio ate part of one, despite his dislike of sweets.

For some reason, the knowledge warmed her further. Which was ludicrous. A few bites of marshmallow and breakfast cereal didn't mean a thing. Like Boris's current behavior, the gesture didn't mean affection, for heaven's sake.

Or even mild like, really. But he had come down here last night. And he'd been kind. Maybe she had touched him in some way. Or maybe she'd just been such a wreck, he decided to accept the offering.

She pushed up from the sofa, being careful not to trip on her insistent cat. She shuffled to the kitchen and reached into the cupboard for a can of tuna. Not only was her cat annoying, he was a very finicky eater. No ordinary cat food for this bossy feline.

Boris meowed plaintively.

"Yeah, yeah, I'm hurrying." She rummaged in a drawer for a can opener. Working the lid off, she tossed the top into the sink, then placed the can on the floor. Another quirk of her cat's. He wouldn't eat from a cat dish. The greedy cat started gobbling before she even moved her hand away.

She tossed the can opener back into the drawer. Then Erika paced over to the door. She opened the door, moving into the sunlight of the glassed-in porch.

The courtyard was beautiful this morning, vibrant and green. Now that the sleepy haze was clearing from her head, she actually felt good. She should take her sculpting supplies outside and work. But instead of doing that, she wandered back to the living room.

Was Vittorio sleeping? She imagined he was. He'd said he kept strange hours, and she'd also kept him up late. Still, she was tempted to go upstairs and check.

Just to thank him, of course. She glanced down at the half-eaten Rice Krispie treat. Or just to see him.

She rolled her eyes at herself. God, why was she making so much of his reaction last night? And of a few bites of Rice Krispie treat.

"I need to just act cool about it," she stated to herself. Or maybe Boris. Or both.

She picked up the remaining treats, tossing the unfinished one on top, and carried them to the kitchen.

Only she could make a couple bites of Rice Krispie treat into a budding romance. She needed to get the notion that he was her predicted prince, out of her head.

"And you need to work," she commanded herself adamantly. But again, she didn't move to gather her supplies. She walked back to her front door, cracked it open and angled her head to look at the staircase to the upstairs.

Without debating it any further, she put her hand on the doorknob and twisted. But the door didn't budge. She frowned down. The old-style dead bolt was latched.

She stared at it for a moment, confused. She remembered locking the bolt last night after going to see Vittorio.

So how did Vittorio get in? And how did he leave and flip the lock back into place? The old bolt either needed a key to lock it or had to be latched from the inside. A chill snaked over her skin.

"Ah!" she let out a startled cry as her cell phone on the table beside the door picked that moment to ring. She clapped a hand over her skittering heart, trying to calm herself, then she picked up the phone.

"Hello?"

"Hey there."

Erika recognized the voice on the other end as her friend Jo's.

"I just bought my plane ticket," Jo said, although Erika was still having a hard time concentrating since her heart was doing circles in her chest like an overexcited dog. Her eyes remained locked on that bolt.

"I'll be coming in for a week. The twenty-eighth to the fifth. I got a great price. Thanks for suggesting that one site. The deals are good."

How had he gotten in here? Had he even really been here?

"Erika?"

Erika blinked. "I'm here."

"Are you okay?"

She debated whether to mention anything to her friend. Jo would definitely think she was crazy. She tended to be very practical—not prone to share Erika's mystical beliefs.

"Yes. It's just that—well, remember Vittorio?"

"Ren's brother, of course."

"Well, he's staying in the apartment above me."

"That's cool," Jo said, clearly not understanding how she was supposed to respond to this information.

"Yeah," Erika said.

"You don't sound too sure."

Erika sighed. "You're right about that. It's just—well, I guess I should start from the beginning."

"Okay," Jo said, then waited.

Erika took a deep breath, realizing this was going to probably make little or no sense to her friend.

"Well, you know since I moved down here that I've been going to see Philippe regularly."

"No. Who's Philippe?"

"He's that psychic I've told you about. The really accurate one."

There was a brief silence on Jo's end of the phone. "Okay."

Erika sensed Jo's censure, but she continued. "Well, he keeps predicting that I'm going to meet a fair-haired, dark-eyed prince. Remember he predicted that way back on our first trip here."

"Okay," Jo said again, clearly not recalling.

"Well, Vittorio fits that description perfectly."

"I know blond hair and brown eyes isn't as common as some color combinations, but it's hardly rare. Vittorio isn't the only guy who'd fit that description."

Erika nodded in begrudging agreement even though Jo couldn't see her. "Well, that might be true. But Philippe also said in my last reading that he was right above me. He was referring to the placement of his card in the reading. But he is quite literally too. He's staying in the apartment above mine."

"Again, that sounds like a coincidence that you are choosing to see as a sign."

"Maybe," Erika agreed. "Maybe." Still she felt like there was something there—some truth.

"Are you interested in him? Is he into you?"

"Kind of." Erika considered last night. Vittorio had been so different than in their other encounters. "I mean, initially he was kind of . . . well, rude."

"That sounds promising. And princelike," Jo said.

Erika knew Jo was teasing, but it still didn't feel good. Rudeness was hardly a promising start to a romance. Was she just seeing what she wanted to see from his behavior last night?

"But last night, I had this horrible nightmare. Honestly, one of the most frightening things I've ever experienced, and I must have been screaming or something, because he came down to check on me. And he stayed until I fell back to sleep."

"Well, that was nice."

"Yes," Erika agreed, although now that she'd said it aloud, Vittorio's behavior didn't sound like anything out of the ordinary. Surely anyone, given the same situation, would act that way.

Then she glanced back to the bolted lock.

"But the weird thing is," she said slowly, "I know my door was locked. It's one of those dead bolts that you either have to lock from the inside or use a key. Yet, he got inside. He left while I was sleeping, and it's locked now too. Isn't that weird?"

Again there was silence, then Jo said, "Erika, he's Ren's brother. If he has a key to the upstairs apartment, then he likely has one to yours, too."

Erika's shoulders, which she hadn't realized had been drawn up, relaxed. *Of course.*

She laughed weakly. "You're right. I don't know why I didn't think of that. I guess the nightmare must have shaken me more than I realized."

Jo made a sound of agreement, then she added, "I do think you are seeing that psychic person too much. And taking too much stock in what he says. Those tea leaf places are just for entertainment. They're a business. You can't believe what they say."

Erika considered mentioning that Philippe had predicted she'd move to New Orleans within the past year, and that her art would finally get some recognition. She glanced at Boris, now sated and asleep atop her crumpled duvet. He'd even predicted her finding a stray cat. And not any cat. A black cat.

But she didn't bother mentioning any of this to Jo. Her friend simply didn't believe in psychic phenomena. Or anything paranormal. She liked a good ghost story as much as the next person, but she didn't believe a word of them.

Jo must have sensed awkwardness in the silence, because she changed the subject to Erika's art show, and her impending visit.

By the time Erika flipped her cell phone shut, she did feel calmer. While Jo didn't understand Erika's belief in mysticism, she had been a good voice of reason about the lock. And Erika wasn't so wrapped up in her otherworldly interests that she really believed Vittorio had some magical ability to undo locks with his mind or whatever.

Ridiculous.

* * *

For the first time in a long time, Erika turned her attention to her art, getting some work done that she was actually pleased with. There was still the lopsided bust that she couldn't seem to fix, but she did finish a smaller piece she'd started earlier.

Pleased, she wiped her hands on one of her ever-ready rags, then checked her watch. It was after 3 p.m. No wonder her stomach was growling.

She wandered to her fridge, only to find a take-out box with a salad that had seen much better days, a twelve-pack of Diet Coke, and some yogurt. She grabbed a soda and headed toward the bathroom.

She'd grab a shower, then a late lunch at her favorite place, The Napoleon House. Maybe when she got back, she'd see some signs of Vittorio. She hadn't heard a sound from the apartment overhead all day.

She caught herself. She wasn't supposed to be thinking about him, having decided as she worked that she wasn't going to search him out. When she saw him, she'd thank him for his kindness last night, and that was it.

If Philippe was right, Vittorio would come to her. If not, he wasn't her prince.

Erika walked into the restaurant, greeted by Jean-Pierre, a short, somewhat stocky waiter with a haircut shorn very close to his scalp.

"Good afternoon, mademoiselle. How are you today?"

"Very well," she said, "and you?"

"Excellent, excellent."

Erika smiled as he led her to her favorite table out in the open courtyard. Some people didn't like to be recognized as a regular, but she did. She liked going to a shop or a restaurant and being remembered. Another reason she loved New Orleans, people made the effort to remember you. And to be friendly.

She was glad she'd made the choice to come here. Even if it

was in part a decision based on Philippe's psychic recommendation.

She sat down and ordered a diet soda. Diet Coke was her biggest vice. Pretty mild as far as vices went.

Picking up the menu, she perused the food choices, although she knew she'd probably order the crawfish étoufée. Her favorite dish here.

"Excuse me?" A deep melodic voice sounded by her right ear. Startled, she twisted to look at the speaker.

"I thought that was you. What a small world."

Erika stared at the large man beside her, unable to speak for a moment.

It was the man she'd run into on St. Louis. Literally.

Chapter 8

"Erika? Right?"

Maksim offered the mortal woman an easy smile. He made sure he tempered himself. On their first meeting, he'd been too intent, too eager to find out what she knew. In retrospect, he now saw he could have easily spooked this woman, even before he entered her mind. Another risk of being a demon, he could come on a little strong.

Actually he did that more often than he should.

"Yes." She set down the menu, returning his smile with a surprised one of her own. "Hi."

"I'm Maksim," he told her, sure she remembered, but wanting to come across unassuming enough to make her think he suspected she'd forgotten his name.

"I remember," she said, as predicted. "How are you?"

"Famished." He smiled, exuding charm from every pore.

She smiled back, timidly, but still a smile. A good sign. "This is the right place to be then."

He nodded, glancing around. "It's my first time here. It's quite—" He'd have gone with *rundown* if he was being honest, but he opted for, "Quaint."

Erika glanced around, an affection for the shabby place clear in her eyes. Humans were such a strange lot.

"It's one of my favorite restaurants in the Quarter."

"Well, you will have to tell me what entree you like best."

He rested his hand on the back of one of the chairs, a signal for her to ask him to join her.

Her eyes went to his fingers, curled casually against the worn wood, but she didn't offer an invitation.

Maybe he had come on too strong with his powers yesterday. He thought the mind-connect had just confused her, like a sudden bout of vertigo when you'd never been dizzy before. But maybe he'd actually scared her. That could happen too. It was never comfortable when someone enters your mind.

He needed to go slowly. Impatience and greed were always his missteps. Of course, he was a demon, and as a whole, his race was hardly known for patience or moderation.

Still, he had to try. He offered her another smile laced with warmth and sincerity.

"I know this is presumptuous, but would you mind if I join you? I hate to eat alone."

Erika looked as if she was going to say no, but then nodded. "Sure." She still didn't sound certain, but that was another trait of demons, they didn't hesitate to capitalize on another's moment of weakness.

"So are you from New Orleans?" he asked, taking the seat to her left. His knee brushed hers under the table and she immediately shifted away. He did make her nervous.

"No. I'm from the East Coast originally."

"Have you been here long?"

She fiddled with her fork. "No, only a few months."

Maksim nodded. He'd been inside her head, and knew all this, but he needed something to use for small talk.

"Are you from here?" she asked.

He shook his head. "No. I'm not really from anywhere. I travel a lot. I did spend a majority of my—childhood in Russia." If demons had childhoods, which they didn't.

"I can hear the accent."

He nodded. "Yes. I guess no matter how much I travel that never goes completely." It was actually a dialect of Malebolge, the eighth circle of hell. But it sounded fairly close to a Russian accent.

She nodded. "Are you here on business?"

"Yes, business."

She nodded again, then there was a lull in conversation. She studied her menu, clearly not knowing what to say to him.

"What do you do?" He knew that too. A sculptor—now. He'd seen other jobs along the way, but in her mind she saw her career as that of an artist.

"I'm a—sculptor."

She was reluctant to tell him. Perhaps because others didn't see sculpting as a real career. But he was a full-time demon, who was he to judge career choices? "Really? That's fascinating." Ah, the sincerity he could portray. Even Orabella at her best couldn't out act him. "How did you get started?"

His "genuine" interest loosened her tongue and got her to relax. Aside from the breaks to order food, then receive it, she told him about her long and rather dull journey to potential success.

Maksim manufactured appropriate interest and impressed reactions, all the while waiting for the thing he wanted.

"That is such a great story. I always relish hearing that creative people are able to use their talents to make a living. Too often you hear that a person has to give up their dream, because of money. You are doing well."

Erika nodded, clearly pleased by his comments. She took another sip of her soda.

"I know this sounds strange," he said suddenly, hoping his approach made his announcement sound unpremeditated. "But I'd love to pose for you sometime. I mean if you use models. If you don't, well . . . I just figured it couldn't hurt to ask."

She shifted in her seat, looking decidedly uncomfortable. "Well, I do. But I generally just take pictures and work from those."

Well, shit. That wouldn't help him. Like he really wanted

an amateur sculpture of himself. Done from photos, no less. He wanted proximity. She was his conduit to finding out more about Vittorio—and maybe through Vittorio more about Orabella, too.

Of course, he was going on the feeble hope that this mortal's sexual interest in Vittorio would lead to some sort of relationship between them. All of it was a long shot, but one he'd been willing to take. Now he just felt irritated with the whole shoddy plan.

So instead, he leaned back in his chair and without any preamble locked eyes with Erika and entered her head.

Erika couldn't say what happened to make her feel so strange, so suddenly. But she did, her heart skipped, almost as if she had a heart arrhythmia. She couldn't pull in a full breath, and her head was spinning. Or rather the room was spinning. Her vision began to tunnel, and for a moment, she was afraid she was going to pass out.

The feeling continued for—she had no idea how long. But finally, she realized Maksim had moved forward on his chair and he frowned at her.

"Erika? Are you okay?"

She nodded, although the bob of her head was slight. She was afraid any sudden movement would bring back the disorientation and dizziness.

An urgent need to leave filled her, an irrational and unrelenting urge to get away. Not from fear exactly, but just a drive to go. Now.

"You don't need to feel badly about not being interested in having me model. I understand that everyone works differently."

Erika blinked. *What?* Then she remembered what he'd been saying just before the vertigo started.

"Thanks—thanks for understanding." Where was Jean-Pierre? She wanted to pay her bill and leave. She knew her abrupt departure would be weird and rude. But she just didn't feel . . . well.

"I'm sorry," she said, her hand going to her head, massaging her temple. "I think I need to go. I'm suddenly not feeling well."

"I hope it wasn't the food." Then he smiled slightly. "Or the company."

"No, no, of course not. I just seem to be coming down with a headache all of a sudden."

"Perhaps it's the heat."

She nodded. "Maybe." She started to reach behind her for her purse, which hung on the back of the chair, but Maksim's hand on her arm stopped her.

"Let me get it. To thank you for the company."

Usually she wouldn't allow that, but the pounding in her head continued to increase and she was afraid if she didn't go now, she'd truly be ill.

"Thank you. That would be lovely." She gathered up her purse and the thin sweater she brought everywhere with her, because she was prone to getting chilled. And she was shivering now, but not with cold.

"It's the least I can do," he said, and something about the tone of his voice caused her to pause. She looked at him, trying to understand what about his tone niggled at her.

She rose, not sure she'd be able to keep her balance. The wooden legs of the chair squawked on the flagstone, and she used the table to center herself.

"Are you sure you are okay?" Again, Erika got the feeling that while his face appeared concerned, his tone didn't quite match his look.

She was rattled from the strange bout of illness, but she certainly couldn't identify anything that should make her feel odd about his behavior. Yet she did. And she just wanted to go.

"I'm okay," she told him. "Thank you for the nice lunch, or early dinner, or—whatever."

Maksim leaned back and crossed his arms over his broad chest. A strange, small smile on his lips. "Not a problem, Erika. After all, I forced myself on you."

Erika still couldn't decide why she felt like there was some hidden meaning behind his words. Or maybe it was just her. It had to be this strange and sudden illness. She really did have to go.

"Okay, thanks again."

He nodded, that little smile not changing.

Erika didn't say any more. She just turned, made sure she was steady and walked slowly out of the restaurant.

The sun hadn't set, but it was low in the evening sky, creating long shadows. She expected the dim light to add to her vertigo. But almost as soon as she stepped outside, her head started to clear.

What the heck was wrong with her? She'd never experienced an overwhelming sense of vertigo like that. Or the weird drive to leave, just get out of that restaurant. But as she slowly took a deep breath, the feeling dissipated.

She started down the uneven sidewalk, feeling a little embarrassed now about leaving Maksim so quickly. Now that her head was clearing, she wondered if the change she'd perceived in Maksim had something to do with her rejecting him as a model. Which certainly did seem more insulting, given her abrupt exit.

But she decided against heading back to the restaurant to explain her reaction to his suggestion. She had to admit, while she didn't dislike Maksim, she wasn't comfortable with him. In a purely aesthetic way he should have appealed to the artist in her, he was truly one of the most handsome men she'd ever seen. Heck, she should want to sculpt him just to have more time with him. But again, she realized she wasn't in the least bit attracted to him.

And for some reason she'd also lied to him. She made it sound like she didn't want to work with live models. But generally it wasn't a matter of wanting to work with them. It was a matter of not being able to work with them. It wasn't easy to find people who were willing to take the time to pose for her. It wasn't as if she could afford to pay a model much, if anything.

Maksim had offered, and she turned him down. But he did

make her uneasy. And if she was being extra truthful, she didn't want Vittorio thinking she was interested in him. She got the vibe that Maksim could be interested in her if she gave him any hint she was attracted. But right now, all thoughts were on Vittorio. Long shot that it was.

If Vittorio offered to model for her, she'd accept without a moment's hesitation. And there was no denying her attraction. Definitely Vittorio. Despite her uncertainty about his feelings, she couldn't deny hers. But she'd play it cool and let things go as they may.

By the time she reached her apartment, the sun had disappeared behind the buildings, and clouds darkened the sky. A storm was rolling in, quickly.

She reached the double doors leading to the courtyard and fumbled with her keys. On the third try, she got the key in the lock. She was still a little shaken from the bout of vertigo— either that or distracted by her own thoughts about Vittorio.

What was he thinking about her after last night? Had he found her reaction to the nightmare odd or too extreme? Was his attention solely because of her nightmare? Or was he a little interested?

She entered the courtyard and relocked the gate. Ren had told her when she moved in that it was never wise to leave the front gates unlocked. Tourists or other undesirables— Ren's words—wouldn't hesitate to come in and look around if the gate was left open to the street.

A chill stole over her skin as she thought about that. She turned and inspected the darkening courtyard. The rising wind rustled the greenery, but aside from that, all was quiet.

She glanced up at Vittorio's apartment. A light glowed from one of the windows—and the tension in her muscles relaxed. Had anyone had asked her yesterday if she'd find peace in knowing Vittorio was near, she would have said no. Peace wasn't what her body ever felt when she was near him.

But tonight, even with the insane attraction and confusing interactions she had with the man, she was glad he was there.

Although between nightmares, mystery vertigo and unreasonable attractions, she couldn't decide what was going on with her. Lately nothing seemed to make much sense.

The key slid easily into her apartment door. She stared into her darkened living room. She suddenly didn't want to face her lonely apartment. She turned and headed up the stairs with none of the hesitation of last evening.

She rapped sharply on Vittorio's door, then waited.

This time, he answered right away, although as before, the door opened without any sound of footsteps. And again, he wore sweats that rode low on his narrow hips, and little else.

She swallowed, loving the sight.

"Hi," she said, greeting him with a smile that she knew was probably too delighted. But she was happy to see him. She felt safe, which again made no sense, given she should have had nothing to feel wary of in the first place. Aside for a dream that was well over and done with. Maybe she was just lonely. And it was nice to have someone there.

"I just wanted to come up and thank you for sitting with me last night."

Vittorio studied her, his dark eyes unreadable. But instead of the cool, or even rude, remark he usually gave her, he nodded. "You had a really bad dream."

"Yes. Terrible. But having you there helped calm me." She wanted to touch him. His hair was sleep-mussed and so tempting. But she simply smiled, keeping her hands firmly at her sides.

Although she noticed his eyes move briefly to her lips, they were back meeting her gaze. Just that short glance made her body react—even more. Her skin tingled and her fingers twitched at her sides.

Lord, she wanted to touch him. His hair, the faint stubble along his jaw. His bare chest.

"I just sat there. Nothing particularly remarkable."

She noted a flatness in his tone, but his words held none of the rudeness of before. This tone was different, although she couldn't begin to know what the difference meant.

"Well, given the way I was feeling, your actions seemed extraordinary and downright courageous to me." This time, *her* gaze dropped to *his* mouth. His bottom lip was plumper than the upper one and sinfully sexy against the square cut of his jawline. Her hands knotted into fists. Lord, she wanted to touch him—and not just with her fingers. She fought the urge to lick her lips.

His full bottom lip compressed against the top one, capturing her attention, then slowly signaled to her amorous mind that something might be amiss. Her eyes moved upward, seeking his, but he wasn't looking at her. He stared at a place on the floor between them.

She didn't want this moment to end with him withdrawing, so she quickly said, "Okay, well, I just wanted to thank you—and let you know that I was really glad you were there."

He lifted his gaze, then nodded, a look in his eyes that she didn't quite understand. Dark irises shadowed with sadness. Or maybe longing. Or maybe just something from her own overactive imagination.

"You're welcome," he said.

She nodded, then lifted a hand. "Okay, I guess I will talk to you later."

"Okay."

As she turned away, she hoped Vittorio would say something to stop her, but with each step she knew he wouldn't. So when she reached the stairs, she stopped herself. She glanced back at him.

His eyes were still on her, giving her a touch of hope. And courage.

"I know this sounds strange, but would you consider posing for me?"

Chapter 9

Vittorio didn't quite understand what Erika had asked. Model? He shook his head slightly, revealing that he wasn't following, because she added, "You know, model for a sculpture."

One of her sculptures. His person immortalized forever. Except his person was immortalized forever already. A living sculpture.

"I—I don't think I'd be a good subject."

She moved closer to him, so her lovely pale skin and dark hair, knotted on the top of her head, glowed in the light from his apartment.

"I think you would be a wonderful subject. You have such a beau—an interesting face."

She'd been about to call him beautiful. Not a word he'd ever use to describe himself. And a word that scared him, because he liked that she found him beautiful. And he couldn't like it.

"I don't think—" He didn't know quite what to say.

"No," he finally said, which he realized wasn't the best response as soon as he said it.

Erika actually backed away as if he'd shouted his answer.

"Oh. Okay," she said, making a valiant attempt to sound blithe about the whole idea. "That's fine. I just thought I'd ask."

He nodded, but she barely saw it as she turned and headed down the staircase into the encroaching darkness.

"Thanks again for last night," she called back, again trying to sound nonchalant.

"Sure," he said, trying to capture his own sense of indifference, although he could already hear her opening the door to her apartment, then closing the door behind her.

He stayed in the doorway, somewhat stunned. She wanted to sculpt him. *Why?*

Then he grimaced. Why was he even considering the idea? Last night, he'd done what he had to do. What he'd have done for anyone. She'd been terrified, and even as cold as he could be, he couldn't leave her shaken and panicked. But he'd known when he left that was the end of their interaction. It had to be. A clean break.

He'd wanted to talk himself out of what he'd come to believe about his past. But he couldn't dismiss it—not yet. He hoped he would be able to, but his hopes weren't too high.

He glanced at the sky through the windows. It had to be close to 7 p.m. The coroner's office would be closed now.

He headed down the stairs.

Erika heard the porch door open and close, but she didn't glance toward her door. She continued to knead the fresh clay in her hands, working all her emotions into the caked earth.

In the silence, she absently smoothed her hands over the existing curves of the lopsided bust, unaware if she was fixing the piece or not.

"I can't believe I asked him to pose," she suddenly announced to Boris, unable to continue her pretense that she was thinking of anything else. Boris opened one eye from where he lounged on a cushion at the end of the sofa.

What had she been thinking? She smeared more clay onto the torso of the sculpture. And didn't she know what Vittorio's answer was going to be anyway? Had she really expected a yes?

Still, she couldn't shake the feeling they should somehow be together. Even though Vittorio had hardly reacted with joy to seeing her. He wasn't as cool as previous meetings, but he was hardly warm either. Why was she doing this to herself?

She slapped on more of the softened clay, then used water to smooth it.

But even without the attraction, she knew she'd want to sculpt him. Something so intrigued her about his face and his eyes. She wanted to capture that. His expression spoke to her in that unidentifiable way that Maksim's didn't.

She reached for her sculpting knife, and shaved away some of the excess clay she'd just added, trying to get the shape she wanted. Wet clay splatted onto the drop cloth beneath the pedestal her creation was perched on.

Her hand paused mid-swipe. *But mostly you just want to be with him.*

She had to face the truth. She wanted an acceptable excuse to look at him. To study the nuances of his features, the build of his body, the hints of emotions in his eyes.

"But instead, you just weirded him out. As usual. Good work." She rasped the palette knife harder than necessary, gouging the side of her creation.

"Crap," she muttered, then tossed the knife down on the table next to her. She reached for more clay, kneading it between her palms. She filled in the hollow.

She had to let go of this crazy idea about him being *the one*, her romantic interest. His behavior last night was simply what he'd have done for anyone. Nothing special. Certainly not a hint of potential interest.

There was a show to get ready for, so she didn't have time to worry about him anyway. She was thankful he'd been there last night, but all other feelings had to go away. They had to stop. Before she made a pathetic fool of herself. If she hadn't already.

She smoothed out the clay, filling in the deep nick she'd made. She wished she could erase her own feelings like she did flaws in the sculpture, manipulating her own thoughts until they disappeared, smoothed out with no signs of ever having been.

She reached for another clump of clay. She was going to do just that. No more of this nonsense. She shaped the clay to the chest of her sculpture, attempting to level out the female statue's breasts. She would focus all her energy into her work—if it killed her. No more Vittorio.

Vittorio moved through the hallways of the coroner's office. Fluorescent lights streaked the hallway in stark bluish light, and he appeared as nothing more than a shadow against the institutional grayish-white of the walls.

He stopped outside the door marked with a tarnished metal sign, the word *Records* etched into it. He passed through the solid wood door, not rematerializing until he was sure he was alone.

Then he appeared like fog, gathering and condensing until he returned to his solid form. He waited, expecting the dizzying disorientation he normally felt when shifting, but it didn't come.

Because he'd fed from Erika, he realized, guilt stealing over him. He forced himself to ignore the emotion and strolled down an aisle of metal shelves lined with cardboard boxes labeled in alphabetical order.

He went down one of the middle aisles, pulling several boxes, flipping through the manila folders until he reached one of the names he was looking for.

The first, Jessalynn Taylor, twenty-eight, reason of death, drug overdose. Jessalynn had been a heavy drug user. She'd had two children, lost them both to the state. She'd been a stripper. Not a good person by society's standards. But she had been good before her husband left her for another woman, skipping out on her, refusing her child support. He disappeared, leaving her destitute with no real skills to survive.

So with three mouths to feed she'd turned to the one thing she could do. Strip. And then the problems snowballed from there. It wasn't an unusual story here. Nor was her death.

Except now, he wasn't sure.

He sorted through the pages, looking for anything. Any

comments and notations that might look out of the ordinary. He did find indications of some bruising and scratches on her back and arms. But they weren't extreme and didn't necessarily indicate a struggle.

He moved on to another box, rifling through, to find Angela Snow's records. She'd been the first of his friends to die. Gone almost twenty years now.

Her death had been declared an accident. A fall down the stairs in her apartment building. She'd had high levels of alcohol in her system, which had led the coroner to pronounce the death the way he had.

Yet, Vittorio couldn't shake the image of a struggle at the top of the stairs, then Angela being shoved, her body landing in a crumpled, broken heap at the bottom of the staircase.

He went on, looking at several more files, finding nothing definitive. But then he knew the individual he suspected of murder was savvy enough to cover her tracks. She'd certainly duped him readily enough.

Finally, he went to the section of the alphabetized files he'd been avoiding since stepping into the claustrophobic room with its towering shelves and the endless records of the dead.

As he walked down the aisle, the room seemed to tighten in around him, making it hard to focus. But he forced himself to go directly to the D's.

Da-Dae. Daf-Daj. Dak-Dap. Daq-Dat. Dau-Daw. He stared at the box he'd been seeking for several seconds before pulling it down. Crouching, he set the container on the floor and flipped off the lid.

With the faint light from the hallway filtering in through the small, square window in the door, he began to thumb through the folders, slower than he had with the others, until he found the one he was looking for—Seraph Davidson.

Date of death, December 25, 1998. God, had she really been dead ten years? He supposed it had been that long. Funny, it seemed like ages ago that he'd played keyboard for The Impalers, but just yesterday that he'd lost Seraph. He'd left New Orleans right after her death. Being here was just too hard.

He opened the folder. Pictures fell to the floor at his feet. He picked them up, making himself look at them. Pale blond hair matted around her grayish, sunken features. Her eyes closed, not showing her pale blue eyes.

He stared at them for a moment longer, then shoved them under the rest of the records. He didn't want to remember her that way.

He moved on to the autopsy findings. The death was labeled a drug overdose. Heroin. The next form was a police report, stating she was found with drugs scattered around her body and a needle still in her arm.

At the time, he'd had no reason to question the findings. Seraph had a long-standing heroin addiction. She'd tried to get clean many times, but her other problems made that difficult.

He'd believed heroin had done the actual killing, but he'd known, even then, he'd been as much a cause of her death as any drug. He felt the same today, but now he wondered if he was to blame for other reasons.

Seraph, an angel. A name that oddly fit her despite the roughness of her upbringing, her lack of proper education, her propensity for overindulgence. Yes, despite all that, she'd had a sweetness. A gentleness. A lost, broken quality.

She, above all the others he'd tried to help, had touched him. Even though he'd known romantic involvement with her wouldn't help fix her, he'd allowed it. She'd drawn him in.

So he'd begun to see her, and their romance was probably as close to love as he'd ever felt, in all his centuries. Maybe it wasn't exactly love, but it was deep affection and a need to protect her. All too quickly, however, it became clear she had problems he couldn't begin to protect her from—not even with his preternatural abilities. Depression, manias, even bouts of psychosis. Drugs were her mask for much deeper-rooted problems.

When she'd been discovered dead the day after Christmas,

he hadn't been surprised. And he'd been riddled with guilt and despair.

They'd had an argument, because she'd wanted them to marry. He'd told her that wouldn't, couldn't, happen. She hadn't even known the truth about what he was. He never planned to tell her. And he certainly wouldn't offer immortality to a woman who suffered like she did. An eternity of mental illness, drugs, self-hatred—that would have been beyond cruel.

He'd known for a while he should end things. But he always wondered if he'd handled the situation better than he had, would she be alive today? Breaking things off on Christmas Eve. It had been terrible timing, and he should have guessed she couldn't handle it.

When he'd discovered she died, the overdose made sense. She'd always turned to drugs when life became too much. But now, he wondered. He read the coroner's report. He studied the autopsy diagrams.

She did have fresh needle marks, but there was also mention of some bruising on her wrists, and two broken fingernails.

Vittorio stared at the notations scrawled in barely legible black ink next to a drawing of a body. Had she fought someone? Had someone killed her, then covered their tracks by making it look like an overdose?

A strange, sick feeling in the pit of his stomach told him, yes. Seraph hadn't died by her own hand. But that knowledge didn't lessen the regret and the never-quite-gone guilt he felt about failing Seraph. His feeble attempt to make it up to her by saving another long-dead woman. By saving them all from their addictions, their awful lives.

But he hadn't saved any of them, had he?

He left the box in the aisle, and moved to find the last file he needed to see. Julianne's file.

What was her last name? Simmons? Sinclair? Yes, it was Sinclair. He went to the S's, and found the correct box. Her file was toward the front. Again, the first things he saw were photos. These were more gruesome than Seraph's, Julianne's death more visibly violent. But both were disturbing in their own way. More disturbing because of his suspicions.

The final outcome of the police investigation and the coroner's report was that she'd committed suicide, jumping from the third story window of her apartment building.

He studied the autopsy report, searching for anything that didn't coincide with the determined cause of death: severe head trauma and internal damage.

On the diagram of the body, marked heavily with the locations of her injuries, he found two interesting notations in handwriting much neater than on Seraph's report. One noted bruising around the neck that appeared to have happened before the other damage. And the other was written at the bottom of the report. Material fibers under her fingernails.

Vittorio frowned. Material fibers? He flipped through the other reports. They had done an investigation. And forensics had determined the material fibers matched those of curtains hanging in Julianne's apartment.

An image flashed in his mind, of Julianne clinging desperately to the curtains as she struggled against being pushed out a window to the street below. Julianne had been a slight girl. Of course, the one he suspected was guilty of her murder was slight too. But then, the murderer had vampirism on her side.

And determination. Vittorio knew full well how much determination she had. He'd experienced it for decade upon decade.

Why the hell hadn't he put this together sooner? After all, he'd always suspected his mother was not above getting rid of anyone she saw as competition for his attention.

Chapter 10

Maksim lounged in the chair across from Orabella, cradling an expensive glass of pinot noir between his fingers, taking in the charm of the courtyard. This restaurant was a far cry from the place where he'd had lunch with the skittish mortal.

Bad demon, he admonished himself. He'd gotten a little impatient again, and sure enough the human had gotten unnerved, disoriented. She was a sensitive little thing—at least when it came to demons. She was wary of him, yet had no idea the being she had the hots for was a vampire.

And while he'd jumped the gun on discovering any really solid information, he did know one thing. Vittorio had gone to her last night. Maybe he was more interested in this Erika than he'd originally believed. And Erika was very interested in Vittorio.

Erika could actually be a way to reach Vittorio.

"What are you ordering?" Orabella asked, looking up from her menu. She looked stunning tonight in a white sundress, her skin a milkier shade against the starkness of the material, her hair swept up in loose blonde curls.

He halfheartedly scanned the menu lying on the table in front of him. "I think I'm in the mood for oysters. They're aphrodisiacs, aren't they?"

Orabella raised a perfectly arched brow. "If they are, you hardly need them, my lover."

He smiled at the way her pale skin colored as she said the possessive endearment. She was quite an actress, although limited in her repertoire. The virginal blushes were becoming a tad of a bore.

"You are right," he agreed. "But I can't help myself. I find you so stunning."

This time the pleased look was genuine—although a little more smug than charmed. She reached across the table and touched his hand, her fingers cold.

He smiled, then took a sip of his wine, debating if he should mention what he knew about Vittorio and a certain human. He longed to see Orabella's reaction—what would a slip in her practiced acting skills reveal to him?

But he didn't say anything. Not quite yet.

"And what about you, my darling? What will you order and push around your plate?"

Orabella gave him a small smile. "The filet mignon, I think."

"Rare, of course," he added.

"Of course."

Orabella loved to go to expensive restaurants, even though she wouldn't take more than a couple bites of the delectable entrees. But she certainly would feed. Taking energy from the other patrons until she was so full it was a wonder she didn't lean back, unbutton her pants, and pat her belly in satisfaction.

Okay, she didn't have on pants, and frankly his image of her would revolt her, which was why it made him chuckle. But the fact remained; she was a glutton, even if she tried to hide her greed.

The waitress approached the table, a pretty brunette in her mid-twenties. Orabella studied her, her dark eyes devouring the girl as Maksim ordered their dinners, her body stealing the girl's energy.

He'd noted that when they dined like this, Orabella always

took the most life force from the young, pretty girls. Of course a woman like Orabella did not like competition. A bit of the "who's the fairest of them all" syndrome, Maksim suspected.

Even now, the waitress frowned as if she was having a hard time following Maksim's words. She touched a hand to her forehead as if she was getting slightly disoriented.

When the waitress finally left, Orabella sighed, content, and relaxed in her chair. Not exactly reclining in a Barcalounger with her stained T-shirt rolled up over a fat belly, but Maksim still found the action humorous.

She lifted her glass of Chablis to her lips, taking a deep sip, then let out another contented sigh. He supposed she was more like a cat, really. Greedy, self-satisfied and disdainful.

"So, what did you do today while I got my beauty rest?"

Maksim took a sip of his own wine before answering. "I had lunch with a mortal woman."

Orabella's eyebrows immediately drew together. "Really? Whatever for?" She tried to sound casual, but her acting skills were wobbling.

He took another sip of his wine. It was a good year. Rich, yet not heavy. A little spicy.

"Well?" Orabella asked, her voice sharp, not the sweet, singsong tone she usually adopted when she spoke.

He smiled again. He enjoyed provoking her. Just a little.

"I believed that perhaps she knew Vittorio."

She sat forward on her seat. "And did she?"

Maksim nodded. "She is an acquaintance. Well," he said, tilting his head, pretending to consider what he'd learned, "maybe a bit more than an acquaintance. He'd been with her last night. Understandably too. She's lovely. Dark hair, skin as white as snow." He waited to see if she caught the Snow White reference, since she did tend to act like the evil queen.

She didn't. Instead, she literally bristled, her posture becoming stick straight, her skin appearing to pull tight against her bones.

"Did you enter her mind? What did you see?"

"He didn't seem to do anything threatening, if that's what you mean."

"It's not," she said, her voice harsher. Then she seemed to hear herself, because her voice calmed, not yet back to its normal quality, but closer. "Well, I mean of course it is. But I just . . ." She frowned. "Well, she must be kept away from him."

Maksim regarded her for a moment over his wineglass. "For her own safety, of course."

"Of course."

She took a sip from her glass, the white wine clearly not as pleasing as before.

"You will follow them," she said. The comment held no hint of a question.

Maksim nodded. "Yes, I'll make sure he does nothing untoward."

"You will report everything to me. Everything."

"Yes."

Orabella relaxed back in her chair, just slightly. The rest of the dinner would be a tense affair. But when his pan-roasted oysters arrived, Maksim didn't let her edgy silence affect his appetite. He dug into the dish. Plump oysters, a savory cream sauce and a hint of paprika. He closed his eyes in pleasure.

Nope, he wasn't letting Orabella's reaction dampen the enjoyment of his meal. In fact, her response actually added to his satisfaction. She wasn't worried about the mortal woman, as he'd suspected all along. She was jealous. Absolutely.

And he had a stronger feeling than ever that these two vampires could lead him to answers about Ellina. Something was definitely amiss here. Soon he'd know whether she or Vittorio or maybe even both of them had something to do with his sister's disappearance.

Lafayette Cemetery was quiet as Vittorio strolled up and down the rows of tombs. He supposed, given what he'd discovered tonight, it seemed strange to find solace in a place of the dead. This was a different place of the dead than the coroner's office, however. These souls were laid to rest. He always found peace here.

He prayed that all the women he'd known, now knew true peace. Peace they'd never found in their earthly lives.

He wandered, the monuments dark, hulking silhouettes in the overcast night. Drizzle fell, dampening his skin, his hair. But still he didn't leave. He just wandered, trying to understand what he could do to make sure no other woman was hurt because of him. Hurt? Hell, they hadn't been just hurt— they were dead. And could he have stopped it—if he'd only paid attention, been aware?

He came to a halt, not seeing the tombs any longer, not feeling the rain, just lost in his own thoughts. What could he do to stop this now? Did he even have that kind of power? He and his mother were bonded, tied together by blood, by energy, and now it would seem by eternal damnation.

Yet, he didn't know for sure if she was guilty. Oh, he was certain she'd sinned enough both in life and undeath to warrant being damned. But could he punish his own mother based on speculation? Pretty substantial speculation, but speculation nonetheless.

God, he wanted to talk to Ren. His brother was the only other being on earth who knew their mother, even in some small way, like Vittorio did. Ren had managed to escape her during his childhood and for his rebirth into his new existence as a lampir, a creature doomed to live off of the living's energy. He'd learned about his vampirism on his own. Not under the tutelage of a sick, obsessive madwoman.

A woman whose blood and DNA did make up part of himself. He blew out a long breath. That was a horrifying thought.

He sighed, frowning into the darkness, noting for the first time where he'd stopped. In front of him was a small tomb, nearly lost among the larger family mausoleums. On top was a bust of a woman, her eyes closed, her face tilted downward as if in prayer.

He immediately thought of Erika and her request to sculpt him. Then he was just thinking of her. Her face, her tall, lithe body. He returned his attention to the grave. The point of the statue's chin, the curve of her cheeks, the shape of her lips, something, reminded him of Erika. Or maybe all things had him thinking of her.

Was she at risk? If his mother was guilty of killing the other women from Vittorio's past, then would she attempt to hurt Erika? After all, Julianne Sinclair may have paid with her life for simply talking with him, trying to find compassion and understanding in a world she wasn't comfortable in.

He turned, his steps quickening as he headed for the front gates of the cemetery. He had to protect this mortal woman. He'd failed the others, but he had to keep Erika safe. Safe until he found out the truth.

Sometimes, she honestly wondered what she'd done wrong. She'd certainly tried to do her best, but for some reason she was being punished.

Orabella gazed at her ghostlike reflection in the mirror. Her beauty, a transparent veil. Although the diaphanous quality only added loveliness to her features. Like a fragile web or a particularly delicate piece of lace.

"How could I have done any better?" she asked her sheer reflection. "I loved him so completely. I was devoted to no one but him."

Yet, Vittorio had forsaken her, rejected her. For decades he'd been pulling away. Until he'd moved to this foul city, with its lowly women, its filth and poverty, its excesses.

She could understand Vittorio's desire to overindulge. But not with the women he chose. Awful, unworthy whores. All of them.

And now he was back, and already with a woman who

could never be what her son needed. No mortal would ever be good enough for him. Never.

She touched her face, running her fingers over the curve of her cheek, down her neck. She was the only one who could love him the way he deserved. When would he realize that?

She touched her fingers to her mouth, closing her eyes, imagining she was touching Vittorio's mouth, nearly identical to her own. The petal softness of his lips, the heat of his breath.

She opened her eyes, meeting her dark gaze in the mirror. She'd have to take care of this. Show him no one could love him like his mother.

That was her only sin, after all. Loving him too much.

Vittorio wasn't surprised to see all the lights out in Erika's apartment. It was after 2 a.m., and her sleep the night before hadn't been exactly restful.

Pausing outside her door, he tried to sense her in the dark, quiet apartment. Maybe she wasn't even home, although that idea didn't reassure him. After a moment, he sensed her energy, surprised he could actually feel it from outside her place. But then, he was very in tune with her. Her energy reached out to him, swirling around him, sweet and enticing.

He didn't let himself stay to take in any of it, however. She was in there. She was safe. Likely sound asleep, and he couldn't take any more of her energy into him. He enjoyed it too much, and that was very dangerous. He'd learned that the hard way, and he couldn't allow himself to take any more of her. As tempting and lovely as she was.

He climbed the stairs, his feet silent on the warped steps. He didn't bother with his key, simply shifting and reappearing inside. The transition back, even after using his powers to enter the coroner's office, didn't disorient him as it normally would. More guilt weighted his chest. Better control of his powers didn't give him any sense of satisfaction. Not when it was Erika's energy that was making him more powerful.

He didn't bother to turn on the light, even though the room was pitch black because of the storm outside. His eyesight was keener too, seeing even without any ambient light from the moon or stars.

He tugged off his shirt as he crossed toward the bedroom. He wouldn't sleep, not until dawn, but he didn't have interest in doing anything but lying down and trying to sort out what to do next.

He dropped his shirt onto the floor, unconcerned with where it landed. He toed off his shoes, kicking those aside too, and collapsed onto the bed, his body so tense his muscles ached, every joint feeling its two hundred and twenty years.

What the hell was he going to do?

Just then a shriek ripped through the blackness. He bolted upright, this time knowing exactly where the cry came from. His shape began to fade even before his feet hit the floor.

Erika's apartment was as dark as his own. But he knew she wasn't on the sofa this time. Her energy was weaker than if she were near. The intensity not there.

She had to be in her bedroom. He started in that direction, when the same black shadow from last night darted past him, nearly tangling in his long strides. This time, Vittorio wasn't startled. In fact, it appeared that her tetchy cat was leading the way to his mistress.

Another scream echoed down the hallway, and the feline zipped back toward the living room.

"Scaredy cat," he muttered, but didn't slow down his pace.

When Vittorio reached the doorway, Erika's broken cry turned to a chant of terrified, "no's."

"Erika," he called, speaking loud enough to be heard over her cries, but not so loud as to scare her even more. Not that his attempt seemed to matter, his voice didn't penetrate the wall of absolute fear that surrounded her. She continued to plead, her whimpered no's filling the darkened space.

He stepped farther into the room. "Erika."

Her body was much like it had been last night, curled on
her side, her knees pulled up into the fetal position, closed in
on herself. Keeping him out, but also keeping her terrible
dream in.

He reached the edge of the bed and switched on the lamp
on her nightstand. The beaded fringe around the rim of the
shade swung, creating swaying shadows on the wall and on
the bed covers.

He leaned over her. Just like last night, her eyes were open,
but they were unseeing. No, not unseeing. She definitely saw
something. Just not anything he could see too. She was
asleep, lost in her horrible nightmare.

He sat down beside her, reaching out a hand to brush back
her hair. The skin of her cheek was cold, but damp with perspiration.

"Erika," he said, continuing to stroke her hair. "Wake up,
sweetheart."

Her arms curled tighter around herself. She whimpered.

He lifted her, holding her like he had before. His arms
around her seemed to calm her. But as he pulled her tighter
against him, she shoved at his chest, her sudden violent
movement catching him off guard. Her fist connected with
his lip, knuckles bashing him hard. He tasted the rusty, salty
tang of blood.

Then she was scrambling backward across the bed, her
back pressing to the headboard, her eerie vacant stare becoming wild-eyed, frantic.

"Don't hurt me. Oh God, please don't!"

"Erika, you're dreaming," he said to her, raising his voice,
knowing that he had to somehow penetrate whatever horror
was going on inside her head.

She gaped straight ahead, none of his words reaching her.

He touched her again, his hand on her knee. She flinched,
but didn't pull away. Didn't try to escape.

"Erika. Sweetheart. It's Vittorio."

She shook her head slightly, and for a moment, he thought

he was connecting with her. But just as he started to reach for her again, she cried out. Her cry, terrified and heart-wrenching.

"Oh God," she panted, absolute terror in her words. "Oh God." Tears welled in her sightless eyes, spilling down her ashen cheeks. "I don't want to die. Please."

Her words hit him like a punch direct to his gut. Hell, his balls. He wouldn't let her die. Damn it, he'd give up his immortality before he let anything hurt her. Even this monster in her head.

No longer willing to be cautious, just knowing she had to wake up, he pulled her across the duvet toward him. Scooping her up, he hugged her close even though she went rigid in his arms, her body unyielding against his.

"Wake up, Erika," he commanded, his mouth near her ear. "Wake up."

She struggled slightly, then froze again.

"Erika, wake up. It's Vittorio."

Her body jerked as if something was physically releasing her. Then she sagged heavily into his arms, her face burrowing into his neck.

She stayed that way for several moments, and Vittorio decided she'd never woken up, but simply slipped out of the nightmare she'd been having. He started to shift her toward the pillows, intending to place her back in bed. But before he could situate her, she lifted her head, staring up at him, her eyes wide and frightened.

"Vittorio, is that you?" She touched his jaw, dazed, as if she was having a hard time telling if he was real.

He nodded.

She touched his face again, cupping his cheek. Then she burst into tears.

Chapter 11

She was going crazy. She didn't even know if what she'd just experienced was real or a dream. She didn't know if Vittorio was there or not. Could she trust this was really him, only to discover she'd imagined him and those things that had been chasing her were back? Trying to kill her.

Erika clung to him anyway, needing to take solace and comfort from someone. Praying she would be okay.

The arms around her held her tight, the pressure one of protection, not of threat, not the grip of horrible claws or gnashing teeth. She burrowed her face deeper into the curve of his neck, trying to escape the images she'd just seen.

"Shh, Erika, you're safe. I'm here. You're okay."

Erika didn't know how long she stayed pressed against him, or how long he repeated those words, his hands stroking her back, his cheek nuzzling the top of her head. Eventually she allowed herself to believe he was real, and he wasn't going to let anyone or anything hurt her.

She also realized she was sobbing, her tears dampening his bare chest. She forced herself to let go, straightening away from him. Even as more reality sank in, she still hesitated to look at Vittorio, part of her afraid she was still dreaming, and another part embarrassed for him to see her so unraveled.

But when she met his eyes, she saw only concern and compassion in their dark depths. His kind expression made him more breathtakingly beautiful.

She began to cry again in earnest.

"Erika? What is going on?"

She shook her head, unable to explain.

"I'm sorry." She swiped at her wet cheeks, pulling in a deep breath to stifle another sob that threatened to escape.

"Don't be sorry." He touched her hair, tucking a lock of her hair behind her ear, the gesture something her father had done when she was young and upset. But this wasn't her father, and her body reminded her of that fact. Even overwrought with fear and confusion, every cell reacted to Vittorio.

As if he sensed her response, his hand dropped.

"What are these nightmares about?"

She shook her head, even now the details blurring. "I don't know. Someone—" She frowned. "No, something—many of them, were trying to attack me. Catch me. Kill me."

Vittorio waited for her to go on, but with every second another memory grew fainter, until she couldn't pinpoint an exact image. But even though the images were disappearing, the fear remained, as if entrenched deep into her marrow.

"Well, it's over now."

She nodded, but it didn't feel over. She glanced around her bedroom with its wealth of rich colors and plush textures, expecting darkness to appear and try to envelop her.

She shivered, wrapping her arms around herself as if she could feel the impending blackness coming.

"Here." Vittorio stood and fluffed the pillows scattered behind her in the tangle of bedclothes. He arranged them, patting them into perfect place. "Lay back."

She did as he asked, looking up at him, feeling childish, pathetic. Still, she was glad he was there and grateful for his strong, steady behavior.

He tucked in one side of the duvet, and her heart made a strange twist in her chest. She longed to reach out and touch the lock of his long hair that fell forward, shielding his features from her as he reached across her to tuck in the other side.

"Okay," he said, straightening, brushing his own hair back in the way she'd wanted to.

She frowned. "Your head. It's healed."

He touched the place where she'd hit him with the phone.

"Oh, yeah. It wasn't much of a cut."

Erica blinked. It had looked bad.

"You are safe. I will check the apartment before I go. And I will be right upstairs if you need me."

Erika sat up, some of the anxiety that had faded under his calm, caring attention, returning with a renewed vengeance.

"No."

He frowned. "I won't be far. Just upstairs."

"No," she repeated. "Please stay with me."

Vittorio eyed the bed, and he seemed to war with the idea.

"I will stay with you until you sleep," he finally said. Then he pointed to the divan against the wall at the foot of the bed. He sat down on the ornate piece of furniture, looking uncomfortable and out of place against the gold and cream brocade.

She rested back against her pillows, watching him. Wanting him closer. She wanted him beside her. And not solely because his nearness calmed her. Her heart skipped, then sped up as she imagined him lying beside her, his body touching hers.

No, he definitely didn't calm her—but he made her feel safe. Safe, if not more than a little turned on.

He situated himself, leaning back, crossing his arms and his ankles, looking even more awkward on the ultra-feminine divan.

Erika actually felt a smile tug at her lips. Then a small laugh crept past them.

Vittorio frowned at her. "What?"

"You look very—cute." She giggled, unable to stop herself.

He raised an eyebrow. "Cute, huh?"

She laughed again. "Yes. Very uncomfortable, but very cute."

This time, a smile curved his lips, which transformed his already achingly beautiful face into something absolutely mesmerizing. "I don't feel cute, I feel a little ridiculous."

"Well, I did offer you a place on the bed."

He glanced toward the unoccupied portion of the mattress, then tried to relax where he was. "This is fine. I don't want to disturb you if you fall back to sleep."

Erika didn't argue, but she got the feeling he was the one who was disturbed by the idea of sharing her bed. And she hoped it wasn't because he didn't want to, but because he wasn't sure what she wanted. Although she doubted he couldn't guess.

"Now, close your eyes," he said, his voice firm, as if he was being resolute with himself rather than her. His reaction made her feel good. Hopeful that there might be interest there after all.

She considered telling him that his presence in her bed wouldn't disturb her in the slightest, but then thought better of it. She wanted him to stay, and pressuring him might just make him leave. With him here, she felt fine, but she knew if he left, the fear would return and she couldn't bear the smothering completeness of her own terror.

Instead she said, "I've never felt as scared as I have the past two nights. I've never been prone to nightmares. I don't get why this is happening."

Vittorio turned his head, regarding her for a moment before speaking. "Maybe something is just bothering you. And this is how it's manifesting."

"Maybe," she agreed. That seemed like a reasonable explanation. "But these are so much more intense than any nightmare I've had before. These feel absolutely real." She shook her head, feeling as if there was no way to give them adequate words.

He nodded, seeming to understand. After all, he probably

saw more of her behavior during the traumatic episodes than she did.

"Who can really say why it's happening. But they will pass."

He sounded positive, and she was thankful for his certainty, she just wished she could believe it too.

Curling on her side, she angled her head on the pillow so she could still watch him at the end of her bed. He stared up at the ceiling, his mouth set, his jaw rigid.

"You're a very nice person, you know that?"

He turned his head to look at her. "Aside from being rude to you on several occasions."

She shrugged against her pillow. "Yes, aside from that." She smiled. "You can run a little hot and cold. But you are more hot than cold." Her cheeks burned at how that sounded. "Not hot, hot. But—you know."

He raised an eyebrow, obviously finding her flustered behavior amusing. "Yeah, I get what you meant."

She smiled slightly, glad he was letting her muddled assessment go. Although she couldn't help being curious about why he put up walls. There had to be a reason. She'd heard Ren talk about how controlled and uptight his brother was, but now she'd started to think that was a defense of some sort. And she wondered for what reason.

"You and Ren are very different," she said, speaking her thoughts aloud.

Vittorio glanced at her again, considering her words.

"Oh yeah," he finally agreed. "Ren is the spirited brother. The creative one. The charmer."

It was Erika's turn to raise an eyebrow. "I think you are very charming when you want to be. You just hide a lot of yourself."

His gaze locked with hers, then he shrugged, donning an air of casualness. "I guess. Maybe there just isn't a lot to see."

But Erika realized she'd struck a chord with him. He did

hide a lot under a cool, distant exterior. But she didn't believe that was the real him. Not when he'd been so caring to her. Not when he cared for his wild brother so much. Not when he was willing to curl into an uncomfortable position on a narrow divan to make sure she felt safe.

She knew she shouldn't say it, but she couldn't stop herself. "Sometimes I think you look a little sad, too."

This time he didn't speak or look at her, and Erika suspected she'd overstepped her bounds. But now that she'd said it, she realized that's what she saw sometimes in his dark eyes, sorrow and regret.

Why? What had happened to him that he carried so much pain? The idea bothered her.

She studied him for a moment longer, wondering what was going on inside his head, behind those often unreadable eyes of his.

Her own eyes drifted shut as she wondered. What did Vittorio hide? Had he thought about her as often as she'd thought about him since their first meeting? Did he think about her at all?

She hoped so. She wanted him, so very, very much—all his sides. All his facets.

Vittorio hated himself for what he was doing as he pulled in some of Erika's energy. Last night, he'd done it to take away the fear in her eyes. To give her peace from her terror.

Tonight, he stole from her to protect himself. He could feel her watching him, trying to understand him. Her eyes moved over his features like the heated touch of her fingers. A touch he craved with every fiber of his being.

And it unnerved him, because he wanted her to understand him. He wanted her to know all about his past and somehow forgive him. Give him absolution in some way. But that kind of redemption wasn't hers to give. Even if she could.

No, he couldn't share his past, his concerns, his own failings with her. That was dangerous, and she likely wouldn't understand, much less grant him clemency, anyway.

And then there was the slight problem of his attraction. He wanted that part of her too. Her passion, her body, her touch. It had taken all of his willpower not to take her up on her offer and lie on the bed beside her. Feeling her body heat next to him. The spicy scent of her skin. Her lithe curves, made to be touched.

He fought back a groan. Goddamn, he wanted this woman. So much. Even holding her as she cried, her body trembling with fear, he'd noticed how perfect she felt against him. That had to be a whole new low for him, feeling attracted while she was wracked with fright.

And now he was stealing her energy, not to help her rest, but to protect himself. He glanced at her. Her eyes were shut, her breathing not quite to the even rhythm of sleep, but close.

He stopped absorbing her energy, even as everything in his greedy body told him, *just a little more.*

No. No.

She was fine, her body and mind calmed. She would rest. He slowly levered himself up and started to swing his legs off the divan.

"Don't go."

Vittorio froze, her sleepy voice low and . . . sexy. He remained still, watching her.

She managed to open one eye. "Please stay. You said you would."

He nodded, sliding back onto the chaise.

She smiled slightly, then shifted to snuggle farther down into her soft bedding.

He wanted her to curl up against him like that. He crossed his arms back over his chest, as if the gesture could close him off and hold all his wayward thoughts at bay.

He shut his eyes, willing his mind to be quiet. Hadn't he learned enough tonight to know that he couldn't be with Erika?

Wasn't the potential of her death enough to rein in his damned libido?

She was floating. A lovely peaceful place. Floating, floating.

"Erika." The voice reached out to her, but she couldn't see the speaker; but she thought she recognized the deep voice. She looked around.

"Vittorio?" She realized she was no longer floating, but standing in the woods. The forest was dark and overgrown. She stayed to the path slicing through the tangle of limbs and underbrush, but searched the woods for the person calling out to her.

"Vittorio?" she called again.

"Erika." The voice was closer now. Erika's skin bristled, and a chill stole away any vestiges of warmth that had enfolded her.

"Erika." The voice was right beside her, the deep tone becoming guttural, eerie, distorted. She suddenly grew apprehensive, as she whipped around trying to locate who was there with her.

"Erika." This time her name was drawn out, singsong, threatening. Her skin grew cold, her heart pounded.

She was no longer floating, she was running. Racing through a strange forest, tangles of weeds pulling at the legs of her pajamas. Low tree limbs jumping out in front of her like long arms and hands grabbing at her.

"Erika!"

A broken whimper escaped her throat as she tried not to worry about the voice behind her. *Just keep running. Just stay on your feet.*

But even as she chanted those thoughts over and over in her head, her foot caught on a bared root, sending her tumbling. When she finally stopped, the cold earth was at her back.

Get up, she screamed to herself. *Get up!*

She tried to stand. But before she could even get her arms under her to push herself up, shadows started to move around her, some swaying like the movement of the trees.

Just trees, she told herself. *Stay calm, get to your feet.*

Then the shadows began to circle her.

Overwhelming dread stilled her movement. Maybe if she stayed absolutely still. Maybe. But her heart thundered in her chest, her breath came in short pants. She shook.

One shadow moved forward, coming closer and closer until she was enveloped in its darkness. Until it weighed down on her, pressing heavily, crushingly on the middle of her chest, though she saw no hands touching her.

She struggled to pull in a full breath, but couldn't quite manage it. Her sight began to blur as if she might pass out. She panicked, writhing on the ground, those invisible hands pinning her in place. Strong hands, brutal hands.

Then directly in front of her face, she began to see a horrifying, distorted face. An evil face. More faces joined it. Faces that only found pleasure in pain, fear and death. Slowly their features mutated, turning from one ghastly, sinister image to another. And she saw in their eyes suffering and torture. She felt it as if it were her own.

"Erika! Erika!" they chanted, until her senses were filled with hideous images, horrible voices and blinding fear.

She began to scream. And scream. And scream.

Vittorio shot off the chaise. Erika's shrieks pierced the air as she struggled violently against her twisted bedcovers, fighting them as if they were a dozen arms holding her down. Her eyes were wide open and unfocused, as they'd been the other times. Yet, she obviously saw something. In her mind, she saw something absolutely appalling.

Vittorio climbed onto the bed, pulling her bucking body against his, ignoring the jabs of her elbows as she thrashed.

"Erika. I'm here. I'm here."

His words didn't lessen her struggles. They didn't breach

her mind and the awful world she was trapped in. It was as if she was too far away to hear him, to know he was there.

"Erika. Wake up. Wake up, darling."

Gradually her violent movements calmed. But just when he thought he had reached her, she began to flail again. Frightened, panicked noise came from deep in her throat. Noises that frightened Vittorio too. She gasped as if she couldn't breathe. Like invisible hands squeezed her throat.

"Come on," he pleaded, feeling the beating of her heart against his chest, his own pulse matching the rapid rhythm. "Wake up." He held her shoulders, shaking her slightly. "Wake up!"

Erika seized, bucking upward in his grasp, arcing as if something forcibly left her body. Then she fell back, limp, half on the bed, half in his arms.

Vittorio stared down at her pale face, terrified.

Her eyes opened, her expression disoriented but not quite that horrible, glazed stare of before. She managed to focus on him.

"It happened again," she said, her voice so hollow it unnerved him.

"I know," he said. "I know."

"What's wrong with me?"

He shook his head, for the first time thinking maybe she was experiencing something beyond a bout of stress-induced nightmares. She'd seemed under the control of something. Something unseen, but no less real.

"I don't know," he said. He touched her face, caressing the silky skin of her cheek. Her skin was cool, yet damp with sweat.

She allowed his touch as he pushed her tangle of dark hair away from her face. She closed her eyes, and he continued to slip his fingers through her hair, willing her to calm.

After a few moments, her eyes opened, their stormy depths welled with tears. "I feel like I'm going mad. That was so real."

The words were said so softly, so calmly, that it took a moment for them to register. His hand paused at her temple.

"No," he said. "No. You've just had another bad dream. That's all." He wished he felt as adamant as he sounded.

She stared up at him, a tear leaking out of the corner of her eye, running down her temple to his finger. Hot liquid burning him.

With no more thought than to comfort her, he leaned down and kissed her forehead. Then he kissed her temple, the salty wetness there clinging to his lips. The taste spurred on his concern, but somehow also ignited a burning need deep in his chest.

He pulled back, shaken that he could still feel desire when she was so clearly upset. Their eyes locked, and he wondered what was going on behind her wide, thundercloud eyes. Then her hand came up to touch him, stroking his jaw, his cheek. Her fingers tangled in his hair.

"Vittorio," she murmured.

Before he realized what he was doing, his head came down and his mouth was on hers.

Chapter 12

Erika didn't even consider stopping him. Nor did she question why it was happening. She simply wanted Vittorio too much. And his lips moving over hers, his tongue tentatively mingling with her tongue. The feeling, the taste just as wonderful as she'd imagined. Hot, slick, and absolutely perfect.

Her arms came up to loop around his neck, urging him closer, and he obeyed, his weight full on her body, hard and strong. His lips supple, velvety. A lovely paradox.

Her fingers tangled in his hair, stroking as she'd wanted to for so, so long. Again reality was as amazing as imagination, the strands silky and lustrous and so sensual.

She moaned, her senses overwhelmed by him. Silken hair, hard muscles, soft lips, strong hands moving down her body.

Even his scent, a rich combination of earthy woods and exotic spice seemed a delicious incongruity. She delighted at the complexity of him. All of those slight contradictions made her want him more. Made her want to discover more.

Then his hands moved, outlining her curves, and all thought, aside from getting him naked against her, disappeared.

He seemed to sense her need, her urgency. His lips left hers, as he moved away to pull at the covers tangled around her. Her hands joined his, pushing the blankets to the floor.

Then his mouth was back on hers, the intensity of his kisses growing. Her own reactions becoming more frantic too, desire building up inside her, swirling into a frenzy of ravenous need.

Her passion for a man had never spiraled so quickly into something so intense, so totally absorbing. She fumbled to touch him everywhere. His hair, his shoulders, her hands tugging at his shirt, frenziedly seeking the bare skin underneath.

Vittorio's actions mimicked hers, his hands moving over her in frantic, desperate touches, a little rough, a little awkward, and stunningly magnificent.

His lips left hers as he straightened up, taking her with him. Then his hands were under her T-shirt, pushing the material upward. She didn't hesitate as she raised her arms to help him.

He paused, the T-shirt knotted around her arms like makeshift handcuffs, holding them up over her head. Her breasts jutted forward, bared for him to see. His dark eyes moved over her, eating up the sight. Her nipples tightened and puckered in response. She was tied and ready for sacrifice to him. Her nipples hardened even more. Dampness pooled between her thighs.

She would gladly be sacrificed to this man. This gorgeous man. She took in his tousled hair, the smoldering burn of his nearly black eyes.

A whimper escaped her, and she bit her lips. Just his gaze on her breasts was the most erotic sensation she could remember. Then he whipped the tee off her arms and tossed it to the floor.

His mouth returned to her, this time pressing sizzling, openmouthed kisses to her neck, to her chest until he reached her breasts, which ached and throbbed for his touch.

He paused again, studying her. She whimpered, wanting his touch so desperately, begging him for it, or maybe demanding. He obeyed, his lips catching the rigid nipple, drawing on it until a broken, ecstasy-filled cry passed her own lips. Her body arced upward, offering him more, watching him take it.

He suckled her hard, his tongue and teeth worrying the pebbled flesh. He stopped only long enough to move his attention to her breasts.

Then, despite the raw, astonishing thrill of his touch, she pushed at him, impatient for more. Her hands snaked between them to again work at his shirt.

He released her nipple and moved back to rip off his own tee. Before he could even finish, her hands were on his jeans, tugging at the button. He leaned back to give her better access. Soon the worn denim was undone, the swollen head of his erection poking out of the parted zipper.

She would have smiled at the image—maybe even contemplated how they got to this point, but she didn't have time for that. He pushed her back down, moving over her. His mouth found hers again and they were once more lost in a delicious frenzy of tasting each other.

As quickly as before, her desire reached a painful peak. Her legs parted to cradle him exactly where she wanted him. The rough grind of his jeans and his hard erection were an agonizing and incredible friction against her aroused, wet sex.

She moaned against his lips, pulling him tighter to her with her legs. He made a noise low in his throat in response, then the hands that were tangled in her hair moved away. He braced one hand against the bed as he levered himself up and snaked the other hand down between their bodies. He caught the leg of her panties and tugged the crotch to one side, baring her.

One finger parted her, touching her already soaking, hot core. She nearly cried out as he found her clitoris, the pad of his finger a teasing torture.

He swirled. Then swirled again. She gasped, instinctively lifting her hips, wanting more. She wanted it all. All of him.

Even though she didn't say it, he seemed to know. His hand left her to adjust the front of his jeans so his erection now rubbed the engorged nubbin.

His mouth returned to hers as he ground his hips against her, mimicking what he wanted to do. And she wanted it too. She nearly panted with her desire. She nipped his bottom lip and spread her legs wider.

That was all the invitation he needed, because his mouth left hers as he met her eyes. His dark eyes so serious and smoldering.

"Tell me where you want me." His voice was deep and almost pleading.

"I want you inside me," she breathed. "Deep inside."

His eyes held hers for a moment longer, then he reared back and entered her, filling her to the hilt in one powerful movement. It should have been too much, too soon.

But it was perfect. His length and his girth filling her totally, stretching her, filling something within her that she'd only vaguely realized was missing.

"Damn," Vittorio groaned, his voice almost reverent. Erika had to agree. It seemed the only word that fit at the moment. Desire swirled and whipped, growing with the intensity of a tornado, ripping away all thoughts, leaving only the heavy wondrous feeling of him.

Then he began to move. And she realized the marvelous, wild eddy was just the beginning.

He plunged deep inside her, filling her to the point of too much, only to pull out, leaving her wanting that depth and power back. Then he gave it to her, and she wondered how she could possibly handle more. But still she wanted more.

She wanted . . .

Violently, that nameless want shattered through her, rocking her body, straining her muscles as her legs wrapped tightly around him, pulling him deep. Her release took total control. Vaguely, amid her own orgasm, she realized Vittorio had joined her. His body thrust deep inside her, his body taut against hers.

Oh. My. God, she managed to think, before the ferocity of their joining slowly faded into the peaceful lull after a turbulent storm. She floated, aware of Vittorio's weight and heat still surrounding her. Even his spicy, woodsy scent added to the lovely calm she felt.

Bliss. Pure bliss.

"One day love will find you . . ."

Erika blinked into the shadowy darkness of her room. *What the heck?* She squinted around, trying to figure out what was interrupting her languid, lovely dreams. Then she realized it was her cell phone, the musical ring she'd programmed for Jo's calls. Journey—a private joke between them. A joke about their often ridiculous search for the right guy.

Of course her stupid phone was holding its charge when she was enjoying such a lovely dream-free sleep. But before she could even get her sleep-weighed limbs to shove at the bedcovers, the ringtone stopped. She let her eyes drift closed again, prepared to give herself back to her deliciously drowning sleep.

Then she realized she wasn't alone. She sat upright, staring over at the man next to her. Only one of Vittorio's eyes—lashes dark against his cheek—his nose, and an almost exotically high cheekbone were visible among the tangle of his long hair and bedding. Still, he looked unbelievably beautiful.

Here was the right guy in her bed, and she'd been thinking about her stupid ringtone. How on earth had last night slipped her mind, even for a second?

She continued gaping at him, now recalling every detail of their lovemaking. Crazed, impulsive lovemaking that reminded her more of randy teens than rational adults. Her disheveled night clothes, the chaos of the bedding, the fact that

neither of them fully undressed to consummate their desire—
definitely that of overeager teens.

But instead of finding the haste of their encounter embarrassing or at the very least, reckless, Erika found it wildly exciting and oddly romantic.

She couldn't recall a time when she'd wanted a man so
much that she hadn't given any thought to the consequences
of taking their relationship to an intimate level. Not that she
wasn't safe—from pregnancy at least. But she'd never before
forgotten to protect herself from STDs.

She studied Vittorio. Somehow she just didn't picture him
as a guy who slept around. She was sure she was safe, although
if any of her friends gave her that reasoning—he looks safe—
she'd have given them an earful. But she just knew she was.
And frankly, she couldn't let anything shadow the perfection
of what had happened between them.

She fell back against her pillow with a sigh. Beyond perfect—if there was such a thing. She rolled over on her side,
face-to-face with him. But Vittorio continued to sleep on.

With careful fingers, she reached out to smooth back his
hair from his face. *He really does have the face of an angel,*
she thought. She'd love to sculpt him if he'd let her.

But she doubted he'd agree to it, even now. There was a re-
serve to him that she knew he would have to drop to allow
her to sculpt him. He didn't want anyone to look too deeply
into his personality and emotions.

Her fingers paused at that thought. Here she was telling
herself last night had been perfect. That they hadn't needed
to question what they were doing, yet she still knew there
was a barrier around Vittorio that he wouldn't let her past.

That didn't sound like the route to a perfect romance. It
sounded more like a direct course to heartbreak. She knew
from her own past that you couldn't change a person. She
couldn't expect Vittorio to suddenly open up to her.

Her fingers left him, and she rolled over to place her feet
on the floor. *What was she doing? What had she done?*

She crawled out of bed and padded over to the velvet wing-backed chair in the corner, where she'd left her robe. She pulled it on. Glancing one more time at Vittorio's sleeping form, she headed to the kitchen for a Diet Coke and a moment to think without Vittorio's beauty shading all her thoughts like rose-colored glasses.

She automatically went to the cupboard and grabbed a can of tuna, not needing to even look in Boris's direction to know he was annoyed that his breakfast was late.

Way late, she realized as she noted the time on the microwave. After 3 p.m.

After the disgruntled and understandably hungry cat was fed, she got a soda for herself and settled on the couch to consider her next course of action.

She supposed she would be dreaming to believe there wouldn't be awkwardness from last night's encounter. Still, the outcome could easily be great. She and Vittorio could start dating, they could be a couple. Philippe could be totally correct in his prediction.

She sipped from her can. Or Vittorio could thank her for a fun and exciting night, and that could be it. A one-night stand.

Erika pulled a face. She really didn't like that outcome, at all. Not when she'd just experienced the most earth-shaking, phenomenal sex of her life. And not when he'd been her hero for the last two nights. And especially not when she knew deep down inside that he was different than any other man she'd ever met.

God, she did sound like a love-crazed teen. She paused at the use of the word *love*. Okay, even she wasn't so enchanted by Vittorio that she could use that word yet, in any context. But she knew there was something there that needed to be explored.

And she'd tell him so when he woke.

She leaned forward and placed her soda on the coffee table. Then she glanced over at her work area. Despite all her confused thoughts, she did feel like working today. That had to be a good sign too, right?

She got up and went to the bin where she kept her clay. Without any design in mind, she scooped out a big hunk and began working it in her hands. As she kneaded the smooth earth, she told herself everything would work out the way she hoped.

She positioned the clay on her work pedestal and began to mold it, adding contours and lines without considering what she was doing, just letting her hands form what seemed right.

Just like this relationship. She'd do what seemed right, and it would work out as it should.

Besides, she told herself, *he wouldn't have spent the night if he didn't want to be with me.* Wasn't it a classic move to leave right away, if it was only a one-night stand? She had to believe that.

Vittorio shot into a sitting position as soon as the sun disappeared over the horizon, doing a fair impersonation of Dracula rising up from his coffin. Except he wasn't somewhere as innocuous as a coffin. He was in Erika's bed.

Shit.

His hand knotted in his hair, swiping it back from his face as he shot a look around the room. Oh yeah, he was in Erika's bed all right. Right where he'd fallen into his unnatural sleep as the sun rose. Right after he'd had sex with her.

Shit.

He glanced around again, making sure she wasn't there, even though he knew she wasn't. He could hear the faint strains of music coming from the living room, and the occasional sound of her slightly off-key humming accompanying the song.

Shit, he thought again, releasing his hair and looking around like he'd find some answer to this situation lying there, like written instructions on how to handle the impulsive, purely selfish act of casual sex. But there wasn't any manual for him to find. And in truth, there was nothing casual about what he'd felt when he was with her. Impulsive and selfish still applied, but casual—no.

Still, he had to tell her that last night was a mistake. A big, huge, colossal mistake.

He groaned and fell back against the pillows that smelled of Erika's spicy cinnamon skin. His body reacted instantly, despite his disgust with himself.

He never lost control. Never. Yet, one damned kiss, and he'd been tearing at her clothing, plowing himself into her like some oversexed animal.

He stared at her ceiling, barely registering the ornate molding, the same that was on the ceiling of his apartment. What had gotten into him? Why did this woman steal all his sense, all his ideas of what was right and wrong and what he had to do?

He started to push back the covers, when the bedroom door opened. Erika stood silhouetted against the hallway light, but Vittorio could still make out her expression.

"Hi," she said, and he could hear the wariness in her voice, matching the look in her eyes.

"Hello," he managed, realizing his own voice sounded stiff, distant, as if it was a habit he couldn't quite control.

"I was just checking on you." She seemed like she was embarrassed to be caught coming into the room. Her room.

"I just woke up."

"Oh," she said.

Good God, didn't the awkwardness of this conversation show her that they had no business whatsoever having sex? Even beyond the fact he was a vampire with a lunatic mother who might actually try to cause Erika bodily harm?

Erika took a step into the room, and he noticed that she was wearing a short robe. Her long legs tapered down to shapely ankles and high-arched feet. Her waist was narrow and her hips slightly rounded. Her small, perfectly rounded breasts hid just behind thin satin.

His penis hardened painfully against his unbuttoned jeans. His damned body certainly didn't see any problems with their relationship.

"Are you hungry?" she asked, drawing his attention away from her body—and his body—back to her face. That sweet, expectant face that made him feel like a total cad. "I have cereal, and bread for toast, or I could make you a sandwich. I don't really cook much. But I—"

"I'm fine," Vittorio interrupted, unable to listen to her nervous kindness. God, he was a greedy bastard. He hesitated for a moment before rising from the bed. With as much normalcy and finesse as he could muster, he fastened his jeans.

When he looked back at Erika, she was watching him. Then she actually licked her lips, the action nearly more than he could stand. He shifted, trying to hide his body's response.

He just had to deal with this situation. End it now, as crappy and awkward as it was.

"Umm—I have to go."

Wow, that was a *really* crappy way to deal with it.

Chapter 13

Erika stared at him, praying that in this particular instance, even though it wasn't remotely manly, he was referring to the need of a bathroom. But those hopes were quickly dashed.

"Last night was a mistake."

She didn't speak for a moment. She couldn't. She should have known better than to believe that after a wham-bam moment, Vittorio was going to profess his love for her.

Now in the stark lamplight of her room, all her happy little fantasies of the afternoon seemed totally ludicrous. Juvenile, really.

Vittorio regarded her with that closed off, reticent expression she recognized well, and truly hated. And she still couldn't think of what to say. Had what she experienced with him only been perfect on her end? Possibly. That idea made her feel more deluded. And more than a little pathetic.

Vittorio's eyes left hers as he straightened his clothes. Then he met her gaze again. For the briefest moment, she saw some emotion there beyond his cool detachment, but she couldn't quite read it. She wasn't sure she wanted to read it. She'd obviously read far too much into everything already.

"Well," she said, and managed to keep her own voice even, calm, "if you have to go, then I guess you have to go."

He nodded, but still didn't move. Again she thought she saw a flicker of something in his eyes. Maybe regret.

That hurt even more. Regret was far too akin to pity. And that idea not only hurt her, it irked her. She could deal with him not feeling the same way, she couldn't deal with him feeling badly for her.

Okay, she hated that he didn't seem to feel the same way. She hated that he was going right back to the same remote guy she had seen that first night. It was even harder to see now, when she knew there was passion and heat under that cold façade.

But ultimately what could she do? In the immortal words of Bonnie Raitt, she couldn't make him love her, if he don't. Or didn't. Whatever.

So instead of saying anything more, she backed away from her door, offering him an exit. "It's probably good if you go. I have an appointment."

It was a lie, but all she could think of at the moment.

Her clipped words seemed to spur him into action. He came around the bed, his walk neither slow nor rushed, more like determined. She supposed it was better than fleeing, but not much. Any way you looked at it he was leaving, and nothing was good about that.

He paused beside her. "You're okay, aren't you?"

Erika wanted to say, no. She wanted to ask him if he'd felt the same way she did last night. But instead, she nodded. "Sure. I'm fine."

He didn't move right away and looked at her as if he was trying to read her expression. She longed to scream. What difference did it make if she was okay or not? He wasn't staying either way. He thought what had happened between them was a mistake. Her feelings weren't going to factor in.

But she didn't break her steady gaze. She wouldn't let him know how much this hurt. How much she'd felt a connection with him, even after such a short acquaintance. Especially after what they'd shared last night.

It was his turn to simply nod. Then he left the room, heading down the hallway. She didn't move as she heard his deep voice rumbling from the living room, apparently saying something to the cat. Then there was a brief moment of silence, and she almost turned to see if he was returning. But she didn't.

Then she heard the rattle of the doorknob. She heard the squeak of the hinges, then the quiet click as the latch closed.

He was gone. Just like that. Without any explanation why last night had happened. Why it was a mistake. Why he'd even bothered to come down here and help her through her horrible dreams in the first place.

Erika wanted to be philosophical about the whole event. She wanted to look at it as something they'd both wanted at the time, and had enjoyed, but the truth was . . . she was mad.

She didn't bother to go check if he'd truly left, she knew he had. Instead she walked to her dresser and pulled out a pair of jeans and a T-shirt. Her movements were wooden, despite her determination to stay strong and get a handle on all the emotions running through her.

Once dressed, she walked to the kitchen looking for her pocketbook. Boris came up as she double-checked to see if she had her keys, twining through her legs as if he was trying to comfort her. The cat's actions made her feel even worse. Even Boris, the most self-absorbed creature on the face of the earth, knew she'd just been dumped after a one-night stand.

She made a face at the cat, then gathered up her stuff and headed toward the front door, not looking in the direction of the sculpture she'd been working on earlier. God, she hoped Vittorio hadn't looked either. If she felt stupid and pathetic now, she couldn't imagine how she'd feel if he'd noticed that the bust she'd been working on held an uncanny resemblance to him.

* * *

Vittorio reached his apartment before he allowed himself to think. He'd just needed to keep his mind focused on making his feet move, one after the other, because frankly every inch of his body was rebelling at the idea of leaving Erika. But he'd had to.

Damn, last night shouldn't have happened. He wandered over to the old sofa, the only piece of furniture in the living area of the dingy, dusty apartment. Collapsing onto the worn cushions, dust motes billowed up around him. Not that he cared. He wasn't here to lavish himself in luxury. He certainly wasn't here to engage in a relationship with his downstairs neighbor. Of course, that concept had been far, far from this mind last night, hadn't it?

Groaning with frustration, he dropped his head into his hands, furrowing his fingers in his hair. How had he let that happen? His intent was to protect Erika. Not to get more involved with her. Certainly not to make her a target, if his suspicions about his mother were true.

And if they were true, sleeping with Erika might as well have put a bull's-eye right on her back. How could he have been that selfish? That totally lacking in restraint?

Because he'd wanted her more than he'd ever wanted any woman in his life. Far more. He'd cared about Seraph, worried about her, but not once had he longed for her with that intensity. With a need that seemed to take on a life of its own when she was in his presence. God, just looking at Erika drove him mad. And now he'd held her in his arms. And felt her moving against him. He'd tasted her and been buried deep inside her.

How was he supposed to let her go?

He groaned again, this time the sound ragged and filled with yearning.

Damn it! He couldn't let himself think that way. He had to let her go. But even as he repeated that in his head, he heard her moving downstairs. He heard the creak of her door and her footsteps on the worn wood of the sun porch, then the outside door opening and closing.

Where was she going? He rose from the sofa and crossed to the window that looked out onto the street. For a moment, he didn't see her as she opened, then relocked, the front gate, but then she stepped into view, heading down the sidewalk toward Jackson Square, her pace quick and determined as if she was on a mission. Her face placid, calm.

She certainly didn't look as shaken by the events of last night as he was. She looked like she had already forgotten about what had happened.

Irritation filled him. Another emotion to remind him how damned selfish he was being. Did he want her to pine, even though he knew he couldn't be with her?

He watched as she walked out of view. Then he turned back into the nearly dark, nearly empty room. *Where was she going?* Then a prickle of fear crept along his skin.

She might not be safe, even now. Even if he did make a pact to stay away from her, his mother might already be aware of her.

He couldn't let her wander around unprotected. Before he even finished that thought, he was moving to the door. He had to stay away from her, couldn't touch her, talk with her, be with her in any way his mother might feel threatened by, but he also had to watch her.

She could already be in danger. Thanks to him.

Erika turned onto Chartres, trying not to let her mind replay what had happened between her and Vittorio. Which was darn near impossible. Okay, it was totally impossible. How could something that had been so perfect for her be so easily dismissed by him? It just didn't make sense to her, and it sure as hell wounded her ego.

The sign over Philippe's shop, in the shape of a teacup and saucer, was lit as Erika moved to try the door. Bells jingled, the door opened easily, and she was immediately enveloped in the scent of incense and coffee. She supposed it was weird that she was so relieved to find the place open. She wasn't sure it would be, given that it was a Sunday night.

She thought a lot of people would find it weird that her first thought after getting jilted was to head to her fortune-teller, but she needed to find out some answers. Plus, Philippe was her closest available friend, with Maggie gone. And Erika wasn't sure she would go to Maggie about this anyway. After all, Vittorio was her brother-in-law, which made discussing the situation awkward for all involved. And Jo made it fairly clear that she found the whole thing a tad odd anyway. So that left Philippe.

As she walked up to the counter, she saw Saffron, a woman in her fifties, who handled booking the psychic's appointments and ran the cash register. She was bent over her usual word jumbles, squinting at the newsprint in consternation. She glanced up as Erika approached, giving the same slightly vacant smile she always did.

And as usual, despite the regularity with which Erika came here, Saffron only vaguely seemed to remember her.

"Can I help you?"

Erika didn't bother to act like she recalled her either, it wasn't worth the effort, really. And she was too distracted this evening to bother.

"Is Philippe in?"

"He is. He's just finishing up a reading. Did you want a reading next?"

Erika nodded. A reading, a therapy session, they were one and the same with Philippe.

"Tarot, palm or tea leaves?"

"Tarot." Tonight she definitely needed the big guns of divination.

Saffron wrote down her information and rang up her bill, then Erika moved to the tables at the back of the shop to wait.

Saffron attempted idle chatter, asking her if she liked to do word puzzles, mentioning how good it was that nights were getting a little cooler, asking if she'd like some coffee. But finally Saffron seemed to get the hint that Erika was too preoccupied to make small talk, and she turned back to her word scramble.

Erika was thankful for the quiet—not that being stuck in her own head with her own repeating questions and thoughts was a great place to be, but she just couldn't focus on anything else so it seemed pointless to try.

Fortunately she didn't have to wait long before she heard Philippe's voice from the back as he walked up with his client. They chatted about the fact that whatever changes were coming were going to be good. The client seemed pleased.

When they stepped out into the main room of the shop, Philippe saw her and gave her a nod to acknowledge her, but he continued to talk with the man whose hair was so curly it was nearly spherical.

Erika speculated on whether his hair was natural or if perming rods somehow came into play. Then she noticed the tight-fitting polyester shirt and Wrangler jeans, and decided perming rods it was. She looked away, feeling bad about being critical. It wasn't fair to take out her irritation with men in general, on a stranger.

Erika tried not to eavesdrop, but it was hard not to, since the shop was empty and not even the usual new-age music played to drown out a little of the conversation.

Overall, the man with the unfortunate fashion sense was going to have a good month. And love was definitely on his horizon. To which he said, good, because he was ready to get back in the saddle.

Erika tried not to shudder. She knew it was unkind, but, given her total brush-off from Vittorio, it rubbed her the wrong way that this guy with bad clothes and a coarse attitude was, according to Philippe's prediction, headed toward a hot romance. And she so wasn't.

But then, Philippe had predicted her love affair too. So maybe this guy was going to have the same outcome. A one-night stand. She glanced back to the permed, polyestered man. Actually a one-night stand seemed like it would be fine with him. Maybe for him that would be the height of romance.

Okay, that wasn't fair in the least. And she needed to stop making judgment calls on this guy because of her own broken heart.

She frowned at herself. Broken heart was too extreme. Battered heart maybe—at the very least battered ego.

Frankly, she just wanted Philippe to tell her she'd made a mistake. Or he'd made a mistake. There wasn't a fair-haired, dark-eyed prince in her future or her present. Not that she'd forget about Vittorio or what she'd experienced in his arms any time soon. But she needed . . . answers.

"Erika, you're back soon," Philippe greeted her, with a big smile.

She nodded. "Yes. I'm . . ." How did she explain how she was feeling and why she was here?

Philippe's smile slipped, then he waved for her to follow him back to his little booth. "Come. Let's look at the cards."

But they only took a few steps down the small hallway before he stopped, casting a worried look at her. "Oh dear, you met your prince, didn't you?"

She didn't even need to answer, because he nodded as if something else answered his question.

"These princes," he muttered, as if he knew all along this situation was going to be hard.

Nice of him to pass that along, she thought grimly, as he ushered her into his reading room.

"Sit, sit." He gestured toward the chair where she always sat, then he angled his bulk around the small round table, reaching for the cards even before he sat down.

He shuffled them a few times, then held them out to her.

She shuffled them too, and although she'd done it many times, her fingers trembled. She wanted answers. She needed them.

Finally, when she felt as if she'd mixed them up enough, or to the right combination, she handed them back.

Philippe laid out the cards in a Celtic cross, his brow furrowing more and more with each flip of the cards.

"Hmm," he finally said, after perusing the major and minor arcana arranged before him. "Well, you have met him. That is very clear."

He gave her a knowing look, raising his eyebrows in an expectant way. "Really met him, eh?"

She didn't nod, but she was sure the heat in her cheeks, probably coloring her skin pink, was answer enough.

If it was, he didn't react. Instead his gaze moved back to the cards. "And things feel like they aren't going well. Not the way you want them to."

He didn't need to be a psychic to tell that, she was sure. She knew she looked hurt and frazzled.

"Princes," he muttered again. "Such a ridiculously noble lot."

Erika frowned at that. She personally didn't see Vittorio's behavior this evening as noble. He'd basically told her all he wanted was a one-night stand. Not that she should have assumed more. That was her own fault. But still Vittorio hadn't acted noble—even if she had misunderstood.

"He's upset."

Erika snapped out of her own thoughts. Upset about what? That he'd had sex with her? That wasn't flattering. Was he upset that she'd clearly wanted more? In which case, oh well for him.

"And he's feeling guilty."

Erika tried not to roll her eyes. Again, guilty over what? She breathed in deeply and tried hard to tamp down her disappointment and annoyance. It wasn't as if she'd asked him about his feelings before she'd jumped in the sack with him.

She was as much a part of this mess as he was. And she knew he ran hot and cold before she'd done what she'd done.

In her past experience, if a relationship was ambivalent from the start, and there was no real friendship, but only lust, then things were doomed from the get-go.

But then again, she didn't want to sit here and hear that Vittorio was having doubts and regrets. She knew that and hearing it again was like poking at her heart with a stick. It didn't feel nice, at all.

"Oh, yes, you are very disappointed with how things played out."

Again, no psychic ability needed there. She was sure disappointment was clear in her whole demeanor.

"He's back here to deal with a major problem," Philippe said. "I didn't see that before. Something that he's really worried about."

What could that be? For a moment Erika's hopes rose. Was that what had his behavior changing so readily? Was there something going on with him that didn't have anything to do with her?

She immediately cast aside that idea along with her optimism. It wasn't wise to think that way. Vittorio could very easily just not be interested in her. And she didn't want to keep looking for signs of interest if they weren't really there.

"But things are not over between the two of you. Not by a long shot." He pointed to the Lovers card. "He will be back."

Erika again felt a wave of hope wash through her, making her heart skip slightly like a flat stone over water. Things weren't over. She wanted to hear that. But then again, she didn't want this roller coaster of aloofness, then lust, then back to coldness.

"Are you sure?" she asked.

Philippe even gave her a pointed look; that kind of insulted, reprimanding look that only an offended gay man could give.

"Don't you doubt me," he said. "I never once said this love affair was going to be easy. I just said that it would happen. It has. And it will continue to happen."

Erika immediately felt contrite. After all, Philippe had been right far more often than not, and he had also become her friend. He wasn't telling her any of this to hurt her.

Still she was scared. Her attraction to Vittorio was too intense, her feelings growing out of control too quickly. And that sex. Even now it was hard not to sigh just thinking about it.

"Now, I know you aren't in the mind-set to believe this," Philippe said slowly, tapping the Three of Cups card as he spoke. "But this card refers to home. To domestic life. He's going to be spending a lot of time with you."

Erika recalled how he'd left. Without looking back. She had a hard time imagining home and hearth with the man who'd beat feet away from her.

"Well, he currently lives upstairs from me, if that's what you mean."

Philippe gave her a pleased smirk. "See, didn't I say he was right above you last time you were here?"

She nodded begrudgingly.

"Well, I can tell you with all certainty that he will be back in your life soon. Very soon. And spending a lot of time with you."

Erika nodded, trying to disguise her skepticism, because she knew it would hurt her friend's feelings.

"I can't see what has him so worried. It's definitely an external problem. Something that was there even before he met you." He studied the cards, then slowly understanding dawned, lighting his eyes. "It is another woman."

Erika's heart sank, dropping to the pit of her belly, stealing her breath. She'd never considered Vittorio would have another woman. Now that Philippe had said the words, she wondered why not. He was a handsome man. A beautiful man. Why wouldn't he be involved with someone? And that would explain his reticence and indecision with her.

"But I can't get a firm feeling of that relationship. It's very complicated."

Erika nodded, even as her mind buzzed with this new idea. Why hadn't she thought of this?

"And did you know there is a large age difference between you two?"

Erika blinked, not immediately following the transition in topic. "Yes, I noticed." She had, since Jo had pointed it out. But really, when they were together she never thought about it. She supposed, however, that it might be an issue for Vittorio. Especially if this other woman was younger, closer to his age. God, what if she was only nineteen or twenty? That could be very likely. Erika was willing to bet Vittorio was only twenty-three or twenty-four himself.

"This idea does bother him, but won't eventually. He just needs to come to terms with it."

Come to terms? That sounded highly unromantic. God, he thought of her as an old lady.

"But he will definitely be back. He can't stay away."

She tried to take comfort in that, but between the idea that he was involved with some cute young thing, and that he saw her as ancient—well, she wasn't feeling the least bit better.

"Hmm," Philippe said, tilting his head and narrowing his eyes as he studied the Queen of Swords card, inverted. "This seems to be very important." He paused for a second. "There is someone around you who you should be aware of. Very aware of. This is not a good person. I see a lot of darkness and . . ." He shook his head. "Just be very aware of anyone new in your life. And careful."

Erika frowned. "Is it a man or woman?" Her first thought was maybe this was the person related to Vittorio. His slighted lover. Again she got the image of a sweet young girl, in love with Vittorio and heartbroken. She couldn't seem to conjure any of her own past love interests who would want to hurt her.

Philippe shook his head again, his gaze distant, as he tried to see, or feel, or however he perceived the psychic realm. "I can't tell. But I do see—" He shook his head again. "I know this sounds overdramatic, but I see evil. You need to be aware and very careful."

She considered that, then for some reason Maksim entered her mind. Why she couldn't say. He certainly hadn't given off the vibe of evil, but he did make her—uneasy. And he was the only new person she could think of having met.

But from the tone of Philippe's voice, she knew she had to be careful, and chills snaked down her spine.

Chapter 14

Vittorio paced back and forth in the doorway across the street from the shop where Erika had been for well over an hour.

A fortune-teller's shop. Likely the same place she'd gone before. He frowned at the teacup-shaped sign with scrolled red lettering, wondering why Erika put so much stock in this type of thing. But she clearly did. And he wondered what the fortune-teller would have to say about his cold dismissal of Erika earlier this evening.

What *was* the person telling her? Vittorio definitely couldn't deny that psychics existed. He'd seen far more incredible things in his long life than a person who could get visions of the future, but he did wonder if this person was legitimate, or just taking the money of a woman needing someone to talk to.

Except Erika had plenty of good friends. Maggie. Her other close friend . . . he struggled for the name, only having met her once before. Jo? He was sure she knew others who would give her sounder advice than a French Quarter fortune-teller.

He was tempted to transform into shadow and go in there, eavesdropping like a nosy neighbor. Or a jealous boyfriend.

He shoved that notion aside and paced again in the narrow alcove of a closed bookstore. As he turned again, beginning to think he'd wear a groove in the cracked cement of the stoop before she finally came out, a movement down the street caught his attention. It was a person.

The figure paused, moving to lean against the wall, trying to appear casual. A person waiting for someone, just like Vittorio was.

Except Vittorio looked agitated and a tad stalker-ish. He stopped his pacing so he wasn't quite so noticeable. Not that his behavior was likely of any interest to the person down on the corner.

The dark figure was tall and muscular, clearly male. Vittorio watched him for a moment, then returned his attention to the shop where Erika was. Nothing had changed there. Except the woman who'd been seated behind a counter by the cash register was now sweeping. Getting ready to close. Erika should be out soon.

Vittorio's attention returned surreptitiously to the person at the corner. The man was situated in a place that would allow him to see when Erika left the shop too. He paused, wondering why he'd even think that. Clearly this person was waiting for someone. Was it Erika?

Vittorio couldn't shake the feeling this guy was up to something. Maybe just a mugger. But quickly Vittorio dismissed that idea. There was something different about him, that went beyond a run-of-the-mill menace.

Vittorio remained totally motionless, concentrating on him. Even with the distance between them, Vittorio suddenly realized why this guy was making him ill at ease. He was not human.

Try as he might, he couldn't pinpoint what type of being he was, but he knew for certain that the tall figure clinging to the shadows of the street corner was not mortal.

Vittorio's already cool skin needled with chills. He'd been prepared for the possibility that his mother could be watching Erika. He hadn't bargained on any other preternatural creature. That worried him.

He regarded the figure for a moment longer, trying to decide if he should approach him, just to be safe. But just as Vittorio would have stepped off the stoop, the other creature casually stepped out into the streetlights and started down the sidewalk in the opposite direction.

Vittorio instantly felt stupid. Was he going to suspect that everyone was out to hurt Erika just because of his own guilt over last night? That didn't make any sense.

After all, humans would be shocked how many preternatural creatures walked among them. Especially in New Orleans, which seemed to be a haven for all beings supernatural. He often wondered if that was because Anne Rice brought the place into vogue with her vampire books, or if they were already here, and she just knew it.

Either way, the only preternatural he needed to protect Erika from was his mother. And of course himself. He was already failing on that count.

"Vittorio? What are you doing here?"

His train of thought froze and he slowly turned to look at the speaker. Erika regarded him with a surprised expression.

"I was . . ." What the hell was he supposed to say? He was standing on the sidewalk like he'd stalked her. Which he sort of had. "I was looking for you."

He nearly rolled his eyes at his lack of originality. He might as well have admitted he'd followed her.

"Why?" she asked, not sounding particularly pleased.

"I wanted . . ." God, he sounded like a stammering idiot. "I wanted to tell you I was sorry for leaving the way I did."

Okay, that wasn't what he'd intended to say at all.

Erika's finely arced brows rose as if she really hadn't expected that. Of course, nor had he. He'd intended to stay away, keeping an eye on her from afar. He never intended to discuss what had happened between them. Talking about it seemed far too much like opening Pandora's Box. Reminding him how much he'd like to be with her again.

Hell, who was he kidding? He wanted to make love to her again right here, right now. With psychics, unidentified preternatural creatures and random pedestrians watching. This was all so dangerous.

"Is that all you wanted to say?" she asked.

If he was smart, yes. But his big mouth seemed to have developed a mind quite separate from his own. "I just wanted to make sure you were all right."

Erika shifted, then wrapped her arms across her middle. "I am. A little confused but all right."

He could identify with that feeling. "About what?" Couldn't he just stop? Did he have to keep getting deeper and deeper into this conversation?

"I'm very confused about you. About what you want from me."

He didn't know either. He kept telling himself all of this was to protect her, yet everything he'd done thus far dragged her in deeper and put her more at risk.

"I mean, one minute you are cold," Erika continued, obviously believing he didn't intend to answer, which, given his loose lips at the moment, would have been a good thing. "The next you are so sweet. And then last night, that was wild and spontaneous and really, really good."

She put a lot of emphasis on those reallys, and Vittorio couldn't squelch the satisfaction that filled his chest. Their sex had been very good. Crazy good. The best.

"I just don't know what you want. And you don't seem willing to tell me. Not even a hint."

His premature feeling of pride vanished as he struggled to find something to say. Something that wouldn't hurt her feelings, but that wouldn't lead them right back to her bed. But nothing came to him.

"Is it because I'm too old for you?"

Vittorio blinked. "What?"

"Well, I mean you can only be twenty-three or twenty-four, right? That makes me nearly ten years older than you. Is that what is putting you off?"

Vittorio stared at her. She was kidding, right? She thought that was what was making him act so inconsistently?

First of all, he tended to forget that he only appeared to be in his early twenties, in spite of all the years he'd lived. Not to mention, he'd never considered her age, period. Which also showed how badly he was doing at keeping a grip on his attraction to her. Because he should have thought about his age.

If she knew the real discrepancy in their ages, she'd be horrified. He was ancient. And a lampir.

"I've never considered your age," he said honestly, but instead of the look of relief he'd expected, she only frowned. "And I am much older than I look," he added.

Her frown changed to a look of skepticism.

"Okay," she finally said. "Why did you leave? Is there someone else?"

Wow, she wasn't pulling any punches. She was also giving him the out he needed. And should take. But fool that he was, he didn't.

"Someone else? No. I just think things got out of hand last night. We barely know each other." God, he sounded like a freakin' prude. Uptight and a little censorious. Which was exactly what his brother always accused him of being.

He considered for a moment that maybe his brother was right, then he discarded the idea. He wasn't as frivolous and carefree as Ren, but then Ren hadn't spent the years he had surrounded with their mother's insanity and obsessive love. Vittorio was cautious.

Or he had been cautious until he met Erika.

"That's true," Erika said, and for a moment he thought she was addressing his thoughts rather than what he was saying. It took him a moment to follow along. "Things did get out of hand, but why can't we get to know each other? Go slower."

She tilted her head slightly, her dark hair falling against

her cheek. His fingers twitched to touch the silky strands, to tuck it behind the perfect shell of her ear.

And that was why. He didn't seem to have a *slow* with this woman. He, who'd spent his eternity thus far, debating his every move. Taking the time to make sure what he did was right. He, who'd prided himself on his control and moderation, after knowing none of that in his youth. He had none of that restraint when it came to Erika. He wanted to act on every impulse in his body. And some of those impulses scared him.

But instead of telling her, no, plain and simple, he felt his head nod. "Maybe—we'll see."

As soon as the words were out, he wondered what the hell he was thinking. Couldn't he come up with some excuse why they couldn't be together? Couldn't he go back to her suggestion of there being someone else? After all, his mother was someone else. And something else, too.

"How about we head back to my place and order pizza? Or we could go somewhere. One of my favorite restaurants is right over on Iberville."

His first instinct was to go with her to the restaurant, to keep them in public, where he couldn't act on his desire for her. Except his mother could be around. She couldn't get too close to him or he'd sense her, but she could possibly get close enough to see them together, especially in a crowded place where all the different mortal energies might mask hers.

Keeping himself and Erika out of crowded places was the best way to keep her safe. Crowd—safe from him. Private— safe from his mother. Privacy was the better option. Hell, the best option was to say away from her altogether. But that wasn't happening. Clearly.

"Pizza sounds good," he said, wondering how on earth this was going to work. Being near her, talking, yet not wanting. Or more correctly, not acting on that want. Even now, he found himself tempted to move closer to her as they started down the sidewalk.

But he would maintain control and keep his distance until he could find out more about his mother.

Erika took down plates, setting them on the kitchen counter, then she busied herself with looking for paper napkins. She wasn't quite sure what to make of the change of events tonight.

Philippe had said Vittorio would be back, which she hadn't believed—funny, given that she'd believed her psychic friend up to this point. Or mostly believed him. But not only had Vittorio come back, he'd been waiting outside the tea leaf shop. Talk about a fast-acting prediction.

Yet, he seemed genuinely confused by her asking about their age differences and the possibility of another woman, though Philippe seemed certain about both those predictions too.

After much rummaging, she finally found the napkins. Behind her, she heard Vittorio moving around the room, pacing like a caged tiger. She wasn't sure if she should be flattered that he was staying, since his agitated movement implied he'd rather not be here. She still didn't understand what was going on inside him. Vittorio was a mystery, and it was driving her nuts.

But she did want him here. Despite the weirdness of their relationship thus far, she wanted him. She wanted more time with him.

"Would you like something to drink?" she asked, feeling as nervous as he was acting. "I have soda. Water. Tea."

She turned away from the counter, not noticing immediately that he'd stopped pacing and was studying the sculpture she'd been working on earlier today.

Finally, he glanced at her. "Nothing for me, thanks."

Erika wasn't sure if he realized what he was looking at. That the bust done on rough, broad curves was actually himself.

She'd hoped the features were too coarse, too rudimentary

to be recognized, but when his dark eyes met hers, she knew he saw who it was.

"Is this me?"

"I hope you don't mind," was all she could think to say.

He stared at it again, then slowly shook his head. "No. It's good. Very good."

She crossed over to stand beside him.

"I like it," she admitted, even looking at it critically, trying to see it from his perspective. She actually liked the primitive quality of the sculpture, although she hadn't intended to keep it that way. Yet, it somehow touched a part of Vittorio she hadn't realized she was capturing.

It somehow showed the starkness underneath Vittorio's breathtakingly beautiful exterior. Not a harshness, but the jagged hurt and pain she saw hidden there. Although she hadn't even realized it was there until she'd started using her other senses to create him. Her sense of touch rather than her sight.

She glanced up at him, suddenly afraid she'd pried too far into his psyche. "Do you like it?"

"Yes," he said simply, and she believed him. Relief flooded her, making her knees a little weak. She stared at him for a moment, then her eyes dropped to his lips.

Suddenly, he was leaning in, or maybe she was, but she knew for certain they were going to kiss. And God, she wanted it.

Then the buzzer from the front gate filled the room with a loud, unwelcomed noise, shattering the moment.

Vittorio stepped back as if coming out of a spell. "Pizza," he murmured. "I'll go get it."

Erika could only nod and watch as he hurried toward her door, disappearing out into the darkness.

What were they doing?

Vittorio reached the front gate in record time for not using his preternatural abilities. The delivery boy, a lanky, black kid with a red baseball hat perched on an impressive afro, waited with a square, greasy box. Fortunately the kid didn't seem to expect conversation, polite or otherwise, because he took the money and headed back to a bicycle with other pizzas bungee-corded to a back rack. He'd already pushed off and sped away before Vittorio could close the gate.

Instead of returning to Erika's as quickly as he'd left, he ambled back, trying to use the cool, wet night air to dampen his desire, which overshadowed every other sensation in his body.

When the buzzer had sounded, he'd never been so relieved and so frustrated at the same time. He had no idea those two emotions could roil within himself in equal portions.

How was he supposed to do this? Remain controlled when he wanted her so desperately? And when he knew how she tasted and what she felt like in his arms. When he wanted another chance to take his time, to explore all of her?

He'd thought the years of his early vampirism were torture. They held nothing on this. Every fiber of his being demanded to have her.

He'd been in the apartment with her less than an hour and he'd already nearly kissed her. He had to get a grip.

But something about her so called to him, and it went beyond her face and her figure, which were both stunning. What really drew him, and now he understood after seeing her artwork tonight, was that she seemed to see him. Really see him.

He'd seen other interpretations of himself, in paint, in marble, but they'd only ever captured his outside. They'd never revealed anything within him.

But Erika had seen inside him, seen something he didn't even know was there. A sorrow he thought he masked behind aloofness and vampiric beauty. The ache and sadness she captured should have upset him, but somehow, it just made him feel closer to Erika. She understood a part of him that he hid. And she didn't seem to pity him for it. She just— understood.

Oddly, her vision of him made him feel almost—normal. Like she'd depicted his pain and in doing so had allowed some of it to be set free.

Someone understood, and that was as powerful an aphrodisiac as anything he could imagine. And he wanted her more, if that was possible.

He hesitated on the sunporch, debating what to do now. Knowing if he went back in there, he'd have to have her. And not just for a night. But how could he risk someone he wanted so much? And he could be risking her life.

He considered what to do a moment longer, then headed back inside. He stood in the doorway, watching her set the table. She looked up at him as he stood there, her expression pensive.

"Are you okay?" she asked, her voice low and uneasy as if she expected him to say something awful. Which was justifiable given his past behavior.

"I'm fine," he told her, meeting her eyes directly. He'd already put her at risk by being with her. So now, would he really be doing her any good by staying away? No. He had to stay close to her. That was the only way to protect her. And in the process, maybe he'd lure his mother out too. But no matter what, he wanted to be with Erika. He wouldn't let anything or anyone harm her.

He walked over to the table, setting the pizza box down. Then he moved closer to her.

"I think I'd like to pose for you," he said, telling the truth.

"Really?" She frowned at him, clearly not following or understanding his change in demeanor. And he wanted to take all that uncertainty from her. He wanted her trust. Her friendship, her affection, her desire. And he wanted to be that normal, and flawed, guy she saw inside him.

"Yeah. I really love what you did with that bust."

She smiled, the first genuine and unguarded response he'd seen since her response to him last night.

"I'd love to sculpt you." She moved closer too. He could

see the varying shades of gray and blue in her eyes. He could smell her spicy, cinnamon scent.

He smiled back, then he touched her cheek. "I'd also really like to kiss you."

She didn't speak this time. Instead she kissed him.

Chapter 15

Erika surprised herself by kissing him first, especially since he'd told her so sweetly what he wanted to do. But she was afraid he'd change his mind.

And she just couldn't let that happen. But as soon as her lips touched his, she realized he had no intention of stopping. He took control of the embrace, his hands, his mouth as filled with wild desire as they'd been last night.

She exulted in the frenzied loss of control, because she knew he was a person who always kept a tight rein on himself.

He broke the kiss, yet didn't release her, his hands holding her waist.

"Do you have any idea how much I've wanted to do this? And for how long? I've thought about it since that first time we met."

Erika smiled, remembered that night at the jazz bar when Ren had introduced them. They'd only shook hands, a brief touch, yet her body had reacted as if it was on fire, inflamed with burning desire, and only Vittorio could have put that fiery desire out. The source and the solution. She felt the same way now.

"I thought about you too. A lot," she admitted, feeling her cheeks redden with the admission.

He smiled, a pleased, slightly smug curl of his lips. Erika

found the look very appealing. Then his mouth was back on hers, and she was only thinking about how turned on he made her.

She made a small, surprised noise into his mouth as he picked her up. A plate clattered as he placed her on the table. He pushed it away. The pizza fell to the floor.

Her legs parted, and he moved between them like there was no other place in the world he should be. And by her way of thinking, there wasn't.

"I've thought of you dozens of times," she admitted against his lips. "Dozens of times."

She felt his smile, then he caught her bottom lip with his teeth, worrying the tender flesh in a way that made every nerve ending in her body tingle and ache. Then his mouth left hers to kiss and nip down the side of her neck to her collarbone.

Their actions grew more frenzied with each kiss and caress. He pushed closer between her thighs. Her jeans rubbed against the aroused, damp flesh between her thighs. The material of his own jeans added to the friction, a maddening and exciting sensation.

She wanted to cry out; it almost became too much, yet not nearly enough. He sensed her frustrated need. A need to have them naked, with skin touching skin.

His fingers found the top of her jeans, and he unbuttoned them. Then he pulled down the zipper. She levered herself off the tabletop so he could work the pants down her legs. He worked them over her bare feet and tossed them aside. Then her panties joined the jumbled jeans.

She sat in front of him, wearing nothing but her tank top, her legs splayed wide, her wet sex offered to him. And she didn't feel the least bit of embarrassment or uncertainty. She wanted him, and she wanted him to know just how much.

His dark eyes grew darker as he stared at her, his hungry gaze moving down her. Then he braced his hands on her hips, his fingers curling possessively over the jut of her hipbones.

He eased her farther back on the table, a plate fell clattering to the floor.

"Sorry," he said, but she simply shook her head, not concerned. Like she could care about her dinnerware when she was splayed before him, desperate for his possession.

He released her hips and leaned forward to kiss the inside of her knee. She leapt at the touch, her body so desperate for him. For more of his touch.

He didn't disappoint. His mouth moved its way up her inner thigh, wet, hot kisses. Her fingers tangled in his hair, her body arcing upward to capture each kiss. Then he was right where she wanted him, his breath hot on her damp flesh.

"Vittorio," she managed, rising up again, offering herself to him.

He lifted his head to raise a questioning eyebrow, but she tugged at his hair, positioning his mouth where she wanted it.

He chuckled, the sound deep and delicious and supremely masculine. Her body reacted, her sex pulsing, her breasts growing heavy.

"Is this what you want?" he asked, then he ran his tongue up the center of her sex, the tip connecting and lingering on her clitoris.

"Yes," she cried, "God, yes!"

She felt his smile against her, then his tongue again. Licking, swirling, plunging into her over and over.

Her fingers tightened in his hair as her arousal grew, more and more intense, so powerful she thought she'd shatter apart. Her body couldn't possibly handle the strength of her desire, the need for her release.

But just as she would have splintered, flying into thousands of brilliant shards of ecstasy, he pulled back. A small strangled sound of disappointment escaped her.

"Don't worry," he told her, his hands moving back to her hips, sliding her toward him until her bottom was on the edge of the tabletop. He positioned himself between her thighs.

"I won't let you go unfulfilled." He nudged her apart with the head of his hard penis. She wriggled, wanting more. Wanting all of him.

He smiled, the gesture breathtaking. She nearly orgasmed just looking at him.

Then he thrust into her deeply, filling her totally, and she did orgasm. Her body shaking with her release. Long, violent shudders.

Vittorio stayed still, buried fully inside her, letting her ride out her release to the very end. But when she would have collapsed depleted against the sunny yellow tabletop, he began to move, slow, fully penetrating thrusts amazingly building her desire again. Each stroke of his penis felt like a thousand hands bringing her back to intense arousal.

Vittorio filled Erika, pulling back then refilling her. He watched every nuance of her face, every reaction. He felt every shudder and vibration of her body. He learned how much she wanted, how long she would wait before demanding him, with her body, back to her.

This was heaven. Utter and total heaven.

And just as quickly as she had with his mouth, she spiraled upward toward release. Her breathing came in short pants, perspiration glossed her skin in a fine sheen.

He leaned forward and licked between her breasts, tasting the saltiness of her skin, breathing in her wonderful scent. Quickly, his own desire rose up, spinning through him in a whirling frenzy.

Her fingers dug into his back as he picked up his pace, grinding into her hungrily.

"Yes," she cried, her nails biting through the cotton of his T-shirt. "Vittorio!"

His name called out in her passion-ragged voice was all he

needed. He came into her. His release wet and slick and filling her.

He collapsed against her, his head nestled between her breasts. Her fingers combed through his hair, stroking him, caressing him.

"Vittorio," she whispered.

He moved, resting his chin lightly on her chest. "Yes?"

"What's your favorite color?"

He lifted his head, frowning in confusion. "What?"

She smiled lopsidedly, the expression so cute, he was momentarily lost in it. "What's your favorite color?"

He smiled back, still confused. "Favorite color?"

She nodded. "Mine is black. And green. I like green a lot."

He considered the question. "I've never thought about it," he admitted.

"Well, you must have a favorite color." She tilted her head in that way that he loved. "Everyone does."

For a moment, those words made him remember how different he was from her. From everyone she'd known. But then he actually thought about it. "I guess I like blue," he said, then shook his head. "Or red."

"Dark or light red? Bright red?"

He studied her for a moment, trying to decide if she was serious, then he laughed. "This is actually important to you."

She nodded. "Of course it is."

"Why?"

"Because I want to know what you like and dislike. I want to be friends."

He glanced down at where their bodies were still joined, his penis semi-erect inside her. "I think we are definitely friends."

She smiled, although he noted some uncertainty had returned to her stormy eyes. "We are. But I do think there's something a little wrong about doing what we've done, and not knowing something as simple as your favorite color."

Vittorio regarded her, realizing that her words should be true. But in his world, sex wasn't something necessarily done between friends, just the mutually attracted. He'd never known something as basic as a person's favorite color.

He'd never been with someone who thought about their favorite things or other people's favorite things. Certainly Seraph hadn't talked about details like this. That was far too whimsical for someone like Seraph. Drug addiction blotted out any normal thoughts, anything so lighthearted. Her addiction had been all she thought about, just like for him, his vampirism became all he thought about.

He hadn't realized that even when he'd been helping those women, he'd thought he'd been doing it to atone for past sins. Now he wondered if he'd done it because they were people he understood and felt comfortable with.

He was drawn out of his thoughts by the gentle touch of Erika's fingers trailing along his jaw. Her eyes looked deep into his. She had a penetrating look that could rival any vampire. Even Bela Lugosi's interpretation.

"Why do you look so serious?"

He stared down at her, wondering what he was doing with this woman. He was risking her safety. He was not the right type for her, even if he weren't jeopardizing her well-being.

Her fingers traced the cut of his jawline, until they threaded into his hair. He let his eyes drift shut, loving her touch more than anything he could recall.

Her lips touched his chin, then his lips. A sweet caring kiss. She stopped, and he opened his eyes to see she was still watching him. They simply looked at each other for a few moments. Then he offered her a small smile.

"My favorite color is definitely blue," he said, studying the hues of blue and gray in her eyes. "Definitely blue."

Then he began to rock inside her, making love to her all over again. This woman he wanted to be his friend, his lover. Just plain, his. Forever. Or as long as she wanted him.

* * *

Sometime during the night, Vittorio must have moved Erika to her bed. She must have fallen asleep, or maybe passed out after their last bout of lovemaking on her sunshiny kitchen table. Because she woke up, curled in her bed, Vittorio asleep next to her.

She touched his hair, silky and spread out over the pillow. Her eyes drifted shut, her body languid, her thoughts muzzy and peaceful.

This was so nice. She floated back into the darkness. She didn't know how long she actually slept that way. Serene, pleasant. But all too quickly that calm, lovely feeling disappeared, replaced by stark terror.

She was running. Her legs pumping, her focus on the uneven ground as she tried to keep her balance. Her neck prickled and she fought the urge to look over her shoulder, but she knew she couldn't without the risk of losing her footing. And she couldn't let him catch her.

She whimpered as she nearly tripped on an exposed root. The woods got thicker, more disorienting. Branches and undergrowth pulled at her clothes.

And she could hear him right behind her. His breath, the pound of his feet.

She whimpered again. He's going to kill you.

"You will die," a voice said from behind her. A deep voice. A familiar voice.

"Erika?" Vittorio managed to resurface from his deep sleep. *God, the sun must be high in the sky,* he realized vaguely, blearily, because it was hard for him to gather enough energy to move. But still he mustered all his strength.

"Erika?"

She was having a nightmare again. Her legs moved under the blankets, as if she were running. Small frightened noises sounded in the back of her throat.

As if he had enormous weights strapped to his limbs, he slowly touched her, running his fingers through her hair.

"Erika."

She struggled a little more against the covers, against her dream. But gradually she managed to sense his touch.

She blinked, seeming to struggle awake with nearly as much difficulty as he had. Although she didn't have the sun to blame for her deep sleep. Again, he did wonder if she had something equally paranormal to blame, however.

"Vittorio?" She cupped her cold, shaking fingers around his hand. She pressed his palm to her face. He saw fear in her eyes, even in the dimness of the room.

"I'm right here. Are you okay?" His voice sounded gritty and slurred even to his own ears.

"Yes. Just another nightmare." She offered him a wobbly smile, obviously trying to comfort him.

"Was it the same as before?"

She didn't respond immediately, instead she nuzzled her cheek against his hand.

"No," she finally said. "Before I was always being chased by creatures I didn't recognize. Monsters or demons or something—several of them. This time it was only one."

Even though the sun pressed heavily on him and willed him to sleep, he kept his eyes locked with hers, a strange wariness filling him.

"Did you recognize who was chasing you?"

Again she didn't respond immediately. Then she nodded.

"Yes, it was you."

Chapter 16

Erika woke with a start. She cast a look around, her gaze stopping on Vittorio asleep beside her. She didn't move for a moment, recalling her nightmare, surprised she'd managed to fall back asleep. But then she remembered that Vittorio had held her, stroked her hair, and despite her agitation she had found herself lulled back to sleep.

Even now, the dream seemed distant, as if it hadn't quite happened. But it had, and as she stared at Vittorio, she couldn't help wondering what her distressed psyche was trying to tell her.

Vittorio had been chasing her. He'd intended to kill her. She knew it. Yet looking at him sprawled out on her covers, hair tousled, face relaxed in sleep, she couldn't see any threat.

He looked like an angel. Not a monster. Definitely not a monster. She could never see him as such. Especially not after what he'd done to her last night. His lovemaking had been generous, and also intense, but not in a way that could even remotely be perceived as frightening. No, fear had been the last thing on her mind when she was in his arms.

So why had the dream changed? Why was she having the dream anyway?

For a split second, Philippe's words about someone threatening being around her flashed in her mind. But she disregarded that idea. At least about Vittorio. He wouldn't hurt her. She knew that.

So what could be triggering these horrifying nightmares? She'd always been prone to vivid dreams, but never nightmares. She supposed it had to be the stress of the upcoming show. Or maybe the move had finally caught up with her.

Then she glanced back to Vittorio. They had started after he arrived. Again, Philippe's words about someone dangerous being near her came back.

Vittorio could be distant. And so abrupt it came across as rude, but he wasn't a threat. And now, Erika couldn't help feeling that his aloofness was a defense mechanism. A way to keep people at bay—and not show the pain inside him. But she'd glimpsed it, even when she didn't realize she had. Not until it manifested itself in her art.

She reached out and touched his hair, letting the silky strands fall through her fingertips back to the pillow. No, she'd never have to fear Vittorio. Well, except maybe fear for her heart, but to think that way was allowing things to go too far too fast anyway.

She touched his hair again, then crawled out of bed. She grabbed her robe and pulled the silky material on as she headed to the living room. Just as she reached the other room, her cell phone on the kitchen counter rang.

She rushed to flip it open, casting a look back at her bedroom.

"Hello," she said, her voice hushed and a little breathless.

"Hey," Jo said. "Am I calling at a bad time? You sound like you're busy."

"No," Erika said, glancing back to the bedroom. "No. I'm just being quiet because Vittorio is still asleep." She waited, expecting Jo to be pleased for her.

"So I guess you are going to stand by the fact that your psychic friend is never wrong."

Erika frowned, surprised at the disapproval she heard in

her friend's voice. "Well, I think he was right about this. But honestly, it's too early to really say." Not to mention, she didn't want Philippe to be right about some of the things he'd said. Other women, age differences, impending threats. Those were definitely a few things she could do without.

"Well, I suppose I shouldn't keep you if he's there."

Again, Erika was confused. Why was Jo so put off by the idea of her and Vittorio? "Well, he's asleep. What's up with you?"

"Actually I have to run, I was just sneaking in a call on my lunch break. Just to make sure you were okay."

"I am."

Jo told her she was glad things were going well, but as Erika flicked her cell phone shut, she didn't believe her friend's words.

What was bothering Jo? Was it the idea of Vittorio or the idea that a psychic predicted it?

She was still holding her phone, trying to understand what was going on with Jo, when the phone rang again. She didn't even look at the number before she answered it.

"Jo? I think we need to talk about all of this a little more."

"I'm sorry," a voice said. "This isn't Jo. I'm trying to reach Ms. Erika Todd. Am I calling at a bad time?"

"No," Erika immediately answered, embarrassed. "I'm sorry. This is Erika."

"Ms. Todd, I'm so thrilled to speak with you. I'm a huge fan of your work."

Erika moved the phone away from her ear to see if she recognized the number. She didn't—although the area code was a local one.

"Thank you."

Erika obviously hadn't kept the confusion from her voice, because the woman on the other end laughed a little nervously, then said, "I'm sorry. I guess I should explain who I am and how I got your number. My name is Isabel Andrews, and I'm a patron of The Broussard. I saw some photos of your work, and I was greatly impressed. I'd like to discuss commissioning a piece."

Erika's heart jumped in her chest. Someone was already showing interest in her work, and she hadn't even had the show yet. This was wonderful.

"I'd love to meet with you and discuss you working on a piece. I realize you must be getting ready for the show, but I was hoping it could be sometime soon."

Erika nodded, even though Isabel Andrews couldn't see her. "Sure, that wouldn't be a problem. What time is good for you?"

Erika heard a noise on the other end of the line like she was thumbing through a datebook.

"How about tomorrow evening?" Isabel suggested.

"Tomorrow evening should be fine. Say, six o'clock?"

"Yes," Isabel agreed. "That would be fine."

"Great," Erika agreed, thrilled that this woman wanted to see her so soon. That had to mean she was very excited about Erika's work.

"Okay," Isabel said. "Six o'clock, and let's meet at Court of Two Sisters. They have such a nice courtyard and wonderful food. Perfect for discussing your work."

"Sounds good," Erika agreed. "See you then."

Erika flipped her phone shut, then glanced around, trying to decide what to do. She felt giddy. Vittorio and she were planning on—dating, she guessed, although that seemed a just a little out of order, given that he was in her bed. And now someone wanted to commission a piece of her art. Things were coming together.

She wanted to go in and tell Vittorio her good news, but he was sleeping so soundly she hated to wake him. He'd be up soon anyway.

Instead she cleaned up the mess from last night. The plate that had clattered to the floor during their lovemaking. The pizza she hadn't eaten. Although from the pieces dragged out onto the hardwood floor, it appeared Boris had helped himself, which explained why he snoozed on the back of one of the chairs in the living room instead of yowling around at her heels, demanding food.

And while the fallen pizza no longer looked appealing, Erika realized she was famished. She'd sort of lost interest in dinner once Vittorio set about satisfying a different hunger in her. But now, she could really use some breakfast.

She glanced at the digital clock on the microwave. Or some lunch. Late lunch. Dang, they'd stayed in bed late today. She finished picking up and then headed to her cupboard.

She really did need to do better with her grocery shopping, she always had only odds and ends, which never made a meal. Well, at least not any meal that appealed to her.

She decided to throw on some clothes and head to the gumbo shop down on the corner. She'd bring back carryout for her and Vittorio. They could celebrate her potential commission.

She grinned at the thought. Her career was taking off, and she was starting a relationship with a man she was crazy about. Life was definitely getting better and better by the minute.

This stakeout crap was getting mighty old, Maksim thought as he watched Vittorio and Erika's building. He tugged at the designer shirt which clung to his damp skin. He came to the human realm to avoid the sweltering heat. New Orleans was a steamy, smelly cesspool. At least in Hell, it was a dry heat. If he ever found Ellina—and she was alive—he was going to insist she move to Vermont. Or Canada.

Finally, he saw movement. The large gates of Erika's building opened, and she stepped out. She had her hair pulled up on the back of her head in a messy bun. Her cheeks were flushed a pretty pink and she sported an inanely pleased little smile.

Definitely the look of a woman who'd experienced some good lovin'. Maksim smiled at the image. He always appreciated the look of a woman the morning after. Okay, he usually liked to be the one who created that sated, satisfied look, but he could still appreciate another man's handiwork.

She started down the sidewalk, not bothering to glance around her. She was obviously lost in her own happy place. Which would make following her easier.

Maksim didn't dare approach her again. Not without setting off warning vibes in her. He'd intended to keep showing up and using his physical appeal to win her over. But she was not interested in him. In the least. He didn't even need to probe her mind to know all her attraction and attention was on this Vittorio. And mortals could be quite amazingly loyal.

Not to mention, she was unusually susceptible to his mind reading. Likely she was very open-minded. That always made mortals more aware of him, even if they never figured out what he was exactly. He knew this would probably be the last time he could enter her thoughts without causing permanent damage. But he had to give it one more shot to find out what she knew about Vittorio.

Although this time he thought he could enter her brain without getting particularly close to her. Once he'd been into a mind, he could usually find his way back.

Not that he was hopeful of discovering anything new. Nor did he think Vittorio was involved in his sister's disappearance. He'd done a little research outside of mind reading, and he'd learned Vittorio was a bit of a do-gooder. Working with addicts.

Maksim grimaced at the idea of hanging out with people so self-consumed and riddled with insecurities and hang-ups. Drug addicts were only entertaining in the beginning phases, when they were still deluding themselves that the drugs were just for fun.

He'd also discovered that Vittorio was close to his brother, Ren Anthony, a vampire with a penchant for women, liquor and classic rock. Well, until he'd recently settled down with a mortal, of all creatures. But Vittorio, up until that point, had been his brother's keeper.

None of these traits added up to a being who'd be involved with the disappearance of a Halfling demon. But then, he did know looks could be deceiving. Just look at himself.

But his gut was telling him that Vittorio wasn't involved. And his gut was usually right. Not to mention, all along his gut had also been telling him if anyone was involved it was Orabella.

He had a feeling that if he was going to get her to crack and show her true colors, he'd have spill more details about the relationship between Vittorio and his mortal object of lust. Or maybe even love. Vittorio seemed like the type who fancied the idea of love.

So he was going back to Erika for more details. Specifics were bound to piss Orabella off. And while he could manufacture the finer points of the mortal and vampire's tryst, sometimes the truth added so much more spice.

Maksim fell into step some distance behind Erika. Besides, he liked the details too. What was the fun of being a mind reader if you couldn't get all the juicy insights?

Erika walked straight to the gumbo shop, lost in her memories of last night, and her excitement to tell Vittorio about her new career offer.

The air was hot and humid, the showers of the day before only adding to the thick dampness of the air, but she didn't mind. She was in far too good a mood to let the heat bother her.

"Hi Allan," she greeted one of the waiters as she entered the narrow hallway of the shop, which led out to a courtyard.

"Hey Erika, eating in today?"

She shook her head, knowing she was smiling broadly. "Nah, I'm taking out today."

Allan gave her a speculative look, as if he could tell what had her grinning ear to ear, then he handed her a menu. She settled onto one of the worn wooden chairs that lined the wall and began to peruse the different entrees. Although she barely saw the names and ingredients of popular Creole dishes as she stared at the dog-eared cardstock page.

She was too damned happy. And that was a good thing.

Allan returned after a few moments. "So what can I get you today?"

"The chicken with red beans and rice. Two of those, and two cups of gumbo. And do you have the bread pudding today?"

Allan nodded. "Sure do."

"Then I'll take two of those too."

Allan gave her another knowing look. "So you're not eating alone."

"Nope," she said with a wide grin.

"Well, crap. And when I've been trying so hard to win you for myself." He winked, and she laughed. Allan was ever the flirt.

Erika continued to smile foolishly as he headed toward the kitchen to put in her order. She leaned back in the chair, absently observing the other patrons.

She knew she was being ridiculously giddy about everything, but the truth was, everything just felt right. She knew she shouldn't get too ahead of herself. But she was just . . . happy. And there was nothing wrong with that.

She sighed, letting her mind wander to the night before. Aside from the irritating nightmare, her night with Vittorio had been perfect. She sighed again. She had no idea making love could be like that.

"You're still smiling," Allan said as he returned with two white plastic sacks filled with delicious-smelling food. "You must have it bad."

She laughed, reaching into her pocketbook for her wallet. "Yeah, I do." For a niggling moment, she considered that she really was feeling too much, too soon. But then she was a believer that when something felt right, why question it?

She waited as Allan ran her money card, hoping Vittorio

would be awake when she got back. She had enough food for an army. He better have an appetite.

She leaned over to inspect the bags, making sure everything was in there, when a prickling sensation crept slowly up her spine. Straightening, she glanced around. The restaurant was relatively busy, but she didn't spot anyone paying her any attention. Yet she felt as if someone's eyes were on her. Watching her. Studying her every move.

Another needling chill ran up her spine. She shivered, her flushed skin suddenly feeling cooled.

"Here you go," Allan said, handing her the leather folder with her credit card receipt inside. She jotted down a tip and signed her name, all the while fighting the urge to look around her again.

She thanked Allan and grabbed up her bags. When she stepped out on the street, she realized the sun had set. Signs that autumn was coming, even if the weather didn't realize it. But she no longer felt the heat—only that creeping, eerie chill.

Someone was watching her.

She cast a quick look up and down the street, but didn't see anything or anyone out of the ordinary. Still she didn't linger. She doubled her steps, hurrying along the cracked and uneven sidewalk.

As she got closer to her apartment her nervousness didn't lessen. If anything it rose, her heart battering against her rib cage, her breathing coming in shallow and panicked puffs.

When she reached the front gates, she fumbled with the keys, nearly dropping them as she searched for the right one. Finally after two tries, she managed to unlock the old padlock and hurry inside.

She leaned against the gates, trying to calm herself. She didn't even understand what frightened her. She was also feeling lightheaded, like she had when she had been at the restaurant with Maksim. Maybe it was restaurants—although that made no sense whatsoever.

The nightmares, these sudden bouts of irrational nervousness and dizzy spells. What was going on with her?

She slowly sucked in another calming breath, then headed to her apartment. The place was dark, which meant Vittorio must still be asleep.

She unlocked her front door, automatically slipping the bolt back into place. She set the food on the kitchen table and continued on to her bedroom, flipping on the hall light as she went.

She reached her bedroom, only to see her bed was empty. *Where was he?* She turned back to the bathroom, but the door was wide open and the light off.

She knew he wasn't in the living room. The apartment was empty. She moved back to her bedroom, staring at the rumpled covers of the bed, suddenly afraid that he'd left again. Gotten scared or distant or, she sighed, or whatever, and just left.

Then she heard footsteps behind her, and she spun to see Vittorio entering the hallway, his hair pushed back from his face as if he'd been running his hands through it. His dark eyes clouded with concern. Eyebrows drawn together in dismay.

"Where were you?" he asked.

She blinked, surprised by his tone. He sounded irritated. "I went out to get food," she answered, hating that she sounded contrite, like a child caught doing something wrong.

He nodded, then his rigid posture seemed to relax, but before he could speak again, she gathered her wits.

"Where were you?"

"I was looking for you," he admitted.

She studied him for a moment. "If you weren't in the apartment, how did you get in? I just locked the front door."

Chapter 17

As Maksim headed up the front steps of the house Orabella was renting, he considered what he'd discovered, and again he was struck with the idea that Vittorio wasn't involved in Ellina's disappearance. Granted, he couldn't know that for certain without entering Vittorio's mind, which he couldn't do. But his gut just told him this vampire wasn't the type to abduct and kill Halflings—or anyone else for that matter.

Maybe it would be safe to approach him and ask him outright about Ellina and Orabella. But still he wasn't sure. He wished he understood the real relationship between the two vampires.

This Vittorio certainly didn't seem like Orabella's type, yet she was clearly jealous of his love interest. Maybe Ellina had been interested in Vittorio too. Which brought Maksim back to Orabella being the dangerous party in this scenario.

"So what did you find out?" Orabella asked as he walked into her lavish bedroom. She lounged on the bed wearing nothing but a demi-bra and panties, both of which were little more than scraps of peach lace.

He stopped briefly to admire her, interrupting his train of thought. Demons were notoriously easily distracted. Then he turned away to hang up his coat in the armoire.

"I read the girl's mind again," he said. "To be honest with

you, I don't think she can handle me doing it much more. She's very open. I could drive her mad if I continue. And we wouldn't want that."

"No," Orabella agreed, a wryness lacing her voice. "We wouldn't want that."

His back to her, he smirked slightly. Her jealousy was showing again.

"So what did you learn?"

He turned back to her, working the buttons on his shirt, regarding her impassively. "She and Vittorio are definitely involved."

She sat up. "You're sure?"

He laughed, recalling the images he'd seen in her mind. Not half bad, he had to say. Erika was indeed a well-pleased woman. "Oh yeah, very involved."

Her lips narrowed, the expression making her look old, hard. He'd never noticed that about her before—she wasn't as young, pre-undeath, than he might have once thought.

"But I've got to tell you, he isn't doing anything that seems creepy or suspicious to me. He really seems quite besotted, at least from what I can tell from her memories."

Her eyes narrowed, but then she managed a look of concern. Well, sort of like concern. A vein in her forehead looked as if it might pop. Acting was getting more and more difficult for her. "Well, he would give her that impression," she stated. Then she quickly added, "He has to gain her trust. That's part of his strategy."

Maksim nodded as if he believed her. But he knew she wasn't going to leave this alone. She'd want him continue to spy, entering Erika's head despite the damage he was causing.

All for her own good, of course. Orabella did have a strange way of protecting this mere mortal.

He shrugged off his shirt, then turned to hang that as well. He heard her move behind him, the mattress making a muffled creak.

"I just don't know what I'm going to do to stop him," she said, pretending to mull over ideas.

He turned and raised an eyebrow as if to say he didn't know either—but he was definitely considering the dilemma right along with her.

She sighed, then stretched, her breasts straining and swelling against the barely-there restraints of her bra.

"I just don't know," she finally said, sounding as if the idea was just tearing at her.

He waited, expecting her request to come any moment. But instead she patted the mattress.

"Why are you staying way over there?"

Maksim frowned. He hardly expected her to have sex on her mind. Not when he'd just dropped the bomb that her precious Vittorio was involved with another. Very involved. Three-times-a-night involved.

But he walked over to the bed, not joining her, still waiting. What did she want him to do now?

She rose up on all fours and crawled toward him. He watched with surprise as she knelt in from of him. She slid her hands up his thighs until she reached the button of his fly.

He simply could not believe she was seducing him, not when he'd just confirmed her fears. "Are you worried about this poor girl?"

"I am. Very, very worried," she said, and for once he couldn't quite read her tone. "And I do have some plans to stop what's happening."

She looked up at him, batting her lashes. "But right now, I just want you to make me feel better."

He watched as she worked free his penis, the damned organ erect, even while he was still confused about what was going on here and her role in it all.

Then she took the length of him deep into her mouth, and he lost track of why he should be concerned.

*   *   *

"How did you get in here?" Erika asked again.

Vittorio shifted slightly, searching for something that would sound believable. "I came in through the front door."

"Do you have a key?"

He considered lying, but he suspected she'd demand to see it, if he did. She watched him with wide eyes, her hands fisted at her sides. Yeah, she'd ask to see the key; she looked truly distressed.

"I guess the door didn't latch right, because I walked right in."

She considered him, doubt in her eyes. She hurried past him, sidestepping him in an obvious attempt to avoid physical contact.

What happened while he slept that had her so shaken? He'd awoken, alarmed to find the apartment empty. He couldn't allow her to go out on her own, especially at night. His mother couldn't get to her during the day, thanks to the old sunlight thing. But at night, Erika had to stay close to him.

Still, he didn't think a run-in with his mother was what had her acting so rattled. What had happened? Where had she gone?

He turned to follow her, knowing she was heading to the door to see if he was telling the truth.

She peered at the lock, then spun back to him. "It's locked now."

He nodded. "I know. I locked it when I came in."

She frowned, clearly trying to decide if she should believe him.

"Erika, what's going on?"

She considered him for a moment, then visibly relaxed, her shoulders lowering, her breathing calmer.

"I don't know," she said, sounding truly confused and troubled. "I just went out to get us some dinner, and while I was at the restaurant, I suddenly got light-headed. And I had this overwhelming feeling of being watched. It was strong enough that I really got a little frightened."

Fear instantly filled Vittorio. Had his mother been out there watching her? "Did you see anyone?" he asked.

She shook her head. "No. No one in particular. And I don't think anyone followed me home. I just can't . . . I can't understand what's going on with me."

Vittorio approached her, stopping at arm's length. He didn't want to make her more nervous. But this time she didn't move away. She just regarded him with those stormy eyes of hers.

"I'm sorry. I know you must think I'm nuts. Nightmares, strange feelings. I don't know." She shook her head. "I don't know what's wrong with me."

He had a feeling nothing was wrong with *her*, but something was definitely wrong. And he couldn't help feeling as if he had something to do with it. Although the nightmares started while he was still attempting to stay away from her. And he didn't know what the bouts of dizziness were—unless his mother was nearby and stealing her energy. Although the waves of her life force filling the room now certainly seemed powerful and undiminished.

So what was going on? Was his mother nearby? Was she causing this fear in Erika? Erika hadn't been plagued with nightmares until his second night back. Were they related to him? Was that why she'd dreamed of him as her attacker last night?

For a moment, he recalled the paranormal creature he'd noticed on the street, but then disregarded him. Paranormal creatures roaming the streets of New Orleans were hardly unusual. The city was riddled with them.

"Sometimes we just get weird feelings," he finally said, knowing whatever the cause he had to keep her calm and make her feel safe. "And the nightmares are strange, but people often suffer bouts of nightmares that are never really explained."

His voice sounded confident; he wished he felt that way.

But she seemed to believe him, or want to believe him. She nodded and moved away from the door.

"What did you get to eat?" he asked. Maybe changing the topic would further calm her.

She glanced over to the table as if just remembering the food. "Oh, chicken, red beans and rice, and bread pudding, Creole-style."

"That all sounds great."

She nodded again, an action clearly designed more to gather herself than to agree, but then she walked to the kitchen.

Vittorio noticed that she still skirted away from him. Given her nerves, he couldn't blame her, he guessed. Although he didn't want that distance. He'd made up his mind to protect her, but on top of that, he wanted to be with her. He wanted to have the closeness they had when they had sex. He wanted to know her. Everything about her.

Okay, even if his mother wasn't a jealous homicidal maniac, he still was a lampir and that was a setback to say the least, but he just couldn't let this woman go. He'd never felt this way in his whole life.

He watched as she got dishes down from the cupboards. Then she moved to the drawers to take out silverware. Then she brought them to the table. She glanced at him as she did so.

"Are you hungry?"

Vittorio nodded. She wanted things to be normal, and being normal for mortals involved sitting down, eating a meal, chatting. And damn it, he was going to give her that—even if it killed him. Or the food did.

He took the plates from her, giving her a small smile. "Let me set the table."

She looked down at both their hands on the brightly swirled pottery dishes. Then she nodded, allowing him to take them. She turned back to the counter to open the containers of food. The spicy scent of red beans and rice filled his nose, making his stomach flip.

The smell of food normally didn't bother him, but then he

didn't usually know he was going to have to eat it. But he would for Erika.

He arranged the plates, also realizing he didn't actually know how to set a table. That sort of thing was done for him when he'd been alive, and since his undeath, plates and silverware just hadn't played a big part in his life.

He placed a fork on the right, then frowned, trying to recall if that looked correct. He changed it to the left, but still couldn't decide if that looked right. He switched it back to the right.

"Here, let me do it." Erika moved close to him and arranged the fork, then the knife. "There."

He studied her, her head close to his. She looked up and smiled. And before he thought better of it, he kissed her.

Instead of pulling away, she kissed him back. Her response gave him hope that she wasn't completely uncomfortable with him or with her earlier feelings.

"Wow," she said when they parted. "I never got that sort of reaction for setting the table."

"Well, you should have," he told her.

She smiled, and he was relieved to see most of the worry had left her eyes.

"So are we going to eat?" He immediately wondered why he didn't just go in for another kiss. That would be much more fun and save him from the dreaded dinner. But mortals needed to eat. And Erika still looked a little wan. Relaxing and food would do wonders for her.

"Yes." She brought the containers over to the table, setting them in the center. "Dig in."

God, he so should have gone with more kissing. But instead he forced a smile and sat down at one of the place settings.

She joined him, passing the white Styrofoam box of chicken toward him. He accepted, taking a fork and spearing one of the grilled and seasoned breasts.

He shook the food onto the plate, regarding the cooked meat warily, as if it might attack him.

"Some rice?"

He took the container and ladled out just a bit.

Erika frowned. "Are you sure you got enough?"

He eyed the small mound, knowing it was going sit in his gut like twenty pounds of wet cement. "No, this is fine. I'm not terribly hungry."

She looked concerned, which he found rather endearing. Then she began to spoon beans and rice beside her chicken.

"I'm starving," she told him. And he couldn't help but grin.

"What?" she asked, pausing, then surveying her filled plate. Her cheeks colored a pretty pink. "I'm really hungry," she said, looking a tad embarrassed.

"Then you should eat," he assured her, making sure she knew he saw nothing wrong with her appetite. "It will make you feel a lot better to have a full stomach."

She nodded, setting down the white container. She immediately began to cut the chicken.

He followed suit, but rather than eat the sawed bit, he pushed it around in the sauce of the rice and beans. He glanced up to be sure she was eating however.

After several bites, she noticed he wasn't eating with the same gusto.

"Do you not like it? I was guessing when I ordered."

"No, it's great." To emphasize his point, he took a bite of the chicken, deciding meat was possibly safer than rice and beans. It felt like wet rawhide in his mouth, but he chewed, even offering her a tight-lipped smile as he did.

She smiled back and continued eating.

Vittorio was thrilled when, after just two more struggling swallows, she asked, "What's your favorite food?"

He took the question as an opportunity to set down his fork. He considered. What had he liked when he'd been able to eat—well, eat for enjoyment?

"I liked—" He had to think. "I liked turkey with dressing. And apple pie." He smiled, recalling how Cook used to put extra cinnamon in the pie, just for him. "And I liked pheasant with new potatoes."

Erika gave him a strange look. "Pheasant? I've never had that before."

"It's delicious," he informed her with a smile. "A bit like chicken, actually."

She nodded, her expression saying she'd take his word for it. She took another bite of rice, then chewed thoughtfully. He wondered what she was pondering.

"Why would you say 'liked' as if you never had it anymore? Turkey and apple pie—why wouldn't you have those? At Thanksgiving at the very least."

He wished he hadn't wondered what she was thinking.

"Umm, no. I don't get them much anymore. I just—order out a lot now."

"Well, you can order out apple pie."

He nodded. "True, but it's not the same."

"Did your mother make it for you? Moms always make things just the way we like them," she said with a rather dreamy look, then she set down her fork. "Or at least that's what I've always heard."

"Heard? Didn't your mother cook for you?"

She nudged the fork with her finger, then shook her head.

"Not that I can remember—I'm sure she did, but she died when I was three."

"I'm sorry."

Erika shook her head, then straightened, as if reciting and trying to believe what she was about to say. "That's okay. I got used to it. After all, I don't even remember much about her. Except she had dark hair like mine, and bright blue eyes. I always wished I'd gotten that color. But I got my dad's."

"I love the color of your eyes. They remind me of thunderclouds and summer rain."

Erika smiled and her cheeks tinged pink. "I like that."

He smiled back, then poked at his food with his fork.

"So you were raised by your dad?" he asked.

She nodded, taking another bite of rice and beans. "Yes. I grew up in Cleveland. In the house my dad inherited from his parents. He likes to tell me I'm like my mom. She was more of a free spirit, artistic too. Dad is pretty cut and dry. He doesn't believe in much that isn't tangible. Just a working joe, really."

Vittorio heard the exasperation in her voice, which he couldn't quite understand. He'd love to have a parent who was solid and there for him. But then it had to be hard to know you were more like the parent you'd never meet.

"Are you close to your dad?" he asked.

Erika shrugged. "I love him, but we've never quite seen eye to eye. He doesn't understand my art and how important it is to me. He finds my interest in the occult strange. We just have a hard time communicating at times."

"He must be proud of your artwork now that it's taking off."

She shrugged again. "I guess. I don't really know, honestly." But then her eyes lit up. "Oh my gosh! I forgot. I got a call today from a woman who is interested in commissioning me to do a sculpture for her."

"Really?" He grinned, finding himself loving her excited expression, so different from the worried one of earlier.

"Yes, she wants to meet me tomorrow evening."

Evening? For some reason that one word roused his suspicion. It couldn't be his mother, could it? Would she contact Erika that way? Would she be that brazen?

Yes. Definitely.

"What time?" he asked.

"At six," Erika said, her enthusiasm not dampened by his wary tone.

She got up and gathered the nearly emptied containers. She placed them on the counter near the sink, then went to the cupboard to get dessert plates. As she placed them on the counter to open the dessert container, she noticed her cell phone, plugged into the wall outlet.

Vittorio watched as she flipped it open and read the caller ID.

"Speak of the devil, it looks like she called again."

He actually rose and came over to look at the phone. He didn't recognize the number, but he hadn't expected to.

Erika pressed the keypad to call her voice mail. The temptation to lean in to try and hear the voice on the other end pulled at him, but he resisted. He could hardly explain what he was doing, hovering over her like a jealous lover. Or a concerned lover. She'd want to know why, and he wasn't ready to explain his worries. Couldn't explain them, and he hoped he'd never have to.

She listened to the call, then flipped the phone shut.

"It was her again. She just wanted to know if we could meet in the afternoon instead—she said only to call if it was an issue." Erika smiled broadly, her face breathtaking.

He felt his own body relax. It couldn't be his mother. She was just like him, constrained to slumber while the sun was up.

He leaned in and kissed her, unable to resist touching her when she looked so happy and lovely.

"I'm really pleased for you," he murmured against her lips. And now he could mean it. She'd be safe during the day.

Chapter 18

Orabella looked down at Maksim as he snored softly from the rumpled covers of her bed. She supposed she should take some pride in the fact that she could screw a demon into utter exhaustion, but frankly, she was too consumed with her own thoughts to care.

So Vittorio was doing it again. Insisting on a relationship with a mortal. *Why?* She wanted to yell it out to the room. *Why?*

But instead she eased out of bed. She wandered to the window, looking out at the street below. Even from this vantage point, New Orleans looked shabby and soiled. She disliked any signs of age, even in cities.

No, that wasn't totally the case. She liked cities that had been maintained, their architecture restored and revitalized. Much like herself. She wouldn't age—nor would her lovely son. So why—why did he insist on being with creatures who would wrinkle and sag and stoop with the passage of time?

After all, she knew he'd never make anyone into an lampir like himself. He resented the gift she'd given him. Acted like she'd harmed him, when in fact, she'd given him everything.

She looked up at the sky. There was still plenty of night left, which would normally be a comfort. But tonight, she was anxious to have the sun rise. Creeping over the tops of the buildings and lighting the sky in a fiery, golden glow.

She looked back at Maksim, debating how she would get rid of him now that she had what she wanted. And she'd put in a lot of time getting this right. But she'd done it, and tomorrow she'd get to test her hard work.

She had to admit, she was a little nervous. If she hadn't done the ritual correctly she could be badly hurt. Or worse than that, scarred. Scars were not something she could survive.

But she didn't think she had done anything wrong or out of order. So tomorrow she would walk in the sun for the first time in over two hundred years.

Maksim roused behind her, but didn't call for her. He was exhausted. Several rounds of wild sex would do that to you even if you were a very powerful demon. And she was counting on him being powerful. Only a demon from the fifth circle or below would do.

She wandered back to the bed, admiring her lover. Or rather her ex-lover. While Maksim was good at pleasuring a woman, she didn't need any more from him. She was done. While she did enjoy good sex, he'd fulfilled his usefulness. Tomorrow she would inform him that they were through.

He wouldn't like it. She suspected that he wasn't the one who got dumped, but then she wasn't the one that got dumped either. So it was going to be an awkward ending any way it went down.

She couldn't really concern herself with that. She had other things to focus on. Like getting rid of her son's lust interest.

And this time making it very, very clear that she wasn't going to tolerate his abominable taste. She'd obviously been too subtle in the past, trying to get rid of them without upsetting her dear boy. But it was becoming painfully obvious that subtlety wasn't working. Nor would Vittorio stop returning to the trough for these odious women.

Oh, he'd learn this time. And eventually, he'd even understand. After all, mother knew best.

* * *

Erika had to admit, after eating she did feel much better. Although she suspected it was Vittorio's calm, steady presence that helped, more than the evening out of her blood-sugar levels.

That and their game of "What's Your Favorite?" So far she'd learned his favorite movie was *Brazil,* his favorite number was thirty-three (for no reason he could think of), and he didn't have a favorite animal—although if he did, Boris wasn't in the running. The cat did seem to glare at him a lot.

And he'd asked her favorites, like who her favorite sculptor was—a tie between Michelangelo (who could beat *David,* after all?) and a modern sculptor, Kira Rogan, who did large pieces with metal and wood and stone.

He'd asked what her favorite fruit was, which was also a tie, between kiwi and watermelon. And what her favorite adjective was, which had made her laugh. Adjective? She'd gone with silky—because she'd been admiring his hair at that moment.

"What's your favorite song?" she asked him from where she sat on her sofa. He'd insisted on cleaning the kitchen for her, although she couldn't help smiling as she watched him. He held a plate in his hand and eyed the dishwasher like he was facing a fully scrambled Rubik's Cube, and if he didn't solve it right the appliance would self-destruct.

Finally, he decided on the proper placement, then turned to her. "That one is easy," he said. " 'Verità Della Vita.' "

She shook her head. "I've never heard of it."

"It's a lesser-known piece by a composer named Renaldo D'Antoni, from the 1800s."

"Really? I'd love to hear it."

He smiled, a small, enigmatic twist of his lips. "I could probably arrange that."

For a moment, she wondered what the little grin meant. But then she got distracted by how beautiful he looked. She loved when he smiled, an action that was still rare enough that she noted each one.

"What's your favorite song?" he asked, then looked back at the dishwasher as he tackled the daunting puzzle again.

"Hmm, let me think about that one. I have to admit I'm a big fan of eighties music."

He placed another dish, then nodded at her. "I like a lot of eighties music too. The eighties really weren't as bad as everyone made out. Well, maybe the pastel linen suits were."

Erika laughed. "They were." Then she thought about it. "But how much of the eighties do you really remember?"

He set in the last plate, closed the dishwasher, then turned to her, his arms across his chest.

"Are we back to the age thing again?"

Erika shrugged, offering a nonchalant smile, even as the idea did niggle her a little, especially the idea that he had a woman closer to his age still in his life. "I guess it shouldn't bother me, if it doesn't bother you."

"Exactly." He walked over to her. "And you'd be surprised how much of the eighties I do remember."

She gave him a dubious look, but let the subject drop. Mainly because he was taking a spot on the sofa very close to her. And she really liked that.

He turned slightly so he was facing her, his knees brushing against hers. Her blood pressure rose at the brief touch. God, she was so attracted to this man.

"So," he said, his voice low. He reached out and touched her hair, pushing a strand back behind her ear. "What song have you always wanted to make love to?"

She couldn't stop her eyes from widening and a big grin from curving her lips. She hadn't expected that question. Not from the man she still expected to be reserved. Even after all the amazing lovemaking.

"Umm . . ." The hand that had tucked her hair, moved to touch her cheek. He leaned closer.

She watched, her lips seeming to pulse with the expectation of his kiss. But instead, he just looked at her, waiting.

"Umm, 'Love Song' by The Cure."

"Very eighties," he said, his lips just fractions of an inch from hers, then his eyes glanced off to the side briefly as if he was committing that information to memory. His hand left her face, moving to capture her hand.

"Where are we going?" she asked as she allowed herself to be pulled to her feet.

He started humming the tune of the song she just named. He sang a few of the lyrics, the ones about being alone with her making him feel young again. She nearly laughed at that, thinking making him feel young again couldn't be too hard. But she pushed that thought aside. He wanted her and she wasn't going to look for trouble.

Vittorio was now singing the lyrics about being alone with her making him feel whole again. He had a lovely, deep singing voice and she liked the idea that she was making him whole. She had a feeling he needed someone to help him with that.

He stopped singing and cast a look back over his shoulder. "Does that get you in the mood?"

His question was so unexpected, she couldn't suppress her laughter. God, he could surprise her! His expression was so hopeful, the question so funny; he just wowed her.

"I don't know. Sing a little more."

He did, with humorous fervor.

She nodded. "Oh yeah. I'm so in the mood."

Vittorio looked pleased, but he didn't stop singing as he led her down the hallway.

Vittorio couldn't quite believe his own behavior. He was the serious one, the uptight one, the stick-in-the-mud. Except being with Erika made him feel light and alive . . . and definitely aroused.

He'd never been one who acted impulsively, yet with her, he couldn't stop himself. As if to punctuate that point, he turned as he reached her room and pulled her into his arms.

She came willingly, her face lifted, prepared for his kiss,

and he didn't disappoint. He pressed his mouth to hers, tasting her thoroughly.

She smiled against his lips as the pressure lessened. "I love how you kiss."

He grinned. "Well, your technique isn't too shabby either."

But instead of smiling like he expected, her face grew serious. She cupped his cheek, her thumb running along the curve of his bottom lip.

"You have the most beautiful smile." She leaned in to place her lips where her thumb had been. Then she pulled back. "You should smile a lot more."

He remained still for a moment, unsure what to say. But realizing it was true. He didn't smile a lot. But since meeting Erika he'd found more reasons to smile than he had in years. Decades.

"Come here," he said, pulling her to the bed. Then he picked her up, placing her among the covers. He knelt beside her, and carefully, reverently, he began to undress her.

She watched him with those big gray-blue eyes. Trust so clear in them.

He pulled away each article of clothing, revealing inch by inch her pale, luminous skin. And he kissed each bit, loving the velvet warmth of her under his mouth.

Her fingers sank into his hair, knotting in the length, arching her body up to press against him. He moved downward, tasting her breasts, swirling his tongue around one hardened nipple, then turning his attention to the other. Then he moved down, down, savoring the soft, heated skin of her belly, her hips, her outer thigh.

She whimpered as he pressed a kiss to her inner thigh just above her knee.

"You are teasing me," she breathed, wriggling as he kissed her knee. "And that tickles."

Vittorio sat back, giving her a crooked smile. "I'm not

teasing. I'm kissing you all over. Which happens to be the song I always wanted to make love to."

He sang some of "Kiss You All Over," focusing solely on the chorus and the objective at hand. He continued to kiss her between lyrics, loving her movements, the taste of her creamy skin.

She laughed, wiggling under his lips.

Then the singing waned as his attention became more focused. On her belly, her hips, her upper thighs. She gasped, and writhed under him. His need jumped with each kiss, with each reaction from her.

"This is lovely," she said, arcing as he nipped, then sucked the flesh of her inner thigh, "but I want all of you."

Then she added with a disgruntled pout, "And you are still totally dressed."

"Hmm, is that a problem?"

Her eyes widened in disbelief. "Of course it is!"

He chuckled, the sound a little foreign to him. He actually felt lighthearted with this woman, which had to be the height of selfish stupidity. If anything he should feel worried and scared for her safety. But that was hard to remember when she was naked in front of him, her expression adorably petulant.

"Should I undress then?"

Again her eyes widened, this time implying he was truly dense. "Yes."

He felt another chuckle building in his chest. But the laugh faded into a shuddering breath as she sat up and tugged at his shirt, working it up and over his head.

"You can be a pushy little thing," he informed her, as her fingers found his nipples, flicking them with her thumb. His penis pulsed at her touch. He had no idea his nipples were so sensitive. But then, he'd never been this attracted to any woman. Never. Erika drove him wild. And she made him behave dangerously. But he would keep her safe. He would protect this mortal. He would.

She stilled, her hands pressing to his chest. "You have gotten awfully serious."

He shook his head, giving her another smile. "No. Just concentrating on what you are doing."

She grinned back at that, her eyes sparkling with pleasure. "Hmm, what else can I do to get you concentrating?"

Her hands slid down his chest, over his stomach to his waistband. She easily undid the button and zipper, and he moved to help work the jeans down. They disappeared off the bed, joining her clothes on the floor.

She started to press kisses along his collarbone, then lower and lower, mimicking his earlier attentions. But as wonderful as her mouth felt, he couldn't let her continue.

"God," he groaned as her mouth moved down to his inner thighs, "that feels so good."

Her lips curled in a smile at his roughly muttered words. But the smile was quickly transformed into a squeal as he caught her around the waist.

"But I'm acting out my favorite song." He pinned her down, kissing her neck, then nipping her ear.

She gasped. "No fair." The words were halfhearted at best.

"I know. I'm awful to make you suffer like this." He kissed her stomach, dipping his tongue into her belly button.

She wiggled, a breathy laugh escaping her. "You really are."

He moved lower, kissing just above the small triangle of dark hair covering her sex. "And I'm about to get worse."

She made a noise of feigned despair. "If you must."

"Oh, I must."

Then he brushed his lips over her. Not parting her, just teasing her with a fleeting brush of his mouth, a breath. Nothing more.

Her hands tangled in his hair, tugging. Urging his mouth to her. But instead he kissed her hip. She wriggled impatiently.

"Kissing you all over is going to take a long time." He kissed her calf. She made a frustrated and purely sexual noise, and for a second he wondered who he was really torturing with this game.

"I can't wait a long time," she informed him plaintively.

He smiled, deciding to have mercy on them both. "You know, neither can I." He pressed his mouth to the core of her, parting her with his tongue, tasting the dewy tang there.

He flicked his tongue, then swirled it, then sucked, repeating the process over and over until he tasted her release, her orgasm a sweet, heady flavor on his lips and tongue.

Erika cried out her climax, amazed at how quickly and how intensely this man could bring her to completion. He was amazing, and what she felt for him, even after such a short time, was amazing too.

Vittorio continued to lick her, seeming to savor what he was doing, and while she did too, and could easily orgasm again, she didn't want it like that. This time she wanted to reach her release with him deep inside her. She wanted the feeling of being one.

She gently tugged at his hair, her fingers still knotted in the silky tresses. At first he didn't follow her lead, his tongue still working its magic between her legs. But after another pull, he looked up at her, his lips rosy and wet, his eyes dazed with his own passion.

The sight awed her, because he truly loved what he was doing to her. He wasn't doing it for any other reason than he wanted her fulfillment, and that certainty was a mighty aphrodisiac.

But she only wanted to feel his thick length deep inside her all the more.

"Come here," she murmured, and with a regretful glance back at her thighs, he obeyed, sliding up her so his whole length was on top of her. The weight and the friction was delicious. Her breasts pebbled and her thighs ached.

"How do you do this?"

He raised an eyebrow, clearly unsure of what she meant.

"How do you arouse me so much? How do you make me forget everything but you?"

He gave her a penetrating look, then he shook his head. "I don't know. But you have the same effect on me."

She kissed him, and tasted herself on his lips, her own juices like a brand, a mark claiming him as hers and only hers. And somehow she knew that was true. She knew, deep in her bones, that he'd never acted like this with another woman. And that feeling was so empowering, so thrilling, she curled her legs around his back, pulling him tight to her, letting him know exactly what she wanted. Not that there was any doubt.

And he gave her what she wanted. He slowly slid his entire length deep inside her, filling her, stretching her.

For a few moments, he simply stayed that way. Just enjoying their connection, not knowing where she started and he began.

She touched his cheek, understanding the intensity and wonder of their union. He nuzzled her palm, closing his eyes, seeming to bask in her caress. Then he started to move, pumping into her, rocking her steadily and easily toward bliss.

She closed her own eyes, her hands sliding down his back, feeling each ripple of his muscles, each hard curve of his shoulders and back.

Then just as the slow rhythm got to be too much in its evenness, he started to move fast, filling her deeper, harder.

Her head arced back into the pillows, her legs locked tighter around his narrow hips, and soon another wave of release flooded her, wracking her body, leaving her limp, washed onto the shore of her own passion.

And Vittorio followed her, his own body writhing in the waves, passion washing over him until he too was limp, his breathing coming in harsh pants, his skin damp from exertion and release.

After a few moments—or maybe many, time lost all meaning—he lifted his head from where it rested on her chest.

"I think I changed my mind," he whispered, and she frowned at him, not following. Then a stark, sharp jolt of fear filled her. What had he changed his mind about? Her? This situation?

But she managed to sound calm as she asked, "About what?"

"About my favorite song."

She tried not sink into the mattress with relief, although her heart still thudded in her chest—and not just from their impassioned lovemaking.

"What is your favorite song now?"

He dropped his head back to her chest, and didn't answer for a moment. Then he raised his head again, lightly resting his chin on her chest.

"It's the beat of your heart."

Erika stared at this man, who she'd started falling for that very first time they shook hands nearly three months ago. God, she was falling in love.

And despite how right it felt, she was still terrified. What if she was feeling more than he was? What if this was going too fast?

She started to open her mouth to ask if he thought that was true, but then she snapped it shut. She didn't want an answer, not if it wasn't the one she wanted. That Vittorio was falling for her too.

Instead she kissed him, and prayed he felt the same way.

Chapter 19

Vittorio watched Erika, making sure that she was sound asleep before he slid out of bed and walked quietly down the hallway. He debated using her bathroom, but decided against the idea. He couldn't risk waking her up, and what he had to do was going to require a toothbrush and mouthwash afterward.

He slipped through the darkened apartment, the only light in the living room that of the courtyard lights reflected in the eyes of Erika's evil cat. The animal practically sneered at him, then curled back in a ball, acting like he hadn't seen him.

Vittorio unlocked her front door and headed toward the stairs. He would have shifted to shadow, but the truth was he was so miserable, he wasn't sure he could manage the concentration needed. And he only planned to be a minute, surely nothing could happen in that brief a time.

Still, he took the steps two at a time, nearly groaning at how vile he felt. Once in his apartment, he beelined to his bathroom. He barely reached the toilet before he wretched, ridding his stomach of the food he'd eaten tonight.

He groaned, reaching for a towel to wipe his mouth. God, that was attractive. Nothing beat a vomiting vampire. Although he had been able to suppress the need for quite some time. He'd been a little too busy having mind-blowing sex to even notice how disgusting he felt.

He turned to the sink, getting his toothbrush and the tube of toothpaste out of the medicine cabinet. He brushed three times and then rinsed with mouthwash for a full three minutes.

As soon as he was done, he felt a thousand times better, although he could feel his own brand of hunger rising up in him. *Damn it.*

He debated sneaking to Bourbon Street for a moment to siphon off some of the energy of the revelers there, but before he could even move toward his front door, he heard Erika. She screamed and screamed as if she was being killed.

His first thought was that he should have locked her door. His next was to race down there, jumping down half the steps in his panic.

He tore through her apartment, heading straight to her bedroom. To his relief, she was still in bed and the room was empty. But like the past three nights, she wrestled with her bedding, her eyes wide open, her mouth open in a horrible, soundless scream.

He quickly crawled on the bed, pulling her close to him. Willing her to wake up. She struggled against him, panting and whimpering as if she thought he was going to hurt her.

"Erika," he called to her loudly. "Erika."

She shook her head back and forth. "No! No!" She stared with that distant, eerily glazed look. She fought him, batting at him with her arms, kicking with her legs, attacking him as if she was fighting for her life.

He hated to restrain her, but he couldn't let her hurt herself. And the way she was flinging herself around, she would. Tonight seemed worse than the others. She struggled and clawed and cried.

"Erika!" he practically yelled, his mouth close to her ear. But still she didn't wake. She screamed and wrestled against him, her scream dwindling down to a high pitched keening sound. A desperate sound. A frightening sound.

Again he thought this was too extreme, too severe to be

just a normal nightmare. Or even night terrors. Fear filled him, matching hers. What if whatever she was battling with inside her head had the power to hurt her? What if it wasn't just imagined, but something real? A psychic attack of some sort.

And he couldn't rule out his mother being involved with this. She had managed to curse Ren. She'd managed to become a lampir. And turn her sons into them too. God he wanted to go back to a time when he didn't believe in anything supernatural.

She screamed again and began to chant, "*Stop!* Please stop. Stop."

Vittorio couldn't handle this. He was afraid for her, very afraid.

He pulled her close, pinning her to his chest, her arms trapped between them. And he began to take her energy, breathing in her essence, which now, laced with her fear, wasn't as sweet, but still pleasant like dark chocolate, bitter yet still tempting.

He breathed in deep, hoping he could take in some of the fear with her energy. He pulled it deep, over and over, his hunger gripping him, his fear that she was at risk making him continue. Eventually her movements calmed and she relaxed against him. He breathed in again, the sensation of her energy calming him too, sending him into euphoria, lovely floating pleasure.

His own hold on her relaxed as pleasure weighted his limbs, making him feel sated and almost lazy. Only then did he realize Erika was limp in his arms. He immediately released the last breath of energy that he'd taken, a new fear gripping him. An icy, horrible fear.

He stared down at Erika, her head lolling over his arm, her breathing shallow.

"Oh my God," he said, his voice panicked, his muscles taut with terror.

What had he done? He'd taken too much. He'd stolen too much of her energy in his own hunger. In his own bliss.

He pulled her close again, angling her head, trying to see the pulse in her neck. She moaned as her head lolled back. More panic filled him, then she slowly lifted her head, blinking blearily up at him like a sleepy child.

Gradually her senses seemed to return, although she was clearly drained. Literally drained.

She smiled sweetly, completely oblivious to the fact that he'd nearly stolen all of her energy. All of her life force. Her life.

He suppressed another bout of nausea. Seeing her like that brought back images he'd tried so hard to forget.

He touched a shaking hand to her face. She caught it, pressing his palm to her cheek. "I think these nightmares are getting to you worse than they are me now." She gave him a worried smile.

He didn't answer, but kissed her, his lips lingering.

"Really," she said when they parted, "are you all right?"

"I should be asking you that." He touched her again, her cheek, her shoulder, needing to touch her and reassure himself she was fine.

"It *was* a bad dream," she admitted. "But waking up in your arms goes a long way to making it a lot better."

More guilt assaulted him, making it hard to meet her eyes. She touched him, brushing his hair away from his face.

"Vittorio, I'm fine. I'm sorry this is happening, but—"

He cut her off, pressing his fingers to her lips. He couldn't listen to her apology when he'd come so close to hurting her.

"I'm sorry too."

"Don't be," she said, then she wriggled off his lap and moved over. She patted the mattress. "Come on, stop looking so worried. I'm fine now. Honestly. I'm just so glad you are here."

He hesitated, feeling like he had no right to get near this woman. First he was risking her safety by being with her when he believed his mother may have hurt others in the past, and now he was endangering her himself.

He should leave her—except he was afraid they were in too deep. How could he walk away, leaving her on her own? The truth was, he couldn't. And he didn't want to.

He slid onto the bed beside her, and she curled her body around him.

"Thank you," she murmured against his chest, her fingers playing with his hair.

God, he felt like a jerk.

Erika tiptoed around her room, carefully opening the armoire and cringing as the door creaked—a loud, tinny squeal of metal on metal.

She glanced over her shoulder, but Vittorio still slept on like the dead. That man really could sleep. He hadn't even moved since she'd gotten up and headed to the shower. She didn't think he'd even twitched.

Then again, she'd woken him again with another of her horrible dreams—this one again about those hideous creatures that chased her, intent on causing her harm. It had been more graphic than any of the others, and she was beginning to doubt they'd go away any time soon.

Although they had started suddenly, so she supposed they could end that way too.

Vittorio had looked as shaken as she was. Actually worse so, really. But then he'd cuddled her, keeping her close to his side for the remainder of the night. Her favorite place to be.

She sighed, just recalling. Her toes curled against the cool hardwood floors. She reflected a moment longer, then forced herself to return her attention to what she should wear today.

She pulled out one of her favorite dresses, a black knit with a little puff to the sleeves and an empire waist. She tilted her head, debating if that would reflect what she wanted it to. Funky, artsy, yet together. She decided with the proper jewelry and cute shoes it would do the trick. She gathered the other items she wanted and headed back to the bathroom to dress and fix her hair and makeup.

Twenty minutes later, she was ready to meet this mystery client. A thrill at the idea of actually being commissioned for her work curled around in her belly. Some of that was nerves too. She really wanted this to work out.

A sale would make life here a little easier. She'd managed to save a good sum over the years, with the idea that she would eventually give at least a year or two solely to her art. But more money would allow her to attempt this career even longer, if necessary.

She supposed her worry could have triggered the worst of her nightmares. She was concerned that this would never be a full-time career. And she did feel the need to prove herself.

But hopefully today's meeting was just a sign of more to come. And it would be a real career after all. She practically wanted to skip around the apartment as she gathered her purse and phone and of course, fed the grumpy Boris.

The cat's nose actually seemed to be wrinkled with condescension as he watched her pour his food, then add a little wet food to it.

"I know," she murmured as she set it down, then checked his water bowl, which was fine. "I've been ignoring you the past couple days. But if you had a hottie like that, you'd ignore me too."

She smiled over calling Vittorio a hottie. That word was too trendy, too adolescent to fit him. Even though he was. But he had maturity to his soul. A cultured, regal bearing. And she really liked that. Yet he wasn't as serious as she'd once believed. Last night, he'd been playful and sexy and funny. She liked that too.

Of course, his serious side had returned with her nightmare. She really wished she could get control of these terrible dreams. She hated to worry Vittorio, and frankly, she hated the dreams too. Even remembering them caused her to shudder.

She sighed, a habit she'd developed since meeting him. Again she regrouped herself and picked up her purse, which she'd placed on the counter while fixing Boris's food, which now held the black cat's full attention.

She found a piece of paper and a pen and jotted down a quick note reminding Vittorio where she was going, leaving it on the kitchen table. Then she hurried from the apartment. She had ten minutes to walk to the restaurant, and she didn't want to be late.

She arrived at the restaurant right at two, as Isabel's voice mail had instructed.

"Can I help you?" the hostess greeted, smiling broadly, her teeth as white as her starched white blouse.

"Yes, I'm meeting someone here, but I'm not sure if she's here yet. Or what she looks like, actually. We've only spoken on the phone."

The hostess immediately nodded, even before Erika finished her explanation.

"She's waiting for you out in the courtyard. Let me show you."

Erika followed the hostess out into the bright courtyard. Sunlight dappled the flagstones and white tablecloths through vines and other greenery crisscrossing overhead. A fountain bubbled in the center. The atmosphere was truly beautiful.

The hostess walked straight toward the far corner, and not until she moved aside did Erika spot the woman who waited to meet her.

The woman sat in the sunlight, her arms resting on the arms of the wrought iron chair, her face tilted upward toward the sun. And Erika's first impression was that of a sun goddess. Thick lustrous blond hair cascaded down her back and framed perfect features, high cheekbones, a nose that was neither too small nor too large, lips that were full and a tad pouty. A small rounded chin.

She opened her eyes as they stopped at the edge of the table. And Erika was struck by the color of them, such a dark brown, they actually looked black. A chord of familiarity struck her, but Erika didn't get a chance to speculate on what seemed familiar to her, because the breathtakingly beautiful woman spoke.

"You must be Erika Todd." She extended a hand, her fingers narrow and graceful, her nails buffed and tastefully polished in sheer pink.

Erika leaned forward to accept her handshake. "It's nice to meet you, Ms. Andrews."

The woman smiled, her smile as lovely and ethereal as the rest of her.

"Please call me Isabel."

Erika nodded, then pulled out the chair across from her. She accepted the menu the hostess offered, then turned her attention back to this stunning woman.

Looking at her, it was impossible to tell her age, her blond radiance could have ranged anywhere from thirty-five to forty-five. Maybe younger, maybe older.

"You are a lovely willowy thing," Isabel smiled, her dark gaze roaming over Erika.

Erika actually felt herself blush. "Thank you."

"Just stating the truth."

Erika smiled, thinking any woman she'd ever met would have a tough time competing with this woman's beauty.

She managed to stop staring and gather her thoughts. "So you are interested in a sculpture? Did you have anything in mind?"

"Right to business, eh?"

Erika's cheeks burned even more. She was honestly so disarmed by this woman, she'd grabbed on to the only subject she could think of, too abruptly, it seemed now.

"I'm sorry. I'm just so thrilled about your interest."

Isabel smiled, then reached out and touched her hand, her fingers cool, despite the fact she sat in the direct sun.

"Believe me," she said with a sweet smile, "it is I who am thrilled to be meeting with you."

Erika smiled back, immediately feeling an affinity with this woman. There was something so comforting in her smile and the sparkle in her eyes. A sense of knowing her, which, given her belief in providence, she saw as a lucky sign.

"May I get you a drink?" the waiter asked, drawing her attention away from Isabel. She ordered an iced tea. The waiter nodded, but Erika noticed his attention was more on Isabel. Not that she could blame the guy.

As the waiter headed back to the kitchen, he bumped into a neighboring table, which Isabel didn't notice. She had to be used to reactions like that.

"I'm very interested in a sculpture of myself," Isabel said.

Erika nodded, immediately wondering if she could do her justice. But her features were so symmetrical, so lovely, she'd love to get the chance to capture them.

"Okay," Erika agreed. "A bust, then?"

Isabel shook her head. "Actually I'd like a full body piece."

Erika paused, trying to calculate how long that would take her. "That shouldn't be a problem. And I can work from photos, if you prefer."

Isabel shook her head. "No. I want to model for it. This is a gift for the love of my life—and I want you to capture my very essence in each curve of the clay. I've seen your work, and I know you can do that. But I would prefer to pose."

Erika nodded, surprised. Not many people liked the idea of standing still for the time she'd require. But she also understood Isabel's reasoning. That was the very reason she'd wanted Vittorio to pose, too. She could attain more of his essence by looking at him, rather than using a two-dimensional image.

"Sure. I can do that."

The waiter returned with tea, nearly spilling it as he admired Isabel. Only Erika's quick catch saved her from wearing the icy liquid in her lap. There were clearly some drawbacks to being so lovely, Erika realized.

The waiter remained at the table, as Isabel ordered a steak, very rare. Erika found the order surprising. Given her svelte form, Erika would have pegged her for the salad and mineral water type, not the red meat and red wine type.

After the waiter left, narrowly missing another waiter balancing a full tray of food, Isabel asked, "When could we start? I'd like to have the piece as soon as possible. How long do you think it will take? I have no idea what kind of time these things involve."

"It varies," Erika admitted. "And of course revolves around when you are available to pose. That could add to the time, if you are busy."

"I have all the time in the world," she said with a small smile.

"Then I will get it done as quickly as I can."

Isabel nodded and took a sip of her wine.

This commission wasn't actually occurring at the best time for her, Erika hated to admit to herself. She had a lot left to do for the show. She wanted to sculpt Vittorio for the upcoming show, a full body sculpture of him as well. And she wanted to finish another smaller piece. But this was her first commission, and she didn't want to lose it.

"I'm willing to pay whatever you think is fair," Isabel added, then took another sip of her red wine.

Erika gave her a figure, half expecting she'd balk, but Isabel simply nodded. "That sounds fine."

Erika tried not to grin like a fool. She truly considered the price fair, given the time a full body piece would take and the time constraints she was under, but she'd expected Isabel to be surprised by the cost.

The money certainly made this far too good an opportunity to pass up. It would be tight, but she'd manage to get everything done.

Then she considered something she hadn't thought of. "As I guess you know, I have a show coming up at The Broussard at the end of this month. It would speed up things if you'd be willing to let me show this piece at the show—then I wouldn't have to be working on other pieces on the side. I could concentrate on your piece." And Vittorio, of course.

Erika had second thoughts as soon as the words were out of her mouth. This was a gift, and Isabel would likely want to keep it a surprise.

But Isabel's eyes lit, gleaming with excitement. "Me? In your show? That would be perfect."

Erika smiled, although she wondered what would be so perfect about it.

Isabel seemed to read the confusion in her half-smile, because she added, "My love would be so thrilled to see me showcased in an exhibition like yours. He's very proud of me, you see."

Erika could believe that. Most men would be overjoyed to have a woman like Isabel on their arm.

As if to punctuate the point, the waiter returned, solicitously placing Isabel's plate in front of her. Only to move over to Erika and set down her plate with a loud clunk on the tabletop. Several pieces of lettuce leapt off onto the tablecloth.

Neither Isabel nor the waiter seemed to notice.

Once the besotted and dangerous waiter disappeared again, Isabel asked, "Do you have a beau? A lovely thing like you must."

Erika was a little caught off guard by the question. She paused, mid-bite, lowering the speared lettuce and chicken back to her plate. Again she felt heat creep over her cheeks.

"Yes, I do. Well, I guess I do. It's a pretty new relationship."

Isabel smiled, her expression somehow different from the other times she'd smiled, but Erika couldn't place her finger on what the actual change was.

"I'm sure he's just crazy about you."

Erika smiled, then took a bite of her salad. She certainly hoped so, because she was crazy about him.

Chapter 20

Orabella continued down the street after leaving Erika at the street corner, right where the damned harlot belonged. Damn her for ruining her delight at seeing and feeling the sunlight for the first time in decades.

She'd expected this woman to be like the others. They had been the dregs of society. Hard women who'd lived hard lives. Killing them had been doing them a favor, frankly. And given who they were, and what they were like, she'd known that Vittorio didn't really love them. How could he?

But this one . . . She fought back the impulse to sneer. This girl wasn't a bit like the others. She'd expected Erika Todd to be a wannabe artist filled with angst, with a drug problem to help her cope. Instead, she was smart, she was irritatingly kind, her goodness written all over her young, optimistic face. And this irked Orabella more than anything else: she was pretty.

No, while that did truly piss her off, there was something that infuriated her far more. Her ridiculous son had indeed slept with this woman. Orabella could smell him all over her skin like a delicious, expensive cologne. And while the smell was like a lure to her, when mingled with the mortal's scent it became noxious.

Oh yes, this one was truly dangerous. Vittorio likely believed himself in love with this one, which made her plan all the more precarious. If Vittorio had feelings for this one, real feelings, then he wasn't likely to understand the favor Orabella was doing him.

And she *was* doing him a favor. That was still the truth, but how to get him to understand that a mortal could never be good enough? *How, how, how?*

What would finally prove to him that only she could love him the way he deserved? Then she paused, feeling the sun, the warm, wonderful heat she hadn't felt for so long, she'd forgotten how brilliant it was.

She'd given him immortality, but he'd resented it, claiming he'd never wanted the change. But she could now give him the sunlight again. Surely he would see the kind of deep love she had for him. She'd make him as human as she could. He'd understand then that her reason for giving him immortality in the first place was totally based in love.

Just like keeping him with her for years was too. She missed those times. When Vittorio had been hers alone. Yes, he'd finally see how much she loved him and come back to her. Even if he did have feelings for this mortal.

Oh, she'd still kill this Erika woman, but it would be just another horrible accident. A tragic death—and Vittorio would ache over the loss. After all, he was her son, and just as sensitive as she was. But that grief would pass. Especially in light of the normalcy she'd return to him.

She and her son would stroll together in the sun. And everything would be perfect.

"That little bitch," Maksim growled, pacing back and forth on the mattress, peering furiously at the floor around the decadent king-sized bed. He made an angry noise deep in his throat.

Oh, had he ever underestimated that little bitch. He stared down at the pentagram that she'd created around the perimeter of the bed with iron filings. More iron filings lined the windows and doorways, creating a barrier that was impossible to cross.

The only trap that could contain a demon—but he hadn't expected Orabella to have the intelligence to even know about that. Much less pull it off.

Damn it! "Damn it!"

"Having a little problem, darling?"

He spun around to see Orabella standing in the doorway. Her lips curved in that sweet smile he'd once considered so easy to read.

"You duplicitous bitch!" He started to jump down off the bed and charge toward her, but stopped short, realizing he'd only end up looking like an ass if he attempted that feat.

"Maksim, it's not like you to have such a temper. I guess what they say about demons is true. Quick to forgive, quick to anger."

Maksim grunted. "You'll see how quick I am to forgive as soon as I get out of here."

She gave him a hurt look. "Well, I guess it's a good thing I took your cell phone before I started this little artwork project." She gestured to the pentagram, then pulled his thin, compact cell phone from her purse. "It's going to be a while before anyone discovers you are missing."

He growled.

She laughed.

"Why did you do this?" he demanded, his fingers twitching at his sides. Damn, he wanted to kill the little liar.

"Well," she said, "as you probably guessed, Vittorio isn't a stalker, nor is he going to hurt that mortal. But I'm going to hurt her."

Maksim gave her a confused and irritated look. "Like I would care if you did." He made a face. "Hello? Demon."

"Oh, I know you don't care about that. But the truth is I don't have any use for you anymore, and I knew you weren't going to take too kindly to me breaking up with you. So I have to take precautions to keep myself safe. And you away from me and my plans."

"Do you really think my ego is so fragile that I would do something petty, just because you want to break up?"

Orabella pretended to consider the idea. "Yes."

Maksim opened his mouth to deny it, but then sighed. Who was he kidding? He so would have done something petty. Not to mention, he was this close to just going to Vittorio and asking him outright about Ellina. He believed he would get a truthful answer from the male lampir.

This one, however, he knew he couldn't trust her to tell the truth. About anything, obviously.

"So what is your plan? To just leave me here indefinitely?"

She gave him a regretful look, then nodded. "I'm sorry to say, but yes."

He growled again, this time unable to control his urge to strangle her. But when he reached the edge of the circled pentagram, he bounced back, like an invisible trampoline blocked his way. He stumbled backward and fell on the bed.

Staring up at the ceiling, he gritted his teeth as her laughter greeted him again.

"Wow, that works very well. When I read about it, I have to admit I had my doubts something so simple would work. Iron filings—they seem so insubstantial to contain a big, brawny demon like you. Funny what constitutes a limitation for the immortals."

His jaw ached as he continued to clamp his teeth together.

"Of course, I can't believe the other demon spell worked just as well."

He sat upright. "What other spell?"

She made a disappointed sound. "Maksim. Haven't you noticed something different about me?"

He frowned, studying her. "No, you look like the same manipulative little whore you always were."

She tsked. "That's not very nice. And I thought you were fond of me."

"Fond of the sex with you, baby. Fond of the sex."

She grinned, his comment seeming to please her. "And thank goodness you were, my darling." She waved to him, and strolled back down the hallway.

He frowned, wondering what the hell she meant by that, then he realized something he'd somehow managed to overlook in his own irritation. And her comment about the limitations of immortals.

He glanced over to the window. The sun was still out. *What the hell?*

Erika stopped on the way home to pick up something for Vittorio to eat. She wouldn't be surprised if he was still in bed. Vittorio didn't seem to sleep during the night at all. She'd woken up again after the nightmare, only to find Vittorio watching her. Again with that unreadable, solemn expression of his.

And if he hadn't gotten up yet, he definitely hadn't eaten, and she couldn't allow him to starve. She'd never been a person who felt compelled to feed others. That was Jo—she always had appetizers and meals and desserts made ahead of time if she had company, whereas Erika just didn't.

So she picked up some turkey po' boys from a small café and headed home. She was excited to tell him about her meeting. She and Isabel had decided to start the sculpture tomorrow at Isabel's place, which was in the Garden District. Not surprising given the fact she hadn't even blinked over the sculpture's cost, and she clearly dripped money. Her clothes were stunning.

And Erika also hoped to start Vittorio's piece tonight. If she could keep her hands off him long enough to actually work with the clay and polymer.

When she entered her apartment, the place was silent. She put the plastic sack of food in the fridge and wandered down the hall. Sure enough, Vittorio was still in bed. And it didn't appear as if he'd moved a muscle.

She smiled. She'd swear that boy was a vampire, if such things existed.

The covers had slipped, leaving his chest and stomach exposed. One leg was bent and uncovered too. He looked like a fallen angel, collapsed to earth and swathed in his torn robes.

Erika suddenly realized that was exactly how she wanted to sculpt him.

Turning back to the living room, she quietly set about creating the scene for where Vittorio would pose. She placed large cushions on the floor near her work area. Then she went out onto the sun porch to get some of the wire framework she used to make the forms for her bigger pieces. The wire mesh would give her the shape and the foundation to add the clay and polymer for the detailed work.

With wire cutters and pliers, she manipulated the metal into the shape she had in mind. She worked for a while, losing track of time, until she realized the room was starting to grow dim around her.

And Vittorio still hadn't gotten up.

She returned to her bedroom, amazed, but not disappointed that he was still in the same position. He lounged back against the rumpled covers, his body all smooth skin and long, lean muscles. His hair tangled against the blue of her duvet, sexy and wild, a paradox to his angelic face. The face of a saint. Yet a body that made her want to experience every sin she could think of—with him.

Her eyes wandered down his body, and she realized one thing had changed. His large erection was clear under the thin cotton of the sheet.

The sight made her breasts ache, between her legs ache. Oh man, did she ever want to sin.

She moved closer, unable not to touch. Her hands immediately went to him, touching his flat, solid stomach, moving downward to the trail of hair, dark blond and swirling around his shallow little navel. Her fingers began to slip under the sheet, when his hand caught hers.

She squealed, surprised. She looked up at him; he grinned, the turn of his lips lopsided and adorably sexy.

"Were you planning to have your way with me while I slept?"

She gave him an innocent look. "Maybe."

"Mmm," he groaned and stretched. "Good thing I woke up then. I wouldn't want to have missed any of it."

So quickly she didn't even see it coming, he caught her around the waist and pulled her down on top of him.

His hand cupped the back of her head and he pulled her down to kiss him. She let him take control for a moment, but then tugged away.

She sat up, her legs straddling him. Her short knit dress rode up, exposing her bare thighs. His hands moved there, holding her.

"I like this," she said, her own hands stroking down over his bare chest.

"Like what?" His voice low, provocative.

"For once you are totally naked, and I'm dressed."

He raised an eyebrow. "Hmm. It's okay, but I do like to see you all pale and nude."

She smiled, then she shifted her hips, rubbing her already damp sex against the hardness of his erection. Panties and sheets separated them, but desire shot through her. Vittorio groaned. The fingers on her thighs gripped her.

She moved again, then again. Each movement more arousing than the last, but not enough. Not even close to enough.

So she stood, her feet planted on either side of her hips and worked off her black lace panties, kicking them off.

From beneath her, Vittorio looked up at her, his eyes moving from her face to her parted legs and her exposed sex. His lips parted, and his breaths came in short, sharp pants. His eyes were hooded, his hair tumbling around his gorgeous face.

Erika's need jolted even higher. She felt powerful, like she was a goddess, and he was worshipping at her altar. Then he sat up, his hands sliding up her legs, over the front of her thighs to curl around and grip her bottom.

He brought his head up and pressed his mouth to her, his tongue lapping up the slit of her sex.

She nearly buckled under that first taste, but his fingers gripped the cheeks of her bottom and he continued to lick and taste her until she couldn't decide if she was his goddess or his sacrifice. An offering to a gorgeous, golden, heathen god.

Either way, it was fine with her. More than fine, absolutely earth-shatteringly perfect.

Her head fell back, her breath coming in sobbing gasps, as he devoured her. Then the hands holding her whole passion-limp weight slid up to catch her waist.

His mouth left her, abandoning her right at the edge of release. She whimpered, but watched as he lay back, pulling her down with him, until she was kneeling over him again, his thick, hard penis poised right at the opening of her vagina.

Their eyes met and held for a moment, then he pulled her down onto him.

She cried out, her head falling back, her aching body impaled fully on his. Her orgasm wracked her body, vibrating through her over and over until she couldn't even pull in a full breath. Her ecstasy was too much.

She remained that way, with him still rigid and heavy, filling her until her release subsided and she could focus again.

She finally opened her eyes and looked down at him. His eyes were heavy with desire, his lips parted, his hair tangled around him, and she knew at that moment she was the sacrifice and he the god.

But then she moved her hips and the tables turned. She was the goddess now, demanding her minion to respond. And he did, his eyes closing and a low groan escaping his parted lips, as she rose up, then down on him.

* * *

Vittorio moaned as Erika slid back down his length, the tight, hot walls of her vagina holding him, caressing him. His own climax was building fast with each writhing movement of her hips, with each stroke of her body around him, with each curl of her fingers on his chest.

God, he wanted this woman. He wanted to do this with her forever, be inside her, feel her heat, her slickness.

His body tightened as suddenly his hunger joined his rising desire, sharpening and intensifying the already powerful sensation, until all he could think about was the way it would feel if he took her energy into him, while she took his cock into her.

Do it, his mind ordered. *Just a little.*

But he shoved the desire away. He wouldn't do that again. Not after last night. He'd taken too much. And she couldn't handle him taking from her again.

He focused on the tightness pulsing around him, squeezing his penis with wet, hot heat. God, she felt so good.

So good. As soon as he felt her orgasm, the long shudders of her muscles, he followed her into her release. His own orgasm pounding through him.

But even the breath-stealing intensity didn't quite take away all of his desire to inhale some of her energy.

This was not good.

Chapter 21

Vittorio had to admit that he didn't feel any better even in the aftermath of fantastic sex. Even with Erika in the living room, and a little distance between them.

He'd used the excuse of needing to use the bathroom to give himself a little physical distance and time between himself and her. But he still craved her energy. Which made no sense.

His hunger was spiraling out of control so quickly. He'd taken from her last night, and that should be enough. He usually went days, even weeks, without having his hunger get out of hand.

But he couldn't seem to stop craving Erika's energy. And that wasn't normal. Not for him. He'd spent his decades mastering his desire to feed until it was almost an afterthought. So why was this different?

A knock drew his attention to the bathroom door.

"Are you okay in there?" Erika's voice reached him, though a little muffled. Her energy, wafting through every crack around the door frame, was loud and clear. And calling to him.

"I'm fine," he managed, realizing he wasn't fine. This was a real problem. The more he had of her, the more he wanted.

A brief silence followed his words, then she said, "Okay.

Let me know if you need anything." Then another pause before he heard her footfalls heading back down the hallway.

He dropped his head back into his hands, not leaving his seat on the edge of the tub. He knew he had been in there a long time, but he was afraid to leave. He knew he'd lose control.

He had to go feed. It was the only thing he could do to be sure he wouldn't just snap and feed from her. Or worse than that, not snap but just siphon a little here and a little there until he'd taken too much.

He sat there for a moment more, then gathered himself. Slowly he rose and opened the door. He knew she was in the living room. A radio played, but he couldn't hear her.

He walked down the hallway, his movements measured and filled with dread. What if he couldn't control this? How could he be with her, protect her, when he was becoming a threat too?

He entered the room to find her bent over a shaped piece of metal that vaguely resembled chicken wire.

"What are you doing?"

She jumped, spinning to look at him, the pliers she had in her hands nearly flying. Not unlike the cell phone from their first meeting.

Vittorio couldn't help wondering if she was aware she should be nervous around him, even though she wouldn't know why.

"You scared me," she breathed, then smiled.

His desire for her flared.

"I'm sorry."

"You are a very quiet walker."

A vampire trait. One of many that were turning out to be a real problem.

She moved closer to him, and he had to fight the impulse to step back. He won, but just barely. He had to do something about this urge that was spiraling through him like a twister.

He could tell by the puzzled expression on Erika's face he wasn't hiding his struggle well.

"I don't know if you are hungry," she said.

God, yes, he was.

"But I picked up turkey po'—"

"I actually have to go out," he interrupted abruptly, his eyes locked on her lips, every ounce of his willpower keeping him from kissing her and tasting her powerful, wonderful life force.

"Oh," she said, her brows drawing together. "Umm, okay."

"Just for a few moments," he added, realizing his behavior was coming across as strange. "Just a quick errand."

She nodded quickly, trying to reassure him it was fine, even though she clearly still didn't understand what was going on with him.

He hesitated, then nodded. "Okay, I'll be back in a few minutes."

"Okay," she said, her confusion evident in the tone of her voice. He didn't hazard a look at her as he skirted around her. He knew his distance would really bewilder, and possibly hurt, her. And he was too much of a coward to look at her and see that.

He hurried to the front door, to get where it was safe to feed. Then he could come back to her and be normal. Well as normal as he got.

But before he disappeared into the night, he paused.

"Lock the door," he said, then slipped out into the darkness, hating the fact that he had to leave, and that he was acting so strangely.

Erika stood there for a few moments, just staring at the closed door. Vittorio's departure was abrupt and more than a little weird. But finally she did as he asked, and locked the door, wiggling the knob to make sure the bolt was secure.

"You know, Boris," she said to her cat as she returned to her artwork, "things have been very odd of late."

What errand did he have to do right this minute? And why had he looked as if he couldn't bear to make eye contact with her?

She wanted to believe his behavior was just typical Vittorio—his usual hot and cold behavior. At least she knew that was normal and he'd get over it. She hoped.

She looked down at her pliers, held forgotten in her hand. She started to reach for another panel of the wire mesh, then stopped, crossed over to the sofa and dropped onto the cushions, her movement jarring Boris.

She dropped her pliers on the coffee table, ignoring the glare of her disgruntled cat. She didn't need to worry about the silly feline. His reactions were always the same, ranging from selfish affection to disdain. If only Vittorio were as easy to figure out.

Where was he going? And why had he stayed in the bathroom for nearly twenty minutes? She hadn't heard the shower, she hadn't heard him moving around in there. Not even the flush of the toilet.

But the crazy thing was that while they'd been making love, she'd truly believed that's what he'd been doing with her. Their sexual encounters went beyond mere sex. She knew it. In her heart, she did. Yet he went off, obviously shaken, obviously in a rush and obviously that rush involved getting away from her more than running some mysterious errand.

Her train of thought returned to what Philippe had said. That Vittorio had another woman. Did she have something to do with this? Did Vittorio need to talk to her? See her? Hell, she didn't even know where this woman was. She could be right here in New Orleans.

Erika sighed. She'd make herself crazy wondering things like that. Maybe that was something she needed to ask him about, not that she'd get a direct answer. Plus she didn't really want to tell him she got this idea about another woman from her psychic. She suspected that, like many people, he didn't buy into psychic phenomena.

Stretching her neck to one side and then the other, she sighed again. Her muscles were strung ripcord tight. Between the enigma that was Vittorio, and her meeting with Isabel earlier, she seemed to have been tense all day long.

Okay, she hadn't been tense while making love, or afterward, but her stress was back. And at the moment, a steaming hot shower sounded like exactly what she needed to loosen her muscles and hopefully calm her overactive mind.

Vittorio would be back soon, like he said he would be, and his behavior had nothing to do with another woman.

And maybe if she told herself that often enough, she'd believe it.

Fortunately Bourbon Street was bustling with revelers. Not terribly crowded since it was a Tuesday night, but Vittorio could find clusters of people to follow. He drained off bits of their energy until he felt in control of himself again.

Then he hurried right back to Erika. He hated to leave her unprotected, even for a few minutes. As he entered the courtyard and approached her apartment, he didn't see her through the windows. Lights burned brightly, but her silhouette didn't dance along the walls as she worked on her art, or prepared her dinner.

Instantly concern rose in Vittorio's chest.

He twisted the doorknob. And he'd told her to lock up when he left. Which was only keeping *him* out at the moment. It wouldn't keep out his mother should she want to get in.

He knocked, but there was no answer. He peered inside again, noticing the cat was on the back of one of the chairs, glaring. But that didn't signal anything. That was all that cat did as far as Vittorio could tell.

He knocked again. Where was Erika? He hadn't been gone more than fifteen minutes, twenty at the most.

He waited, concern growing. He looked back through the window; he saw no movement.

Where was she?

Without further thought, he dematerialized and reappeared on the other side of the door. The place was quiet, which made him all the more nervous.

Had someone or something come in and carried her away? He had just reached the hallway, when Erika stepped out of the bathroom, her back to him.

"Erika," he said, relieved.

Erika screamed, spinning toward him, her towel threatening to slide down.

"Vittorio," she gasped. "You scared me! Again. How do you do that?"

"Sorry." Why did this again seem an insurmountable problem to overcome? Stealth—the demise of a grand affair. Of course, it was just a small part of the problems they'd have to triumph over.

But all too easily, Vittorio's attention was drawn back to Erika and the fact she was wearing nothing but a towel, which was in imminent danger of slipping. She tugged at it, tightening it around her lithe body. Vittorio watched, his body reacting instantly to her long legs, her pale shoulders, and the other incredible attributes hidden under pale blue terry cloth. And all thoughts of insurmountable problems were lost.

God, he was insatiable—in every way—for her.

"I'm sorry. I keep doing that, don't I?" he said.

She nodded, then frowned. "You also keep coming into my apartment when the door is locked."

Shit. Vittorio shifted, then grabbed on to the only idea he could come up with. "When you didn't answer, I got concerned, so I got your spare key from Ren and Maggie's."

"Oh," she said, seeming to find that believable. But then her brows drew together. "Why are you so worried about me? I mean, I've been living here alone for months before you got here."

She had a valid point, and he needed to come up with a viable excuse for his concern. "Well, usually Ren and Maggie are here. And you've been having those nightmares. I just don't want you getting nervous."

She smiled. "That's sweet." Still holding her towel, she leaned forward and pressed a kiss to his lips.

God, she tasted so good, like mint and warmth and a sweetness all her own.

"Thank you for caring."

He did care, just not enough to stay away from her. And he couldn't make himself do it now.

He caught her hand. He couldn't stay away and that had been clear from the moment she'd clocked him in the head with her cell phone. So the only hope was to keep her safe.

She started to pull away, smiling.

He caught her by the front of the towel, holding the edges together for her. "Where are you going?"

She laughed, looking down at the terry cloth, which slipped even further down her body, exposing more of the swell of her breasts. Vittorio followed her glance, his penis pulsing at the swell of pearly white flesh revealed.

"I was going to get clothes on so I could start working."

He shook his head.

"I'm not." She laughed again, the sound husky and sexy.

"Noo . . ." He began tugging her toward the living room.

"Where are we going?" she asked, smiling broadly.

"I noticed the cushions you arranged by your work area. I thought maybe we should practice a few poses there."

"Poses with me?"

He nodded. "Of course."

"But I can't sculpt myself." She raised an eyebrow as if she'd caught him on that one.

"No. So I guess this will be my opportunity to sculpt you."

She tilted her head, clearly intrigued.

"I'll show you."

He pulled her toward the spot she'd arranged earlier. Carefully, he eased her down among the downy cushions and sheets. She lounged back against them, her eyes intent behind her lowered lashes.

"So how does your sculpting begin?"

"Like this." He kneeled beside her, and carefully unwrapped the towel, revealing her perfect body. She breathed out, a slow hissing sound as the cool air hit her still shower-warmed skin.

He breathed in, mimicking the sound, in awe of how truly beautiful she was.

"What next?" she whispered, watching him.

Vittorio pulled in another shuddering breath, then moved his hands to her sides. Slowly he shaped them over her body, caressing the slight flare of her hips, then the narrow indentation of her waist, the subtle ripples of her rib cage. Committing each curve of her body to his memory.

She squirmed slightly as his hands reached her armpits.

"Tickles," she said with a smile, but the smile vanished on the wave of a gasp as his hands moved to mold her breasts.

"Oh," she gasped, closing her eyes and pressing herself more firmly into his palms.

"You are so breathtakingly beautiful," he murmured, splaying his hands upward to stroke her chest, her neck, then back down to her breasts.

"Vitt—"

Her words were cut off by a sharp rap at the door. Vittorio immediately angled himself so that he was blocking Erika from view of the window beside the door. She scrambled for the sheet draped underneath her, yanking it over herself.

There was another knock, then a muffled, "Erika?"

Erika looked at Vittorio. "Is that Ren?"

Vittorio nodded, very, very disgruntled by his brother's timing.

Another knock.

"I'll get rid of him," Vittorio said, deciding he'd have to answer the door to get rid of the pest. "Stay right here. I'm so not done with you."

"I'm not sure that's a good idea," Erika said, but Vittorio rose anyway, heading to the door.

He unlocked the bolt, opening the door just enough to peer out at his brother. Which was unfortunately all the invitation Ren needed.

"Vittorio? What are you doing down here?" he asked as he shoved open the door and walked into the room, followed by Maggie.

"Hi Vittorio," she greeted with her usual bright smile.

"So what are you doing . . ." Ren's voice trailed off as he spotted Erika on the pile of cushions shrouded in a white sheet. ". . . Here."

"Wow," Maggie murmured, her cheeks flushing to a deep red.

"Hi," Erika said sheepishly, waving from amid the sheets.

Vittorio glanced from Erika to his brother, fully expecting Ren to quickly make an exit. Maggie had already caught his hand, and was pulling at him, trying to move him back toward the porch. But Vittorio should have known his brother well enough to know he wasn't going so easily.

Instead he smiled broadly, and asked, "Bad timing?"

Vittorio glared at him. "You could say that."

"I'm not even going to ask why you opted for cushions on the dining room floor."

"Good," Vittorio said, moving to open the door wider, a less than subtle hint, which Ren ignored. Ren sauntered to the sofa, easily tugging Maggie along with him. He sat down, even as Maggie hissed that they should really be going.

Ren smiled at her, then kissed her nose as a way of appeasing her. "But we've obviously missed a lot while we were away."

"And now isn't the time to get brought up-to-date," Vittorio snarled.

"Well, we couldn't have interrupted much. You still have all your clothes on," Ren said.

Vittorio snarled. He should have guessed his smart-ass brother would enjoy this far too much.

"Umm, if you all will excuse me," Erika said, managing to struggle to her feet and keep the sheet wrapped around herself, "I think I'll go get some clothes on."

Oh yeah, Ren was going to pay for this little stunt.

Vittorio watched with a combination of regret and irritation as Erika hurried down the hall.

"Ren," Maggie admonished.

"What?" Ren said, giving her a wide-eyed, innocent look.

Maggie rolled her eyes. "It's a darn good thing you are so cute." She pressed a kiss to his lips, and then stood.

"I give you permission to punch him," she said to Vittorio.

"Thank you. I will."

"I don't think so," Ren stated, then he caught Maggie's hand as she started to walk away. He tugged her back and pulled her down for another kiss. "I can't believe you'd give anyone permission to hurt me."

"Only when you deserve it, my love." She smiled sweetly and slipped out of his grasp. She headed to the door, leaving the brothers alone.

"Well, this was a surprise," Ren said to Vittorio. "You sly dog, you."

Vittorio crossed over to the chair, dropping into it, realizing all hope of being alone and naked with Erika was lost for the time being.

"You are a pain in the ass," he stated to Ren.

"Mmm," Ren nodded. "So how did this all come to pass?"

Vittorio considered not answering him, but decided maybe Ren could be of some help, as unlikely as that seemed.

"What was it like when you met Maggie?"

Ren frowned. "How is this answering my question?"

"It's not. So how did you feel?"

"Most of the time? Hit by a two-by-four—and helpless to stop myself from being with her."

Vittorio nodded.

"Which is clearly where you are too, given that moony look on your face. God, I hope I don't look so ridiculous."

Vittorio didn't bother to answer. "How did you handle all the weirdness of being what we are?"

"As you may recall, I sort of took the pressure off the lampir thing by nearly ruining my relationship with Maggie by being a total idiot."

Vittorio nodded. That had been true. Ren had come up with the worst plan ever to protect Maggie. It still amazed Vittorio that Ren got out of that mess.

"If Erika is the one, she will understand who you are." Ren paused after he spoke, then grimaced. "My God, that sounded so adult, didn't it?"

"I don't know about that."

"So is she the one?"

Vittorio didn't even pause. "Yeah, I think so." Of course, aside from his overwhelming need to feed from her, being a lampir wasn't his major concern.

Vittorio stared at Ren for a moment, then asked, "Do you think Mother is capable of killing anyone?"

"Our mother?"

Vittorio nodded.

"Oh hell, yeah," Ren said. "Definitely."

Chapter 22

Erika wasn't ashamed to admit that she was hiding out in her bedroom, waiting until Ren and Maggie cleared out. It wasn't that she was embarrassed about being caught in the act with Vittorio—okay, that was a little embarrassing—it was a combination of things that had her closeting herself away.

The embarrassment of being naked was one, but what worried her more was what Ren and Maggie would think of this whirlwind relationship. And then there was what she thought about it, which was definitely confusing.

When Vittorio left earlier, and she'd had time to think, with the water from the shower raining down on her and clearing her mind, she decided to just ask him about this other woman.

When she'd asked him outside of Philippe's, he'd seemed genuinely confused by the question. But Erika couldn't help feeling as if someone else had to factor into his hot/cold behavior.

Yes, she'd been determined to talk to him about all of this. Then he'd returned, pretty much crooked his finger, and she was tumbling back into bed with him, or rather into a pile of cushions.

She needed to get a rein on her desires. She did need to understand him better before she got involved. Or more involved. It was clearly too late to claim this was casual.

She pulled on pajamas, which consisted of cotton lounge pants and a matching T-shirt. Then she sprawled on the bed, trying to gather herself before heading back out there.

She was surprised that before long Vittorio appeared in the doorway. He leaned on the door frame, looking slightly dazzled and definitely sheepish.

She pushed up, resting on her elbows. "Ren and Maggie left?"

He nodded. "Yes. Sorry about that."

Erika shrugged, giving him a small smile. "I've gotten to know your brother pretty well since arriving here and I know he's a tease."

"I guess that's one word for him."

Erika studied him for a moment, realizing that now that his sheepishness had diminished, he was pulling away again. There was a distant look in his dark eyes, his arms crossed tightly over his chest.

"What did you two talk about?" she asked.

He shifted, then his arms tightened even more, if that was possible. He was definitely withdrawing.

"Vittorio?"

He blinked at her, lost in his own thoughts.

"Can I ask you something?"

His expression immediately became apprehensive, but he nodded.

"Is there another woman?"

Vittorio didn't know what he'd expected her to ask, but that wasn't it.

"Another woman? No. Why?"

Erika fiddled with the edging of her duvet. "It's just that— well, Philippe told me that you had a woman from your past that you were still involved with."

"No," he said automatically, then wondered who Philippe was. Then his mother, who was on his mind anyway, popped back into his mind.

"Well, he was rather insistent that you were still involved with a woman from your past."

Vittorio took a step toward her, then paused. He did have a woman in his past, one that not only was he involved with, but now Erika might be involved with as well. Ren's immediate affirmation as to the deadliness of their mother was doing nothing to dissuade him from believing his mother was a threat to Erika. But he didn't know what to do.

Instead he asked, "Who is Philippe?"

Erika didn't answer right away. "My psychic," she finally said, her tone flat, as if she expected him to mock her.

"Ah," he said with a smile, but not one of judgment. He moved over to the bed and sat down. Erika didn't move away, but she didn't look at him either. She studied the edge of the duvet where a little of the velvet had worn away.

"Well." He started to open his mouth to explain at least some of the situation, but he couldn't. How could he make any of this understandable for her when he would have to leave out half of his problems? Vampirism, crazed mothers, and other mortal women who likely lost their lives because of him.

So instead, he caught the hand plucking at her bedding. She looked up at him.

"I know you put a lot of stock in Philippe, but I can assure you there is no romantic interest from my past." He pressed a kiss to her knuckles. "You don't have to worry about that."

There were other things to worry about, but he'd take care of those too. When he figured out how.

Erika's stormy eyes searched his, then she nodded. "Okay. Are you hungry?"

She obviously needed a change of topic, which he also welcomed, even though it involved feeding him again. Food was really becoming the bane of his existence.

"Turkey po' boys and chips," she added when he didn't speak right away.

"That sounds great."

She rose and he followed her. She moved around the kitchen, readying plates and the food. He could tell she was still distracted and he didn't want that. When they were together, things should be okay. He'd fed, he was here to keep her safe. It would all work out.

"How did your meeting go with the woman who wanted a sculpture?" he asked, watching as she placed an enormous sandwich on one of the plates. She heaped on a mound of potato chips.

He swallowed, then focused on her.

She actually smiled. "Good. She is interested in a large piece, a full body sculpture of herself."

He raised an eyebrow. "Interesting. What does she want it for?"

She smiled at that, following his train of thought. "For her boyfriend or husband, she didn't say what he was exactly. But anyway—" She wiped her fingers on a napkin after she arranged her plate with food. "She wants a big piece, which means big money for me. That's always good."

He nodded, pleased for her. He knew she wanted her art to be her sole career, and he wanted that for her too.

"So was she nice?"

"Very." She handed him his plate. "Nice, sweet and stunningly beautiful. Easily one of the most beautiful women I've ever seen."

Vittorio raised his eyebrow again. "Well, I doubt she has anything on you."

Erika smiled, although he could tell she didn't believe him. He accepted the proffered plate and leaned in to steal a kiss. She tasted salty and sweet.

She smiled at him when they parted, but he still sensed reservation, uncertainty, in her expression. She still wasn't certain he'd told the truth about the woman from his past. Which he hadn't—completely.

She pulled away from him, returning to the counter to get her own plate. She sat down at her yellow table.

"The best part," she said, waiting for him to take a seat with her, "is that she said I could use her sculpture for my show, which means I can start on hers right away and still have enough pieces for the show."

"That's great."

She nodded, taking a bite of her sandwich. They were both silent for a moment, she chewing, he poking at his chips.

"I don't know how you do it. You have the body of a competitive swimmer, and I've seen you eat virtually nothing."

He looked up at her, a wave of guilt nearly choking him. Oh, he ate. Just not food. Not sure whether it was for her or for himself, a little punishment for what he was, he took a large bite of the sandwich. The bread stuck to the roof of his mouth, turning to salty paste, thick and hard to swallow, but he managed.

She took another bite of her own sandwich.

"Are you willing to start posing tonight?" she asked after a moment.

"Of course," he agreed. He forced down more food, this time a chip. Not much better.

Erika nodded, then smiled. "Good." Suddenly the air changed as some of her uncertainty lifted. Oh, he knew she still had her doubts about him. And she should, but ever selfish, he didn't want her to.

"You think Ren will burst in again?" she asked.

He laughed. "You never know."

Again, they were silent as they both ate. Then Erika stood, leaving her plate on the table and going over to her work area. Vittorio followed, glad the meal was done.

She rearranged the pillows, fixing them after what had happened earlier. His body reacted, recalling how her curves

had felt under his hands. Until they had been rudely interrupted.

He couldn't stop himself from going up behind her and
wrapping his arms around her waist. She froze, but didn't
pull away. In fact, after a moment, she leaned back against
him.

He nuzzled her, kissing the side of her neck.

They remained that way for several moments, pressed
tightly together. Then Erika turned in his arms, meeting his
eyes. He expected her to speak, but instead she pressed her
mouth to his, kissing him sweetly.

"Vittorio," she murmured against his lips. "What are we
doing here?"

He pulled back, without fully releasing her, to meet her
eyes. She wanted to understand their relationship too.

And what could he tell her without making the situation
more involved, more dangerous? Then he reconsidered. Who
was he kidding? They were already involved—completely.

"I'm falling in love with you," he admitted, saying those
words for the first time in his whole eternity. He'd never even
said that to Seraph.

Erika had the dubious honor of being his first.

She stared at him, her gray eyes totally unreadable. Then
they slowly welled, tears making them seem larger, glittering.

"Vittorio," she whispered, and he still wasn't sure what
her reaction meant.

Then she kissed him, the sweet cling of her lips saying
what she felt.

But he was still relieved to hear the words.

"I'm falling for you too."

Her eyes shone with happiness, but instead of a matching
joy, all he felt was shame. He was putting her at risk. The
first woman he'd ever loved, and a woman who loved him
back—he was risking her life.

Chapter 23

Erika's feet might have been on clouds versus a grimy and cracked sidewalk as she made her way to the address Isabel had given her. She was so happy.

After their little talk last night, Vittorio and she had finished what they started among the pillows on her dining room floor. Then she'd started her sculpture of him, working until the wee hours of the night, capturing exactly what she saw in him.

She should have been exhausted, but she was too giddy to be tired. She and Vittorio had gotten off to a shaky start, but he had opened up to her totally last night, and she was hopeful any remaining coldness and aloofness were gone.

She knew she was grinning like a fool, but frankly she just didn't care. Life was good.

She double-checked the street address written in broad, flouncy penmanship on a napkin from the restaurant yesterday. Even Isabel's handwriting was beautiful.

She searched the house closest to her for a street number. A few more houses up. She hastened her steps, then slowed as she reached the place where Isabel's house would be.

Except house was an inadequate word. Isabel's home was a mansion. Surrounded by wrought iron gates and cascades of flowers that still bloomed colorfully even this late into the autumn months.

She pushed open the front gate, the iron creaking as she did so. She gaped up at the beautiful verandas lining both the first and second floors, more flowers draping down over the railings.

She supposed she shouldn't be surprised by the apparent wealth and opulence. Isabel had an air of class that had to have been bred into her at a young age.

She took the steps slowly, still busily admiring every detail of the architecture and the landscaping. It was just lovely.

"Ah, you're here."

Erika paused in the middle of the porch and turned to see Isabel coming, her arms filled with fresh-cut flowers in bright shades of orange and red and yellow.

"I'm not early, am I?"

Isabel's smile was truly breathtaking above the wild array of flowers. "No, no. Right on time. I was out in the garden." She held up the flowers slightly. "I've gotten so little chance to enjoy it over the past years. And the sun is just so lovely." She smiled wider. "I believe I could easily turn into a sun worshipper."

Erika smiled back, finding her impish smile endearing.

"Follow me," Isabel said, stepping past Erika to the large oak front door. She wrestled with the huge bunch of flowers to reach for the doorknob, laughing as she did so, her laughter like the inviting tinkle of chimes.

Erika laughed too, moving around her to get the door.

Isabel thanked her and breezed into the foyer on a cloud of glistening blond hair, gauzy, flowing dress, and scent of wildflowers.

Erika watched her for a moment, again having the strangest sense of recognition.

"Let me drop these off in the kitchen, then we can get to work."

"Great," Erika said, moving to admire the portraits that lined the walls of the foyer. Old paintings of family members maybe. She peeked into the rooms on either side of the entryway. One was a sitting room with gorgeous brocade furniture and immaculate Persian silk rugs. A gilded chandelier with at least fifty small bulbs hung in the center of the room like one perfect earring on a flashy yet stylish woman.

The room on the other side of the foyer was a dining room still equipped with the old pull fans they used in the plantation houses, pre-electricity. A long ornate table took up a majority of the room, surrounded by matching chairs with curved backs and intricate carving.

Erika sighed. She'd love to live in a place like this. The history, the style, the utter magnificence.

They walked farther down the hallway that bisected the house, the walls covered with portraits, most done in dark heavy oils.

"I'll be right back," Isabel said, disappearing through the door into what Erika imagined was the kitchen.

Erika returned her attention to the paintings. Relatives maybe? She tried to identify any similarities between the vivacious blonde in the kitchen and the faces of the past. But interestingly, these people were mostly dark haired, with hard, cold eyes and grim, tightly-closed lips.

Erika grimaced. Definitely not a happy-looking lot.

"Okay." Isabel strolled back into the room and it was as if the sun returned with her. "Are we ready?"

Erika smiled at her and nodded, but she couldn't help asking, "Are these relatives?"

Isabel gave them a cursory glance, then nodded. "Yes. Several generations."

Erika looked back at the dour faces. "Wow."

"Your art supplies arrived this morning, and I had them placed in a room upstairs." Isabel waited at the bottom of the curved staircase, her hand resting on the banister, her smile sweet and patient.

Erika followed, but as she climbed the steps, she looked back to the stern faces watching her from the walls and had the strangest sense they were trying to tell her something.

The room Isabel picked for Erika to work in was perfect, a bright space with pale gold wallpaper and gleaming hardwood floors. Three floor-to-ceiling windows allowed sunlight to flood the room and warm the air.

"This is lovely," she said, wandering into the center and slowly turning to take in everything.

"I thought it would be nice. I love the sunlight here." Isabel walked over to the window, looking out, lifting her face to the rays.

Erika watched her for a moment, wondering if that was the pose she should use to sculpt her. She looked stunning in profile, her long hair in curling waves down her back, gleaming gold in the light, her small, lithe body in a pale blue wispy sundress.

"Did you have any place in mind to pose? Right there is lovely actually," Erika said as she moved to begin opening her bags of art supplies. She spread out a canvas tarp and pulled out a large sheet of the same framing wire she'd set up for Vittorio's sculpture, waiting for Isabel to say what she wanted.

Isabel moved away from the window, a thoughtful look on her face. "I do sort of have an idea of what I might like."

For the first time, Erika noticed she already had a stool in the room. Isabel pulled it to the center of the room. Then she perched on it, her hands behind her back, holding the seat. The pose was oddly sensual and demure at the same time.

Erika considered it for a moment, getting the idea in her mind of how she would create it. Then she nodded. "I think that will look great."

Isabel sat up, a pleased grin on her lovely face. "Good."

Erika smiled back, then returned to her supplies to find the wire cutters and the pliers. Locating them, she spun back around to refocus on the mesh, the design already clear in her mind. She actually made a few snips in the metal, before Isabel caught her attention from the corner of her eye.

Slowly she looked up. Isabel held her pose, except now she

was naked. Utterly and totally nude. Erika's mouth fell open, but she quickly recovered, although apparently not quickly enough.

Isabel straightened up from her pose, her cheeks staining to a bright pink. She clapped her hands over her breasts and crossed her legs.

"I—" Her blush darkened further. "I thought . . . You don't do nudes, do you?"

Erika's eyes remained on her face, both for Isabel's sake and her own. "I do. I just wasn't aware that you were expecting one. But that's—that's just fine."

Isabel relaxed, her hands falling away from her breasts.

Erika nodded, giving her a reassuring look, which was far from what she felt. She really wasn't unnerved by sculpting nudity—but for some reason, in this case, she was caught off guard.

Maybe because Isabel just assumed Erika would know that's what she wanted. Or maybe because Isabel hadn't necessarily struck her as the kind of woman who'd have no reservations about taking her clothes off right away in front of a virtual stranger.

Or maybe it was how utterly stunning she was. That kind of perfection was unnerving.

Erika couldn't quite pinpoint it, but the room suddenly felt uncomfortable. She pushed the weirdness of the moment away, and concentrated on her work.

"So how are you and your beau?" Isabel asked, and Erika suspected she was trying to lessen the awkwardness.

"Really good." Erika glanced up at her, but she quickly looked back down at her work. Why was this so embarrassing? She had done many nudes, from art class on. This shouldn't be so strange.

"Does your beau have a name?"

Erika smiled at that, but she didn't look up from the wires she was twisting together with the pliers. "Indeed he does. A very nice one. Vittorio."

Isabel made an approving humming noise. "That is a nice one. What does he look like?"

"Beautiful." Erika's smile widened at the thought of him. She thought about how he looked last night as they'd lain face to face, just touching each other.

"Beautiful? How so?"

Erika glanced up at Isabel again, but this time not seeing her nudity. Now she only saw Vittorio.

"He has the darkest eyes. The eyes of an old soul. I can just get lost in them. His hair is a shade somewhere between golden brown and honeyed blond. It's long, down to his shoulders." She touched her own to demonstrate the length. "And he has the sweetest smile. A gentle smile."

Erika fought back the urge to sigh. She really was crazy about the man. Totally mad for him.

And he'd said he was falling for her. That idea had the ability to make her instantly euphoric. She grinned to herself as she clipped more of the metal threading, then bent and molded the mesh.

She glanced up to see if she was getting the size and general form right. Isabel regarded her, her eyes narrowed, as if she was speculating about something not necessarily pleasant. But then the expression disappeared, and Erika wondered if she'd even seen it. But Philippe's warning about a dangerous stranger suddenly popped into her mind. Then she dismissed the idea. Isabel was turning out to be a tad odd—but not dangerous.

"He does sound lovely," she said.

"What about you? What is your partner like?"

"Partner," Isabel laughed. "That sounds so formal. So unemotional. My love is just that. The love of my life. My other half, my world."

Erika considered her words. Vittorio felt like her other half too, she understood that. He made her feel safe, protected, loved. When they were together, she just felt whole and right.

"Yes. Vittorio is like that to me too. Or at least he's becoming that way, very quickly."

"Isn't that lovely," Isabel said, her voice low and filled with emotion.

Erika threw her a quick smile, then concentrated on her work. Isabel fell silent, allowing Erika to give all her attention to manipulating the metal into the framework she wanted.

And the atmosphere suddenly felt less awkward, which was good.

Orabella watched Erika work, the way her hands molded the metal wiring. Those same hands had touched her son. Stroked him, caressed him. Satisfied him.

She wondered if the little whore had used those pink lips to satisfy him. The idea enraged her. And she wanted to just kill her now. But she couldn't—yet.

She had to convince Maksim to cooperate with her plan. Which would not be easy. Her demon lover was very, very angry. And an angry demon was ever so hard to get to be obliging. Such ornery creatures.

But once she got him to agree, which he'd soon see was his only way out of her bedroom, he'd do whatever she asked. And then she would have what she needed to lure Vittorio back to her. She'd then deal with this pathetic mortal.

She could bide her time, she had for this long. And she was so close to getting what she wanted. It wouldn't do to lose her temper and act rashly.

She needed to have her lure for Vittorio in place before Erika's awful accident occurred.

Besides, it would be nice to have a sculpture of herself. A nice reminder of the woman she defeated to get her son back.

Erika dashed down the sidewalk, some of the giddiness she'd felt earlier in the day replaced by exhaustion. Isabel had been insistent that they work until the upstairs room lost all of its natural light.

Now it was already dark and because of her stupid cell phone, which was dead when she actually needed it, as usual, she hadn't been able to contact Vittorio all day. He was probably wondering where she could be. He seemed to worry. Although last night was the first night in days she hadn't had those nightmares. So maybe he'd stop fretting.

She unlocked her door to be greeted by Ren and Maggie sitting on her sofa. They both turned to look at her as she stepped into the room.

"Hey," she greeted, "what are you guys doing here?"

"We don't know," Ren said.

Maggie shrugged, forced to agree with that assessment.

Erika frowned. "Where's Vittorio?"

"We don't know," Maggie said. "He just asked us to wait here. For you to come home."

"And he tore out of here like the hounds of hell were after him," Ren stated.

Maggie seemed to sense Erika's alarm at that description, because she quickly added, "He was in a rush, but it wasn't that bad."

"How long ago did he leave?"

"Not too long ago," Maggie said. "How was your day?"

"Fine," Erika said distractedly, going back to the front door to peer out. Dark filled most of the courtyard now.

"Are you sure he was okay?"

"Sure," Maggie said.

"As okay as he ever is," Ren said, which was followed with an "oomph" as Maggie elbowed him.

Erika frowned. "Then why did he have you wait here for me?"

Ren and Maggie looked at each other, clearly as confused as she was.

"What's going on?" Erika asked, moving over to the sofa.

But before either of her friends could answer, the door opened and Vittorio barged in.

"I should have gotten—" His words halted as he spotted Erika standing there.

"You're back." His tense stance relaxed instantly.

"I am," she said. "What should you have gotten?"

Vittorio glanced at his brother and sister-in-law, then back to her. Why did she get the feeling everyone was struggling for answers, not just her?

"I should have gotten the address of where you were working," he finally admitted, when it was clear that Ren and Maggie weren't going to provide him with another excuse.

"Okay," Erika agreed, "I probably should have told you where I was, just in case. But this isn't the first time you've been panicked when you couldn't find me. Why?"

"Umm," Vittorio shifted from one foot to the other, "I'm—"

"He's just a huge worrywart," Ren said, shaking his head. "He does the same crap to me." He looked at his brother. "You got to mellow out, dude."

Vittorio nodded. "I know."

Erika looked back and forth between the brothers, trying to understand what was going on. She wasn't a fool. Vittorio's agitation when he came into the apartment went beyond merely worrying. He actually seemed scared.

Of what?

"Maggie, Ren, I think I need to talk to Vittorio alone."

Chapter 24

If Erika thought her friends would just get up and leave, she was sadly mistaken. Ren rose, but instead of leaving as she asked, he turned to Vittorio.

"Little brother, I think you need to chat with me for a minute."

Vittorio looked toward Erika and evidently decided Ren's questions would be easier to deal with.

"I'll be right back," he told her. Erika nodded. She could wait, but she would still have plenty of questions for him.

"Maggie, why don't you stay with Erika," Ren suggested.

The two brothers exited the apartment, going out into the darkness.

Erika watched them until they stopped in the courtyard, facing each other. She crossed over to the sofa, dropping down beside Maggie.

"Was he really worried about me?" she asked Maggie.

Maggie nodded, but added, "He is a worrier. He watches out for Ren all the time. In fact, if he didn't, Ren and I might not be together now."

Erika considered that. "But he seems almost afraid for me when I'm not in his sight."

"These boys are just a little different than your typical guys."

Erika already knew that. Vittorio was different from her

on so many levels. She'd never been so crazy about, so attracted to, and so cared for by another boyfriend. But instead of saying all those things—which just sounded too extreme for a relationship that was only a few days old—she asked, "How so?"

Maggie didn't answer right away, clearly looking for the right words. "They are just different." Not exactly the explanation Erika hoped she'd get. "But they are such good guys. Amazing, really."

Erika didn't need to be sold on that idea. She'd seen for months now what a good and kind and loving partner Ren was for Maggie. He was all the things her friend needed. And Erika certainly didn't need to be told how special Vittorio was.

She knew she was already in love with him. And maybe that was what had her feeling as scared about his reaction as he'd been about her being gone all day.

After all, she'd probably be nervous if he was gone all day and she didn't know where he was. New Orleans could be a dangerous city. And he was a protective guy—not controlling, but cautious.

"Maggie, I think Vittorio is the prince that Philippe kept predicting I'd meet."

Erika waited for Maggie to express the same reservations Jo had about the idea. But Maggie only said, "I know you've wondered about that." She moved to hug Erika. "And I think it's wonderful. And always remember these are men who would never hurt you. No matter what."

Erika frowned, wondering why Maggie would even say that, but before she could ask, Maggie pulled away.

"Did you tell Jo? Your dad?"

"I haven't talked to my dad," Erika said, "but I did tell Jo. She didn't seem too happy about it."

Maggie frowned. "I'm sure she is. Maybe she's just feeling left out. It's got to be hard for her to still be in D.C., while we are here. And seeing brothers, no less."

Erika hadn't thought about that.

"Maggie, do you know if Vittorio has a girlfriend that he's still in touch with?"

Maggie thought about it. "No. Not that I've ever heard about. Why?"

Erika shook her head, feeling silly and insecure for asking. He'd told her more than once there was no other woman, but still she had a niggling feeling there was. She couldn't say why.

"It's just something Philippe told me. But I don't think it can be true."

"I don't think it is. Ren mentioned he'd been seeing some-one years ago, but not since. In fact, he often commented to me that Vittorio didn't usually involve himself with women, period."

Erika thought about that. There had been a woman, but years ago. Yet, he'd stayed away from women since. That sounded like someone who was still emotionally involved.

She wondered if she could get this woman's name. Just to see. She put an end to that train of thought. Here she was, finding Vittorio's protectiveness weird, yet she was consider-ing acting like a jealous lover. Tracking down past girlfriends.

Maybe they both needed to discuss things, before both their behaviors got stranger.

"What the hell are you doing?" Ren asked Vittorio as soon as they were in the courtyard and out of earshot.

"What do you mean?" Was Ren concerned because he shared Vittorio's concern about Erika, or because Vittorio was deeply involved with Maggie's friend?

"Why are you acting like a panicked, controlling aristo-crat?"

"I'm not," Vittorio said, not necessarily disagreeing with the panicked part. When the sun set and Erika wasn't back, he of course had grown concerned. Perhaps panicked.

But he had no intention of trying to control her. Only protect her. And he supposed the aristocrat thing could apply too. After all, he was born into royalty, although he didn't think many of those aristocratic behaviors remained after all these years.

"Okay," he admitted. "I was worried about her."

"Why?" Ren asked.

Where to start? Vittorio guessed it was best just to jump in. "I came back here to do some research. Remember when I worked with drug addicts here?"

Ren frowned. "No. Not really."

Vittorio fought the urge to roll his eyes. "Well, I did. And I continued to do so for a while in other cities. When you misunderstood the outcome of Mother's curse, I realized that maybe what you considered your curse was actually my curse. Maybe the women I helped were being killed because of our mother. Many of the women I worked with have passed away."

"Okay," Ren said, "but they were drug addicts—so their deaths were not all that unusual."

"True, which is why it took me a while to realize just how many of them had died. Twenty-six in as many years. That's high, even for the lifestyles they led."

Ren nodded. "I suppose that is."

"I really believe Mother killed these women."

"Why?" Ren asked.

"Because she's jealous and petty and always wanted me to herself."

"That is true," Ren agreed. "And I think she's more than capable of murder."

"So do I," Vittorio said.

"And you are worried that she might try to hurt Erika?"

Vittorio nodded.

"That makes sense."

Ren's agreement didn't make Vittorio feel better. "But the problem is, I don't know how to stop her."

"A stake through the heart could work," Ren said.

Vittorio had thought about old-school tactics like that one, but the truth was, he didn't think he could bring himself to kill his own mother. Evil as she may be. Something about killing her made him feel as if he would be becoming just like her.

But he didn't say that to Ren. Ren wouldn't understand. Then again, Orabella had never been any sort of mother to him. Not that she'd been much better to Vittorio.

But Orabella did fancy herself a loving mother to her second son. Even if it was a weird love, to say the least.

"So are you using Erika as bait to draw Mother out?"

"No!" Vittorio cried. "I wouldn't do that."

"But it could work—and then we could be rid of the crazy old bat—hey, that's quite literal now." Ren refocused. "We could be rid of her forever." He smiled at the prospect.

"I'm not using Erika to lure her out. I'm trying to keep her safe from Mother while I try to have a relationship with her."

Ren nodded. "Well, if that's the case, then you know you can count on Maggie and me to help as well. None of us will let anything happen to her."

"Thank you," Vittorio said honestly. It did make him feel better to have their support. Three vampires against one seemed like decent odds. Even if the one was bat-shit crazy.

"She will be okay," Ren assured him. "But you do need a plan if Mother tries anything."

Vittorio knew that. He just didn't know what the plan could be. And was luring his mother out and getting rid of her once and for all the only way to protect Erika? That seemed risky, and he couldn't think of using Erika as bait.

But he knew he did have to know the truth. What was Mother capable of?

"She's truly vile."

Maksim lolled on the bed, an arm resting behind his head, his foot wiggling to some unheard beat. He stared at the ceiling like he had been for hours. Many long, long hours.

"I found her to be a very sweet girl," he said placidly. "And like Vittorio, I've actually been inside her. Well, her head, that is."

Orabella made a noise close to that of a growl, and Maksim didn't suppress his smile. If he was going to be trapped here indefinitely at least he could get some entertainment out of goading her. His smile quickly faded. It wasn't much of a consolation, really.

"She's wretched, weak, and pathetic," Orabella said, not masking her venom—there wasn't much point now. "Just like all mortals."

Maksim turned his head to look at her where she sat on a chair in the bedroom doorway, being ever so careful not to scuff a break in the iron filings lining the floor.

"You seem to forget you were a mortal once too."

She made another noise. "Well be that as it may, I was certainly never one so worthless and silly."

"I think you are mistaking kindness for silliness and goodness for weakness."

"Maksim," she said sharply, clearly irritated as he hoped she would be, "I don't have time to chat. And I'm sure you are tired of having so much time on your hands. So let's get down to what I want from you."

Maksim rolled over onto his side, resting his head on his hand. "You didn't already do that?"

"Oh, I did," she said with a sweet smile. "Thank you. But I have more that I want. And if I get it, I'll let you go."

"If you let me go, I think I'd be forced to hurt you. Even as a demon, I'm not a big fan of hurting women, but in your case, I'm not sure you even constitute a woman."

She made a tsking noise. "Insults really aren't going to help your cause."

He didn't react. He just waited for her to continue, which she did.

"As you have had time to figure out, I've found the spell that vampires can use to basically create a sunscreen."

Yes, he had figured that out. Demon semen, when taken internally, acted as a heat repellent and sunscreen, keeping vampires safe from sunlight.

After all, something kept demons from burning up in the bowels of hell. It just happened that not many knew what it was. Yet, Orabella had figured it out. A fact that irked him to no end. He had really underestimated her.

And Maksim had also had time to figure out where she might have discovered such a spell.

"So you know my sister, Ellina?"

"I've met her," Orabella said. "Nice girl. And a great writer. It was in her research that I found this spell. I'd heard rumors of it, of course. But Ellina actually had the spell written down. As part of a book on demon lore."

Now that, Maksim hadn't known. He guessed Ellina probably had something do with Orabella finding the spell, but he hadn't known she was writing a book. About demons, no less.

"Which leads me back to what I need from you. I need a female demon who is strong enough to make this spell work on Vittorio."

That was right. The spell would only work with a demon from the fifth circle of hell downward. And those demons were always harder to summon. The farther down the more workload a demon had. Hell was a busy place with quite an involved system of delegation. Demons didn't have time for trifling conjurers.

"So you want me to summon a demon for you?"

"Exactly. And as soon as you do, I'll let you go," Orabella promised.

Maksim raised an eyebrow. "You have to know I will kill you if I get out of here."

"Temper, temper," she said to him. "Now is that going to get you released? I think not."

"So say I help you do this, what's the final outcome for you?"

"I get to walk in the sunlight again with my son."

"Your son?"

Orabella smiled, a broad grin filled with desire. "Yes. Vittorio is my son and my only true love."

Maksim actually shuddered. God, this chick just got creepier and creepier.

"You are in love with your own son?"

Orabella blinked at him, obviously confused by his expression of disgust. But hell, even a demon had limits. And the romantic love of your own child definitely was one of them.

His grimace deepened.

"Yes. Vittorio is my perfect man. Begat from me. Part of my soul, my body, my heart.

Maksim found he couldn't keep his opinion to himself any longer. "That is truly repugnant, and I will not help you in any way. You are going to have to figure out how to summon your own demon."

Orabella practically shrieked, "*I can't!* And I won't let you leave here if you don't do it for me."

Maksim flipped onto his back again, staring up at the very, very familiar ceiling. "That's fine. I'm cool with just hanging out here. Relaxing."

She made another discordant, frustrated noise. And he could feel the daggers her eyes were throwing in his direction. He ignored them. He could hold out as long as he needed to. Hell, he'd done time in the abyss. Lounging around on a bed with lots of pillows, comfy bedding and air conditioning wasn't close to the worst that he'd suffered.

And he'd be damned if he'd help this crazy bitch. Of course, that was after the fact, being damned already.

"You think you can out-wait me, but we'll see about that," Orabella finally said, and he heard the scrape of her chair's legs on the wooden floor as she rose.

"You will give in to me eventually."

He didn't respond, but they'd just see about that.

Chapter 25

"I think we need that talk now," Vittorio said to Erika as soon as he stepped back into her apartment. He half expected her to be furious and not want to talk, considering he'd spoken with Ren first.

But she simply nodded.

"Okay," Maggie said, quickly rising from the sofa and heading toward Ren, who waited in the doorway. "See you later then."

Erika waved to them, remaining where she was on the sofa.

Vittorio walked over to her, taking the place Maggie had just vacated. He wanted to pull Erika into his arms, but he didn't. She deserved some sort of explanation for his erratic behavior. And from the firm set of her jaw and the serious glint in her eyes, she wasn't going to accept anything less.

"I'm sorry I panicked like I did."

"Why did you?" she asked.

What could he say? He wasn't willing to tell her about his mother. He supposed that would be the best defense, to just give her the truth, but how could he make her understand that his mother wasn't like the average matron of the family. To do that, he'd have to reveal more than he wanted to about himself.

Yet, what was holding him back? He wanted to be with

Erika—forever. So eventually he'd have to tell her the truth. But he couldn't. Not yet.

"I guess it's true what Ren said, I'm a big worrier. I had a different"—*and that was putting it mildly*—"childhood, and I guess that's made me wary." All of that was true, as close to the truth as he could get without really saying anything.

But he should have known that explanation was only going to raise further questions.

"What was your childhood like?"

Vittorio had a hard time meeting Erika's eyes, because he knew that serious, no-nonsense look was gone, replaced by compassion.

"I had a different"—*there was that word again*—"family. And my childhood was just rather strange."

Of course it wasn't exactly his childhood that had him messed up. Oh, that hadn't helped him out either, but it was the time after his undeath that had him truly mixed up.

"How so?"

He shook his head, unsure, unable to tell her. He met her eyes, and realized what was holding him back. He couldn't bear to see her looking at him with the same fear other women had. Women from the early days of his vampirism who had seen him for what he was. He couldn't go back there.

"I don't want to talk about it," he said. "But just know when I get concerned for you, it's because I care so much about you."

Erika wanted to pressure him to tell her more. She knew that whatever he had gone through in his past had created all the shifts she saw in his personality. All the worries that plagued him, which she did understand. Hadn't she fretted after her mother died? She was sure she was going to lose more people she loved. She didn't understand what he'd been through, but she did understand that kind of irrational, consuming worry.

And she did believe his reactions tonight were out of concern, not control. That alone was enough to make her willing to wait and gradually learn all there was to know about him. When he was ready to share.

"Okay," she said, reaching out to capture his hand. She squeezed his fingers in reassurance, and he did the same in response.

They were silent for a moment, then she just wanted to make things right. Make him smile and relax and realize she was there for him, however he wanted her.

"So the first day of sculpting Isabel went well," she said.

He immediately lost a little of the haunted look that had plagued him since he came back into her place.

"Oh yeah? She was a good subject?"

She nodded. "Very good. A very nude one, but very good."

"Nude? Really?"

Erika smiled at his stunned expression. "Yep. Totally."

"Did you know that was how she wanted the sculpture done?"

"Not until she'd already stripped down."

Vittorio chuckled. So did she, and suddenly the air felt much lighter.

"And I thought I was doing something scandalous the way I was posing for you."

Erika remembered last night and how he'd stretched out among the cushions, a sheet draped over his lap, his hair cascading around his broad shoulders. He'd been beautiful and sensual and oddly heartbreaking, not scandalous.

"You aren't embarrassed about it, are you?"

He considered it for a moment, then shook his head. "No, I actually quite enjoyed it."

"Good. Want to start again?"

"I think I need some warming up first."

She grinned, giving him a speculative look. "How would you like to warm up?"

He tugged her hand, which he still held, drawing her closer to him on the sofa. His mouth found her, showing her in nips and sweeps of his tongue what he'd like to do to warm him up. It was certainly warming her up.

She linked her arms around his neck, her fingers sinking into the thick silkiness of his hair.

"So did you spend the night with your beau?"

Erika glanced up at Isabel, both to acknowledge her question and to study the exact curve of her cheek. She looked back to the sculpture, using her fingers to shape the gentle fullness.

"I did. We are pretty much living together." She smiled, mostly to herself. The past couple of weeks had fallen into a wonderful routine. During the day she met with Isabel, which was always an experience, and she worked on her sculpture. Then at night she was with Vittorio, sculpting him, making love with him, learning about his talents as a musician. Learning everything she could, although she always sensed there was still a barrier there. Things he didn't tell her.

"Living together? In sin?"

Erika glanced up again, not sure if Isabel was disapproving or not.

Then the lovely blonde grinned. "How delicious."

Erika chuckled. "You know, I've never asked, are you and your partner married?"

Isabel smiled. A strange, enigmatic little smile that Erika had long since given up trying to decipher.

"My love and I are joined in every way two people can be. We are one."

Erika nodded, turning her attention back to her work. She was becoming accustomed to Isabel's overly dramatic way of answering questions. Not to mention, she often didn't really answer them, like now. So Erika chose to believe they were indeed married.

"And what of you? Do you intend to marry this love of yours? Do you think he'd be interested in marrying you?"

Ah, and here was another of Isabel's interesting traits. For all the questions she didn't directly answer, she didn't mind asking pointed ones of Erika.

"I haven't thought that far ahead," she told the blonde as she smeared more wet clay on the torso of the sculpture. "Maybe one day."

"Yet, you are willing to live with him? Have relations with him?"

Erika glanced up, giving the woman a slight, unashamed shrug. "Yes, I guess I am."

"And you don't feel any shame in it?"

"Isabel, I'm in love with him, and he is with me. That's enough for now."

Erika had to admit she was growing tired of answering Isabel's relentless questions about Vittorio. The woman was inordinately intrigued by their relationship.

Of course, Isabel had no sense of personal privacy. She didn't like to answer direct questions, but she had no problem telling Erika all about the love of her life, expounding on all his amazing attributes. Beauty, intelligence, kindness—although she often lamented that he was too generous and considerate for his own good.

Erika also realized Isabel never actually said her lover's name. She always referred to him as "the love of her life," "her lover," "her soul mate." Erika was even beginning to wonder if this man really existed. There was something distinctly delusional about the woman.

She'd also stopped seeing Isabel as the stunning beauty she once had. There was a hardness to her that Erika hadn't noted at first. And a coldness to her eyes. Again Phillipe's warning returned to her mind—Erika had to admit she would be glad when she was done with this project.

And she would be finished soon. This afternoon, to be exact, and just in time for the show. And while she was still pleased to have her first commission, she was getting a little tired—and uncomfortable, frankly—with Isabel's company.

She had a hard time seeing Isabel as "evil"—but "odd" certainly fit.

"We will be done today," she said, stepping back from the piece to study her work.

"Today?"

Erika nodded. "Yes—and just in the nick of time. I will have to let this set tonight and tomorrow, and then hopefully I can get one of the people from the gallery to move it over there. My show opens Friday night."

"I know," Isabel said, her voice sharp.

Erika frowned. She truly didn't understand this woman. She could appear so sweet, then shades of a creature acerbic and unpleasant seemed to lurk beneath her pretty surface.

"I'm sorry," Isabel added, clearly aware that she'd sounded sharp. "I guess I'm just nervous about the whole thing. To be a part of your show, that is such a great compliment. And my darling will be so surprised."

Erika forced a smile, letting the previous reaction go. "So I will finally get to meet him."

Isabel gave her an impish, almost sly smile. "Yes, you will."

Vittorio stretched among Erika's soft bedding, waking to hear her out in the kitchen. Dishes clattered, and he could hear her muffled voice. Probably talking to her eerie cat.

He smiled, not about the cat, but pleased Erika was home already. She usually came in after he'd already risen for the night. It was nice to have her here when he awoke.

He flung his legs over the side of the bed and padded down the hallway, coming up behind her and pulling her back against him. Unfortunately his embrace startled her and she dropped the coffee mug she was holding, the ceramic clashing to the floor and smashing.

"I'm sorry," he apologized, releasing her to bend and gather the broken pieces.

Erika, who had become quite accustomed to and tolerant

of his stealthy appearances, threw him an amused, yet long-suffering look.

"I should be used to your creeping by now," she said, squatting to help pick up the pieces. She leaned over and kissed his cheek.

"You're in a good mood tonight."

She smiled. "I am. I finished my commission piece today. And not a moment too soon."

"Isabel is still being strange?"

Erika straightened and placed the broken pottery in the trash can under the sink. "She is odd. I can never quite pinpoint what it is about her, but she'd a weird duck."

Vittorio moved beside her to cast away the fragments he'd cleaned up. "I guess you'll get to see for yourself on Friday." He leaned in and stole a kiss. "I can't wait. And I can't wait to see all your work displayed in a gallery."

She grinned. "Me too. I've wanted this for so long."

"Are you nervous?"

"A little. But mostly excited."

"Really? Excited tends to work out well for me." She laughed and he kissed her again, her giggle fading into a pleased moan.

But the kiss was interrupted by a knock at the door. They reluctantly moved apart, and glanced at the door.

"It's probably Ren," Vittorio muttered. "The pest."

Erika chuckled. "He does have impeccable timing."

Vittorio had to agree with that one. In the past couple weeks that Erika and he had been living together, Ren had interrupted them on the build-up to, or in one case right in the middle of, sex at least three times. Which delighted his warped brother to no end.

Then again, to be fair, it wasn't terribly hard to interrupt them. They were insatiable for each other. And while Vittorio still struggled with his desire to take her energy, he was handling it, taking only a little now and then to satisfy himself.

Recently he felt a new desire—he wanted to give his energy to her. But thus far he hadn't.

Another rap sounded, and Erika pulled away from him to go answer it. As soon as the door was opened, Erika squealed, the sound shocking Vittorio and sending him around the kitchen table toward her.

But when he got closer, he realized Erika was not scared. She was pleased. She hugged the person on the other side of the door, the two laughing and rocking. Vittorio just watched, curious about who this could be.

When the two parted, he realized this must be Erika's friend, Jo. He'd met her at the same time he'd met Erika, but honestly, he didn't recall much about her. He'd been too entranced by Erika.

"When did you get in? You were supposed to call," Erika admonished her friend.

"I've been trying to call you for three days."

Erika groaned. "I really need to get a new cell phone. Mine is a piece of junk."

"Well, I e-mailed too. Do you ever check it?" Jo narrowed a glare at her.

"Not much," Erika admitted. "But I can't believe I forgot anyway. I don't know where my mind is."

"Don't worry about it," Jo said easily. "Maggie knew I was coming and left a key for me out front. And she informed me exactly where your mind is most of the time these days."

As soon as she said that, Jo spotted Vittorio over Erika's shoulder. Her cheeks stained pink, but she managed a smile. "Hi."

Erika glanced back at Vittorio. Her cheeks grew pink as well. Who knew blushes were contagious.

He stepped forward, holding out his hand. "Hi, you must be Jo."

Jo shook his hand. "And you are Vittorio."

He nodded.

Then the apartment became a whirlwind of rolled-in luggage, chattering, laughter, some wine. Vittorio simply watched, enjoying how happy Erika was to see her friend, joining in, but also letting the two friends get caught up.

"So let's go," Jo suddenly said, looking at her watch.

"Where?" Erika asked.

"Down to the bar where Maggie and Ren are playing. She made me promise we'd come see them. And I really want to see Maggie working the keyboards for a Bourbon Street rock band."

"I've wanted to see her too," Erika said, and Vittorio didn't miss Jo's surprised look.

"You haven't seen her yet? She's been playing with The Impalers for a few weeks, hasn't she?" Jo asked.

Erika nodded, looking embarrassed. "She has, it just seems like time has gotten away from me recently." She glanced at Vittorio and blushed, and he knew she was thinking about what had kept her so busy the past week.

They'd definitely been the best weeks of his life. Making love, watching Erika as she sculpted him, making love some more. Oh yeah, it had been perfect.

But he couldn't keep her locked away forever. That wasn't realistic no matter how appealing. And comforting.

But the back of his neck prickled at the idea of their first major outing being in a crowded bar on Bourbon. What if his mother was near? What if he lost sight of Erika?

Yet, he couldn't think of anything to dissuade her that sounded even mildly reasonable. One of her best friends was in town, of course they'd go out. He couldn't cut her off from the world forever.

"Do you want to go?" he asked, even as every fiber in his body wanted to talk her out of the idea.

She gave him a huge smile that made him feel even guiltier. "I'd love to," she said. "I just need to get ready."

"Me too," Jo said, and both women hurried off to get all

gussied up for a night out on the town. And Vittorio sat there feeling like he wanted nothing more than to whisk Erika away to some secluded, and safe, place.

"God, I love Bourbon Street," Jo said, taking a sip of her hand grenade, which came in a large, tall, fluorescent green cup, the bottom shaped like a grenade.

Erika laughed, sipping her own far more subtle lite beer in a plastic tumbler. Vittorio held a drink, a whiskey and water, but his cup was nearly full. He'd been too busy casting nervous glances around the crowded bar to actually think about his drink.

Erika leaned toward him and asked in a low voice, "Are you okay?"

He blinked, like he was being pulled back from some faraway place. "Yes. Just a little tired." He took a swallow of his drink, offered her a smile, then cast a look around the bar again.

She frowned, but before she could question him further, Jo caught her hand and dragged her out to the floor in front of the stage, where Ren belted out the chorus to "Carry On Wayward Son," and Maggie played the keyboards, grinning like she'd never been happier.

Jo started singing along, nudging Erika with her shoulder to join in, which she did. Although she kept sneaking peeks at Vittorio. Something was definitely wrong.

Again he glanced around the room, looking decidedly agitated, as if he expected to run into someone he really didn't want to see.

Even though she told herself not to read into it, her thoughts went back to Philippe's prediction about a woman from his past. He'd denied it, but Philippe had been too accurate, and Vittorio was acting strange.

In fact, he'd been a bit odd about going out in general. A few times she'd suggested going out to dinner, and while he didn't ever say no, he always seemed to find a way to distract her from the idea. Always in a very enjoyable way, which she'd liked very much, so it hadn't really mattered that they never seemed to leave her apartment. But she had noticed.

"So what do you think?" Maggie said, and only then did Erika even notice the music had stopped and the band was on break.

"You were great," Erika said, meaning it, even though she'd been distracted.

"You look so good up there," Jo said, hugging their friend. "You look so happy."

"I am," Maggie beamed, her flushed cheeks and sparkling eyes making her absolutely radiant.

"She's a rock goddess," Ren said, coming up beside Maggie and looping his arm around her shoulder. "And I'm the one who gets to take her home every night."

Maggie made a face and her rosy cheeks brightened further, which just made her look cuter. Ren stole a kiss, then excused himself to go talk to Vittorio.

"What's going on with Vittorio?" Maggie asked, regarding him through the crowd.

"He seems edgy," Jo commented.

Erika nodded, then shrugged. "I don't know." He definitely did seem ill at ease, but she didn't understand why. After all, he'd played with The Impalers for several years, so he had to be used to the Bourbon Street scene. And she did wonder if he'd been avoiding public places—and if it was because of her.

Or someone else.

She tried to put those kinds of ideas out of her head and focus on what her friends were saying. She really did.

"Will you chill and have another drink or something?"

Vittorio stopped scanning the bar, and looked at his brother. Ren frowned, looking mildly exasperated.

"Why?" Vittorio asked.

"Because you are being ridiculous. Mother isn't going to attack Erika in a crowded bar with you, me and two of

Erika's closest friends around. Mother likes success, and that would be a colossal failure."

Vittorio supposed Ren was right.

"Not to mention," Ren said, "Erika is clearly aware of your weird behavior."

Vittorio looked at where Erika danced with her friends to the music played by a DJ. She slid him a sidelong glance, but when she realized he was watching her, her eyes darted away as if she was uncomfortable to be caught regarding him. Not the reaction he expected. His anxiety was affecting her. He didn't want that. Not when she should be out with her friends, celebrating Jo being here, celebrating her art show. Hell, celebrating their relationship, which was the best and potentially the worst thing that had ever happened to him.

"So," Ren said, watching the girls as they danced and chatted, a half-smile on his own lips, a drink held absently in his hand. "What makes you think Mother is even around, aware of your relationship with Erika, and willing to kill to end your happiness?" He shot a look at Vittorio.

"I'm not sure. But I do know there has been a lot of death around me, and I know Mother is a jealous woman."

Ren nodded. "But maybe that was all coincidence. I mean, the other women were rough, right? With dangerous habits and hard lives?"

Vittorio nodded. "They were." Except Julianne. She had been unhappy with her life, but he still couldn't quite bring himself to believe she'd killed herself. But it wasn't beyond the realm of possibility.

"At any rate, she's safe here tonight. So why don't you just enjoy yourself." Ren downed his drink, then moved to join the women.

Vittorio watched them. They danced and laughed and clearly shared an easy companionship that didn't include worry.

No, that wasn't quite true. Erika kept directing covert glances in his direction, and he saw confusion and worry in the brief looks.

The realization that his behavior was affecting her good time and making her more focused on him than her friends bothered him. In effect, he was letting his mother affect their relationship without even being there.

And, Ren had a point. Vittorio didn't have any definitive proof that their mother had killed those women. It was still only a hunch. And nothing strange had happened to make him think she was here and aware of Erika.

As he strode toward Erika and her friends, he decided he was being too cautious. And he needed to loosen up. Which was what Ren always said, and had said again here tonight.

God, he hated when his brother was right.

But as he stopped beside Erika and smiled at her, and she smiled back, seeming very pleased he'd joined the group, Vittorio realized he was being too cautious.

Erika was perfectly safe.

Chapter 26

"Hello, lovey."

Maksim gritted his teeth at the lilting sound of Orabella's voice in the doorway. He kept his back to her, not bothering to acknowledge her presence. He'd learned over the past few weeks that she'd just keep on chattering, no matter what he did.

"How are you today? Are you hungry?"

He was starving. Demons didn't have to eat to survive. But that didn't mean he didn't still crave food. And he ate when he was bored. And this was about as boring as anything got. He'd been trapped in this room, on this bed, for days. And days. He was going mad.

"Well, you'll be pleased to know this is all almost over."

That got his attention. He rolled over onto his back and sat up. "You've finally realized I won't help you, have you?"

"Yes." Orabella nodded from her usual spot in the doorway. As was often her custom, she wore white, obviously an odd little bit of irony she enjoyed. Although he noted her skin had a darker glow than it had had before. She was clearly enjoying the sunlight these days.

He gritted his teeth, but otherwise hid his irritation. "So are you going to be reasonable and let me go now? I promise you I will be reasonable too." Oh yeah, the punishment he had in mind seemed perfectly reasonable to him.

But she startled him out of his fantasies of a torturous retribu-tion, saying, "No, silly, of course I'm not going to release you. I just thought you'd like to know that I no longer need your help."

He glared at her, then snorted at her announcement. She didn't have the ability to conjure the kind of demon she needed for her purposes. She'd just lucked into getting him. Using both him and his sister like pawns.

"Where is my sister?" he demanded again.

She tilted her head, her blond hair falling forward over her shoulder. "I've told you before, I have no idea. I got what I needed from her—the spell and the access to you, and I was done with her. You know that."

Yes, that irked him to no end that she'd played him so eas-ily. Leaving her name in Ellina's apartment. He still didn't know why there had been a second scrap of paper with Vit-torio's name on it, but now he knew Orabella did leave her name behind. To get him to come to her.

"So how exactly do you think you are going to conjure a demon of that kind of power? She will never come to you."

"Well, you did," she said sweetly, obviously unable to re-sist the jibe.

He gritted his teeth. They were going to be worn down to nubs if this continued much longer. But again, he didn't let her see he was irked. Beyond irked.

"So what is this brilliant plan?" he managed to ask.

Orabella sighed. "Well, you know it was very, very hard to think of anything that might lure a high-powered demon to me. Not all of them are so oversexed and underobservant as you, my dear."

The teeth. Gritting.

"But then it dawned on me, I needed to discover the most generous and yet evil gift I could bestow on a powerful demon. And it came to me. A human sacrifice."

She giggled with glee and Maksim nearly groaned. Of course the little bitch had hit on the one thing, sans magic, that she could do to summon a demon.

In fact, he knew the very demon who couldn't refuse an offering like that. Aosoth. She'd be there in a heartbeat and do whatever bidding necessary to see a good old-fashioned sacrifice.

"And the beauty of this idea is it really kills two birds with one stone. I show my son that I'm willing to do anything for his love. And I get rid of that pesky mortal whore, who is somehow convincing my lovely son she is worthy of him."

She laughed again. "Brilliant, isn't it?"

Maksim just stared at her. This chick was nuts, yet somehow she had managed to figure out a way to call a demon to her.

He doubted Vittorio would agree to the rest of it. But Orabella would have a demon in her control and Erika would be dead.

He dropped back onto the mattress and closed his eyes. This had to be a gigantic joke.

Erika curled against Vittorio, grinning. She hadn't thought it would be possible to feel more for this man than she already did, but she was wrong. She nuzzled her cheek against the smoothness of his chest. Last night and this evening had been perfect.

After his initial nervousness, or whatever had been bothering him at the bar, passed, he'd joined her and Jo. He danced a little—although it was clear that wasn't necessarily his favorite thing. They'd watched Ren and Maggie and the other Impalers. Then when the band was done, they'd all hit the street, having a great, carefree time.

Then she'd spent the afternoon at the gallery getting all her pieces set up like she wanted them. Including the one of Vittorio.

The piece had come out stunning, if she did say so herself. And she hadn't even let Vittorio see the finished piece. Even the sculpture of Isabel had turned out fabulous, although because of Isabel herself, Erika didn't consider it her favorite. But the work was good. She thought Isabel would be pleased.

When she'd gotten home, Vittorio told her to dress up, and he took her and Jo out to Brennan's for a delicious and extravagant dinner, which had included crawfish and several bottles of champagne.

By the time they got home, she and Jo had been full, tipsy and very happy. Jo had immediately dozed off into a satisfied and blissful sleep on the sofa, while Erika and Vittorio had retired to the bedroom.

But they definitely hadn't slept. And now, Erika was very, very satisfied. She idly toyed with Vittorio's hair, smiling to herself.

"What are you thinking about?"

Erika lifted her head to look up at him. He watched her with those dark, dark eyes of his, looking breathtakingly beautiful.

"I'm thinking about how much I love you."

He smiled, although it had that heartbreaking quality that she saw every now and then.

"I love you too." He kissed her, and even though they'd just finished a toe-curling, earth-moving round of lovemaking, the kiss quickly deepened, becoming more intense.

Vittorio shifted their positions so he was over her, pressing her down into the mattress with his delicious weight. Erika's hand left the tangle of his hair to smooth down over the satiny skin of his back and the hard, undulating muscles underneath.

She wrapped her legs around his hips, urging him closer to her core, where she wanted him, buried deep inside her. But instead he skimmed downward, leaving a trail of kisses in his wake as he positioned himself between her legs.

Then his mouth was on her exposed flesh.

"I've wanted to do that for so long," he murmured against her lips, and she could taste the tang of her own sex on his lips. A thrill, primal and possessive, filled her.

She kissed him again before saying, "You've done that lots of times before."

"Not like that," he said, and she realized he was right. She didn't understand what he'd done to make the experience different, but it was more intense, more overwhelming, more wonderful than any time previously, which she couldn't quite believe. He was always good, but this . . . this was just more.

She smiled at him, blinking to keep her eyes open. The combination of the intensity of her release, the champagne and her hard work of late had finally caught up with her.

She fought back a yawn. "I'm sorry. I'm trying to stay awake."

"Don't. Tomorrow is a big day. You need your rest."

She nodded, her eyes closing almost instantly.

Vittorio watched her sleep, wondering if he'd done the right thing. It had sure felt right when it was happening, and God knows, he'd wanted to do it so many times before now.

He'd given her his energy. As he'd used his tongue and lips to satisfy her, he'd breathed his own energy deep inside her. And that had been as amazing for him as anything he'd done in his life.

He'd bonded with her. Made her his. And while he knew he should be worried, he couldn't bring himself to feel that way. It was too perfect and he didn't want to ruin it with more of his concerns.

He could care for her. And he would.

He pulled her tight against him. He would.

Fantastic didn't even begin to cover how wonderful Erika was feeling today. She seriously had the sensation of walking on clouds. Big puffy perfect clouds.

She'd woken up early, showered, eaten a quick breakfast and then had headed to the gallery.

She centered one of her pieces on the pedestal, the original work she'd done of Vittorio. Stepping back, she studied it. She hoped the roughness of the piece would speak to people in a very visceral, elemental way.

Satisfied with how it was arranged and where it was placed among the other works, she then moved to the larger piece she'd done. The center of the whole exhibit. Unlike the smaller sculpture, this one of Vittorio was all smooth, perfect lines. Each curve of the clay and polymer showed the flawlessness of his features, of his body.

This was how she saw him as her lover and friend and as her—prince. Lounging among pillows and draped with cloth, the Vittorio of her artist's mind was indeed a royal being. There was haughtiness and grace, but there was also just a little uncertainty in the curve of his lips, in the tilt of his head. A prince who isn't sure he wants to be one.

She loved the piece. She knew it was the best thing she'd ever done. Stroking the curve of his bare shoulder, she then moved to the other significant piece in the show. Isabel.

Erika had to admit that despite the frequent awkwardness of working with the strange woman, she had managed to create something truly beautiful. She'd captured what she'd initially seen in the lovely blonde. The etherealness, the sweet curve of her cheeks and full lips. The piece was stunning, if she did say so herself. And she was very proud of it, and very glad it was completed.

She moved the sculpture just slightly, then moved back to see how the two main pieces looked together. They made a definite impact. And looked somehow as if they belonged together.

She frowned, seeing for the first time how almost similar Vittorio and Isabel's faces looked. Their jawlines, the shape of their lips. She glanced from one to the other, surprised she hadn't noted the similarities before. Then she wondered if she'd just managed to give them similarities when they didn't really have them. Her artistic license shining through.

As she continued to ponder that idea, her cell phone, tucked into the front pocket of her purse, began to chime. She hurried across the glossy wood floor, reaching the phone just before it went to voice mail.

"Hello," she said quickly, expecting to be greeted by dead air. But a voice replied.

"Erika?"

"Yes." Erika didn't immediately recognize the voice. Maybe because she was expecting it to be Jo or Maggie or Vittorio. Although she knew Vittorio was probably still asleep. Lazybones.

"Erika, it's Isabel."

"Isabel?" She couldn't say exactly why she was surprised.

"I'm sorry to bother you, since I'm sure you are getting ready for your show, but I was hoping you could come over to my place."

"Come over? Why?" Erika was busy. It was getting late, nearly 3 p.m., and she had to go back to her place, meet up with Jo, who wanted to take her to a late lunch/early dinner to celebrate. Then she had to get dressed in the gorgeous black Betsey Johnson she'd splurged on for this event. And frankly, she didn't want to rush getting dressed up, or be back here too close to the opening of the show. She wanted to enjoy every moment of this day.

"I'm having some problems with my love that, well—" Isabel sighed as if she were just at her wit's end. "I just think I need you here to make him understand why I've done what I've done."

Erika frowned. That was ever-cryptic Isabel for you. "Is he not pleased with the idea of the sculpture?"

"No, he's not."

Erika glanced at her watch. If she ran over there, talked to this guy, although she didn't know how her talking to him would help, she could still get home with enough time to meet Vittorio and get ready.

"I really think if he just heard the truth from you, it would make everything so much easier."

Erika hesitated, still not understanding what exactly Isabel thought she could do. But she did sound sincerely desperate.

"It will only take a few minutes," Isabel added, her voice nearly breaking with emotion. "He just won't listen to me."

"Okay," Erika heard herself say, wondering why on earth she was getting involved. What could she say to this guy? But she couldn't bring herself to say no.

"But I can only stay briefly," she did say.

"Thank you, Erika."

The phone went dead, but Erika stood there with it still flipped open for several moments. Why had she agreed to do this?

Sighing, she snapped the phone closed and tossed it back into her purse. Taking one more look around the gallery, she went to find the owner to let him know she was finished and would be back at least half an hour before the show. Then she gathered her stuff and hurried out the door.

This better be quick and not involve too much drama.

Vittorio paced the living room of Erika's apartment. It was 6:18 p.m., and Erika still hadn't returned. She'd left a note on the table, saying that she'd be back at 4:30 p.m. or so to get showered and dressed. At 6:30 p.m., they were supposed to meet with Ren, Maggie and Jo to go to dinner before the show. Vittorio had expected the time frame to be tight for him, Ren and Maggie, what with their need to wait for the sun to set, but he hadn't expected Erika to be late.

Where was she?

He gave up his pacing and headed over to Ren's. The lights in the carriage house were on, and he could see shadows moving inside. Maybe she was over there. Jo was staying there, so maybe Erika was visiting her while their nocturnal friends slept on.

He hoped.

He knocked and indeed Jo did answer the door.

She was already dressed for the evening in a vintage-looking dress with a full skirt, like something Audrey Hepburn would have worn.

"I know," she said with a smile, "the two rock stars are running late."

"Not me," Ren said from behind her, coming down the stairs, rubbing his damp long hair with a towel. "I'm ready. It's Maggie who's running late." He tossed the towel onto the banister at the bottom of the stairs.

Vittorio didn't respond to his brother, instead he scanned the room. "Is Erika here?"

"Erika?" Jo said. "No. Isn't she getting ready?"

Vittorio shook his head. "No. She hadn't come back from the gallery." At least he didn't think so. Damned his unnatural sleep.

"She must have gotten hung up there with something. Did you try her cell phone?" Ren said.

Vittorio nodded. "No answer."

"That phone of hers," Jo said. "It only works half the time."

"Hey, Vittorio," Maggie greeted as she came down the stairs in a red dress with a plunging neckline and black high heels. "You look snazzy."

Again Vittorio didn't respond, nor did he acknowledge her compliment on the suit he wore. Instead he asked, knowing it would be in vain, "Have you heard from Erika?"

"No," Maggie said, pausing at the bottom of the stairs. "She said she wanted to get back from the gallery early so she'd have plenty of time to get ready."

Vittorio nodded. "That's what she told me too."

"Well, she has to be at the gallery," Ren said, giving him a reassuring look. "Let's just go there and see if we can help her out."

"These things do always take longer than you think," Maggie said, also giving Vittorio a calming smile.

Vittorio nodded. "Let's go then."

"Wait," Jo said. "Let's get her dress and stuff and bring it with us. She's going to be upset if she's late because she still has to get dressed."

"Good thinking," Maggie agreed. "She'll want to look perfect."

Chapter 27

"**P**erfect."

The smug voice managed to reach Erika through the blurry fog that seemed to fill her head. She tried to sit up, her first instinct to escape the strange, muzzy feeling. But she couldn't seem to move.

You're having another nightmare.

But this didn't seem quite the same. She tried to move again, but something seemed to be restraining her.

"Don't bother to struggle," the voice said, again reaching her through the fuzzy darkness. The voice was familiar, and she tried to remember if it was from the other nightmares, but she just couldn't be sure.

So she let herself drift for a few moments, maybe hours, she really had no idea. No, this wasn't like the other nightmares. There was nothing chasing her, no impending feeling of doom, no blinding fear. Just heavy blackness.

She remained still for a few more seconds, or maybe longer. Time was as hazy as her inky surroundings. Then she attempted to open her eyes, this time managing to peel her lids open.

She blinked, still feeling dazed and bleary. But slowly her surroundings came into focus. Not that her slowly returning vision gave her any more sense of her location. Nothing looked familiar. The walls were in shades of gray, then she realized they were bare stone. The light overhead was a bare bulb hanging from a black electrical cord. And she lay on a table, her hands bound and pulled over her head.

Where was she? Panic that reminded her of her previous nightmares swelled upward in her stomach. This had to be a nightmare. Didn't it?

She tried to pull at the bonds holding her, but they didn't budge. She struggled, only to realize her ankles were similarly bound.

"I told you to stop struggling. Aosoth doesn't like her sacrifices injured until she is summoned and allowed to enjoy it—just a little—before the actual killing."

Erika craned her neck, trying to see who was speaking, but the restraints at her ankles and wrists allowed her very little movement. It was definitely a female, although Erika couldn't quite place her.

"Who are you?" she demanded, trying to sound less frightened than she felt.

"Oh, silly girl, you must know who I am." The speaker came into view from Erika's left, her first impressions blond hair and flowing dress.

"Isabel?"

The blonde smiled, not the sweet smiles of their past meetings. No, this time the malevolence Erika had thought she'd glimpsed beneath the surface of Isabel's ethereal beauty was on her face, so clear and intense, it was hard to imagine Erika hadn't seen it all along.

"I'd think you'd know me by now," Isabel said, her lips curling into a cruel twist. "After all, you have seen all of me for a couple of weeks now."

Obviously she hadn't. Or not as clearly as she should have, because Erika got the distinct impression this was the real Isabel.

Erika tugged at the restraints holding her wrists. The tightly lashed cords didn't give, except to dig into the already tender skin of her wrists.

"I did warn you about marring yourself. I don't want Aosoth to be disappointed with my offering."

"Who is Aosoth? What are you talking about?" Erika was trying desperately not to panic, but she wasn't doing well. Her heart pounded painfully in her chest, which made it difficult to pull in a deep breath.

Isabel sidled closer, that coldly malevolent smile pinned to her lips. "I guess before I explain who Aosoth is, I should probably tell you who I am. You see, my real name isn't Isabel. It's Orabella." She said her name as if it should make some big impact on Erika.

It didn't.

"Okay," Erika said. "I don't really care whether you are named Isabel, Orabella or Svetlana—" *Svetlana?* Where had she gotten that? "I just want to know why you have me strapped to this table."

Isabel's, or rather Orabella's eyes narrowed and a muscle in her jaw ticked. "You will care who I am." She started to move slowly around the table.

Erika started to open her mouth to ask yet again why she was here, but the blonde's next words stopped her.

"So Vittorio didn't tell you about me."

Vittorio knew this nutjob?

Isa— Orabella paced around the table, her eyes focused somewhere faraway. Then she stopped down by Erika's feet, and smiled nastily.

"Well, he wouldn't mention me, would he? Why would he even bother trying to make you understand the relationship we have? Clearly you couldn't."

Erika stared at the woman. Was this the woman from Vittorio's past that Philippe told her about? Of course it was. And very obviously, she was crazy.

"Isa— Orabella, Vittorio is no longer interested in you," she said.

Hard, cold eyes, black, with hatred, pinned her, and Erika

questioned her strategy. Ticking off this woman wasn't going to help her cause here.

"He wouldn't tell you about me because I'm so far beyond your understanding. What we share a mere mortal couldn't begin to comprehend."

Erika frowned. Mere mortal. This woman was utterly nuts, a realization that didn't give her any comfort. Instead her panic rose.

"What is doing this going to prove to Vittorio?"

"It's going to prove my love. It's going to prove that I only ever wanted to make him happy. And," she said as she touched Erika's leg just below the knee, "I'm going to show him I can give him everything he could ever want or need."

Erika tried to jerk away from the brush of her fingers moving slowly upward.

"And how are you planning to do that? By keeping me here tied to a table?"

Orabella giggled. "Oh no, that wouldn't show him anything but how easy it is to capture a human. Not exciting enough."

"So what do you plan to do?" Erika wasn't sure she really wanted to hear what this nut had planned.

"I'm going to sacrifice you, and give Vittorio back the sun. Killing two birds with one stone. Or rather killing one bird and getting exactly what I want. My beloved Vittorio." Orabella giggled. "Isn't that clever of me?"

Erika gaped at the woman, not quite believing what she was hearing. This crazy lady intended to sacrifice her? How?

But before she could ask yet another question she wasn't sure she wanted the answer to, Orabella began to move around the table again, this time chanting in a low singsong mumbling, words Erika didn't understand.

She thrashed against the cords binding her, feeling the unforgiving ropes bite and burn her flesh. Dear God, she had to get out of here.

This woman really intended to kill her.

*   *   *

Maksim lay in the center of the king-size bed, staring at the ceiling like he'd done for days. He'd always loved lounging in a comfy bed for hours with no need to go anywhere, but there were two other things he loved which he didn't realize until this moment. He did enjoy leaving the bed eventually, and while he didn't need to eat to survive, he liked to eat. Maybe more than lounging in a bed all day. Alone.

Growling, he rolled over onto his stomach, that position no more comfortable than the one before, or the one before that. Which led to another thing he'd learned in the past days—even a comfy bed got uncomfortable eventually.

He punched the pillow, then dropped his head onto the fluffed feathers. This was hell. And since he was from hell, he certainly knew it when he experienced it.

"This is worse than hell," he muttered to the empty room. What he wouldn't give for his portion of hell with all its fire, and molten rock and sweltering heat.

He closed his eyes, trying to will himself back to sleep again, but that wasn't working either. Even unconsciousness wasn't an escape.

So instead his mind moved on to his new favorite pastime, thinking of ways he was going to punish Orabella when he finally got free. He liked to play out scenarios that she would find intolerable. Things like forcing her to work for all eternity as a carny, surrounded by the smell of fried food, animals and the unfortunate aftermath of some of the more dizzying amusement rides. Or there was the one where he imagined her as a fishmonger, flinging smelly carps in the broiling sun. Or his personal favorite, the person who empties out the Port-a-Pottys for construction crews.

Oh, he knew his little fantasies were petty, but they did help to pass the time. And made him smile.

He was lost again in the Porta John scenario, when a noise caught his attention. The sound of footfalls coming up the staircase toward his room.

He flipped over onto his back just in time to see a small, middle-aged woman, struggling to carry a large canister vacuum cleaner. She was so focused on the monstrous machine, she didn't notice him through the partially closed door.

"Excuse me," he called.

The woman squeaked, dropping the heavy vacuum, the hose curling around her feet.

He levered himself up, plastering a mild, hopefully appealing smile on his face. The last thing he wanted was to scare this woman away. She was the first being, other than his evil undead captor, that he'd seen in two-and-a-half weeks. He had to play it cool—and charming. Which wasn't exactly easy since he was chomping at the bit to get out of this bed.

"I'm sorry," he called to the lady, offering her another smile. He levered himself up more, trying to look lazy and charming. Too much charm might unnerve this woman.

"That—that's okay," she said, returning his smile with an uncertain one.

He tried to gauge her reaction to him, trying to decide his best course here. He could jump into her head and find out exactly what she was thinking, but for the first time ever, he didn't want to do that. He didn't ponder what was stopping him from doing what was so natural to him.

Instead he tried to read her expression. For just the briefest moment her eyes, half hidden behind dark-rimmed glasses, flicked down to his bare chest. Then her cheeks, lined with wrinkles, a testament to the hard work she'd clearly done her whole life, tinged faintly pink. The reaction had been so slight, he was lucky that he'd been watching her, rather than focusing on getting into her head. Because of that insignificant little glance, he knew exactly how to play his hand.

He sat up and stretched, flexing the muscles in his pecs and his shoulders. The woman's eyes again darted for a split second to his upper body, but she quickly turned her attention to fumbling with the vacuum and the hose.

"I'm sorry to be lazing around like this so late in the day," he said, drawing her attention back to him. He dropped his arms. "Actually Ms. D'Antoni would be very upset with me for forgetting you were coming to clean today. She reminded me, but it slipped my mind."

The woman nodded, now looking everywhere but at his bared chest. Not good. His plan to draw her in because of her obvious attraction to him might not work. She could get flustered and run. In fact, the way she was rearranging the vacuum looked as if she intended to pick it back up and move along. He couldn't have that.

"She'll be very upset with me if you don't clean this room," he said, then smiled sheepishly.

"I will," the woman assured him.

"Well, maybe it would be best if you started with this one. Perhaps you should start here. Just in case she comes home." Comes home and stops this woman with her blessed vacuum.

"Okay," she agreed, although he could tell she wasn't understanding his urgency on the matter. Of course, the cleaning woman certainly wouldn't go right to—*oh, you need that pentagram around the bed cleaned up*—now would she?

"I'll just let you start here, that way if she does come home, the room will be done and she won't ever guess I was here when you arrived. Our little secret."

He smiled, turning on the full charm.

She smiled back and nodded, tugging the huge vacuum into the room. The wheels marred the straight line of the iron filings running along the doorway.

He smiled again, then fell back against the pillows, stretching as if he was taking a lazy moment before getting up for the day.

There was some quiet shuffling as she prepared to clean the master bedroom, or his jail cell, as he now considered it.

But not for much longer, he thought with a small smile at the ceiling he knew better than he ever wanted to know a ceiling again. The vacuum rumbled to life, and he knew he'd finally found the way to make his prison break.

*   *   *

Vittorio tried to keep his pace somewhat in line with the others, but Ren, Maggie and Jo were simply walking too slow. Didn't they feel the same sense of urgency he did? And something was wrong, he could feel it in every cell of his body, like she was calling out to him, yet he couldn't quite hear her or sense where she was.

Finally they reached The Broussard. The place was fully lit, and a full color sign announcing the show tonight was propped on an easel beside the doorway, but otherwise things were quiet.

Vittorio tried the door, and it pulled open easily. They stepped into the gallery. The place was silent. They all looked around, trying to see any signs of Erika.

Ren walked over to the center of the room. "I don't think she's here."

"Wait, I hear someone," Maggie said.

As she said that, a shadow appeared on the wall and Vittorio's heart leapt with hope. Maybe she was here. But it was an older man with glasses and a neatly trimmed beard who greeted them.

"Good evening. I'm glad you could make it to the show tonight. Although the actual reception doesn't begin for another half an hour or so. But please feel free to look around."

Vittorio nodded, eager to just cut him off and ask about Erika. "Yes, we know. We are friends of Erika Todd's and we are actually looking for her. We thought maybe she was still here getting ready."

The man shook his head. "No, she left hours ago."

Cold fear prickled Vittorio's skin. He glanced over to Ren, who also looked apprehensive.

"She did mention something about getting a call from one of her models. The woman said she needed to see Erika before the show. It sounded a little urgent. Maybe she is still there."

"Do you know who the woman was?" Vittorio asked.

The man shook his head. "No. But I think I know which model it was. And maybe you can recognize her from the piece."

He waved for them to follow, which all four did.

"Oh, Vittorio," Maggie said, pausing by the full-size sculpture Erika had done of him. "This is wonderful."

The piece was amazing, no thanks to him. Erika had captured something in him, yet again, that he hadn't even realized was there. But his attention was quickly pulled away from the piece as Ren murmured, "Holy shit."

Frowning, he followed his brother's gaze.

"I believe this is the model who contacted her this afternoon," the gallery owner said.

"Holy shit," Ren repeated.

And that didn't even begin to do the moment justice. They were all staring at the sculpture, Ren and Vittorio aghast, while Maggie and Jo just looked, trying to understand the two brothers' reactions.

"Do you know this woman?" Jo finally asked.

Ren nodded, then laughed, the sound more shocked than amused. Vittorio wasn't amused at all. He was scared, deep-to-the-marrow-of-his-bones scared.

"Yeah, we know her," Ren finally answered. "She's our mother."

Chapter 28

Erika watched Orabella as she circled and circled the table, now holding a sheet of tattered notebook paper, reading something from it that sounded like gibberish.

Erika had also noticed that there was something like an altar to the left of her. The small table was covered with a black tablecloth, and two black candles burned in heavy silver candlesticks. A chalice was centered between the two candles along with some bottles of what appeared to be herbs and oils. In front of all of that was a large, very menacing-looking dagger. The edge glinted in the candlelight, sharp and deadly.

"What are you doing?" she demanded of Orabella, getting the distinct feeling that when the chanting portion of this ritual ended, bad, bad things were going to happen.

Orabella ignored her, still mumbling her incantation or whatever it was.

"Vittorio will come for me," Erika said, knowing her voice sounded high and panicked.

That did cause Orabella to pause, losing her train of thought, but only for a fraction of a second, then she continued on, her voice louder than before.

"He will come, and he's going to be very angry with you."

More chanting was Orabella's only reply.

"Do you really think all of this will get him to be with you?"

More chanting, then when Orabella had circled around the table to stand behind her head, the chanting in that awful singsong tone stopped.

Erika tried to tilt her head back far enough to see her, but the bindings were too tight and she couldn't angle herself enough to see anything. And the silence was even worse than the weird words half spoken, half sung.

Her breath came in short, harsh puffs, and she tried to calm herself. Hyperventilating and passing out were not going to help this situation in the least.

She needed to slow Orabella down. Down from what, she wasn't sure, but she knew something bad was going to happen. Clearly no good could come of being strapped to a table by a madwoman who also had a sharp knife.

Orabella then appeared to her left, at the altar. Where said knife waited.

Erika swallowed, trying to calm herself. "There have got to be better ways to try and reach him," she said. "I just don't think this is going to have the effect you want from him."

Orabella remained with her back toward her. She had the dog-eared notebook paper set up against one of the candlesticks and she worked with the herbs and oils, mixing them. She didn't appear to hear a word Erika was saying.

But Erika had to keep trying. "Orabella, don't you think just talking to him would work better? How is he going to forgive you for this?"

As she babbled on, saying anything she could think of to reason with this crazy woman, she kept trying to move her wrists, hoping to loosen the cords.

"You are making a big mistake."

"Do you think so?" Orabella said, turning toward Erika, the chalice and the dagger in her hands as she approached the table. "Why?" she asked, her tone more bored than curious.

Erika glanced at the dagger—it glistened dangerously in

the candlelight. Erika swallowed. "Vittorio is the type who hates violence."

Orabella paused. "Yes, I suppose that's true."

"It is," Erika said, moving her gaze away from the frightening knife to Orabella's face, trying to read her expression.

The blonde seemed to be considering the idea. She slowly twirled the stem of the silver chalice between her fingers.

"What is he going to think? How is this going to make him want to be with you?"

Orabella continued to twist the chalice, lost in her thoughts.

Erika tugged at the restraints. "Please, Orabella, don't do this. Vittorio won't understand. He won't be able to forgive this."

Orabella's eyes flicked back up to her. "Now that's where you are wrong. I'm going to give him something that will finally make him understand how much I love him. He will forgive me."

Erika shook her head, preparing to tell her that he wouldn't. That he'd been very angry. But those words never made it to her lips. Only a scream reached them as Orabella, with a speed so lightning-fast Erika could barely register the movement, was at the table. Orabella placed the chalice on the table beside her, and captured Erika's hand.

Erika struggled, but her captor easily turned her hand palm up, and with that same blinding swiftness, sliced her.

Erika cried out again, this time the sound laced with pain.

"There, there," Orabella clucked. "This is nearly done."

She positioned Erika's bleeding palm over the chalice, and they both watched, one with horrified shock, the other with smug satisfaction as the blood dripped into the cup.

After how long Erika didn't know, Orabella released her. "That should do."

She didn't look at Erika as she strolled back to her makeshift altar and began to add herbs and oils to Erika's blood.

Now Erika squirmed on the table, yanking violently at the cords which cut into her skin, oblivious to the pain. She was too terrified, too desperate. She had to escape.

She began to scream, shouting out for help.

"Do be quiet," Orabella hissed over her shoulder. "Not a soul can hear you."

Erika didn't stop.

Orabella turned back to her work, then after several moments, turned back to Erika, the chalice cupped between her two hands. She began to chant again.

"Please, Orabella, please don't do this." Tears rolled out of the corners of Erika's eyes.

Orabella didn't look at her. She began to circle the table again, lost in her chanting.

"Please," Erika begged. She knew she sounded pathetic, her voice cracking with her fear. "Please."

The chant continued, then finally Orabella stopped at the end of the table. She stared at Erika for what seemed like minutes, though it was likely only seconds.

"There's no point begging," Orabella said with an almost apologetic look on her face. "It is done."

She raised the chalice, shouted out two more words, then the room was filled with deafening noise, like lightning striking right there in the room. Blinding flashes, huge booms that shook the walls and caused Erika to scream. And even above all that fury, she could still hear Orabella laughing. A triumphant laugh.

"It is done!"

"What's going on?" Maggie asked, her gaze going back and forth between the two brothers.

"It's our mother," Ren answered, because Vittorio couldn't. He was too filled with sickening dread.

"What about her?" Jo frowned, her gaze moving to each of them, trying to understand. "What does she have to do with Erika?"

"Vittorio thinks our mother may have—"

"We have to find her." Vittorio cut him off, his unwilling-
ness to hear Ren say the words forcing him out of his stunned
state. He couldn't hear, couldn't believe she wasn't okay. But
they had to find her—quickly.

"How are we supposed to do that?" Ren asked. "We don't
have any idea where she could be."

Panic rose in Vittorio's chest. "We have to do something."

Before Ren could respond, the door to the gallery opened.
They all turned to see who entered. Vittorio prayed it was Erika,
but instead it was a tall man, looking a little disheveled and
rumpled. Clearly out of place for a catered art show.

The man glanced around, then his eyes centered on Vittorio. He didn't hesitate, but walked straight toward him.

"Your mother has her."

Vittorio stared at the man. Then he quickly sensed this
wasn't a man. Preternatural vibes radiated off this being like
heat waves off hot tarmac.

"Where?" Vittorio had many more questions, but this was
the one of most importance at the moment.

"A house in the Garden District—that's all I know."

That was all Vittorio needed to hear. Erika had told him
about the house where she'd been going to sculpt this Isabel
Andrews. How lovely it was.

Vittorio started toward the door, when Ren caught his
arm.

"Where are you going?" he asked.

"I know where she is," Vittorio said.

"I'm coming with you," Ren said, releasing his elbow and
falling into step beside him.

"Shouldn't we all go?" Maggie asked.

"No," Ren said instantly. "We will be fine. We've had to
deal with this woman for years."

Vittorio agreed, but he didn't say anything. He just doubled his steps. She had to be okay.

* * *

Maksim didn't speculate too closely on why he'd come to find Vittorio. The deed certainly wasn't one that would normally come naturally to him. Altruism and demon were two words rarely used in the same sentence.

Perhaps the two weeks stuck in a bed with nothing and no one to do had caused him to snap. Or at the very least forced him to think.

And he'd want someone to come to him if they knew anything about Ellina. And he supposed Orabella's sons truly hating her was enough punishment for the crazy bitch.

"How do you know where Erika is?"

Maksim turned his attention away from the doorway to look down at a petite, curvy, strawberry blonde. Maggie, he realized from being in Erika's mind.

"I know their mother."

"Do you know Ren and Vittorio?" The woman was clearly confused about where he came into all this.

"Not really."

Maggie frowned, studying him. She knew he was preternatural, and she was suspicious. Smart woman. But in this case, he was really only trying to help.

"Is she okay?"

For the first time, Maksim noted the woman just behind Maggie. Jo, he recognized, again from Erika's memories.

Although her memories hadn't done this mortal justice. She was lovely. And she narrowed dark brown eyes at him, clearly trying to decide if he could be trusted.

Not most of the time. "I hope she's okay," he answered, and realized it was the truth. All this concern and sympathy—weird.

"So how do you know her?" Jo stepped forward to stand next to her friend. This mortal obviously couldn't sense he was something other than human, but she still found him suspect. Smart woman, too.

"I've met her a couple times. And I used to see Vittorio and Ren's mother."

Jo raised an eyebrow and he imagined that she thought he was a tad too young for the mother of children as old as Ren and Vittorio. Little did she know.

She studied him with those coffee-brown eyes, trying to read him. Which he found strangely unnerving—and a little arousing too. Clearly fallout of being trapped in a bed for days. Alone.

He turned away from the two rather intense women, only to be greeted by two life-size sculptures of Vittorio and Orabella.

He blinked at the image. Then glanced back at the women.

"Wow, that's a nice addition to a bizarre few weeks."

Vittorio moved rapidly through the streets, trying to cling to the shadows so no mortals would see how fast he was moving, if they could see him at all. Ren followed.

He reached the address Erika had mentioned.

"Is this it?"

Vittorio double-checked the number, then took in the grounds. It fit her description perfectly. And he could sense Erika nearby, could sense her fear. Still, fear was better than other options. If he could feel her fear, then she was alive.

"Yes, this is it."

He pushed open the gate, and hurried up the front walk. As was to be expected, the front door was locked. He didn't even hesitate, but faded to shadow, slipping under the door.

Once inside, he rematerialized and looked around. The place was dark, no lights on. Ren materialized beside him.

They both listened. The house was quiet. But Vittorio could feel Erika there. Somewhere.

"I don't hear anyone," Ren said, "but I think Mother is here."

Vittorio nodded.

They took a few steps farther into the room, when a loud crash like a thunderclap sounded from above them. The ceiling vibrated and the chandelier overhead swayed, the crystals jangling.

Neither brother spoke as they swiftly moved through to the sweeping staircase in the center of the main level. Once up the stairs, it didn't take them long to locate the room where Erika had to be. Light and her energy, riddled with terror, seeped around the door frame.

Vittorio glanced at Ren before reaching for the doorknob. His brother shook his head and gestured for him to simply break it down. Vittorio only debated that idea for a second, then decided maybe a surprise entrance would be the best bet. Maybe the commotion would throw off their mother, making it harder for her to escape. And shifting and rematerializing would waste needed energy.

He looked at Ren again, then held up his fingers to count to three. When his third finger came up, he rammed his shoulder into the oak door. The wood splintered, and both brothers raced inside.

But instead of creating the surprise they intended, they were the ones stunned by the scene before them.

Chapter 29

Erika lay lashed to a rectangular dining table in the center of the room, her eyes wild and disoriented. She didn't even appear to know Vittorio was there.

Orabella was positioned at the end of the table, a wide, pleased smile curling her lips, not appearing the least bit surprised by the arrival of her sons. She was with a tall woman—at least Vittorio assumed it was a woman from the breasts evident under the encasement of leather that made up her clothing. Other than breasts and a semblance of clothing, the creature looked only vaguely humanoid, with reptilian eyes and skin, and her lower half was that of a goat.

"Just in time, my pet," Orabella said cheerfully to Vittorio. Her smile slipped slightly when she noticed Ren. But she didn't let the appearance of her disliked son dampen her joy. She walked over to Vittorio.

Raising a hand, she tried to stroke his cheek, but he jerked away.

"My love, don't be that way. We haven't seen each other for so long. Does our reunion have to be like this?"

Vittorio's eyes widened. "How else would you expect it to go? You abducted the woman I love and have her tied to a table."

"And I don't even know what's up with the reptile chick," Ren commented, eyeing the creature warily.

"Shut up," Orabella hissed. Then she moved away from Vittorio and toward the creature. But she stopped several feet from the lizard chick, as Ren had aptly dubbed her. Then Vittorio noticed a pentagram created from iron filings—the creature was a demon.

"I'm not impressed either," the creature said, her voice surprisingly beautiful and elegant, given her appearance.

"Aosoth, this is my son. The one I want you to be with," Orabella said by way of introduction.

"Mmm, not my usual type, but quite lovely nonetheless." The demon licked her lips. Her tongue was forked.

Vittorio stared, appalled and confused. "Mother, you are mad. This is your plan? To matchmake me to a demon?"

Orabella laughed as if he'd just said the most delightful thing. "Oh, hardly, dear." Then she touched a finger to her lips. "Well, you will have to—well, you know, be with her— to have the ritual work."

Vittorio made a face. "What?"

"Yes, Mother, what ritual? What fabulous idea have you come up with now?" Ren asked mockingly.

Orabella turned her attention to her other son, sneering at him. "You have no part in this. Just leave."

Ren moved a little closer to her. "No way, Mumsie. I want in on this scheme. What's the plan? Do tell."

Vittorio glanced over at Erika. Her skin was pale, tinged gray. She watched the scene, but from the distant look in her eyes, it was clear she wasn't taking it in. She was in shock. Which at the moment might not be a bad thing. He wanted to move toward her, but didn't dare. Mother had clearly snapped.

"So the plan?" Ren prodded. "I want to know. And if it's good, I want in."

Orabella laughed humorlessly. "Not hardly."

Ren moved closer, getting between Vittorio and his mother.

"It's the least you can do, having ruined my ability to write original music."

Orabella laughed again, although this time the sound was smug and gleeful. "That was brilliance, I have to admit."

"You are such a petty, pathetic woman," Ren stated.

Vittorio stared at his brother. What was he doing? They needed to be focused on Erika. The two of them could take Orabella and then go to Erika. But Ren was too busy arguing to be of any help.

"I can just as easily have Aosoth take you as a sacrifice too," Orabella gritted out, her full attention on her hated son.

"As long as I get someone for this irksome interruption," Aosoth muttered as she apathetically inspected her long, clawlike nails. Then she glanced at Ren.

"You will, my exalted one," Orabella assured the creature.

While Orabella's attention was turned to the demon, Ren gave Vittorio a quick sidelong glance, then looked toward Erika.

Ah, that was what Ren was doing. Creating a diversion. Sometimes his older brother surprised him.

Carefully, Vittorio took a step toward the table, not wanting to draw any attention to himself.

"So what do you get for giving Erika to—what was it . . . Asshole?"

The demon growled low in her throat. "Aosoth! Oh, yes, I'd like to take this puny vampire back to hell with me."

"Sorry, Aosoth-baby, I'm already spoken for," Ren said sweetly.

Vittorio continued to move closer and closer to Erika. Ren was remarkably good at keeping the attention of both their mother and the demon. And soon, without anyone but Ren realizing, he'd reached Erika.

He touched her arm, and she flinched. Her eyes were unfocused, like they had been during her night terrors.

"It's okay, darling," he whispered, his lips barely moving. He hoped since they were bonded she could hear him, take comfort from him. But he couldn't tell. The shock was too much for her.

He carefully reached for the cord around the wrist closest to him, working the tight knot, noting the red welts and bits of blood from where she'd struggled.

Erika, I will keep you safe. You have to trust me.

Erika heard Vittorio's voice in her head. His voice was smooth, soothing. Even though her mind had shut down, he still reached her, through the panic and horror that clouded her mind and numbed her.

She felt his hands at her wrist, working the restraints free.

Trust me.

Erika wanted to, but she couldn't comprehend what she'd just seen. Flashes of light, blue and blinding. Noise like being trapped in a thundercloud. And then the appearance of that . . . thing. This couldn't be real. It couldn't.

She forced herself to focus on the gentle touch at her wrist. At the voice in her head.

I will take care of you. I'll protect you.

She compelled her eyes to blink. Then blink again until slowly the cloud of terror lifted enough for her to see outside of herself.

Slowly she turned her head. Vittorio was there. At least she thought it was him. She wasn't sure what was real at the moment.

"I'm really here," Vittorio whispered, although she was fairly certain she hadn't spoken.

She felt the cord around her right wrist loosen and drop away. Then Vittorio's fingers were gently rubbing her wrist. She vaguely registered the sting of her tender skin.

For a moment, Vittorio moved out of her line of sight, and she panicked, making a frightened noise low in her throat.

"Shh." His fingers returned to her, working on the other wrist. She tried to calm herself, to gather her stunned wits.

Beyond Vittorio's calming words and touch, she recognized Ren's voice. And Orabella's. They snipped at each other, Ren's tone mocking and derisive, Orabella's sharp and angry.

Then she heard a smooth, cultured voice, the one that had to belong that . . . that creature.

"I believe my trussed chicken is being set free."

Orabella and Ren did react immediately. Then all hell seemed to break loose. Vittorio's hands were gone. Ren shouted and Orabella made a noise like an enraged banshee.

Erika, even though she felt oddly disembodied, braced her free arm against the table, struggling to roll so she could see what was happening.

A scuffle had ensued with the two brothers trying to subdue the slighter, petite Orabella. The small woman was giving them a run for their money.

"Mother," Vittorio growled as the woman came at him with clawed hands. "Stop this now."

Hearing Vittorio's reference to this woman was like icy water dumped over her head. Mother? Isa—Orabella was Vittorio's mother? Nausea rose up in her throat, gagging her.

"I'm doing all this for you," Orabella cried. "Can't you see that? I've found a way to give you back the sun."

Vittorio shook his head, clearly not following.

"I can," Orabella said, looking at him hopefully. "I can give you back the sun. I can make you what you were before your undeath."

Erika blinked. Undeath? She knew what she'd seen here wasn't normal, wasn't even possible, at least in the world where she'd come from. But she'd never believed that Vittorio was somehow a part of this. She'd never thought Vittorio was not—human?

"Mother, you can't ever make me like I was," Vittorio said, glaring at the little woman in front of him.

"I can," she said, sounding almost pleading. "I can. And then you can stay with me. Like we once were."

"You can't make it like it was. That was gone the moment you selfishly made me like you. That was gone when you forced me to take energy from women until they were nearly dead. When you forced me to take energy from you."

"Which is really sick," Ren added.

Orabella whipped around to glare at her other son. "You know nothing of this."

Erika watched as Ren seemed to be pinned to the wall by an invisible force. Color drained from his face.

"You'd do well to remember I am your mother. And I'm your creator. You can never be stronger than me."

Ren actually began to slide down the wall, his eyes rolling back, his limbs falling limp, unable to hold him.

"You're going to kill him," Vittorio shouted and Orabella's attention turned back to him.

"Perhaps I should kill him. The liar has poisoned your mind against me. Filling you with all this nonsense about what I did for you when you were newly changed. Your brother doesn't love you. He's jealous of you. You were my favorite, he knew that. He was an accident. You were my love."

"Ren is the only reason I've managed to go on. He actually taught me how to survive. How to survive without hurting others," Vittorio said, his voice low.

"See, more of his lies," Orabella shot back. She turned back to Ren, hatred clear in her expression. Ren had crumpled to the floor.

"Is that what happened to my father?" Vittorio suddenly asked, an almost stunned quality to his tone. "Did you kill him too, for not agreeing with your ideas of parenting? For making it clear how selfish and manipulative you were?"

Orabella's eyes returned to Vittorio. "I did what I had to do to keep you with me. I love you, darling. You and I are the same person. Two halves of a whole."

Vittorio made a noise of disgust. "We are nothing alike.

Just tell me, Mother, what about the women? What happened to them?"

Erika listened to the exchange, only half comprehending what they said. Her eyes kept returning to Ren, praying he was just faking. That he wasn't hurt. He needed to help Vittorio. Help her.

She heard a movement down by her feet. Her eyes darted in that direction. The lizard-looking creature stood there watching the scene along with Erika. Her yellow eyes met Erika's and the creature smirked. Erika suppressed a frightened whimper.

God, she had to escape, and while she didn't understand what Vittorio and Ren were, they were her only hope. She did understand that Orabella and the lizard-thing were deadly.

Her look returned to Ren, who still lay motionless on the floor. She glanced back to Vittorio.

"What about the other women?" he demanded again.

Orabella hesitated, her hand going out as if she wanted to touch him, but she didn't.

"I had to do it, Vittorio. They weren't good enough for you. They weren't worthy."

"So you killed them."

At Vittorio's flatly stated words, more fear chilled her. *Killed? This had happened before?* And from the sound, it was several women. She closed her eyes briefly, trying to gain some calm.

"I had to," Orabella said as she held out her hands in a beseeching way. "Just like with *her*." She turned slightly to gesture to Erika. "I have to do it. For your own good."

She stepped forward and touched Vittorio's cheek. "I'm the only woman who can truly be worthy of you. Who can love you as you should be loved."

She rose up on her tiptoes and pressed her lips to Vittorio's. Erika stared in silent horror. Everything about this was unnatural and horrific. It was like every nightmare, every horror movie, every V. C. Andrews novel rolled into one.

Erika stopped watching the disturbing scene in front of her and tried to work on the cord holding her other wrist. Vittorio had managed to unknot some of the tight bonds, but from this angle and without being able to see what she was doing, she couldn't get the knots undone.

She whimpered in frustration. She couldn't just lie there listening to this, watching the bizarre drama taking place before her, and wait to be killed.

She crammed her free hand into her jeans pocket, hoping, praying for something that she might use to saw at the knot. The only thing in her pocket was her ancient cell phone.

She wrestled with it, her hand getting caught in her pocket because of the awkward angle. Finally she pulled it out, nearly dropping it over the edge of the table. Fumbling to wedge her thumb under the cover, she flipped it open and peered at the screen. No backlight, no graphics, nothing. The damned thing was dead.

She made a whimpering noise, then her attention was drawn away from the dead cell, back to Vittorio.

Orabella no longer touched him. Instead he'd switched positions and had her pinned to the wall, his hand at her throat. From the bulging eyes and gaped mouth, Erika could see Vittorio was using powerful strength on the woman—the whatever she was.

"When are you going to realize I hate you for what you've done. Taking away my father, killing people I cared about, making me believe I was only able to survive through you."

Orabella made a choking sound and dug her fingers into the hand clamped to her throat. "I—I did it—all—for you."

Vittorio laughed, the sound a harsh, humorless bark. "No, you did it all for yourself."

She continued pulling at his fingers. "I love you."

Vittorio shook his head. "No, you love yourself. Only yourself. And you aren't even worth my contempt."

He released her, his shoulders slumping as if he just couldn't take anymore. "Leave me alone. If you don't, I will find some way to kill you. I will."

She collapsed back against the wall, her hand to her throat, rubbing the place where he'd strangled her. "You can't mean that."

"I do. I never want to see you again. And I want you to stay away from Erika, or I will find some way to stop you for good. Even if it takes a stake through your goddamned heart."

Orabella's eyes welled with tears, but she didn't say anything. Even as he turned away from her and crossed over to Erika, she remained leaning against the wall, tears rolling down her cheeks.

Even attacked, deranged and denied, she still managed to look beautiful, Erika thought vaguely.

Slowly Orabella slid down to the floor, her knees pulled up, her forehead resting on them, like a broken, lost child.

"Are you okay?" Vittorio asked Erika. His tone was soft, regretful, his dark eyes filled with concern and maybe trepidation.

She managed a nod, even though she was still scared witless and aghast at all that had happened here tonight. But she needed to trust someone, and no matter what she'd seen and heard here, Vittorio—and Ren—were still her best bets.

Vittorio touched her shoulder, just a brief brush of his fingers against the cotton of her shirt, and she wasn't sure if the caress was meant to comfort her or himself.

He leaned across her to undo the cord binding the other wrist. As he worked, he murmured to her in the same calming voice he'd used when she'd had her nightmares. But this went beyond mere nightmares. This was real.

"It will be okay. I swear. I love you. I'm sorry."

His words were all things she wanted to hear, but at the moment she couldn't process them. She couldn't comprehend what had just happened.

She let her eyes drift shut, trying to gather herself, to calm herself enough to walk back into the world, now knowing things she didn't want to ever know.

Yet, she did know Vittorio and Ren. She knew they were good and decent, and she loved the man leaning over her. She did.

She opened her eyes to reassure herself this was the same Vittorio she'd spent hours with, talking and laughing and making love. The man who knew all her favorites, right down to her favorite vegetable, zucchini, and her favorite animal, the aardvark, just because she liked the word.

She looked up at him, his lovely long hair, his too-serious eyes, the sensual shape of his lips.

She started to reassure him that she was okay, when she saw a movement over his shoulder. Then suddenly he was jerked away from her, bodily flung across the room. Erika screamed, watching him fly through the air like a discarded rag.

Orabella stood there, glaring down at him where he landed in a heap close to Ren. She no longer looked like a shattered child, but rather a furious goddess hell-bent on destruction.

"Vittorio," Erika called to him. He struggled to sit upright, but didn't attempt to stand. Instead he swiped the tangle of hair from his face and regarded his mother with dead-looking eyes.

"You have to stop this now," he told Orabella.

Orabella laughed, the sound cruel and sharp. "You have to understand that you can't stop me from having what I want. Neither you nor your lowly brother are strong enough to stop me."

"Then you are going to have to kill me," Vittorio said evenly, "because I will never do what you want."

"If that's what you want, then I guess as your mother I will have to try and give you what you want."

She didn't move, but clearly she was doing something that was affecting Vittorio. In the same way Ren had seemed to simply fall unconscious, Vittorio began to droop, his arms falling heavily to his sides, his head bobbing, then falling to his chin.

Fear overtook Erika. Orabella was going to kill them all. She tugged at the binding Vittorio had been working on and her wrist slid free. She sat up, reaching for the knots around her ankles.

"Don't tell me you are going to give me trouble now," Orabella said from beside her. "Can't you see I already have had a rough day?"

Erika didn't pause, slowly looking at her. "Please."

"Please. Please," Orabella mocked. "No amount of your pathetic begging will save you. And if I hadn't promised you to Aosoth, I'd take great pride in killing you myself."

"But you did promise," Aosoth said, reminding Erika for the first time in some time that the creature still waited, boredom clear in her pale yellow eyes.

"I did," Orabella agreed, but she didn't move.

"And I want her now," Aosoth said, her voice losing some of its cultured refinement and growing guttural. "I grow tired of this drama. I want my sacrifice, and then I want to go back to hell. The place doesn't run itself."

Orabella didn't seem to be listening to the demon—at least, given the hell talk, Erika assumed it was a demon.

Suddenly a ripple of confusion coursed over Erika. She blinked slowly, trying to get her bearings. Then another wave hit and another, until she was feeling muddled and weak and unable to focus on anything.

"You cannot have her. You brought me here and I demand payment."

Erika could tell it was the demon talking, but it seemed very far away, like she was drifting away under the effects of anesthesia.

"I will have her," the voice repeated, and though it was distant, Erika could hear the fury in its voice.

Erika stopped trying to fight the heavy, lulling sensation and closed her eyes. This didn't feel bad. Maybe this was as bad as death was going to get.

Then she forced her eyes open. What was she thinking? She couldn't just give up. She didn't want to die.

She lolled her head to the side and squinted at Orabella, her form a blur of blond hair and the pale material of her dress. A hazy ghost. A deadly ghost.

Erika's limbs felt like she was underwater, as she used the only thing she had to fend off Orbella—the ancient cell phone in her hand. She tried to aim and threw it, her attempt more like a lob than a well-aimed pitch.

Orabella's laughter reached her ears.

Then Erika heard her mutter, "Pathetic." And Erika had to agree. She let her eyes drift shut for just a moment, but knew she couldn't give in to this warm, weighted feeling. This was death, no matter how nice it felt.

Erika lifted her eyelids as much as she could, trying to center on Orabella, who was nothing but a fuzzy blur like a person seen through a frosty window. Then behind her a dark form appeared. And then there was a scuffle, although Erika couldn't see who was fighting.

This is too difficult, she thought, and her eyes closed again. Maybe she could give in just a little. Just a little death.

Vittorio half shoved, half fell into his mother. Not the most agile move, but his unexpected assault did send her flying. Her head cracked against the edge of the table and she crumpled to the floor.

He caught his balance and stood over his mother's prone body. She didn't move and he used the little time he knew he had to check Erika. She was breathing, thank God, but the pulse at the base of her throat was weak, erratic. He could still be too late.

Vittorio sensed rather than saw a movement from beside him. He spun, poised to fight. To attack again if necessary.

But it wasn't his mother that he saw coming toward him. It was the demon. Aosoth.

Then he noticed that the demon, who'd been contained in the circle of a pentagram, stepped outside the boundary, the spiked heels of her boots clacking on the wooden floor. He studied the circle, realizing Erika's phone had slid across the floor, disturbing the iron filings, leaving a break in the circle. Allowing the demon to escape.

Vittorio positioned himself between the demon and Erika, shielding as much of her as he could.

"You can't have her," he stated.

The demon stopped, surveying him from narrowed, yellow eyes. "It's brave to deny a demon."

"You can't have her," Vittorio repeated.

Aosoth smiled then, a wide curl of her lips that almost made her look human. Almost.

"I don't want her," the demon said, and for a moment, Vittorio thought he'd imagined the response.

"What?"

"I don't want her," Aosoth repeated slowly. "I want her." A long, claw-tipped finger pointed toward Orabella, just as she came to, struggling to sit up, disoriented.

"I will take that one in place of your mortal."

"Why?"

Aosoth smiled, again taking on a human air. "Call me a hopeless romantic. Or call me a demon smart enough to take the one who will do my bidding best."

Vittorio glanced at his mother.

"Give her to the lizard," Ren said groggily from his place on the floor. "She deserves to be in hell."

Vittorio couldn't deny that. His mother had killed so many. She'd rejected one son and tried to dominate the other. She'd done everything with only her own needs and desires in mind. And she'd never stop.

Not unless she was finally taken where she belonged.

Vittorio nodded, a small bob of his head.

The demon moved forward, easily lifting Orabella by the neck.

"You are mine," Aosoth growled.

Orabella finally seemed to be aware of what was happening. She threw Vittorio a wild-eyed look. "*No!* Vittorio, don't let this happen. Don't let this happen."

Vittorio didn't move, or even breathe. This was the right thing to do. The only way to stop her. And she had to pay for her deeds.

"Please," Orabella begged, her voice breathy, scared.

Aosoth glanced at Vittorio, just for the briefest second, then the room was filled with blue flashes of light and deafening thunder.

Vittorio leaned over Erika to shield her as plaster shook down from the ceiling. Just when Vittorio decided he had to carry Erika out of the shaking room, that it wasn't safe, the noise and lightning stopped.

The room was almost harshly silent. He immediately lifted his head, which had rested on Erika's stomach. Her pulse still fluttered in her throat, but it seemed even weaker than before.

Ren appeared at his side, leaning heavily on the edge of the table.

"That bitch nearly drained me," he muttered. Then he eyed Erika.

"Is she breathing?"

Vittorio nodded. "Just barely." She was alive, but for how long? Had Orabella taken too much?

"She's not doing well," Ren said, pressing his fingers to her wrist. "You've got to give her some of your energy."

"What if she's too close to the edge? What if I change her over?"

"What if she dies," Ren stated.

Vittorio stared down at Erika's pale, almost translucent skin. The faint, delicate veins in her eyelids. The whiteness of her lips. She would die. That knowledge pierced him, like a knife slicing deep into his chest and twisting.

Without thinking any further, he leaned forward and pressed his mouth to her, her lips slack and cold against his. He made a frightened noise deep in his throat, then he let his energy enter her, filling her.

God, please let me be doing the right thing. The thing Erika would want. The thing that she could forgive.

Erika woke. What a weird dream. Definitely the worst of the nightmares she'd had thus far. Well, maybe not the worst because Vittorio and Ren had made an appearance in this one. And Isabel had made an appearance too. Craziness. Definitely not the worst, but definitely the oddest. And very vivid. And Vittorio had been some sort of monster—a vampire or something.

She started as someone knocked on her door.

"Come in," she called, expecting it to be Vittorio. She would have to tell him what she'd dreamed. He'd get a kick out of that image. An angst-filled vampire. And that Isabel had been his evil mother.

But instead of Vittorio, it was Maggie. She poked her head in the doorway, looking almost sheepish.

"Hey there. How are you feeling?"

Erika smiled, giving her a confused shrug. "Fine. How should I feel?"

"Fine," Maggie agreed. "I just wanted to check."

That didn't add up. "Why? What happened?"

Maggie didn't answer, looking decidedly uncomfortable as if she had no idea what to say.

"What's happened?" Erika asked again.

Maggie hesitated, more confused emotions reaching Erika. "Do you remember last night?"

Erika shook her head. "Not really." Then her eyes widened. "All I recall is some crazy dream where Vittorio—and Ren's—

mother was the woman I've been sculpting. And she was evil. And there was a lizard creature."

Maggie smiled but didn't seem to share her amusement.

"I guess I was so tired from all the work I've been putting into my show that I just zonked out."

Then Erika paused. She didn't remember being at the gallery, putting the last touches on her pieces. Oh God . . .

"My show was last night, wasn't it?"

Maggie hesitated, then nodded.

Erika put a hand to her head. "I don't remember it."

"No," Maggie said, shifting from one foot to the other, clearly uncomfortable.

Erika groaned. "Did I just get sloshed on too much free champagne at the show? What happened?"

Maggie gave a smile that was a little sad. "You know, I think you should talk to Vittorio about all this. He's just gone out for a few moments, but he'll be back soon. I just wanted to be sure you are okay."

Erika nodded, even though she had no idea what was going on and she wanted answers now. But she didn't think Maggie was going to give them to her.

"I'll be out here if you need anything," Maggie said, and Erika nodded. She heard the door latch as Maggie left her alone.

What had happened last night? She fell back against the pillows, trying to decipher what events she could recall. She'd been at the gallery. Then—Isabel called, she suddenly remembered. She'd gone there and Isabel had invited her into her huge, beautiful house and then . . .

She sighed. Then the weird dream.

Another knock sounded at the door, this one light, as if the person on the other side was unsure.

"Come in."

This time Vittorio poked his head in the door. "Hey."

"Hey," Erika replied, waiting for him to come in.

"Are you feeling all right?"

Erika nodded, feeling a little exasperated that no one would just tell her what had happened last night. "Why shouldn't I feel all right? Tell me what happened last night."

Vittorio didn't know how to tell her the truth. She didn't seem to realize last night hadn't been just a dream. She did know she missed her show, but according to Maggie, she had written off the whole confrontation with his mother and the demon as a strange nightmare. Like her other ones.

Vittorio stepped into the room, wanting to go to her, but he stopped just short of the bed. He couldn't touch her. Not when what he was about to tell her would scare and likely repulse her.

But there was no avoiding it. "What do you remember?"

She told him about being at the gallery and Isabella's call to come to her house. Then she told him about the dream.

Vittorio wished he could assure her it was all a dream. That she'd gotten sick or something and missed her showing and all the rest was a dream. But he couldn't. He loved her, and the truth would come out eventually.

He needed to tell her and let her decide what she wanted from there.

"Erika," he said slowly, "that wasn't a dream. Everything really happened."

She stared at him, her eyes wide. "What?"

"All of it. Isabel really being my mother. A conjured demon from the seventh circle of hell. Me—being a vampire. Or rather a lampir, which is just a vampire who—"

Erika held up her hand. "You can't be serious."

"Sadly, I am."

She just stared at him for several moments, then shook her head. "I don't know why you would tell me this."

Vittorio gave her a helpless look. "Because it's true. And I love you. And you need to know the truth."

"You love me? And you are telling me *this*?"

Vittorio knew it couldn't sound true to her. But he was

tired of lies and he was who he was. He couldn't change that fact or hide from it any longer. Not with her of all people.

"Erika, I want to spend all eternity with you. And it just happens I can do that. For real."

Erika didn't know what to say. This was crazy, and she couldn't . . .

"I can't deal with this."

Vittorio nodded as if he expected that answer. Maybe that was the answer he'd hoped for. But this was one convoluted way to get a person to dump you.

"So if you are a vampire—is Ren one?"

He nodded.

Then a thought hit her. "And Maggie?"

He nodded again.

Erika stared at him. This was nuts. Totally nuts.

"Vittorio, I'm not sure how I'm supposed to deal with this. This is . . ."

"Unbelievable," Vittorio supplied.

"Yes. Yes." She blinked, feeling the urge to cry. How could this be real, how could she have fallen for a . . . vampire?

"I know it is way more than anyone could ask a person to understand. But I am still the same person who had pretty much fallen in love with you from the moment I first met you."

His words made her heart dance and jump in her chest, but they were also bittersweet. He was a vampire. A vampire with a mother who wanted her dead.

"I don't think your family approves of me," she said wryly.

"Ren loves you. Maggie is your best friend. They are the only family who needs to approve."

"What about your mother who wanted to—" She couldn't believe she was about to say this aloud. "Sacrifice me to a demon?"

"Would you believe the demon took her instead?"

"That was fortunate, I guess," Erika said wryly.

Vittorio started to sit on the bed, but the wary expression

on her face must have stopped him. Instead he crossed his arms over his chest.

"I know this is a lot to handle. But my mother was the only reason we couldn't be together and she's gone. I am crazy in love with you." He cringed at his wording. "Okay, I'm madly—" he paused. "I'm head over heels in love with you. And I want us to be together, but I do understand if you need some time."

"I do," she said. "I—just do."

Vittorio nodded and took a couple steps toward the door. "I'll be around. Just call for me and I'll be right there."

Erika frowned as he stepped out the door, closing it quietly behind him. Call him and he'd be right there? Somehow she didn't think that he meant with her phone.

She stayed in bed for several minutes, just trying to sort out what she had just heard. What she felt about it. What she was supposed to do with all this information.

Finally she rose and headed to her dresser. She found a pair of jeans and a sweater and tugged both on. Her apartment was silent as she tried to locate her purse, which she was surprised to find on the coffee table.

Near-sacrifice to a demon by a crazed vampire, and still Vittorio thought to locate her purse. That had to make him a keeper, right? Even with the fangs?

She laughed to herself, the sound slightly hysterical. What was she going to do? Then she noticed Boris sitting on the windowsill.

She walked over and stroked the grumpy animal. "What would you do, Boris?"

The cat meowed, but that didn't clarify much for Erika.

She patted the cat one more time, then headed to the door. She knew this was a weird place to go—at least many people would think so—but it was the only option she could think of.

*   *   *

"Hey, girl, where were you last night? I was there all gussied up and you weren't. Were you sick?"

Erika forced a weak smile at Philippe. "I had—something come up."

Philippe raised an eyebrow. "Really? Good or bad?"

"That's what I'm hoping you can tell me."

Philippe made a face that she didn't quite understand, then nodded.

"Tea leaves or tarot?"

"Tea leaves, I think."

He nodded and prepared the cup. After she'd tipped the cup up and he lifted the saucer off the top, he paused without looking at the leaves clinging to the side of the stained porcelain.

"Erika. I know you come here because you want answers. You like answers. But the truth is, the future is always uncertain."

Erika's heart did a funny flip in her chest. Wasn't that essentially what Vittorio had said to her on the night they'd admitted they were in love? That there weren't always answers and you had to trust yourself to make the right choices.

"You know your own emotions," Philippe said. "You know what you want and what you need. And while I can tell you what's ahead of you, you have to ultimately decide what you want."

Erika stared at him, not sure what to say or do.

"Like with your fair-haired, dark-eyed prince, I knew he was coming, but it was up to you to go for him or not."

And she had gone for him. And she didn't regret that.

She stood, the wooden chair bumping the wall in the small cubicle as she did so. "I think I need to go."

Philippe smiled as if he knew she would do that. Probably he did.

"I'll catch you at your next show."

"Absolutely," Erika said, suddenly feeling giddy. She pushed aside the curtain batiked with stars and moon that served as a door, and practically dashed from the shop.

"She'll come around," Maggie assured Vittorio, who sat on the sofa in the carriage house. "She just needs some time."

"Not everyone can just go with this concept. Except for Maggie, who didn't apparently have the sense to be scared of a lampir," Ren said with a teasing smile.

"True enough," Maggie agreed, then touched Ren's knee with affection.

Vittorio somehow didn't think he'd be getting a reaction like that from Erika anytime soon.

"Well, it probably helps that our mother didn't try to sacrifice you to the demon, Aosoth," Vittorio pointed out.

"That was one time when being her least favorite came in handy," Ren said.

"There were plenty of times," Vittorio said. "Believe me."

Ren sighed, and Vittorio knew that his brother was truly bothered by what Vittorio had suffered at the hands of their crazy mother.

"I think it's over," Vittorio finally said. "How can she get past all that?"

Just then the front door flew open, and Erika dashed into the room, her cheeks flushed, her hair coming out of the knot she had on the top of her head. Her chest rose and fell as she tried to catch her breath.

Vittorio stood. "Erika? Are you okay?"

She brushed back a lock of dark hair that clung to her cheek and she smiled. "I am. Just a little breathless." Then she paused. "Crap, I could have just called you to me, couldn't I?"

Vittorio nodded, confused by her words and her sudden change in mood.

"I've got to remember that."

"Okay," he said, not knowing what else to say.

"So does that mean I'm becoming a lampir too?"

Vittorio shook his head. "No, no it just means I've—bonded to you."

"Bonded—like we have a connection."

He nodded, feeling miserable. He was probably the last person she wanted to be linked to.

"Is that how you found me last night?"

He nodded again. "Well, in part, some—demon . . ." Damn, he hated to say that aloud. "Who was involved with my mother told us that she took you, and that's how I located you once I knew you were in danger."

"That's a good trick. It's like OnStar, but in your head."

Vittorio stared at her, having no idea what she was talking about. Maybe last night had driven her mad. It *had* been horrifying.

When neither of them said anything more, Ren stood. "Maybe we should go. So you can talk."

Erika turned her attention to Ren and Maggie. "So you are vampires too."

They both nodded, Ren looking rather blasé about it, Maggie looking sheepish.

"Maggie, I can't believe you didn't tell me. You suck at keeping secrets."

"I know," Maggie said in a rush, "but I didn't think you'd believe me."

"Probably not," Erika admitted. "It is a little far-fetched."

Maggie nodded, then let Ren take her hand and lead her to the stairs. But Maggie stopped at the bottom, making Ren stop too.

"It's really not scary," she said to Erika. "It's the best thing that ever happened to me."

Erika smiled and nodded. "I believe you."

Maggie smiled back, then she and Ren disappeared upstairs.

Erika turned back to Vittorio. "So how does this all work for us?"

Vittorio frowned. "What do you mean?"

"This vampire thing. This relationship."

"I'm not sure," he admitted. "This is the first time I've been with anyone who actually knows what I am."

Erika moved closer to him, then rested a hand on his chest. His breath caught at the simple touch.

"Well, you are my first vampire." She moved closer, her body nearly touching his.

"And your last," he said, then realized that probably his roughly muttered words sounded more ominous than possessive.

But Erika smiled. "I agree." She then rose up on her tiptoes and kissed him. "I love you, Vittorio, no matter what you are. All I ever wanted was for you to want me."

"That's all I ever wanted too."

He kissed her again, long and deep and filled with everything he felt for her.

"I have to admit your mother might have been a deal breaker though."

Vittorio nodded. "Understandably."

"Thank God for demons."

Vittorio laughed. For the first time ever, he felt like he was going to be okay. He pulled Erika tighter to him. Better than okay.

Epilogue

Maksim had to admit he'd never been to a wedding before. It was all too romantic and based in commitment and loyalty and fidelity and stuff he wanted no part of. And it was all a little too—white.

He shoved at a bit of white tulle that kept sticking to the top of his head from where it was draped on the courtyard walls.

He took a bite of the crawfish étoufée that was being served. The food was good though.

He glanced over at Erika and Vittorio dancing in the center of the courtyard. The fountain behind them silhouetted them, like the image of a romantic photograph. Friends and family also danced and chatted and ate. Well, some ate. Vampires really got screwed in that department.

He sighed. What a strange combination of beings. Vampires, lampirs, a werewolf, humans—and a demon of course.

Just then Erika's black cat—Boris, he believed he was called—jumped onto his lap. The cat perched on him, staring up at him with unblinking, glowing eyes.

"You are a weird animal," Maksim muttered, stroking it once then pushing it off him. He dusted the fur from his Armani pants. The cat took no offense, and sat on the cobblestones watching him.

Maksim ignored the animal and returned his attention to

his food. He still hadn't found any information about Ellina. But he didn't think Orabella was involved with her disappearance.

He just couldn't find any leads, period. But something had happened to her.

"Enjoying yourself?"

Maksim looked up to see Erika's friend, Jo. She looked lovely in a red dress with a full skirt and off-the-shoulder neckline.

"Yes," he said, setting down his fork.

"Good." She smiled and his blood pressure shot up. God, she was stunning.

"Jo, care to dance?"

Maksim recognized the man touching her arm as one of the members of Ren's band, The Impalers. Chuck? Maybe Buck? Something like that.

"Sure," Jo said, then offered Maksim another smile, one he couldn't quite read. "Enjoy your dinner."

Maksim nodded, knowing what he'd enjoy even more as he watched the sway of her hips as she walked to the dance floor.

His gaze returned to Vittorio and Erika, who held each other close, talking and laughing and clearly so smitten with each other that they could have been alone.

Not for me, he thought as his gaze returned to Jo. He wanted good sex, good food and to find his sister.

That's all he needed.

As if reading his mind, and finding his desires lacking, the black cat at his feet meowed.

Maksim laughed and continued to watch Jo with hungry eyes.

Get in the holiday spirit with
TO ALL A GOOD NIGHT,
A sexy anthology from
Donna Kauffman, Jill Shalvis, and HelenKay Dimon.
Check out Donna's story, "Unleashed."

She was quite thankful for the addendum maps, as she'd be hopelessly lost without them. Actually, even with them she'd gotten herself somewhat turned around at the end of the west wing—at least she was pretty sure it was west. Even the dogs had given up on the adventure and trotted off some time back to God knew where. She was sure they'd find her when they got hungry or wanted to go out, so she wasn't too concerned about that. But she was getting hungry herself, and she had no idea how to get back to the kitchen area, much less the garage, or the rooms she'd been assigned to stay in.

She was stumbling down a dark corridor, unable to find the hall light switch, when a very deep male voice said, "If you're a burglar, then might I direct your attention downstairs to the formal dining room. The silver tea set alone would keep you in much better stealth gear for at least the next decade. At the very least, you'd be able to afford a flashlight."

She let out a strangled yelp, as her heart leapt straight to her throat, then froze in the darkness. Except for the animals, she was supposed to be completely alone. Not so much as a valet or sous chef was to be on the premises for the next twelve days. Of course the notebook did say that Cicero had a lengthy and amazing vocabulary. But he was at least two floors away. And she doubted he knew how to use the house speaker system. Armed with a notebook and not much else, Emma decided offense was the best defense. "Please state who you are and how you got in here. Security has already been alerted, so you'd best—"

Rich male laughter cut her off. "You must be the sitter."

"Which must make you the burglar, then," she shot back, nerves getting the better of her.

More laughter. Which, despite being sexy as all hell, did little to calm her down. Because though she'd been joking, the idea that she'd been on the job of a lifetime for less than two hours and had already allowed a thief into the house was just a perverse enough thing that it would actually happen to her.

The large shadow moved closer and she was deep into the fight-or-flight debate when a soft click sounded, and the hallway was illuminated with a series of crystal wall sconces. Emma's first clear glance at her unexpected guest did little to balance her equilibrium.

Whoever he was, he beat her five-foot-nine height by a good half foot, which made the fight thing rather moot. Flight probably wasn't going to get her very far, either. He had the kind of broad shoulders, tapered waist and well-built legs that her defensive-line coach dad would recruit in a blink, and charming rascal dimples topped by twinkling blue eyes that her Irish mother would swoon over as she served him beef stew and biscuits.

Emma, on the other hand, had absolutely no idea what to do with him.

There's nothing more irresistible than
EVERLASTING BAD BOYS.
This sexy anthology from
Shelly Laurenston, Cynthia Eden, and Noelle Mack
is available now from Brava.
Check out Shelly's story, "Can't Get Enough."

"Ailean," she somehow managed to squeak out. "Good morn to you."

"And to you, Shalin. You look awfully beautiful today."

The fact he could say that and sound like he meant it was probably why so many females fell under his spell. Yet, Shalin couldn't be fooled. She had mirrors, did she not?

"Thank you. So why are you—"

"Och!" he cut in as he always did. The dragon rarely took a breath, it seemed. "You won't believe my morning, Shalin. You truly won't. Mind if I sit?"

"Uh—"

"Good. Thanks." He dropped down beside her. All that dragon as naked human male. It took every ounce of her strength not to reach out and touch him. Like that solid thigh brushing against her robe-covered leg, to see how it felt under her human hands. She'd never been with a male as human. She'd heard it could be . . . entertaining.

"So there I am, taking a bath, as she said I could, when suddenly her father comes in."

"Oh, that must have been—"

"Horrible, right. Because she told me that we were alone in that house. But apparently not. I think she wanted me to claim her or marry her or whatever they call it."

"Even though you're—"

"A dragon, right. She doesn't know that bit, you see. Best to keep her in the dark about that, don't you think?"

"Well—"

"Especially for just a night of entertainment. Why she'd want me as a mate, I have no idea. So what are you reading?"

It took her a moment to realize he'd asked her a question he expected her to answer. "*Alchemic Formulas from the Nolwenn Witches of Alsandair.*"

"Is it interesting?"

"A—"

"I don't know how you can read so many books. I get bored after a few pages."

"So," Shalin found the courage to ask, "you've never read the books about yourself?"

Ailean groaned, rested his elbows on his raised knees, and dropped his head in his hands. "Tell me you haven't read those."

Read them? She'd devoured them.

"Well—"

"Because I didn't authorize those to be written."

The books had begun to show up among humans and dragons nearly ten years before. She'd only just finished reading volume three the previous night and word of volume four being available soon had her nearly breathless. Each volume had two editions. One for humans and one for dragons written in the ancient language of their people. A language the humans of this world could never hope to learn with their much weaker minds, ensuring the fact that dragons roamed among them freely remained a well-kept secret.

"The books aren't true, then?"

Based on his wince, she knew they were as true as they could be.

"I never said those things didn't happen. I just said I never authorized them being written about." He turned his head and looked at her, those silver eyes hot on her face. "I don't want you to think I run around telling tales about my relationships, Shalin. I can keep a secret quite well."

And how tempted she was to take him up on his unspoken offer, but that would be cutting her own throat. She'd officially be an enemy of Adienna then, and she simply wouldn't risk her life for any male.

"I—"

"Perhaps I could tempt you away from your interesting book with the promise of a delicious meal at one of the nearby taverns?"

Shocked, Shalin gripped the book in her lap tightly. He wanted to take her out? In public?

What should she say? *I'd love to? How about dinner in my room? Forget that, let's go for it right here, right now?*

Instead what she heard herself stuttering was, "I . . . I can't."

"Can't or won't?"

"Both." She shot to her feet, the book still in her hands. "I have to go."

He stood and towered over her as no human could. "Don't go, Shalin. Spend the night with me."

She should be insulted. He'd just left another female's bed and now, still naked and wet from the woman's bath, he'd asked Shalin to warm his bed. But this was Ailean the Whore. He wasn't doing anything out of character. She actually felt kind of proud he'd asked her at all. Although she knew that to be pathetic. And she'd never admit it out loud.

Shalin focused on the book in her hands. "That's very kind of you, but . . . but I—"

Big fingers lightly gripped her chin and tilted her face up to his.

"Gods, Shalin. You do so tempt me."

She nearly melted at his words. Melted right into a big puddle at his feet.

"Ailean, I—"

Shalin stopped talking when she realized guards stood behind him.

"There you are," one of them said, slapping his hand down on Ailean's shoulder.

Ailean gave a short snort. "And such a good job finding me, since I've been standing here for the last twenty minutes."

With a snarl, the guard motioned to the others and large steel manacles were locked onto Ailean's wrists.

"Don't look so, Shalin." Ailean grinned. "I have every intention of coming back for you."

Shalin opened her mouth to say something, but no words would come out. He'd rendered her completely speechless. But since he really didn't let her get a word in edgewise, this wasn't exactly an incredible feat. Holding the book close to her chest and pulling the hood of her acolyte robe down over her face, she nodded, turned, and fled.

And keep an eye out for
Katherine Garbera's latest,
BARE WITNESS,
coming next month from Brava . . .

Justine arched an eyebrow at him. "Are you making fun of me?"

"Never. I was trying . . . trying to tease a smile back on your lips.

"Why?"

"I like your smile."

"You do?"

"Yes."

"Why?"

Nigel shook his head this time. "You mustn't get many compliments."

She shrugged. "Honestly, I don't trust them."

"Why not?"

"What's with you and all the questions?"

"I'm a CEO. I thrive on information."

"So do bodyguards," she said.

The teasing note was back in her voice and he felt a little thrill of victory at having done that. "Why are you a bodyguard?"

"Well, to be honest, I'm usually more of a weapons expert and marksman. For most assignments we take on, Charity functions as the bodyguard."

"Why is that?"

"She's tall and gorgeous, just the sort of person that makes most assailants think they don't have a thing to worry about."

"And you're not."

She gestured to her short frame. "Height is one thing I've never needed."

"No?"

"No," she said. "I learned early on that if I don't quit, I can take anyone."

"Can you take me?"

"Easily," she said.

He took two steps toward her. The plane rocked and bucked and all the playfullness that she'd had a second ago disappeared as she used her body to take him down to the floor and braced both of their bodies.

When the plane leveled itself she knew it had to be turbulence and not an engine out or any other danger. But her heart was racing and it had nothing at all to do with the security of Nigel Carter of his daughter.

Justine closed her eyes but that just made everything . . . better. All of her other senses came to life. The feel of his hard body under hers, the scent of his spicy aftershave, the sound of each exhalation of his minty breath against her cheek.

She opened her eyes as Nigel's hands settled low on her waist. This time it wasn't different. His hand was in the exact same spot that had worried her when they'd been standing toe-to-toe. But now it didn't bother her.